Titles by K S Ferguson

Rafe & Kama series:

Calculated Risk

Hostile Takeover

Family Owned

River Madden series:

Touching Madness

Undercover Madness

The Hellhound series:

No Place Like Hell

Novella:

Puncher's Chance (with James Grayson)

This is a work of fiction. Names, characters, places, and incidents either are the product of the author's imagination or are used fictitiously, and any resemblance to actual persons, living or dead, business establishments, events, or locales is entirely coincidental. The publisher does not have any control over and does not assume any responsibility for third-party websites or their content.

No Place Like Hell

Copyright © 2014 by K S Ferguson

Contact the publisher: http://www.ksferguson.net

ISBN: 1-938179-22-6
ISBN-13: 978-1938179-22-8

No Place Like
HELL

K S Ferguson

K S FERGUSON

ACKNOWLEDGMENTS

I would like to thank the many people who assisted with this novel. First, thanks to my daughter for her unfailing support and thoughtful suggestions. Thanks to James for his suggestions and assists. Thanks also to my beta readers, especially Pam, and to Luke for his sharp editorial eye.

If you enjoy this book, please consider leaving a review at your favorite online retailer or social library site.

If you'd like to be notified when the next volume of the hellhound series is released, you can sign up for notification at my website: http://www.ksferguson.net/sign-up-for-news.html.

1

June 1968

Bricks-for-brains at the wheel of the Camaro in front of us revved his engine. It roared through his glasspack mufflers like a rocket taking off.

"You want to bet he's going to do something stupid?" I asked my partner, Dave, who rode shotgun in the patrol car.

"We can't bust him just because your female intuition says he's trouble, Nicky," Dave replied.

His gibe barely made a ripple in my concentration. I kept my eyes on the Camaro and hoped I'd be wrong about the punk at the wheel.

We crawled down Santa Domingo Boulevard amidst a sea of teenagers cruising in their muscle cars. Exhaust choked the airless summer night as we drove past the stucco façades of businesses lining the Solaris commercial district.

The brake lights flashed on a beat-up Ford Falcon ahead of the Camaro. The Falcon's driver had spotted our cherry top, and traffic slowed further. At the intersection, the light cycled from green to yellow.

The numbskull in the Camaro jerked his car into the open right lane, downshifted, and peeled rubber. The chirp of his tires cut through the rumble of motors. After a quick glance in my rearview mirror, I changed lanes to give chase.

"Idiot." Dave flipped on the light and siren.

A pedestrian came out of nowhere and charged in front of the Camaro. With a squeal of brakes and a thud, the Camaro smacked the guy, who bounced down the pavement like a wad of Silly

Putty.

"Hell!" I slammed on the brakes, shifted into park, and jumped out. Dave called in while I dashed ahead.

Traffic had lurched to a halt. People got out of their cars to gawk. Bricks-for-brains sat frozen in the Camaro, his face white through the side window. His girlfriend covered her mouth as though holding back a scream.

I should have flashed our light at him, should have whooped the siren. Should have done something before the kid got himself in so deep.

The poor schmuck he'd hit looked dead lying so still on the pavement. My breath caught in my chest, and my feet seemed to move in slow motion. Knowing that I'd followed the rules didn't assuage my guilt over the outcome of my inaction.

A couple of toughs burst from the door of a building to my right and pulled up short at the edge of the street, staring at the body. More young turks driving muscle cars got out to watch and point and elbow their companions.

"Stay back!" I raised a hand to warn them off.

I reached the victim, and the world spun down to a halt. He was of average weight and probably average height, although it was hard to tell, the way he was crumpled on his side. His shiny wing-tips were scuffed and streaked by his slide across the pavement. The right pant-leg of his gray dress slacks was shredded from mid-thigh to mid-calf, and bloody, ragged flesh showed in the gap.

All those first-aid lectures played like a reel-to-reel tape on fast forward. My first coherent—and useless—thought was that I should have grabbed the first-aid kit from the trunk. Like a first-aid kit could fix this mess.

Dave joined me. I shifted the victim onto his back and positioned his head as gently as I could, mindful that if he ever woke up, he'd be pissed if I'd made him a quadriplegic.

The right sleeve of his white dress shirt was rolled up above his elbow. The left was still fastened by a glittering green cufflink. I loosened his green-and-gray striped tie.

He had close-cropped brown hair and a face scraped raw and pebbled with grit. I put two fingers on his neck where his pulse should be. Something jumped. Or maybe it was wishful thinking. He definitely wasn't breathing.

I tilted his head back, pinched his nose, and put my mouth over his to start artificial resuscitation. Inflating his chest seemed impossible.

"Oh, man!" Dave crouched beside me. "It's Tad Newell, the mayor's son."

I didn't care who he was; he wouldn't die on my watch. His lips tasted of bourbon and his cheeks smelled of aftershave and blood. His chest, rippling with hard muscle under his shirt, didn't crunch or grind as I compressed it. I took that as a hopeful sign.

His picture had been on the front page of the paper. He'd recently returned from a tour in 'Nam. According to the article, a group of anti-war protesters spit on him while he made a speech at a veterans' picnic.

"Where the hell's the ambulance?" I gasped between breaths and compressions.

But Dave was gone, taking control of the scene. The hot Southern California smog transferred from my lungs to Tad Newell's, one breath at a time. My hands willed his heart to beat. The night stretched while I counted to five over and over.

"Okay, lady, we got it."

A white-clad ambulance attendant elbowed me aside and checked vitals. A second attendant rolled a gurney up before joining his workmate. The first one peeled back an eyelid and flashed a penlight over the eye.

"Dead," he said.

My stomach heaved. I'd locked lips with a corpse. I wanted to wash my mouth with soap. It was hard to see through the mist in my eyes. Hard to believe the man in front of me was dead. If only I'd done something about the kid in the Camaro.

"Maybe you want to rethink that," Dave said at the attendant's shoulder. "You want to be the one who pronounced on the mayor's son?"

The attendants exchanged a look. In a heartbeat, they had Newell fitted with an Ambu bag. While one of them squeezed the bag, the other applied a neck brace. Together, they whisked him to the ambulance. They pulled out fast, siren wailing.

I dug a hanky from my pocket and wiped Newell's blood from my lips. I wanted to swipe at my tear-filled eyes, but as the first—and only—woman patrol officer on the Solaris force, I couldn't afford to show weakness. A uniform might make a man, but it didn't guarantee respect for a woman. If I wanted financial independence, I needed this job.

"Have you taken statements?" I asked.

"All done. Unit two picked up the kid driving the Camaro."

Dave waved off the last of the bystanders, and we returned to the patrol car. I looked around the scene once more, imprinting it in my mind. When I reached for the door handle, my hand shook.

"You drive. I want to make notes while it's fresh." I dropped into the passenger seat with a thump.

Dave grinned. "You should be a novelist. You love writing reports. They sound just like those gritty crime novels. Or maybe an episode of *Dragnet*. Hey, you ever thought about writing scripts for them?"

"That's how you spend nights off? Watching Joe Friday catch crooks or reading detective stories? No wonder you can't find a girlfriend." I tsk-tsked a few times while Dave's face turned red. All the guys at the station harassed him about his lack of a girlfriend despite his good looks. I'd overheard ribald jokes about how his being assigned a female partner was as close as he'd ever get to having a wife.

I hoped the EMT was wrong and Tad Newell wasn't dead. He'd gone off to war half a world away and returned safe. He didn't deserve to die in an accident in his home town.

"We should have stopped that kid before he hit Newell," I said.

"People have free will, Nicky. They make their decisions, and they face the consequences. We can't arrest them before they act."

"It's a stupid way to run a world," I muttered.

I flipped open my notebook to a fresh page and documented the accident scene in all the detail I could remember. After two years at a desk and two weeks on patrol, I finally felt like I'd done something useful. But I should have done more.

Despite my shaking hands, I'd managed six pages when the radio crackled.

"Unit five, respond to a 10-53 at Clark's Books, 1511 Bueno Ventura."

I snatched the radio. "Unit five to dispatch. Is there another unit available? We're still finishing our last assignment."

"Unit five, be advised we have a pile-up on the 101. You're the only unit in the vicinity of the 10-53."

"Unit five, 10-4."

Dave groaned. "Great! A silent alarm and no backup available."

My first serious criminal bust. The winds of change blew through my open window, and a little chill rippled through me.

2

Kasker's mouth watered at the thought of tasting Decker's soul. His breath came in short, quick gulps, and his loins engorged like they did when his corporeal vessel lay with women. But the climax of this hunt would bring a hundred times the pleasure of the flesh.

He got out of his Mustang and gazed about. Music throbbed from around the corner, and a few cars breezed by, stirring heat with their tires. But mostly, the business district, after another scorching day, had succumbed to the somnolence of exhaustion and darkness.

His otherworldly senses told him no other souls lingered in the alley to his right. In fact, for the last several minutes, he hadn't detected the sweet scent of Decker's damned soul, either, which seemed odd. Decker's date with death wouldn't come for another half hour, and even then, his soul couldn't escape.

Kasker trod down the potholed asphalt alley between the old brick buildings. Distant streetlights cast faint illumination, and deep shadows cloaked the building walls. Rats scurried around the battered garbage cans dotting the sides of the alley. Warped lids let the stench of the cans' rotting contents waft in the night air.

The thrill of the hunt coursed in Kasker's veins. He suppressed the urge to throw back his head and bay his excitement. Every muscle tingled with anticipation.

The light over a shop entrance threw a dirty gray pool on the pavement under it. An ancient wooden door stood partially open. Faint luminescence flickered through the gap.

Kasker moved closer with silent steps. Burning candle wax

and blood overrode the miasma of the garbage. Curious rats drawn by the scent retreated at his approach. He pushed through the back door of Clark's Books and stopped short.

Decker's naked body lay spread-eagled over a pentagram scrawled in charcoal on the warped hardwood floor. Black candles flickered at each point of the star. Runes circled the corpse and spiraled inexorably out until they stopped at Kasker's feet.

Curses and cantrips! Where was Decker's soul? It had to be here. The pact Decker signed kept it anchored to the body until collection. How could it have broken free?

He scented the air, swung his eyes over the storeroom. Cardboard boxes and rows of books lined tall shelves circling the walls. An electric coffee pot stood on a worktop, along with packing supplies. An unlit bare bulb hung from the ceiling. A narrow door led to a tiny bathroom jammed by a sink and toilet.

No soul. No hint of it or any other in this room or in the front of the shop beyond the dusty curtain.

Kasker wiped a hand over his brow and blinked at what remained of Decker. *I've lost my touch.* It must be the constant distractions of wearing flesh. But he'd found other souls since he'd taken it. Why couldn't he find Decker's?

He stepped into the room, careful to keep his Jesus boots off the runes and the splatters of blood. Not an easy task. Whoever helped Decker from this world had opened him from sternum to groin.

From the arcs of blood painting the walls and shelves, he'd still been alive when it happened. A fitting end for a power-hungry cheater. Nothing less than the man deserved.

Was this the death Fate prescribed for Decker? Kasker didn't think so. If it was, it had come well ahead of schedule. Seve's foretellings were never wrong.

Kasker knelt beside the body for a closer look, making sure he didn't step into the final circle. Goats only knew what dark magic might be at work here. He could be vulnerable.

Decker was a short, corpulent man of forty. A thick mat of dark hair covered chest, arms, and belly. He had a blockish head, uneven eyes, fat lips, and a double-chin.

No bruises or scrapes marred Decker's face or hands. No needle marks left their tracks on his arms. His expression was serene.

His face was clean shaven, his short brown hair tidy. Under the odor of blood and offal, the scent of soap and clove oil drifted. He'd been ritually prepared for his ritual sacrifice. It was as if Decker lay down for a nap and was gutted while he slept.

Black threads circled the wrists and ankles, their loose ends trailing down to disappear under the candles. A ragged hole gapped where Decker's heart should be. Kasker scanned the room. No sign of the missing organ. The hair rose on the back of his neck, and a low growl rumbled in his chest.

He stood and danced around blood pools to step beyond the curtain separating the back of the shop from the front. A large window let in dim streetlight. Bookshelves covered the outer walls. More tall bookcases stood in ranks down the center of the space. A counter with a cash register—drawer open and empty—blocked access to the storeroom.

Kasker's senses told him no one lurked in the aisles, but he walked a serpentine path through them anyway, just to be sure. Book dust tickled his nose until he sneezed. The hot, close air made sweat break out on his body.

Nothing seemed amiss. No additional corpses lay waiting to trip him. No stack of books was adorned with a bloody heart.

Kasker returned to the storeroom. He rubbed his chin and stared at the body. Never in the eons he'd collected souls had he seen anything like this. He crouched by Decker.

Candlelight danced on the rune-inscribed ivory hilt of a dagger embedded in Decker's throat. Kasker hovered a hand over it but didn't touch. Like the symbols on the floor, the dagger vibrated with strange energy.

He sniffed, just to be sure. No more soul scent here than from the tasteless burgers his meat puppet craved. But from the dagger, a tendril of essence wafted up, a trace of the practitioner responsible for Decker's lost soul.

Holmes.

A slow smile spread Kasker's lips. A trail at last.

3

I sucked in a deep breath. "Drop me here. I'll take the back."

Dave gave me a sideways glance. If I'd been a man, there'd be no hesitation about us splitting up.

I'd joined the force because I wanted a good-paying career and economic independence. The idea of spending a quiet life looking after a husband and kids made me nauseous. But I hadn't expected the mean-spirited resistance I'd met from many of my fellow officers. While Dave mostly supported me, in his glance, I could feel his lack of faith in my abilities.

I wouldn't admit it to him, but I was nervous about facing my first burglar. I'd practiced physical restraint with cop partners twice my size. I shot at the range regularly and had earned expert marksman status. Shooting paper targets was one thing; they didn't bleed. Shooting a fellow human? Not something I looked forward to.

Dave pulled up behind a maroon Mustang parked near the alley and scowled at me. "You cover the exit. The owner's on his way to unlock the front."

I jotted the Mustang's license number in my notebook and hopped out. You wouldn't think burglars would be so stupid as to park right outside the scene of a crime, but they did. Jails were full of brainless morons who'd intended to enjoy life on someone else's dime.

Dave rolled around the corner.

The alley yawned before me. I wiped sweating hands on my pants. Rustling drifted from the dark, and I gulped. Rats. I hated rats.

Idiot! I should have grabbed my flashlight off the seat before

Dave pulled away. I tiptoed over the asphalt, ears straining. Flickering light shone from an open door. A faded stencil on the brickwork overhead read *Clark's Books*. Small bodies scurried deeper into darkness.

Nothing in the alley offered cover, at least nothing I wanted to snuggle up to. A garbage can wouldn't stop a bullet from a burglar's gun. The best I could do was stay in the shadows.

Footsteps scuffed inside. There'd been a rash of burglaries in Solaris, purportedly all done by the same theft ring. Nabbing the ring in the act would show the brass what I could do. It would be an important step toward building my policing career. *No pressure, Demasi.*

I itched to peek in, see what was happening. I drew my pistol, eased to the door, and stepped into the flickering light.

The sick son-of-a-bitch knelt beside a mutilated body. My stomach did handsprings at the sight. But the guy sucked up the scent of the blood and offal like a new Hoover.

And that smile. It reminded me of a kid waiting for the Thanksgiving turkey to hit the table—the anticipation sparkling in his eyes. Definitely not the burglar I'd expected. My hand tightened on my gun.

One long finger touched a puddle of blood on the floor beside his victim. Then he raised it to his mouth. The tip of his pink tongue flicked out for a taste.

My gorge rose. I choked on the malodorous fog hanging in the hot, stuffy room and fought the urge to turn away. Arresting this jerk was my job, and I'd damn well do it no matter how revolting the suspect.

"Police! Hands in the air!" I sighted down my service revolver, ready to plant a round in his chest if he made a wrong move. The steadiness of my hands surprised me.

His head jerked toward me, flipping his blond ponytail the opposite direction. Ice-blue eyes raked my police uniform. He stood, lifting his open hands to shoulder height. The smile turned sultry.

He was tall, tan, and in his twenties with a movie-star hero's square jaw and a dimple on his chin. Sexually charged charisma oozed off him, the kind that would have women ripping off that skin-tight tank top and unbuttoning his bell-bottomed Levi's. I struggled for breath and pushed the feeling away. *Eww.*

He had to be strung out on LSD. What else could explain the cruelty on the floor? Or the smile? The sucker was staring down a life sentence.

Surprise lit his eyes, and he glanced over his left shoulder toward the front of the shop. My throat closed on an indrawn breath. Did he have an accomplice?

A second later, the door rattled, a bell tinkled, and footsteps sounded on the hardwood. The lights came on, dispelling the eerie shadows cast by the candles. Dave's voice mingled with another, probably the shop owner.

"Dave, in here!" I called.

Dave drew back a dusty curtain. One look at the scene and his revolver rose to point at the hippie. The sickness I felt was mirrored on my partner's face.

An older man in an undershirt, rumpled pants, and bedroom slippers stared over Dave's shoulder at our vic and gasped. An arthritic hand flew to his mouth. He turned away to vomit.

The cold blue eyes swiveled back to me. The killer wasn't smiling now.

"I found him like this." He gestured toward the body.

His voice startled me. It was low and melodious with a 'come hither' quality that promised pleasure. I shivered. His eyes narrowed, and he ran them from my feet to my head. I was struck with the thought that he suddenly found me less appealing.

I'd studied my detective handbook. I knew what we could ask without advising the hippie of his rights—and what we couldn't. I phrased my question with care.

"You stumbled over him while shopping for the latest issue of Rolling Stone?"

A hint of frustration hardened his face. "I heard someone cry out. The door was open, so I looked in."

He glanced at Dave again. Something about my partner worried him.

"What's your name?" I wanted to ask why he'd done it, understand how someone could perpetrate such cruelty on another individual. But that wasn't allowed.

His lips set in a straight line, like a dam holding back an internal torrent that threatened to explode from his mouth. A hand drifted down to point at a back pocket. "It's on my license if you want to know."

Was he trying to lure me closer so he could make a grab for my gun? Dave holstered his firearm and frisked the guy. The hippie carried no weapons. Of course he didn't—the knife was still stuck in the victim's throat.

A wallet bulged in the hippie's pocket, and Dave handed it to me. The driver's license said his name was Kasker Sleeth. It listed a local address in a neighborhood of quality apartments.

He didn't look like he could afford the lifestyle. And he didn't act like a drug-crazed maniac. Crazy for sure, but a careful, thoughtful crazy.

"So, Kasker Sleeth, who is he?" I nodded toward the vic.

His eyes darted down and lingered on the mess on the floor. It didn't seem to bother him in the slightest. Every glimpse caused a tsunami in my gut.

The hippie opened his mouth, closed it, shrugged. "It isn't anybody now."

His twisted answers were as bent as his psycho behavior.

"What about you, sir?" Dave asked the store owner. "Is this man a customer of yours?"

The old guy spoke over his shoulder without looking into the storeroom. "No. Not one of my regulars, anyway. I never seen the other guy before, either. I'll be out front if you need me."

He shuffled away.

"Let's get out of here," Dave said. "We're contaminating the crime scene."

Dave took a firm grip on Sleeth's arm and marched him through the front of the shop. Our suspect didn't protest, didn't resist, didn't act at all like he should in the presence of such horror. His cool demeanor gave me the creeps.

Outside, I swore I could still smell the blood despite the fresh air. The faint strains of country music drifted from a bar across the street, too normal for our macabre situation. We stopped by the cruiser, and Dave opened the back door.

"Get in," he ordered.

Sleeth's brows pulled down and belligerence stiffened his face. "Why? I had nothing to do with this."

The hippie kept secrets; I wanted them exposed. "Of course you didn't. We run into upstanding citizens every day who just happen to stumble over bodies while taking midnight strolls down dark alleys to visit closed businesses." I flashed him my pearly whites.

"Don't talk to him. Leave it to the detectives." Dave glared at Sleeth. "In."

Our suspect's jaw tightened while another battle raged across his face. "I know my rights. You can't hold me. 'Sides, I have places to be."

I stepped closer. "Where would these *places* be?"

The cold eyes gazed down into mine, and his lips quivered in a snarl. We stood locked in a stare-down while I waited for an answer. In a few seconds, he'd confess. I could feel it in my bones.

"Nicky, call it in. I'll take care of Mr. Sleeth."

I didn't understand how someone so cold could give off so much body heat. It was like standing next to the old coal furnace in my parents' basement. He smelled like sweat and sex and cannabis. He didn't smell like brutal death. There wasn't a speck of blood on his clothes. How'd he done it?

Dave shot me an irritated look. "Nicky, leave it. Let the detectives handle him."

Sleeth's eyes slid to Dave, and something feral flashed in them. His breathing picked up, and his frame stiffened. I grabbed his bare arm. The muscles were thick and bunched.

His pulse skipped under the pressure of my fingers, and his skin burned in the cool night air. His attention returned to me, a new sharpness showing.

He leered at me. "Yeah, Nicky, leave it to the men. This is no job for a woman."

He said it as casually as if he'd commented on the weather, but he watched for my reaction like there was nothing more important in the world.

The urge to pepper him with questions squirmed in me. I was so close to making him admit to his crime. Wringing a confession from a murderer would shut up all the naysayers who believed women couldn't succeed as cops. Then I could get on with the job without all the drama and debate about my gender.

But if I screwed up the interrogation and a killer went free, I'd prove the doubters were right. Despite my better judgment, I'd follow the rules.

"It's *Officer Demasi* to you, buddy. Now get in the car."

4

A guardian angel. That was the last thing Kasker expected. The angel seemed oblivious to Kasker's true nature. Not surprising. Goats knew the lower forms of angelic hosts were mostly blind followers with little power.

But if the woman, Officer Demasi, was important enough to warrant a guardian as her companion, they should send some badass seraph, not dorky Dave, especially considering the power of the demon that called Solaris home. A demon Kasker was now late reporting to.

He looked out the window to where the angel's ward unfurled yellow police tape. What an interesting ward she was. Unfashionably short dark hair tucked under her hat. Long face, thin nose, piercing brown eyes, and strong hands whose touch made him burn.

Her dark blue uniform slacks had razor-sharp creases, her shirt was wrinkle free despite the heat, and her shoes were spit-polished shiny. Even her gun belt gleamed. She was perfection.

She smelled like spring sunshine and hot iron, of choices well-made and true. A neat package of female explosive ready to napalm anyone who crossed her. His little test temptation had bounced off without a hint of indecision.

A little shiver crept up his spine. Her words had power. He'd almost spilled everything when she'd asked why he was there. It had taken all his evasive guile to avoid giving straight answers.

And even though she stood half a foot shorter, she hadn't backed down from him. Impressive.

Did his master know about her? What prophesy was she tangled in? The angels liked their prophesies. He didn't worry overmuch about it. Let the demonic horde concern themselves with the machinations of Heaven. That was their purpose, after all.

The hunt was his. The hunt was all that mattered, all that sated. But the presence of the angel and his unusual ward could complicate the hunt. Hunting in flesh was forbidden.

Maintaining the uneasy peace between Heaven and Hell required strict adherence to rules of conduct. To break those rules was to restart the conflict, and Hell hadn't sufficiently stacked the deck yet. But to find the escaped damned soul, Holmes, some rules had to be bent.

He'd followed Holmes on his flight from Hell. The trail went cold once Holmes entered the realm of the living. Now Kasker was stuck in this loathsome mortal vessel searching this goats-begotten city.

The loss of Decker's soul was little more than a blip on the radar. If it led him to Holmes, he'd welcome it. Decker was nobody special, but Holmes had performed the unthinkable when he'd escaped the confines of Hell.

To add insult to injury, Holmes had eluded recapture for three months, making Kasker look more the fool. Kasker would gladly sacrifice Decker's harvest if only he could fetch Holmes' soul back to Hell.

Kasker sat in the back of the stuffy car, irked at his confinement. He had a clue to Holmes' whereabouts at last, and instead of following it, he was detained while the trail grew cold. Perhaps that had been the point? He'd underestimated his quarry.

The annoying flesh craved a joint, after which it would crave another burger, and then a woman. How did humans cope? Masochists the lot of them, with their backward social rules that denied them everything their corporeal corpses demanded.

Two police cars and a black sedan pulled up. Uniformed officers leaped out and scurried away like picnickers from a wasp attack. A heavy-set man stepped from the sedan. He scanned the scene and barked orders. Everyone scurried faster.

Unlike the rest of the pigs, the new arrival didn't wear the dark blue uniform of the Solaris PD. His sweat-soaked white shirt was tucked in ill-fitting brown peggers, and his thin navy tie hung crooked. Close-cropped brown hair dusted with gray hinted at military service, maybe in the Korean War. He was too old for 'Nam.

He spent a few minutes talking to Officer Dave in quiet tones before opening the cruiser door and sliding into the front seat. The acrid smell of his sweat filled the interior. Kasker wrinkled his nose.

"Kasker Sleeth, I'm Lieutenant Mack. I have some questions."

Kasker smiled. Time to pay back the delay they'd caused him. "Do I need a lawyer?"

The detective mirrored his smile, including the lack of warmth. He had crooked, yellow teeth and bad breath that carried through the wire separating the front and back seats of the cruiser. If he'd been laid in this decade, he'd paid for it.

"At this time, we consider you to be a witness. We're asking for your help to solve the heinous crime committed in the bookstore. Nothing you say now in response to questions can be used in evidence against you. If we move on to a formal interrogation, we'll inform you of your rights, and then you can have an attorney present."

Kasker snorted. "I already told that cute little bitch in the uniform everything I know. Anyway, you're the Man. Whether it's legal or not, if you don't like my answers, you can beat me bloody, lock me up, and throw away the key."

Mack's face grew hard, and he crossed his arms. "Don't play smartass hippie with me. A man's dead. What were you doing in there?"

Crossed arms, a sign of a soul's repression. Kasker smirked. "Being a Good Samaritan."

"How's that? You think that man needed to be put out of his misery?"

Kasker rubbed a thumb and finger over his chin and looked contemplative. "Was he miserable? I suppose, once the knife went in."

Mack's jaw worked back and forth. "Last time. What were you doing in the bookstore?"

By now, word of Decker's demise must have reached Kasker's demonic cohort, not someone to anger. Time to cut the crap and cut out.

"Answering a plea for help. Guess I was too late."

Mack's mouth sagged open. "You telling me you heard the guy on the floor call for help?"

"I heard..."

When the woman questioned him, he'd snapped off an evasion without thinking it through. Goats! She had a disturbing effect on him.

Decker hadn't been dead more than a few minutes when he'd entered the shop. That serene face—the man had probably been drugged, or he would have screamed in agony, and Kasker would have heard that sweet music. But would anything show up in

Decker's blood work that could have prevented him from calling out? Best to be vague if Kasker didn't want another visit from the pigs.

"...something strange. Strangled. The door was open. So I went in to check."

Mack leaned back. "I'm not buying it. What were you doing in the alley?"

"I wasn't in the alley. I was on the street by my car. That's still legal, right?"

"And what were you doing on the street by your car at midnight?"

Kasker gave a lazy smile. "Hanging out."

"A guy like you hanging at your car like a chump when there's a bar across the street?" Mack said, a frown creasing his forehead. "Were you waiting for your supplier?"

Kasker glanced out the window. Where had the guardian angel and his ward gone? Best to keep an eye on them. They could be trouble.

"I was waiting for a chick."

"This *chick* have a name?"

"Alice? Amanda? We met at a party. Or maybe it was a bar. She said she'd catch me later."

In truth, he hadn't asked the pretty redhead in the skimpy halter top and mini-skirt her name when they'd hooked up earlier. They'd balled and split, her with some dude promising great weed and him on the hunt for Decker, the yammering meat puppet temporarily sated.

"Why on the street?" Mack asked.

"Maybe she wanted me to do her in the car before we went in the bar." Kasker pointed across the street. The flesh desired a cold beer. If the police let him go soon, he could get one before the bar closed, and then hunt for Holmes—and Decker's soul, although devouring it took a back seat to the recapture of Holmes.

Mack grimaced. "You see anyone in the alley?"

An interesting question. When had he lost the connection to Decker's soul? Before he'd parked? How long could Decker last, split open like that? No more than a few minutes. Only seconds after his heart was removed. But the alley was empty when Kasker arrived. Where had the killer gone?

"It was dark, man."

Mack shifted in the seat and squinted at him. "You seem pretty cool about what you saw in there."

Kasker shrugged. "Shit happens. Can I split now?"

5

——————

"Demasi, Chief of Ds wants you in his office." The duty sergeant jerked his thumb toward the hallway door.

I tossed a glance at Dave, who labored over paperwork at the desk opposite me.

Dave grinned and whispered, "Probably going to give you a medal for catching a killer."

I wished I had his confidence. It was blind luck that we responded to the call at the bookstore. I also wasn't sure we'd caught a killer. I had so many questions.

How'd Sleeth done it and remained pristine? Why the bookstore? How'd he gotten in? We saw no sign of forced entry. If the owner was to be believed, neither Sleeth nor the vic had a history there. What was Sleeth holding back?

I trudged down the dingy corridor to Chief of Detectives Lenny Greene's office, the end of my twelve-hour shift weighing heavy on me. Two of Lt. Mack's guys hurried by, squeezing me against the wall without a whisper of apology. I was used to their careless disregard and sloughed off their rude behavior. It was the most fascinating day of my life. I wouldn't let anyone ruin that.

I was about to rap on Greene's door, but it swung open before I connected. Lieutenant Mack stood on the other side. His eyes narrowed, and a frown deepened the downward curl of his lips. I stepped back, and he brushed past without a word.

Greene's office was small and cluttered and shabby. An ashtray overflowed on the desk, and the air in the room would set off a smog alert. Pictures of Greene with famous villains he'd collared plastered the walls. Pictures with politicians—and family—were absent. Not many cop marriages survived. That would never be a problem for me. Single and independent, that was my mantra. If only I felt more confident I could make that happen.

Greene sat in his battered swivel chair behind an equally battered wooden desk buried in case files. His ruddy face looked darker than usual, and he ran a hand through gray hair thinning on top. His hazel eyes squinted into mine. They weren't warm and welcoming. He didn't ask me to sit. No surprise there.

"What did you think you were doing questioning Sleeth? You're a beat cop, for Christ sake. You detain suspects, and you secure the scene. Period."

My face felt like a three-alarm fire. My usual unflappable mask failed me. Words of protest slipped out my lips before I could lock them in. "But, sir—"

"Mack told me you questioned our prime suspect. If you weren't the poster child for those bra-burning women's libbers, I'd fire you right now." He waved an arthritic hand in the direction Mack had gone. "Leave the detective work to the detectives."

The heat in my face migrated to my gut, and my shoulders got tight. How would I pay my mortgage if I lost this job? I'd be some homeless person living on the streets and eating meals at the mission.

"I know how to interrogate a suspect without crossing legal boundaries, sir. If Lt. Mack said I did, he's wrong."

A moment too late, I realized I should have taken my lumps and kept my mouth shut.

Greene leaned over his desk. "You thought you could use your feminine wiles to trick Sleeth into confessing. How would that look in front of a jury? Or did you plan on batting your big doe eyes at the jury, too?"

Greene's jaw tightened. "How you became a patrol officer is beyond me. Just because you talked your way into the job doesn't mean you have the skills to do it. When the bullets fly or some drug-crazed maniac comes at you with a baseball bat, pretty words won't stop them. You endanger the good officers you serve with because you have neither the brawn nor the guts to be a cop or the good sense to do as you're told."

Greene turned his attention to the stack of files on his desk. "Now get out."

I spun on my heel and rushed from the office. Down the hall, I darted inside the ladies room. I gripped the edge of the sink so hard my fingers turned white. Bitter disappointment churned in my stomach.

I'd never failed at anything, never been fired from a job. I'd used my brains and my initiative to exceed expectations. Deep inside, I heard doubt whisper that no woman could get along without a man to support her. Sure, the feminist movement might say women were the equals of men, but out in the working-world trenches, very little had changed. Women were still paid a pittance even when they did a man's job.

Would I end up one of those desperate women who snagged a man—any man—to keep a roof over my head and food on the table? Would I stay with a drunk or a wife-beater because I relied on him for security? I'd vowed I wouldn't, knew I could make it on my own. But men like Lenny Greene amplified the whispers of the little voice that said I'd fail.

The door swung open and Maggie Tisdahl dashed in, throwing a worried glance over her shoulder.

"You all right, honey? I heard that brute Greene was gunning for you."

She glanced in the mirror and swept a finger over the thick makeup on her cheekbones that disguised four decades of sun damage. She still wore her civvies—a cream peasant blouse and blue jeans with green paisley insets that made the jeans flare at the bottom. The style looked ridiculous on a woman in her mid-forties.

Black and white yin and yang earrings dangled from her earlobes, and gold rings flashed on her thumbs. I'd heard she'd embraced counterculture mysticism after her husband cleaned out their checking account and ran off with a younger woman, forcing her to moonlight at a security company to pay the mortgage. She was a prime example of how single women struggled without a man to support them.

If Maggie knew about Greene's lecture, then everyone would soon know. I groaned inwardly. How could I face any of my fellow officers now? I'd be the laughingstock of the force.

Maggie put a motherly arm around my shoulders and squeezed. "It's okay, sweetie. You're the sharp end of the stick poking those macho men in the behind. They're just a bunch of fraidy-cats worried we women will replace them. You know all us girls are with you, right?"

Maggie's eyes shone with her own frustration. She'd served fifteen years with the Solaris PD, never giving up hope that one day she'd earn the responsibility and the pay of a patrol officer. That one day they'd appreciate her intelligence and loyalty and reward her with the job she deserved. At her age, she'd never see service on a beat.

She knew her dreams had passed her by. That hadn't stopped her from organizing a rowdy celebratory party at the Longbar when the chief announced my promotion. She'd generously seen my advancement as success for her own perseverance.

Shame crept over me. I had a duty to prove that women had the talent and the moxy to do the job. I'd let them all down. I'd try harder, work smarter, prove Greene wrong. That was my style.

Maggie watched me in the mirror, dark and assessing. Her hand touched my sleeve, and her voice dropped into a low register. "Listen honey, you've had a lot of stress. Why don't you come to my meditation group tonight? It would do you good to be surrounded by positive energy for once."

For a moment, I was tempted, but I didn't believe in all that hooey. I splashed cold water on my face, dried it with a paper towel, and practiced my serious, unflustered expression. I straightened my spine and tucked a stray hair behind my ear.

"Thanks, Maggie. I've got to work. Maybe another time. What are you doing here so early? I thought you didn't start until eight?"

"Greene called everyone in to 'provide logistical support' to the detectives. For us clerical gals, that's code for 'fetch coffee and sandwiches.'" She gave me a friendly pat. "Gotta change into my uniform. You keep your chin up."

Maggie swept out.

After a last glance in the mirror, I strode back through the hallway to the squad room, head high. I'd messed up by arguing with Lenny Greene. But I wouldn't let that stand in the way of doing my job, of protecting the good citizens of Solaris.

Dave rocked in his chair, pencil tapping in his hand while he chatted in a low voice with one of Mack's detectives. When they saw me, their conversation stopped, and the detective sauntered out. From the sympathy on Dave's face, he'd heard about my reprimand.

I yanked my chair out and sat.

"Sorry, Nicky," he mumbled.

My fingers clattered on the typewriter keys.

Dave dropped his eyes to his own unfinished report. "It's still your collar, no matter what anyone says."

I sighed. "You can't collar an innocent man. I'm not convinced Sleeth did it, but he's hiding something. I could have cracked him, before he had a chance to think up anymore lies."

My partner poked at his typewriter with his forefingers, finding one letter at a time. "It's a stretch to believe he showed up in the middle of the night to find our vic dead on the floor."

"Decker. The victim's name was William Decker. No prints on the knife, and no blood on Sleeth. Mack couldn't break his story about finding Decker like that, so he turned him loose." I stopped typing, still regretting that I didn't push the hippie harder. "Sleeth's an animal. You saw him. He looked... excited. He gets off on cruelty. But the ME said Decker hadn't been dead more than a few minutes when we arrived. No one could have gutted the man, ripped out the heart, and still been pristine."

Dave sat back in his chair and scratched his chin. "Good observation. Maybe he wore coveralls. Or a surgical gown. It's probably in a garbage can outside the door."

"Mack had me check all the garbage cans for a two-block radius. No sign of bloody clothes, and none in Sleeth's car, either." I suspected Mack got a kick out of assigning me garbage-can duty, but I wouldn't complain. At least he'd let me work the scene.

"Then he had one or more accomplices who took them away before we got there. Or they did the slice and dice while Sleeth watched from the door. After all, he'd need help to restrain a man the size of Decker." Dave lolled in his chair. "Still, we can't hold Sleeth if there're holes in the case."

All my unanswered questions whirled like a tornado in my brain. Sleeth's pale blue eyes stared out from my memory. "He's cold. Cold like a hard frost. Cold like an ice age. If he ever had any humanity, it's dead. It froze over."

"Is that your female intuition talking? Detectives aren't allowed to use intuition." He grinned and gave me his Joe Friday imitation. "All we want are the facts, ma'am."

His words stung. I'd thought I could count on Dave, that he could get beyond gender bias. No matter what, partners supported partners.

"Laugh all you want. Sleeth's criminally insane. We have a duty to the community to get him off the streets even if he didn't kill Decker."

"Our job is to get the evidence so the DA can convict. We can't lock up psychos until we have proof they've committed a crime."

"And to get that proof, if we can't nail him for Decker, someone else has to die. Doesn't that strike you as wrong? I wish I could have asked him more questions."

"They should have turned you loose on him. You can talk anyone into doing anything. It's your gift. Have faith, Nicky. The righteous will prevail, and the unjust will be punished." Dave pulled his report from the typewriter and checked his watch. "Shift's over. I'm going home. The watch commander wants us at the hospital at three."

"What for?"

"Photo op. The mayor's son made it, and the mayor's going to thank you personally at a press conference. You're a hero." Dave winked at me. "If you want a promotion, nothing beats having the mayor in your debt."

I groaned.

6

Kasker pulled his Mustang to the curb in front of the Luna Azul, sure that Seve Calderon would be in the restaurant even though the place wouldn't open for hours. The rising sun already heated the pavement, promising another scorching day.

The burly Latino door guard took note of his arrival but kept his eyes on two men walking on the opposite side of the street. When Kasker approached, the man held the door open.

Inside, a whip-thin Asian and a scruffy white dude lounged at a table by the door. They rose as he entered, hands straying toward guns holstered under jackets. Kasker strode past without acknowledging their presence.

Cool and dim, the interior was a welcome refuge from the heat outside. Salsa music played from the doorway to the bar on his left. Kasker glimpsed a busboy polishing glasses.

In the dining room, vacant tables had upturned chairs stacked on their red checkered tablecloths. Orange walls were decorated with sombreros, fans, and painted gourds.

The clanging of pots and pans came from the kitchen at the back of the room. Kasker threaded between tables, making his way toward a booth by the kitchen door. The place smelled of fried food, and his stomach growled, reminding him that he needed to feed his protoplasm overcoat soon or suffer its distraction.

A tall, muscular Negro and an equally impressive Latino flanked Seve Calderon, a diminutive Latino who sat in the vinyl-padded booth and sipped cinnamon-laced coffee. The bodyguards scrambled up, and the Negro put himself in Kasker's path.

Kasker stopped, toe-to-toe with the man, a slow smile forming. Silent, he stared into the bodyguard's eyes, waiting, one ruthless hunter challenging another. The bodyguard flinched and stepped back.

Seve pursed his lips and waved a hand at the bodyguards. "You two, help with the deliveries out back."

Kasker waited while the hired thugs obeyed their master. When they'd gone, he slid into the booth and turned his attention to the demon clothed in the flesh of a rich, middle-aged crime lord. The muscles of the demon-inhabited tenement were stiff and the eyes hooded.

Kasker's embodiment tensed in response. While he didn't fear the demon, a certain wariness was called for, and diplomacy was not his strong suit.

"I expected you sooner."

"Decker escaped."

Thin black brows pulled down, and the fine wrinkles at the corners of Seve's frigid brown eyes deepened. "No soul escapes the sabueso del infierno—unless the sabueso permits it. Or have you become weak and incompetent now that you walk among flesh-clothed souls?"

A flash of heat blossomed in Kasker. For a moment, his grip on his corporeal transportation loosened. Huge jaws fitted with long, sharp fangs thrust forward from his face. Heavy lips wrinkled in a snarl. Massive leg bones that ended in enormous paws lifted from his arms. His skin, his *true* skin, burned black with the flames of Hell.

Seve's face darkened, overcast by the emergence of a black skull with long spiral horns and empty eye sockets. A forked tongue slithered over the demon's pointed teeth—teeth that gnashed in angry response to Kasker's loss of control.

"We are not for the eyes of mortals, sabueso," the demon said.

The demon faded, and Kasker struggled to submerge his own true nature, envious of how quickly Seve looked fully human again. But the demon had worn the form of souls for many years, whereas Kasker had only a few months' experience.

Seve's lips turned up in a smug smile. He'd shown his superiority over Kasker just as Kasker had dominated the overeager guard. Kasker vowed he wouldn't let the demon humiliate him again.

"The pact was broken, the soul untethered," Kasker said.

The demon rubbed his thumb and finger over a mustache no thicker than a pencil. "You're sure?"

"I tasted the blood."

"This is not good news, mi amigo. Could you follow?"

Kasker squeezed his hands into fists on the tabletop. "I was nabbed by the pigs and held until this morning."

"Few untethered souls survive long. By now, he will have escaped his fate." The demon scowled. "You owe me a debt. How will you repay it?"

"His escape wasn't my fault. Find another to take his place," Kasker shot back.

The demon straightened, a challenge in his eyes. "You think it's easy? Then you do it. Find another, bind his blood."

They glared at one another. Kasker needed the demon's support to continue his hunt. There would be consequences for them both if he failed. He looked away.

Seve must have had similar thoughts. The steel in his voice was gone when he spoke.

"How did the police catch you?"

"I still wore the flesh when they arrived at Clark's Books moments after me."

Seve smoothed the tablecloth. "How did they know to come?"

"Silent alarm, the pigs said. It was a trap. He set me up to look responsible. But why? It wouldn't save him."

"Blood and sacrifice," the demon muttered.

"Exactly."

The demon's eyes widened. "It was a *sacrifice*? Decker didn't die of natural causes?"

"There were runes drawn on the floor and imbued with power. A bewitched blade was used to cut the soul free. The magic carried a trace of Holmes."

Seve sucked in a breath. "Decker and Holmes are linked?"

Kasker nodded.

"Did Decker fight?"

"No sign of it."

"The blade, it was white? And the runes spiral out to a portal?"

Kasker stared at the demon. "To the back door. You've heard of this?"

"Si, many years ago. I thought the knowledge lost."

"Is it of the angels? Why would they save a man like Decker?"

"No, sabueso, of the *universe*, and therefore much more dangerous, especially in the hands of a soul like Holmes."

Seve sat back in the padded seat and sipped his coffee while Kasker considered what the demon had said. Magicks loose in the world... they could have consequences greater than the salvation or damnation of a few souls.

"What do you know?"

Seve blotted his lips with a white linen napkin. "The ritual severs the binding and frees the soul."

Kasker chafed at the demon's reply. This much he knew already. "So the soul escapes into nothingness instead of being swallowed by Hell. Humans cling to their lives. They would agree to die this way to escape their fate?"

The demon put his fingertips against his temples. "The soul still yearns for existence. The rune path guides it in a search for new blood, new sanctuary."

"The loosed soul has the power to kill?" Kasker asked. He wiped a wrist across his forehead.

"No, no. It is weak and blind. It seeks warm, unoccupied flesh, just as we do when we manifest here. There may have been a second sacrifice nearby, one that prepared a new vessel for occupation. Did you sense it?"

Kasker frowned at the table and thought back to the night before. "How near?"

"In the past, the receptacle waited on the other side of the door."

"If Holmes sacrificed another so Decker could take its body, it had to be done near the bookstore. I sensed no dispossessed souls in the alley, and I would have smelled Holmes if he were nearby."

Kasker rubbed a hand across his mouth and wondered if that were true. He'd broken the rules and taken this annoying form because he'd been unable to trace Holmes since his escape from Hell. He'd caught whiffs of his prey in the Solaris area, but never enough to track. How was Holmes hiding the scent of his damnation?

"Then perhaps the transfer was unsuccessful and the universe has taken the soul owed me. If this was Holmes' first attempt to wield the power, he may not have mastered it yet."

"How does Holmes come by this knowledge?" Kasker asked.

The demon pushed his coffee cup away. "There is a tome, thought destroyed. The freeing of souls is but one secret it illuminates. Great harm can be done with the knowledge in it. Perhaps even the unmaking of Heaven and Hell. To find it, you must seek answers from another, one who stands outside our paradigm."

Kasker shifted on the bench. "I'm a simple hunter. Saving Heaven and Hell is beyond my purpose."

"You are sabueso del infierno, the greatest hunter in Heaven, Hell, or the universe. The one who can help will not wish to be found, but no one is better qualified than you to locate the Oracle."

7

My feet ached, and I wished Mayor Newell would get on with it. The conference room at the hospital was hot and stuffy. Antiseptic tainted the air and burned my nostrils. We stood on a low stage at the front of the windowless room. A bevy of reporters and photographers gathered before us, jostling for places in the front row.

Dave and I were to the mayor's left. His son sat in a wheelchair to his right. No way the mayor would allow himself to be trimmed from any photos. He might be short, bald, and chunky, but he looked sharp in his fancy three-piece suit, gold ring flashing on his pinky finger.

Mayor Newell was running one sentence of thank you to twenty sentences of his usual political propaganda. He bragged about how he'd increased the number of officers on the streets, how he'd cut the crime rate. No mention of last night's horrific murder, although I was sure the press would ask if given the whisper of a chance.

"And here she is, folks. Officer Demasi, the first female patrol officer on the Solaris PD and the person responsible for saving my son."

Flashbulbs blinded me. Too late, I wiped the automatic smile from my face. I didn't want people to think I was a bit of fluff. Stern female Officer Demasi doing the same job as all those men, and doing it well.

"Can we get you and the mayor's son together?" one of the photographers shouted.

The mayor took my elbow and guided me to a place behind his son's wheelchair. He pressed close to me and smiled. The smell of

cigarettes mingled with his overpowering cologne to create a nau-
seating odor. I thought I might barf in his son's lap if we didn't
finish soon. My partner stood on the other side of the podium,
stifling his amusement.

"Okay, folks," the mayor's rat-faced press secretary said.
"That'll be it for now. The mayor's a busy man."

The press grumbled but took their cue and dispersed from the
hospital conference room.

The mayor patted his son's shoulder. "Remember what the
doctor said. No strenuous activity, which means you can't chase
your nurse—or Officer Demasi."

Newell gave a forced chuckle and grimaced once his father's
back was turned. He'd been silent throughout the press conference.

The mayor hurried away, the press secretary scurrying behind. I'd intended to make my own hasty exit, but Newell caught
my forearm.

"Thank you," he said. He held out a hand, opened his mouth.
Nothing came out for ten seconds. "Tad. Tad Newell."

I took his battered, sweating hand. "Officer Demasi. Just doing
my job. Are you okay?"

Newell blinked. "Yeah... yeah. I hit my head. Everything's still
a little muddled."

He looked like hell. One side of his face was masked in
scrapes, and the other was purple edging into green. I couldn't
imagine how Dave had recognized him.

He smiled through puffy lips. "Thank you for being expert at
your job and saving my life."

"Glad I could help. It's not every day that I get to work with a
celebrity." I flashed him an encouraging smile. He looked like he
could use it.

"Celebrity?" His brow furrowed. "Oh, you mean because I'm
Tad Newell, the mayor's son. Everyone acts like that's such a big
deal."

Dave and I exchanged a glance.

"Mr. Newell, if you wouldn't mind, I do have a couple of questions." I pulled my notebook from my shirt pocket.

"Of course. Anything I can do to help."

"Can you tell us how the accident happened?"

"Well... no." Newell studied his hands where they lay on a red
plaid robe. "It's all gone. I don't remember anything about yesterday. I don't remember getting up. I don't remember having lunch
with my dad, although he says we did. Can you tell me about it?

They said you saw it happen."

I cleared my throat. "You stepped off the curb in front of a Camaro just as the driver accelerated to make the light. You seemed to be in a hurry. Any idea what you were doing in that neighborhood?"

"Is that relevant? If I stepped in front of the car, I was in the wrong."

"You know how it is," I said softening my voice. "We have to dot all the I's and cross all the T's or the duty sergeant will be on our case for not being thorough."

"I don't remember why I was there, although I'm sure I had a good reason when I set out." Newell hung his head. "Sorry. The doctor says my memory might come back eventually. Maybe you could help me?"

"Me?" It came out shrill. "I'm not a psychiatrist."

Newell laughed. It was a low, throaty sound that resonated all the way to my bones.

"You were there when it happened. I thought maybe if you told me about it over lunch tomorrow, it might jog my memory."

"Lunch?" I'd become a monosyllabic mimic. But somewhere, deep down, my curiosity twitched. Could I really help him recover his memory? Wasn't it my duty to help people?

"They're discharging me tomorrow morning. Let me buy you lunch. I have to do something to repay you." His fingers took mine, and he gave me a hangdog look. "You wouldn't turn down an injured vet would you?"

Dave seemed terribly interested in the carpet. My face had blazed into a forest fire.

"Travo's at one?" Newell suggested.

I looked into those sad, swollen hazel eyes and felt my resistance drop all the way to my uncomfortable uniform dress shoes. The guy needed my help. Who was I to say no?

"Okay, Travo's at one. Now we have to go. Duty calls."

Newell rubbed his hands over the lap robe. "Yes, you must be very busy. I saw in the morning paper that they found Bill Decker horribly murdered in a bookstore."

"Did you know him?" I asked.

His eyes clouded over, and he took his time answering. "No, I guess I didn't. Maybe he's a friend of my father's. The name's familiar, that's all."

I pulled my hand from Newell's grip and hurried down the aisle to the exit doors. Dave's footsteps thudded on the carpet behind me. At the last minute, I wondered whether Newell needed help to get back to his room. I stopped a candy-striper in the hall and suggested she check on him.

In the parking lot, the afternoon sun felt hot enough to bubble the paint on the car. Dave grabbed the driver's side before I could react. We both slid into our mobile oven.

"Lunch, huh?" Dave waggled his eyebrows before he maneuvered us onto the road.

"What was I supposed to do? He insisted. It's just lunch. In a public restaurant."

"Just remember, he's the mayor's son. That gives him power. If he doesn't get what he wants, he can torpedo your career."

8

———

Kasker stared through the open car window at the storefront. Sweat dampened his forehead and trickled down his ribs to form dark circles on his tank top. His back stuck to the Naugahyde upholstery. He barely noticed his discomfort.

Hawaiian Mike's Meditation Center the overhead sign read. The window displayed an image of some Indian god or goddess, seated, with one pair of arms held palms together over the head, and another pair resting on the knees, thumb and middle finger forming Os. Printing at the bottom of the window advertised incense, candles, yoga mats, and meditation classes.

Kasker shifted position. A sense of unease kept him in the stifling heat when he should be inside seeking the Oracle. He hadn't slept since sometime yesterday morning, and the flesh yearned for rest. He couldn't drive it much further before it would stop responding to his will. Already, behind his eyes, sharp pain throbbed.

After his discussion with Seve, he'd visited bookshops to ask about texts on fortune telling, astrology, magic, prognostication. Bookshops always attracted the believers. They came seeking arcane volumes and assurances of their own worth. They came to learn about life after death.

After he'd expressed an interest in such things, it was easy to strike up a conversation about practitioners of the arcane arts in the area. Solaris seemed to draw them like maggots to a rotting carcass. He'd tracked one after another through the long, hot day. They were all shams.

Seve was right. The Oracle was a bitch to find. But Kasker was the hunter. He never quit. Eventually, he always located his prey.

He'd ended up here, on the doorstep of what must be the most powerful creature in the universe. It masqueraded as a human, which seemed implausible. Why would any creature with a choice take the flesh?

He didn't understand how he knew, but in his gut, he could feel the weave of the life, the texture of the choices made. This one was beyond the reach of Heaven or Hell. This one brought danger.

Two attractive co-eds strolled down the street, opened the shop door, and went in. His worry was such that the meat puppet failed to respond to them despite their long shapely bare legs and jiggling breasts.

He lost sight of them between the display shelves, but tracked their souls to the back of the building. He'd wait until they left. Then there'd be no one inside to see should he need to shed his human disguise.

Over the next few minutes, ten more people arrived, some male, some female, all upper-class and ranging from late teens to middle-aged. Twelve souls inside, and with the proprietor, thirteen. Thirteen, a number of power.

He wiped moist palms on his shirt. Perhaps they were a coven. If so, whatever magic they practiced gave off no strange vibes like the knife. Still, he didn't want to risk going in while they were at full strength.

Forty-five scorching minutes passed before the occupants trickled out in ones and twos. The strange soul of the proprietor lingered in the middle of the shop. Then it moved through the front door and onto the sidewalk.

The shopkeeper stood five foot nine. Dark hair framed a round face with Asian eyes, and a huge belly billowed a tent-sized floral-print shirt. Khaki shorts peeked out below the shirt, and flip-flops finished the attire.

He stretched his hands over his head, surveyed the cloudless sky, and faced Kasker's direction. His dark eyes found Kasker's, and the hint of a smile touched his lips. Kasker slumped in the seat.

The man stepped back inside, turned the Open sign to Closed, but didn't lock the door. He shuffled from view toward the interior of the shop.

Kasker drew a deep breath, got out of the Mustang, and crossed the street. He stood in front of the shop door gazing through the glass.

Light spilled from lava lamps strategically scattered through the space. Black lights illuminated glowing wall posters of fairies, dragons, and fantastical ships sailing starry skies.

Display racks piled with merchandise filled the space between the door and a counter behind them. A beaded curtain hung across an opening to a second room. The shopkeeper-who-was-no-shopkeeper fussed with paperwork at the counter.

Kasker hovered his hand over the door handle, checking for magical emanations. Nothing. He stepped inside to the tinkling of bells.

Cool air washed over him, raising bumps along his skin. Jasmine, sandalwood, and dozens of other exotic scents filled his nostrils. His empty stomach churned from the sickening mix, and the ache behind his eyes worsened. The closing door bumped his butt.

"You should take better care," the shopkeeper said without looking from his paperwork.

Kasker tensed. Was that a threat? How should he answer? As though he could hear Kasker's thought, the man continued.

"Of your body. All that time in the heat. It's dehydrated."

Kasker glanced over his shoulder. The shopkeeper couldn't see the car from behind the counter. How had he known Kasker waited outside?

A prickling crept up his neck. He wanted to back away, but he pressed against the door already. Cornered, he straightened and thrust out his chest. He was the hunter, not the hunted.

"You're the Oracle."

"Sure. Whatever you say." The shopkeeper's pen tipped to a sign on the counter.

The customer is always right.

Kasker frowned. "I've come for information."

"We only offer *enlightenment*, Angra Mainyu. And it takes a lot of work. Gonna cost ya. You prepared to pay?"

Was *that* a threat? If the Oracle could wield the magicks of the universe and knew one of his names...

Kasker looked over his shoulder again to be sure the Oracle's followers didn't lurk on the street, although his senses told him no souls hovered outside the storefront. Was the man so powerful that he didn't need seconds?

"You won't find any cult followers *here*. Just little old Hawaiian Mike trying to make a living amongst the haoles." The Oracle rubbed his expansive belly and chuckled. "Okay, maybe not so little."

Kasker stared. *Could* the man read his thoughts?

The Oracle placed his hands on the counter and stared back. "I owe you money or wot?"

Kasker looked away and wished he'd never come. But Seve said Decker's escape could be the unmaking of Heaven and Hell. He needed information. He swallowed hard and took a tiny step forward.

"No, you don't plan to stay long enough to find enlightenment. You want to buy something?" the man asked, waving his hands at the merchandise.

So the Oracle demanded payment for information. Kasker understood greed. His mouth was too dry to speak. He nodded, wary about the price.

The Oracle came around the counter and into an aisle between the display racks where he patted his cheek and studied the candles, packets of joss sticks, and brass incense holders.

The closer the man came, the worse Kasker felt. The room seemed to tilt and melt like a bad acid trip.

"Hmm, seems I'm outta wolfbane." A twinkle shone in his dark eyes. "That's a joke."

Kasker's grip on his corporeal transport loosened, only it wasn't his doing. He'd become insubstantial, powerless. His very existence flickered.

When Kasker didn't laugh, the Oracle shrugged and wheeled around to peruse the opposite display. "Maybe some brimstone to make you feel more at home, yeah? Oh, sorry, outta that, too."

The Oracle faced him. The jocular banter dropped away, and a serious intensity filled his voice that penetrated to the center of Kasker's being—what remained of it. "There's a chance I'll have a supply next Friday afternoon, after the solstice."

Kasker put a hand on his throbbing head. He had to get out. Had to get away from the fat Hawaiian and his bad jokes. He backed into the door, snatched it open.

"The winds of change may blow away all that you know. You want to prevent that, Fenrir, you go with the non-believer," the Oracle called as the door swung shut.

Kasker fled.

9

I drove along Santa Domingo, eyes flicking left and right. Business hours were over, and it was still too hot for anyone to stroll the deserted sidewalks. Kids in their muscle cars wouldn't start cruising until sunset.

I'd been thinking about what I'd wear to lunch. I had that little black dress, but Travo's in the early afternoon in the summer probably wasn't the venue for it. I'd play it safe and stick with my uniform. I didn't want to give Newell the idea that I was interested in anything more than helping him with his memory loss.

"What do you suppose he was doing here?" I asked.

"Who?"

"Tad Newell. Mostly businesses along here, and they're closed by six. Not even any bars."

Dave shrugged. "What does it matter? Pedestrians have the right-of-way, even when they jaywalk, and the driver of the Camaro tried to run the light."

I took a left at the light. Newell's amnesia intrigued me. What was it like to simply lose a whole day from your life? Could I help him find the missing time? I didn't want to give Dave the idea I had an interest in Newell, so I changed the subject.

"You think the Solaris Slasher will strike again?" That's what the press had dubbed our killer. The title had Lt. Mack tearing out his hair. I chuckled at the image.

"Well?" I said when Dave didn't reply.

"What?"

I frowned at him. "The Slasher. Think he'll do it again?"

"Maybe."

I made another left. "Anyone with the stomach for such a brutal killing won't stop."

Dave glanced sideways at me. "You sound like you want someone to die so you can be right."

"I want to question Sleeth. He's the key. I know he is."

"If we arrest Sleeth when he didn't do it, we're leaving the real killer out there to strike again."

"If we let Sleeth walk away when he knows something, more people will die. I can't stand by and witness innocent deaths."

"You've already had one warning. Leave Sleeth alone."

I clamped my jaw. I had a lot to offer the Solaris PD, but all they wanted was an automaton who kept her mouth shut and followed orders. If I didn't need the paycheck, I would have quit after the first month. At least as a patrol officer, I had more latitude to apply logical thinking and make a difference instead of endlessly shuffling papers.

At the next left turn, Dave sat a little straighter. "This isn't our usual patrol route. You're running a search pattern."

I slowed as we cruised by a half-empty parking lot. "Newell drives a blue '65 Chevy Impala. If he can't remember where he left it, then it's probably still here somewhere."

"What's with you and Newell?" Dave folded his arms over his chest. "Do you have the hots for him?"

Dave and I had known one another since first grade. We were best friends and partners, nothing more. He was the kind of guy I ought to date: strong, dependable, almost sensitive. But there was no spark. Was he suddenly jealous?

"I just think we need to find out what happened. Too many things don't add up," I said.

Dave threw his hands in the air. "He's the mayor's son. What do you think he's into?"

I took the next corner a little too fast. "I just want to be sure he isn't mixed up in something. He didn't step off the curb. He ran into the street. Why?"

Had Tad been trying to kill himself? Was he messed up from serving in 'Nam? I'd only spoken to him for a few minutes, but he seemed like a nice guy, a man of substance. According to the papers, he'd been working to help other veterans. There were rumors he'd run for city council come the next election. I didn't want to believe he had a death wish.

Last night's tableau replayed in my head, and just like that, I had the answer. He wasn't trying to kill himself—he was running away.

"Those two guys." My voice climbed. "They were chasing him."

"What guys?" Dave shot me a perplexed look.

"Two thugs ran to the curb just after he went down, one white and one Negro. I didn't see where they went. Did you get their names?"

"They must have split. I didn't interview them."

"I'm going back to Santa Domingo. I want to see where they came from."

I drove back to the accident site, pulled to the curb, and got out to walk the sidewalk to the intersection.

Smeared blood still marked the pavement. I turned my back on it, took a deep breath, and started the previous day's scenario playing in my head.

The Camaro roared. Newell flashed into my vision and jumped in front of it. I ran up the street towards him. The two men had come from...

The Carlisle Hotel. It was a seedy brick affair on the corner, rising seven stories, home to strapped pensioners, destitute widows, and newly released convicts.

I walked back to the car, my gut churning. If that's where Newell came from, what was he doing there? Why were the men chasing him? My mind shied away from the possible answers, all of them involving criminal activities.

"Well?" Dave asked.

"The hotel."

Dave craned his neck to see its façade through the windshield. Then he looked at me. "Maybe he has friends living there. You can ask him when you have lunch. He should be able to remember that much."

"If those two guys I saw were his friends, he needs to keep better company," I said.

"If those hoods were after him, he could be in big trouble. Keep your distance until you know what's up, okay?"

"He might need our help."

I returned to the search for Newell's car. We meandered through the business district into the commercial district where the streets were lined with a mix of big department stores and small boutique shops. Most of them stayed open late on Friday, and shoppers ambled through the heat picking up last-minute bargains.

"There it is."

Newell's car sat among a dozen others in a pay-by-the-hour lot, a boot on the back tire, and a yellow notice jammed under a wiper blade. We'd driven a good twelve blocks from the accident site. Three movie theaters and a dozen restaurants or bars were scattered in a six-block radius.

Dave surveyed the neighborhood. "Funny place to park if he was going to the Carlisle."

"Let's ask around, see if anyone remembers him," I said.

A fuzz of static came from the radio, followed by a dispatcher's voice. "Unit five, respond to a 10-37 shoplifter at the Stop 'n Go, 2212 Maple."

I ground my teeth and vowed that I'd come back. I'd find out what Newell had been doing before he'd been mowed down by the Camaro—and why he was of interest to two hoodlums.

10

An unmarked cop car stood in the cracked asphalt parking lot outside Decker Industries. Kasker assumed they were here to interview Decker's staff. He eased the Mustang past and parked around the corner. Then he walked back to the intersection and stood in the shade of a building, watching.

The grubby neighborhood didn't provide much cover. The shining six stories of Decker's flagship rose in the midst of grungy warehouses, import companies, and vacant lots. No coffee shops, bars, or other businesses in which to loiter unobserved.

On the other hand, it looked like everyone had already gone home for the day. His senses found no souls working late in any of the nearby buildings. Once everyone was gone from Decker Industries, he could have a look around to see what Decker had been up to before he died. With luck, he'd find something to point him towards Holmes.

He took a noisy pull on the straw of his Coke cup, sucking up the last of the melting ice. The Oracle had been right about the dehydration. Too bad the rest of what he'd said was gibberish. Goats! Why had he been so frightened of a middle-aged, overweight shopkeeper?

The flickering glow of a woman's soul firmly attached to its fleshy vessel paced around the sixth floor. Two male souls rode down in the building's elevator. The men came into view at a side door and walked to the cop car. They lugged double-stacked file boxes, which they put in the trunk before they pulled away.

Carbuncles and covens! The pigs were already carting away all of Decker's valuable information? Now how would he track down Holmes?

A beat-up green Dodge Dart coupe sat alone in the parking lot. The woman who remained in the building wasn't a cop then. Decker's secretary?

Kasker tossed his empty cup in the gutter and trotted to the Dart. The woman was coming down in the elevator. He fished a penknife from his jeans, unscrewed the valve cap on a rear tire, and let the air out. He hurried from the lot to the doorway of the next building.

Her high heels clicked across the hot asphalt. A blonde beehive topped her head. Her white cotton blouse stretched tight across her buxom breasts and plump torso. A wide floral print skirt swirled around heavy legs. She carried a huge white purse, large enough to hold a week's shopping, slung on her shoulder.

Kasker waited.

She got in her car, backed from her place, and gunned toward the exit. For a minute, Kasker thought she might drive home without noticing the flat.

At the exit, she stopped, got out, walked to the rear of the car. She smacked a fist on the rear panel above the deflated tire. Her tirade of cussing carried to him through the hot air.

He wiped the smile from his face, stepped out of the doorway, and sauntered down the street until he reached her. Close up, she had a plain face, buck teeth, and way too much blue eye shadow. She gave him a ferocious glare, hands on ample hips. He looked at the flat.

"Man, that sucks," he said.

"Tell me about it. First my boss, then the cops. Now this."

Kasker ambled closer. "I could change that for you."

She twisted toward him, and her eyebrows rose. "You'd do that?"

He shaded his eyes and peered at the sun dropping slowly behind Decker Industries.

"Bitchin' hot out here. Why don't we get a drink somewhere and come back when it's cooler? You look like you could use one. My car's just around the corner."

"I don't generally get in cars with men I don't know," she said, eyes full of suspicion.

"Kasker Sleeth." He held out a hand. "We're neighbors. I work next door."

She reluctantly took his hand and glanced over his shoulder to the building he'd come from. When her attention returned to him, her eyes swept him up and down.

"Susan Brown. Friends call me Susie."

Kasker smiled and took her elbow. "What's this about your boss and the cops, Susie?"

"The bastard got himself killed." She sucked in a squeaky breath. "Sorry. I shouldn't speak ill of the dead."

"It's cool. The guy musta been a real spaz to get you riled up so bad."

She ranted all the way to the car, about how Decker was a miser and wouldn't pay her a living wage, how he made lewd remarks and ogled her, how he gave her ridiculous tasks to complete on impossible deadlines.

Kasker tore his eyes from her generous breasts, which had already caused the first stirring in the flesh. On the way to the bar, he tried to turn the conversation to Decker's business, but each time he did, she changed the subject. She must have some moral objection to spilling her boss's secrets even though he was a lecher and dead.

Two beers later, she admitted she'd had sex with Decker. She'd done it because she thought he was about to fire her. What had it gotten her? She had no job now. Kasker consoled her with an arm around her shoulders and comments about how Decker was a jerk.

He wanted to touch more than her shoulders but practiced restraint while chafing at the passing time. If he spooked her, he'd get no information. There must be a way to speed up her seduction. The hippie girls he screwed were so much more willing. But Susie seemed inhibited.

"You know, I've always wanted a family," he said. "I thought I'd found the perfect woman. We were high school sweethearts. Then, while I was in 'Nam, she sent me a Dear John letter."

He cleared his throat and brushed a hand over his eyes. Her lips parted, and she put a hand on his thigh. He congratulated himself on a smart move.

"Kasker, that's horrible! How could she do that to someone as gentle and considerate as you?"

"I've been so lonely. I thought I'd be married by now, with my first child in my arms." He tucked his chin, cleared his throat again, and looked around as though embarrassed to have made this admission in such a public place. "I'm sorry. I shouldn't be prattling on to you about my problems. Not with the kind of day you've had. It's just—well, I miss having someone to hold."

She pushed a stray strand of his hair away from his face. "It's too noisy here. Why don't you come back to my place? We can talk over a glass of wine."

11

Between the shoplifter, a kid spray painting graffiti on a train trestle, and a drunk urinating in public, we had no time to check the bars, restaurants, and theaters near Newell's car. They were all locked up tight when our shift ended. Our relief had rolled onto the streets, our co-workers had headed home, and the station was dead quiet.

I dropped our final report in the night-shift basket and trailed Dave to the back stairs. Our path took us by the incident room. The door stood ajar, the lights off. I ached to peek inside.

"What should I tell Cindy? You coming to dinner tonight?"

We trotted down together. I'd been so absorbed with thoughts of my lunch date that I'd forgotten Dave's invitation to join him at the christening party for his sister's baby.

"Okay, but only if you promise Cindy didn't arrange a blind date for me."

"Would I do that? Let Cindy set you up, I mean." Dave grinned and opened the station door.

My ache for a peek at the incident room blossomed into an itch I had to scratch. I had to know about the Slasher case. I couldn't sleep with all my questions still unanswered. I might never sleep again if he claimed another victim while I did nothing.

"Damn! Left my keys upstairs," I said. "You go ahead."

Dave waved his goodbye as he pushed out. I waited for the door to slam and took the stairs two at a time.

The hallway was empty. I placed my hand on the door and stopped. I shouldn't go in. This wasn't my case. I stepped back. If I got caught inside, I'd be kicked off the force.

But the murder pulled at me. I'd seen Sleeth. Something

was off about that guy. The nagging feeling that, while he hadn't killed Decker, he was somehow mixed up in the killing, wouldn't go away. He'd hesitated too long answering my questions—if you could call his responses answers.

I slipped into the incident room, closed the door, and switched on the light.

Six desks were littered with file folders, empty coffee cups, and overflowing ashtrays. The place reeked of cigarettes and the moldy remains of sandwiches tossed in the trash. A mobile blackboard at the far end had photos taped to it, with illegible scrawls between them.

I walked to the blackboard. No need to look at the crime scene photos. I saw the bookstore every time I closed my eyes. There was a picture of Decker pre-slice-and-dice: dark hair going prematurely gray at the temples, low forehead, flat cheekbones, bulbous nose, staring eyes. He didn't look much better alive than dead.

Sleeth's photo was taped below Decker's. It looked like some movie studio publicity shot. Jeez, didn't he ever have a bad hair day? The scrawl beside it read *Suspect*.

They were still interested in him, but what else were they investigating? Every moment the killer walked the streets increased the chance he'd kill again. We had to move faster.

To the left of Sleeth's photo was a picture of Solaris' mob boss, Seve Calderon. What was his picture doing on the board? Vice and Narcotics were both after him. As an equal opportunity employer, he was the first to hire across racial lines and recruited the worst from the Los Angeles gangs. No one knew how he got them to work together without going at it chain and switchblade.

Someone had drawn an arrow from Calderon's picture to Decker's and written *Doing business*. Another arrow connected Sleeth and Calderon. The label on it read *Associates*.

"Associates?" I breathed. Was the hippie Calderon's hit man? He had the stone-cold vibe of a killer. I wanted details.

I turned to the file folders on the desk. A bit of pawing netted me Sleeth's jacket. He was a California native, born and raised in Solaris in a middle-class family. He'd enrolled at UCLA, probably to avoid the draft. By his sophomore year, his grades were in the crapper even though he was an acting major. Acting. With his looks, how hard could it be?

He'd gotten in hot water for a drugs-related incident on campus, and UCLA had given him the boot. He'd held a number of menial jobs since, none for more than a month or two, and mooched off friends for a place to live.

By all accounts, he spent any money he earned on drugs. He'd been picked up a couple of times for possession or drunk and disorderly, but he always talked his way out of charges.

Three months ago, everything changed. He'd moved into a swank apartment building and registered that sweet little Mustang in his name. He still didn't have a job, but he wasn't short on cash. His only contact with law enforcement had been over complaints that he played his stereo too loud.

Noise complaints? No arrests for assault and battery? Not the description of a killer. More like a pantywaist.

I set his jacket aside and picked up Calderon's thick file. If there was a connection between Calderon and Decker, the mob boss got my vote as the most likely killer, if not directly, then because he'd ordered one of his thugs to make the hit.

Calderon was careful. Narcotics and Vice had followed him for a year without a result. Last month they got permission to tap his phones. They couldn't get a snitch inside his organization; everyone was too afraid of him.

The file included pictures of people who came and went from his restaurant, the Luna Azul. Decker had dropped by once. Just once? And that made the lieutenant think Decker and Calderon were in business together?

Sleeth hit the place weekly, mostly when the restaurant was closed. He never stayed long. Maybe he didn't like Mexican food.

The fat jacket included a lengthy list of property owned by Calderon. He had his fingers in some surprising pies. Someone had circled the name and address of Sleeth's apartment building.

In my book, the evidence made Sleeth and Calderon more than associates. The mob boss was looking out for the hippie punk. Hell, if I'd been running the investigation, Sleeth would be clapped in irons because of the company he kept.

Footsteps sounded in the hallway. I held my breath. If anyone found me in here, my career was finished.

The clip-clop of feet continued past the incident room to the squad room. It must be a late-returning patrol unit. A hiss of relief escaped me. I'd wait until they left, and then I'd slip out.

The footsteps came back. They stopped outside the incident room door. My teeth clamped so tight I thought they'd break. The doorknob rattled. No time to hide. The door swung open.

"Dang it, Nicky, do you know what will happen if Mack catches you in here?"

Dave pushed the door closed behind him.

Escaping air whistled from me. "Jesus Christ, Dave, give me a heart attack."

I picked up Decker's file.

Dave snatched it from my hand and waved it in my face. "You want to get suspended?"

"I want to catch a killer. And Sleeth has mob connections. It was no accident he showed up at the murder scene."

"You may be able to talk down raging wife-beaters, but you won't talk down Chief Greene if you get caught."

I picked up Sleeth's file and swapped it for Decker's. "Read this. Sleeth's in bed with Seve Calderon."

"I don't care if he's in bed with John, Paul, George, and Ringo all at the same time. You can't come in here and snoop. You're not on the case, and it's against the rules." He put the folder on the desk.

I flipped open Decker's file. He had some Better Business Bureau complaints for delivering dodgy goods and three outstanding parking tickets. Otherwise, he wasn't any more crooked than most of the business owners in Solaris.

"Look at this," I told Dave. "Those clowns Stutzman and Arndt questioned Decker's secretary, and she refused to cooperate. I bet she would have talked to me."

Dave snatched the file from my hands and slapped it on the pile tottering on the desk. "You're not on the murder squad, and at the rate you're disobeying rules, you won't be on patrol much longer either."

I waved a hand at the blackboard. "The squad thinks it's a pro hit. Calderon's a target they can't resist. Their desire to nail him will taint the whole investigation."

Dave grabbed my arm and dragged me to the door. "They'll follow the evidence, which is what they're supposed to do. Your job is to carry out your duties as a patrol officer. That doesn't include sneaking into the incident room."

He cracked the door and checked for activity in the hallway. The floor was still as quiet as a crypt.

"Sleeth's the only suspect on the board. There's something not right about him, but they have no evidence he's the killer," I said. "Why aren't they casting a wider net?"

Dave pulled me out and shut the door. He didn't let go of my elbow until we were at the top of the stairs.

"Calderon is dangerous. Promise me you'll stay out of this."

We trotted down a second time. I couldn't make a promise I knew I wouldn't keep, so I hedged.

"But I could help. People talk to me. Sleeth would talk to me.

The secretary would talk to me."

Dave swung the door open. "No, and that's final."

We exited into the cool night air and walked across the lot to our waiting vehicles. Dave stood beside his Dodge pickup and watched while I started my Corvair. I gave him a wave and phony smile.

The idea that Decker's death was a mob hit didn't sit right. It left too many open questions. What if Decker had other enemies? Who would know about that?

Decker's secretary, of course. She might open up to another woman, one-on-one. It was worth a shot. If I got information from her that broke the case, Chief Greene would have to eat his words—and it might save the life of another innocent victim.

12

Susie's pad turned out to be a tiny Craftsman home on the north side of Solaris, a long, long drive from Decker Industries. She left Kasker in the cramped living room with its blue plaid overstuffed sofa and chair. A table beside the chair displayed pictures of an older couple and a foo-foo dog.

Ancient, sun-faded brocade curtains hung at the front window. A blue and brown braided rug covered most of a hardwood floor. The lamp on the table with the pictures provided soft light.

She returned with two glasses and a bottle of cheap white wine, which she placed on the coffee table. She sat down and fussed with her hair. Kasker sat beside her, close enough that their hips touched.

He poured the wine and raised his glass. "To the nicest woman I've met in a long time."

Susie blushed and raised her own glass. "To the knight who rescued me."

He smiled and stroked her upper arm. "I don't understand how a man like your boss could let you get away."

"Let's not talk about him." She took a long pull on her wine.

Kasker topped up her glass and estimated the minutes until he could have her clothes off. His flesh screamed its desire to take the woman now. He'd never restrained the meatbag from its wants before, not for this long. Trying to pry information out of her at the same time he screwed her might be a challenge.

"You have a dog?" He nodded toward the photo on the table.

She glanced at the picture. "Not anymore. Pepe passed away two years ago."

"Tragic loss," he said, glad he didn't have an ankle biter to contend with. He didn't like dogs, and the feeling was mutual.

He stroked a finger down the side of her neck. She took another swig of wine. He leaned in and kissed her cheek. She faced him, her eyes huge. He kissed her lips, quick and light, to test her readiness. She didn't pull back.

Kasker set his glass on the coffee table. He took her empty glass and set it beside his. Her chest heaved with her rapid breathing. He kissed her again. When their lips were firmly locked, he closed his arms around her. She stiffened, but only for a moment. Then their tongues were probing each other's mouths.

Her arms wrapped around him and stroked his back. In a minute, she had her hands under his shirt, stroking his skin. He reciprocated. She stopped moving. He nibbled her neck, and her hands moved again, slowly. Goats! Couldn't she make up her mind? He should have encouraged her to drink more wine.

Kasker pulled back. "I have a confession to make. I've never been with a woman." At her incredulous look, he hurried on. "Oh, I've made out, kissing and stuff, but I've never gone all the way. I was saving myself for someone special. For someone like you."

Her bleary eyes went soft. "You want me to be your first?"

He hung his head. "Would you?"

"Okay," she said. "But not here."

She wobbled as she stood, and Kasker reassessed her drunkenness. He needed her alert enough to answer questions. She giggled and led him to a bedroom decorated in frothy pink.

Once in the door, she fell against him and kissed him full on the mouth. She tasted of wine and smelled of desire. He ran his hands under her blouse and unclasped her bra. She pushed him to arms' length.

"I'm not that kind of girl, you know," she slurred. "I don't fall into bed with any stranger who buys me a beer. Or fixes my flat."

"I can tell you're a good girl, Susie. But you're so lonely. Why should you be lonely?" he whispered, pushing temptation at her. "You deserve a man, one you can brag about to your girlfriends."

He kissed her again, thrusting his tongue into her mouth. She sucked hard. His dick was a steel sabre and ached for release. Now how could he bring up Decker?

He unzipped her skirt and let it fall to the floor. She pulled his tank top over his head. He did the same with her blouse, ducking the time-consuming buttons. Her bra dropped on his feet. He still hadn't come up with a strategy to work Decker into their strip tease.

Kasker captured a breast in his hand and rolled her nipple between his thumb and middle finger while she unbuttoned his fly. Had he known in advance he'd be in a hurry, he would have worn jeans with a zipper. Never mind. They were off.

Decker. What of Decker? He ran his tongue across her breast and onto her belly while he bent to remove her panties.

She groaned and buried her hands in his hair.

He had it. He'd bring her to the edge, make her beg for more. He'd exchange her pleasure for the information he needed. He stood.

She clutched him for another long kiss while she used her soft belly to grind against his woody.

It was too much for him. He scooped her into his arms and onto the bed, her flab straining his shoulders and back.

In a moment, he was in her, stroking, stroking while he licked her face, nibbled her ears, and moaned his desire. She writhed and urged him on, adding squeals of delight.

At last, release. He collapsed onto the bed beside her, panting.

Horns and hooves! They were done, and he'd learned nothing. He'd been bested by the weakness of the borrowed housing. He was a fool. He had nothing left to bargain with, nothing to withhold, at least not for another half hour.

Susie rolled onto her side and laid her head on his shoulder. The fingers of her hand twined in his chest hair, bringing a gentle pleasure. He wrapped an arm around her torso and traced curlicues on her arm with a forefinger. What else could he use to bargain with?

"That place next door to Decker Industries went bust six months ago," she said. "Who are you really?"

Kasker stopped drawing on her arm.

Susie propped up on an elbow and looked at him. Her fingers continued their grooming.

This wasn't at all how he'd planned the evening. He thought he understood human motivations. He'd screwed up.

"If you knew I was lying, why did you come with me?"

She flopped back and sighed. "All us fat girls have fantasies of being swept off our feet and making love with a valiant knight. But the hunks like you never give us a second look."

She propped up again and grinned at him. "Tonight, my fantasy came true. Sorry I used you. Why do you want to know about Decker? It's all you've talked about. You should learn to be more subtle."

Using people. He understood that. A glimmer of hope sparked. He resumed drawing on her arm.

"Decker had something that didn't belong to him. Whoever murdered him took it. If I can find the killer, I can get it back."

"You want to know about his business rivals and enemies. I already told the police, they're one and the same. To know Decker was to hate him. If you had something he wanted, he took it. He had the most amazing luck. Or rather, his rivals had such bad luck."

Thanks to Seve. Decker's luck came at the price of his soul. Too bad he hadn't lived long enough to enjoy his wins.

She put her head on his shoulder again. Her fingertips stopped their exploration of his chest hair and drew little rings around his nipples.

Kasker pushed the tingling in his nipples away. She was talking at last. He needed to get what he came for and get home for a night's sleep.

"Whoever killed Decker was someone he knew and trusted, not someone he thought of as an enemy. Where did he go? Who did he trust?"

"The police took everything from his desk." Her fingers walked to his bellybutton, lingered, and continued south, grooming the hair as they went. "He always feared an IRS raid, so he didn't leave the important stuff where they could find it. Like his appointment diary."

Kasker quivered. "But you know where it is."

"He had a secret safe installed behind a bulletin board in the janitor's closet. It has the same combination as the decoy safe in his office: 11-05-30, his birthday."

"How do you know?" His rising excitement warred with his rising flesh. Goats! Was it never satisfied?

"Because I tried it." Her nails trailed across his thigh, and warmth rushed to his groin.

"Why didn't you tell the police?"

"Those jerks treated me like shit." She withdrew her hand, sat up, and sighed. "I guess you'll be leaving now that you have what you want."

He needed sleep. But in the morning, he'd awake with a hard on and lose time seeking another female. If he stayed the night, he could quench his corporeal cloak again before he left. Much more efficient.

The sight of her dangling breasts hardened him. He pulled her down and kissed her. When he released her, she drew back, eyes glowing with anticipation. He rolled her on her back and slid on top.

"No rush."

13

The sun crested the horizon as I arrived in Susan Brown's low-rent neighborhood on the north side of Solaris. I'd managed only a few hours' sleep, and my eyes burned, but I hummed along with the radio.

Neat little houses lined both sides of the street, each with dead brown grass in their front yards. Curtains were drawn over windows left open to allow in the cool night air. The cars in the driveways were older model compacts bought during the last recession.

I slowed to locate Brown's place. I'd park out front and sip my coffee until I saw movement. I didn't want to wake her and start on the wrong foot.

Then I noticed the maroon Mustang. I'd memorized Sleeth's license number. The plate matched.

I pulled in across the street three houses down and walked to the pony car. The temperature of the hood told me it had been there for hours. I returned to my Corvair.

My first stakeout. A little thrill lanced through me. I flipped open my notebook, licked the tip of my pencil, and wrote the date on the top of a fresh page. Too bad I hadn't brought my Instamatic camera to document my observations.

The sun rose, the shade from the palm tree I'd parked under crept across the hood and up the windshield, and I sipped my coffee, now gone cold. I shifted in my seat and checked the time. The paperboy cycled past, tossing folded papers on porches.

At the next house up, a little old Asian man tottered onto his porch and surveyed his domain. Unlike the other places, his yard sported a profusion of summer flowers around which birds and butterflies swirled. The riot of colors made a beautiful collage.

He picked up his paper and tottered inside. Ten minutes later, he emerged juggling a teacup, the newspaper, and binoculars. He eased down into an old rocker and set the cup and the paper on a wicker table beside the chair. First he sipped tea, then he studied the wildlife in his front garden with the binoculars.

Binoculars? For birds and butterflies twenty feet away? He must be blind. Having perused the garden, he unfolded the paper in his lap.

The temperature climbed. I rolled down all the windows and squirmed more. I'd learned my first important stakeout lesson: Never drink a large cup of coffee when you don't know how long it will be until you find a bathroom.

A glint caught my attention. The little old man had his binoculars pointed at me. He set them down, fished a pencil and paper from the pocket of his blue denim work shirt, and jotted something. The pad and pencil went on the table next to the cup.

My heart climbed into my throat. What if Mack had the secretary's house under surveillance? She hadn't rated a file, but if that was Sleeth's car... And now I'd been seen here.

My jangled nerves were too much for my full bladder. I had to find a service station with restrooms before it burst. I started my car.

The house door opened. Sleeth stepped onto the porch. Behind him, an overweight woman in a flimsy robe stopped in the doorway. He turned to say goodbye. She hooked a finger in the waistband of his jeans, pulled him close, and buttoned his fly.

He laughed, pulled her closer with a hand behind her neck, and kissed her with so much tongue action I thought she'd choke. Watching them made my panties damp. I looked away.

Sleeth got in his Mustang and pulled out in a hurry. I gave him a two-block head start and drove away, certain he hadn't spotted me. The little old Asian man waved goodbye.

I didn't know the neighborhood. It took me fifteen minutes to find a restroom and another five to get the service station attendant to cough up the key. When I'd taken care of business, I filled up with gas. The attendant cleaned my windshield and checked my oil while I tapped on the steering wheel.

I returned to Miss Brown's house. The curtains were still drawn. I knocked anyway. And knocked. No answer. Maybe she was in the bath.

I waited in my car for fifteen minutes and tried again. Still no answer.

As I walked back to my car, the little old man caught my eye. I strolled to his house and stopped on the sidewalk. He smiled and nodded. Encouraged by his greeting, I joined him on his porch.

"Good morning," I said. "I couldn't help admiring your beautiful garden."

He smiled and nodded. I wondered whether he understood English. Or maybe he was hard of hearing.

I took a few steps closer. The pad on the table listed my license plate number right under Sleeth's. I swallowed hard.

"I was hoping to catch my friend Miss Brown at home this morning, but she isn't answering."

More smiling and nodding. He glanced down at the front page of the paper before he turned his attention to me.

"Y'all a friend of Miss Susie's?" he asked with a thick Texas drawl. "Or is this official police business?"

I stared. I wasn't in uniform or driving the patrol car. How did he know? Was he one of Mack's undercover agents?

He held up the paper. There was the picture of me with the mayor and his son. He put it back in his lap.

"If this is official, I'll need to see your badge so I can write down the number." He picked up his pad and pencil.

"This is a social call. We went to school together," I replied.

His sharp eyes looked me up and down. "A social call at sunrise? Didn't your mama teach you better manners?"

"Okay, okay," I said. "It's not an official investigation, but her boss was murdered night before last. That guy she was with is a person of interest. What can you tell me about him?"

If the information about the murder surprised him, he didn't show it. Of course not. He read the paper.

"Not much. He's never been here before."

That tidbit was unexpected. They'd looked damned friendly when they kissed. Had they been going to Sleeth's place instead? Was he worried that his apartment might be under surveillance? I hadn't noticed anything in the file to indicate Mack had men following the hippie.

"Anything else you can tell me about her?"

"She grew up in that house. Her folks died in a car accident two years ago, and she inherited it. She keeps to herself."

Time was marching by. If I was going to question Miss Brown and get back for my lunch with Newell, I had to get moving.

"Guess I'll give her doorbell another try."

"You won't get an answer." He reached for his cup. "She went out not long after you and that young man left."

14

Kasker navigated the deserted Sunday morning streets on his way to Decker Industries. He blinked dry eyes. He hadn't gotten much rest. Susie's appetite for sex exceeded that of his flesh, something of a novelty.

Too bad her house didn't have air conditioning. He could stop trawling for willing females at parties and use her exclusively if only her place were closer to his apartment and more comfortable.

How did humans cope with all the nattering distraction? Food, drink, drugs, sex. To deny the body was to be miserable. Perhaps that was why so many humans sold their souls to Seve and his brethren.

His true form had but one desire—to hunt the damned. The diary would provide the clue he needed to Holmes' location. He'd devour Holmes' soul and return to Hell where he belonged, free at last from the torturous realm of humans.

Susie's car still blocked the driveway of the Decker Industries parking lot. As before, Kasker left the Mustang around the corner and walked back. He glanced at the flat tire as he passed. She could find some other sucker to change it.

The key he'd lifted from her purse opened the rear door. He slipped into the stuffy interior and strode to the elevator. On the sixth floor, he stepped out and prowled for the janitor's closet. It was tucked in next to the restrooms just a few steps from the elevator. It was locked.

Goats! Susie hadn't said anything about a key for the closet. He walked all the sixth-floor offices looking for something to help him break in. Most of them weren't used.

He found Susie's desk, another picture of her scruffy dog and a pamphlet for some hippie commune on the desktop. The drawer held five bottles of nail polish in various shades of pink and a long, sharp letter opener shaped like a jeweled dagger.

The phony dagger proved ineffective on the door. The blade snapped off when he tried to pry the latch back. He kicked the steel-clad door, more from anger than a test of its strength.

His Moses moccasins were no match for the metal. He hopped away bruised and cursing. Decker had done an excellent job protecting his private stash.

Flummoxed, he walked each floor on his way down. These offices, too, were vacant. None provided the necessary weapon for his next assault.

He went to his car and returned with the tire iron. Prying with it got him no farther than prying with the dagger. He took aim and bashed at the doorknob. Each contact sent an unpleasant jolt up his arms. After five or six blows, the knob surrendered and crashed to the floor.

By fiddling with the internal workings, he drew back the latch and pushed open the door. He stepped in and wished he hadn't. The place stank of noxious cleaning compounds.

He flipped on the light. The narrow slice of back wall visible between the metal shelving was covered by a bulletin board plastered with health and safety notices. He crossed the dinky space, gripped the edge, and tugged. The board didn't budge.

Kasker didn't bother hunting for a latch. He jammed the tire iron under a bottom corner and pried. The lower half of the board snapped off and dropped on his toes.

After more cursing and hopping, he levered off the remaining half to expose the safe. He twirled the knob, entered the combination, yanked the handle. The door swung back.

The safe was empty.

Kasker flung the tire iron to the floor. It bounced against a shelf, toppling a bottle, which fell and broke. More noxious fumes swirled.

Coughing and squinting through watering eyes, he ran to the elevator. The stinging odor followed him. He gave up on the elevator and plunged through the stairwell door, running down all six flights.

When he came out in the parking lot, he realized he'd left the tire iron behind. He wanted to use it on the windshield of Susie's car. The bitch had lied.

He had no doubt that the diary *used* to be in the safe. The question was whether Decker removed it before he died, or whether Susie had taken it. If Susie had it, why had she told him it was in the safe?

Sex, of course. When he didn't find it here, he'd go back to her. She'd use it as payment for another fantasy evening with her knight errant. He'd hunted souls for thousands of years. The females were always the more devious.

The day had warmed to an unpleasant temperature. The flesh nagged for food, and he'd need forty minutes behind the wheel to return to Susie's. A pox on the woman.

The drive to Susie's was hot, boring, and a waste of time. Susie wasn't home. He waited down the block for a useless hour. The neighbors began to stare—especially the little old man with the binoculars.

Seve expected him. He needed to feed the meat puppet. He'd come back later, and then he'd settle the score with Susie. He'd get the diary. Right after they screwed.

15

I tucked my uniform hat under my arm and pushed through the door of Travo's.

Who would have guessed that Italian brothers would decorate their upscale restaurant Indian style? Sun lanced in west-facing windows and glittered off tableware and white linen tablecloths. Little crystal vases held pink carnations and a sprig of fern leaf.

Bold pastel pink and green stripes zigzagged the tan walls. A mural by the door showed an Indian brave mounted on a rearing pinto pony, a teepee in the background. His nocked arrow aimed at my heart.

The place buzzed with conversation from two dozen tables filled with women in town to shop. They wore breezy cotton dresses and carried designer purses. I wore my dark blue uniform and carried a gun. I'd never had any fashion sense.

The place was jammed. How had Newell gotten a reservation so quickly? As the mayor's son, I supposed he could call in favors.

Cool air sent a shiver down me. Or maybe it was the sight of him sitting in a booth near the back. Dave was right. Hanging with the mayor's son was a bad idea. It wouldn't endear me to the upper echelons. They'd think I was trying to leverage our acquaintance into a promotion. But I wanted to know what he was doing at the Carlisle Hotel.

I gritted my teeth and wove between tables until I reached him. For a guy who'd bounced down the asphalt just the day before yesterday, he scrambled up with surprising speed.

"Officer Demasi, I'm glad you made it." He helped me into the booth and took his seat. He stared so hard I thought I'd smeared my lipstick.

"Mr. Newell, it's good to see you up and around."

He chortled. "Listen to us. We sound like complete strangers. It's Tad. 'Mr. Newell' is my dad."

"We are," I blurted. It felt a lot warmer by the kitchens. "Strangers, I mean."

Belatedly I added, "Nicky. Friends call me Nicky."

The waitress arrived with menus. I scanned for something that wouldn't slop on my uniform or get stuck in my teeth. Tad ordered a beer and asked if I'd join him. A tall cold one sounded wonderful.

"Not while I'm in uniform." I regretted again my choice in attire.

"You wear it well. It's about time the Solaris PD realized what an important contribution women can make."

"I'm delighted to hear you think so." I was surprised by his progressive attitude. "Now if only the old boys' network would come around."

Dave's words of caution danced through my head, and I bit my tongue. I didn't need Tad tattling to his dad how the lowly patrol officer whined about the brass.

"You have all the qualities of an excellent officer. You're smart. You keep your head in an emergency." He reached across the table to touch my hand. "If you didn't, I wouldn't be here now. I can't thank you enough."

The little metal cream pitcher reflected the red in my face. "Any officer would have done the same."

"Of course I wasn't awake to appreciate it, but I'm glad it was your lips locked on mine." He winked at me.

I focused on the menu. His flip-flops from serious discussion to smarmy quips left me without a retort. From the expression on his face, he seemed as confused as me. Maybe the hospital let him out too soon.

He cleared his throat and read his menu, a little scowl forming on his brow. "I recommend the tomato bisque with the bread sticks."

The waitress returned, and he ordered the soup for both of us. I placed the napkin on my lap and adjusted the cutlery.

"Tell me what happened," he asked in the silence. "The accident, I mean."

"Not much to tell. The kid in the Camaro accelerated to make the light. You stepped off the curb in front of him." We'd gone over this in the hospital, and I wondered why he still had questions. Maybe he didn't remember my previous answer.

"I walked against the light, in front of an on-coming car? I'm a combat vet. How could I be so stupid?"

"You seemed to be in a hurry."

"Oh." His shoulders relaxed, and he glanced around the restaurant. "Maybe I was preoccupied."

"Do you know someone who lives at the Carlisle Hotel?" I asked.

Tad frowned and pursed his lips. "Doesn't ring a bell. Why?"

"The accident happened right in front of it. Given your trajectory, you may have been coming from there. Do you know anyone who lives in the hotel?"

The waitress brought our order. Tad dipped a breadstick in the soup, chewed, and swallowed.

"I don't think I know anyone there." He sighed. "My brain is all jumbled up. Thinking feels like wading through molasses. The doc says I have to give it time."

We both spooned up soup. If Tad had trouble thinking, I didn't want to press him with small talk.

He looked over his beer glass as he sipped. "This Slasher case sounds nasty."

"It is. I'd never imagined one human could do that to another."

Tad's face shaded to green under his yellow and purple bruises. He swallowed hard, and a sheen of sweat broke on his forehead. "You were there?"

"My partner and I were first on the scene. We got the call right after you left in the ambulance."

"I hadn't realized..."

He frowned down at the fork that he rubbed with a forefinger, and I got the impression he'd gone a million miles away. Or perhaps he'd gone only as far as the killing fields of the war.

"But I can't talk about the case."

"No, of course you can't."

Tad rearranged the salt and pepper shakers. "You must be excited to work such an important case."

I snorted. "I'm not part of the investigation team. I don't have the experience. Besides, Chief Greene doesn't think a woman can handle the job."

"You graduated at the top of the class from the police academy, and you've been on the force for two years. You found the body. Why shouldn't you be involved?"

"It's my second week on patrol. How did you know about my academy record?" My voice climbed.

Tad grinned. "The mayor mentioned it in his speech yesterday.

I guess you weren't listening."

My cheeks got hot enough to singe my eyelashes. "I was listening... sort of."

He laughed. "He can't open his mouth without making a speech. I usually tune him out, too. But I listened to what he said about you."

Tad's merriment fell away. "The person responsible is a fiend and has to be caught. No one deserves a death like that."

I placed my spoon in my empty bowl. "We have a witness, but he's not telling us the full story."

"You mean that hippie Sleeth? You're the only cop on the force who thinks of him as a witness. To everyone else, he's the prime suspect." Tad stirred the remains of his soup with a breadstick. "Lt. Mack's report says there's no connection between this Sleeth and Decker."

"Ha!" I laughed. "Turns out Sleeth's enjoying 'free love' with Decker's secretary."

Tad's eyebrows bounced up. He dropped the soggy breadstick in his bowl. Confusion clouded his face while his eyes bored holes in the table. "That information wasn't in the mayor's briefing."

"Well..." I cast around for a way to explain how I'd come by this tidbit.

"Aren't most murder victims killed by people they know?" His voice carried a hint of anger. "Decker's secretary will have a list of his contacts, and I bet you'll find the killer's name on that list. Has anyone questioned her? From the report given to my father, it doesn't sound like they've focused on Decker enough."

"If she knows anything about Decker, she isn't sharing it. She handed over a couple boxes of files, but nothing interesting turned up."

"You should talk to her," Tad urged with surprising intensity. "You're both working women. You two would connect. Secretaries are snoops. They always know what their bosses are up to."

"I'm not on the case. If Lt. Mack found out—"

A look of determination settled on his face. He didn't say anything more.

"We found your car," I said. "It's three blocks from here in that lot next to the State Theater."

A smile flitted across his face. "Thanks. I'll pick it up."

16

Kasker drove by the Luna Azul and muttered curses under his breath. Cars filled every parking spot for blocks, their occupants attending a street fair ahead. Strains of guitars and marimbas floated in the open window, and the scent of barbeque filled the air.

He circled back at the next corner, rumbled two blocks, and pulled into a fifteen-minute loading zone. From there, he strode through the climbing afternoon heat to his destination, keenly aware that he was already half an hour late.

A couple with two children slipped into the Luna Azul ahead of him, and the sound of dozens of voices drifted out. Customers packed the restaurant. When Kasker tried to enter, the burly door guard put up a hand.

"Mr. Calderon isn't here. He says you should wait."

A curse on Susie for making him late. The sumptuous smells from inside caused his empty stomach to growl. A double-curse on the flesh for its incessant demands. But he had time. He'd eat now.

He nodded and started through the door.

The guard stepped into his path. "We're full."

Kasker ground his teeth. He would make do with beer and peanuts.

"I'll wait in the bar." He moved sideways.

The guard moved with him. "Bar's full, too."

Kasker's eyes narrowed. "How long will he be?"

"Mr. Calderon couldn't say for sure, but he thought it would be real soon."

Seve left him blistering his heels on the burning sidewalk for half an hour—precisely the amount of time he'd been late. By then, his shirt was soaked in sweat and he'd do anything for a drink. The demon sent the big Negro bodyguard to fetch him to his inner sanctum. The man smirked as he delivered the summons.

Seve sat in a tiny office off the kitchen looking cool and comfortable. He waved Kasker to a chair on the opposite side of a heavy mahogany desk and took a sip of a tall iced tea. He didn't offer any to Kasker.

"What progress, sabueso? Did you find the Oracle?"

Kasker shifted in the hard chair. "He's a crazy man who tells bad jokes."

The demon leaned forward and folded his hands on the desk. "Did you ask him about the ritual?"

Now that he thought about it, Kasker realized that he hadn't asked anything. Remembering their meeting brought back the uncomfortable feeling of melting away. He suppressed a shiver.

"He speaks in riddles. He's useless."

Seve leaned back. "You fear him."

"Get real. I'm not afraid of anything."

He grabbed the demon's glass and drained it. *How does anyone drink this stuff?* Had he been less desperate, he would have spat it on the floor.

Kasker slammed the glass on the desk. "Decker left a diary. Somewhere in it, I'll find Holmes. Holmes will lead me to Decker, and if Decker lives in the mortal housing of another, you'll get your soul."

The demon's eyes narrowed, and his hands tightened on the chair arms. "Our master is not pleased. You will return to the Oracle and learn about the ritual."

"I have better things to do." Kasker's lips twitched into a sly smile. "But if you believe the Oracle has important information, I'll tell you where to find him."

Seve's eyes slid away, and his knuckles whitened. *So even a creature as powerful as this demon fears the crazy Hawaiian.*

Seve seemed about to make a retort. Instead, he reached into the bottom drawer. He withdrew a yellowed scroll and tossed it on the desk between them.

"Lester Renquist. A man willing to do anything for money."

"Another collection so soon?" Kasker asked.

"Their fates are written at their birth. It's only the path they take to their ends over which they have free will." Seve leaned back in his chair and steepled his fingers. "This time, no mistakes."

The hackles on Kasker's neck rose at the implication that he was somehow responsible for Decker's escape. He grabbed the scroll and unrolled all three feet of crumbling parchment.

A spidery scrawl of ink crawled down the page, one line after the other, describing in great detail what each signatory would receive. Kasker skipped over the text. The human always wanted power of some kind: wealth, influence, dominion over others. Seve always wanted a soul. Boring and predictable.

Two signatures written in blood blazed at the bottom of the page. Kasker ignored Seve's. Blood from demon-worn flesh was meaningless, and the demon hadn't signed his true name, only the moniker of the envelope he occupied. The human who co-signed didn't know how he'd been hoodwinked.

The human signature was unreadable, not that it mattered. Signing was a ruse to willingly get the human's blood on the contract. The instant a drop hit the parchment, the soul was doomed.

Kasker raised the paper to his nose and sniffed. Soul-scent wafted to him. He flicked out his tongue to test Renquist's blood. His senses ignited with the sweet burn of damnation.

He closed his eyes and savored the experience, gradually narrowing his focus and following the pull of the blood to its source. There it was, three miles southeast in a high-rise office building. Renquist's soul glowed like black fire.

"When?" he whispered, breathless.

"Tomorrow night at 11:13. Don't be late."

Kasker let the admonishment go unanswered. He could already taste the soul, and his mouth watered. His true form fought for release from its earthly binding.

"Go," the demon ordered. "I have work to do."

Kasker opened his eyes and growled his displeasure. The demon turned his attention to papers on the desk, unfazed.

Kasker kicked back his chair as he rose. It ricocheted off a table behind him. He yanked the door open and considered slamming it. No, he'd leave it open and make the demon rise to close it.

On his way past the surly bodyguard, Kasker caught the man with an elbow in the solar plexus and thumped him back against the wall. He stormed on, listening for the sound of footsteps.

The guard recovered and pursued him into the kitchen. A hand grabbed Kasker's shoulder. He spun, seized a beefy wrist, and twisted. Pain blossomed on the bodyguard's face.

Kasker grabbed the giant's shirt front and slammed him into a counter. A stack of plates crashed to the floor, drawing shrieks from the kitchen staff. Kasker bared his teeth.

"Your time will come," Kasker said in a quiet voice. "And then I will devour you."

The bodyguard struggled, panic filling his eyes, but Kasker didn't let go.

Seve broke them apart and faced Kasker, arm pointing to the door.

"Enough! Go."

For an instant, the demon's true face flickered beneath the mask of skin. Kasker turned away. As he passed a counter, he snatched a taco from a plate.

"I warn you, sabueso, don't lose this one," the demon called.

Kasker strode through the restaurant dropping a trail of crumbs as he ate. Heads turned at his passing, and waiters scrambled to get out of his way. A murmur of disapproval followed him. By the time he reached the door, he'd polished off his meal and licked his fingers clean.

Outside, a wave of heat and regret swept over him. He shouldn't have antagonized Seve. He relied on the demon for money, drugs, and a comfortable place to rest. He smiled. If Seve withdrew his support, he'd crash at Susie's.

Thinking of the woman roused the flesh. He walked faster despite the heat and cursed the street fair for causing so much congestion. If only Susie's place had air conditioning. Or perhaps a swimming pool. Then they could shag in the cool water.

A yellow traffic ticket fluttered under the wiper blade of his Mustang. He laughed, pulled it loose, and tossed it on the sidewalk.

Only then did he notice the slashes in the sidewalls of the front and rear tires.

Kasker cursed the souls who'd done the damage, and then for good measure, he cursed the entire human race. The nearest service station was six blocks away, and he had only one spare.

He popped the trunk. The spare was bolted to the floor. His tire iron was missing. He'd dropped it in the janitor's closet at Decker Industries. He cursed more and slammed the trunk.

It was eight blocks to the service station, not the six he'd thought, and a sign in the window announced that they'd closed for the fair. Kasker stopped a man passing by and was told he could find another station five blocks west.

Sweat poured down his face by the time he arrived at the second station. The mechanic agreed to help, but he couldn't go until the other attendant returned from break. He suggested Kasker buy a Coke from the machine by the door. The Coke—like the day—was hot.

Forty-five minutes later, the attendant returned. Kasker climbed into the mechanic's beat-up Ford pickup. The mechanic chatted amiably while he drove, oblivious to Kasker's silence. They parked a block from the Mustang, the closest empty space the mechanic could find.

"She's a beaut," the mechanic said as he circled Kasker's car. He clucked at the damaged tires. "Someone has it in for you. Where's your spare?"

Kasker opened the trunk and pointed.

The mechanic looked inside. "Tire iron's missing."

Kasker ground his teeth. "I lost it up the ass of my last mechanic."

The man blinked. Then he grinned. "No problem. I'll get mine from my truck."

The mechanic fetched the tire iron and changed the spare for the front flat. When he'd finished, he lowered the jack. The car dropped until the rim sat on the asphalt.

"Huh. Looks like your spare's flat." The mechanic wiped a greasy hand across his sweating brow, leaving a dark streak. "I'll have to charge you extra for changing that one again."

Kasker clenched his jaw and nodded his acceptance. He glanced up at the sky. Mid-afternoon already. That made him grind his teeth more.

They rolled the two flats to the truck and drove to the station. The mechanic got to work mounting new tires. Kasker squatted in the shade and craved a cold beer and a joint. And Susie.

The mechanic charged an exorbitant fee. Kasker pulled a thick wad of Seve's money from his wallet and counted bills. If the demon cut him off, he hoped Susie could feed him as well as provide a bed.

The mechanic placed the new tires in the truck and drove to the Mustang. The nearest parking space was three blocks away. Now that he had his money, the man moved slower with each passing minute. Kasker wanted to bite him.

The mechanic replaced the jack and the spare in the trunk. A greedy glint lit his eyes.

"Not much good having a spare that's flat. Swing by the station and I'll fill that up for you. Sell you a tire iron, too."

"Maybe later." Kasker got in and fired up the engine.

"Mind giving me a lift back to my truck?"

The mechanic reached for the passenger door. Kasker shifted down and laid a patch on the pavement as he pulled away. In the rearview mirror, the mechanic shook an angry fist.

17

I pulled up at Cindy's house a few minutes after seven. The place looked like a Spanish hacienda with its stucco siding, tile roof, and big palms waving in the on-shore breeze. Dave's banker brother-in-law must be climbing the white-collar ladder.

A little flash of envy blossomed. I'd never afford something like this on a cop's salary. I had a cozy two-bedroom bungalow on the east side. It was a step up from Susan Brown's place, but only a short one. If I wanted to live better, I needed a better job—or a rich husband.

The feminist movement might preach that women deserved equal pay for equal work, but the employment market mostly wasn't listening. I'd seen so many unhappy housewives stuck in loveless marriages and unable to escape for economic reasons. I swore I'd never be one of them. Could I make it without a man to support me?

I'd thought that going to Miss Brown's would net me a vital clue to help solve Decker's murder and show Greene I could be an effective officer. What I'd learned wasn't enough to offset the trouble I'd created for myself by going there. I had to tell, but I couldn't. My initiative had always gotten me ahead in the world. Now it threatened to cost me my job and my independence.

The street was jammed with cars. I abandoned my pity party and walked to the door. A sign directed me to a side gate. When I reached the back yard, I figured half the parish must have come.

Three barbeque grills smoked and flamed on the patio. Cindy's husband minded a whole fishery's worth of salmon steaks. Beer nestled in ice-filled tubs beside the grills. Nearby, a picnic table groaned under the weight of a fancy cake, a dozen kinds of salads, condiments, plates, and utensils.

I helped myself to a beer and looked through the crowd of strangers for Dave. He waved from across the yard. A pretty blonde in a halter top, floral miniskirt, and sandals had a hand on his arm. Her attention turned to me, and her soft pink lips pulled into a pout.

Dave extracted himself from her clutches and threaded between people until he reached me.

"Boy, am I glad to see you." He bent to peck my cheek.

I pulled back in surprise. His arm went around my shoulder, and he steered me toward the house. "That woman sticks like Elmer's Glue."

"So you told her I was your girlfriend?" I asked, feigning outrage. I couldn't keep the laugh out of my voice.

"Hardy har. Wait until some shark sets his sights on you."

Once we were in the kitchen, Dave released me. I nibbled chips from a bowl on the counter while he wiped a forearm across his sweating face.

"How was the date?" he asked.

"It wasn't a date! We just had lunch." I pressed my beer against my face, hoping to cool the rising heat.

"I stand corrected. How was the lunch?"

Dave's eyes had a twinkle in them. I wanted to turn it into a big black shiner.

"Not very productive. But listen, I saw Sleeth this morning. He lied about not knowing Decker. He spent last night with Decker's secretary."

Dave lifted his chin. "You promised you'd stay out of the investigation."

I'd counted on Dave to see a way out of my prickly situation. I'd gotten myself stuck between a lie and a catastrophe. The tone of his voice flushed my hopes away.

"I wasn't chasing Sleeth. I thought maybe I could get the secretary to talk, one woman to another."

"Nicky, Greene will put you on report when you tell him. You've been warned not to interfere."

I focused on Cindy's kitchen floor, looking for scuff marks while I fumed. The floor was immaculate, as always.

"I thought I might not tell Greene just yet," I said in a small voice.

When I glanced up, Dave stared at me with his mouth open. My hand tightened on my beer.

"We signed on to obey orders," Dave lectured. "You're frustrated, but you can't be a renegade. You can't withhold evidence to cover up your own bad behavior."

"If they'd done their job better, I wouldn't have gone to the secretary's house! If they had a tail on Sleeth, they'd already know he was there."

"I know you're concerned about showing the brass a woman can do the job, but you can't run off on your own. You do your job and let the detectives do theirs."

We glared at one another until Cindy stuck her head in and called us to eat. Dave held the door for me, and we lined up with the rest of the guests.

The blonde bombshell positioned herself next to Dave and gave me a condescending look while she ran her eyes over my sneakers, pedal pushers, and seersucker shirt. I'm sure she wondered what he saw in me. Occasionally I asked myself the same question, especially when I'd done something as stupid as going to Miss Brown's house.

Dave seemed more inclined to talk to his new sidekick now that he and I were on the outs. Fine by me. I needed to decide on my next move.

We ate on opposite sides of the yard. My anger faded, and I had to acknowledge that Dave was right. I needed to tell Greene and Mack about Sleeth and take my lumps. My party spirit fizzled.

It wasn't until Cindy cut the cake that Dave extricated himself from his blonde shadow and came to stand by me.

"I'm sorry," he said. "I shouldn't have gone off on you like that. You're a good officer and a selfless person. But lately, you've stopped following the rules. I know how important it is for you to lead the charge for women. Haring off on wild hunches isn't the way."

A little tickle of guilt wiggled through my gut. Dave had such high expectations of me. I hated to admit I'd let him down and changed the subject.

"I found out where Tad was before the accident."

Dave's mouth twitched into a frown. "You went looking without me?"

"Memories fade and get confused. I didn't want to delay any longer, so I made the rounds this afternoon. It's not like I was in any danger."

Dave wasn't mollified.

"The bartender at The Shack says he came in for happy hour and didn't leave until eight."

Dave scratched his jaw and stared into space. "That still

leaves three and a half hours unaccounted for."

"But here's the interesting part. Those two guys I saw on the sidewalk came in just after Tad did and left right behind him. The bartender didn't like the look of them. He thought they were casing the joint for a stickup."

"You and Mr. Newell are on a first name basis now?" He had his hands on his hips and watched me like a mother watches her toddler in the candy store. "Did he say why he was at the Carlisle Hotel?"

"He says he isn't familiar with it. If things are slow tomorrow, I thought about checking theaters to see if anyone remembers him. If he caught a show, it would fill a hole in the timeline."

"Good idea." Dave passed a hand over his hair and examined his own shoes. "You know, Nicky, if you want to prove your worth, you should forget about Sleeth and focus on Newell. If you collar someone who's after him, it'll prove what a good cop you are, and you won't have to do it behind Greene's back."

I was torn between pursuing the thugs stalking Tad or a mad killer gutting his victims. If I chased the Slasher, I risked losing everything.

"Tomorrow, I'll go through mug shots, see if I can recognize those two guys," I said. "That'll tell us who's after Tad."

18

The streetlights in Susie's neighborhood came on as Kasker turned down her block. Steppenwolf's *Born to Be Wild* blared from the radio, and his thumbs tapped the steering wheel in time to the music. Things were finally looking up.

Susie would have Decker's appointment diary. She'd haggle over what she wanted for it. He'd promise her anything. Then they'd screw because that would be a bargaining chip in Susie's offer.

In the diary would be the clue he needed to locate Holmes. When he'd found Holmes, he'd learn how Decker had been released and where he was now, assuming his soul hadn't been swallowed by the universe. Then he'd devour Holmes and shed this goats-begotten mortal wrapper. And his promises to Susie.

Already, an uncomfortable lump in his crotch strained the zipper of his jeans. Bang Susie first, then take the diary. No more lies. No more tricks. In and out, he told himself. In and out. The lump hardened at the thought.

But Susie was dead.

Kasker killed the radio and cruised by without slowing, all his senses heightened. No lights shone through Susie's windows. Inside her house, the last remnants of her soul faded from existence.

He slammed a hand on the wheel. He had to get into the house and look for the diary, but he couldn't afford to be found at the scene of another death, especially one connected to Decker. Bad enough he'd been seen here earlier. He turned at the next corner and parked.

An hour later, when the last light faded from the sky, Kasker considered his options. He could sneak through back yards to Susie's, but one of the houses had a dog, and all of the houses had five-foot chain-link fences. The dog would bark before he got close enough to silence it.

Approaching from the other end of the block meant more fences and more dogs. Souls and their annoying pets! He hissed his displeasure.

The residents of the house directly behind Susie's enjoyed the cool evening air on their back patio. He could wait to see if they went inside, but waiting wasn't for him. He was a hunter.

He'd have to go to the front door. He wished he'd stolen all Susie's keys instead of only the key to Decker Industries, in case her door was locked. He should have taken the mechanic up on the offer of a new tire iron. It might come in handy.

Kasker strolled quietly along the sidewalk, hands jammed in his pockets, head down. No one seemed to take note of his passing. Except that old guy on the porch, a candle flickering on the table beside him. How could humans live like that? All day, just sitting. He shuddered.

He turned up Susie's drive, cut across the lawn, and mounted the two short steps to the door. He didn't bother with the bell, didn't knock, didn't hesitate to turn the knob.

Locked.

Horns and hooves! How would he get in? Then he remembered Susie's open bedroom window at the side of the house. It had done little to cool the room while they'd had sex, but it would allow him access.

He hurried through the creaking side gate and tripped over a rake, falling on the dry, prickly grass. He cursed Susie for leaving the rake and whoever killed her for depriving him of release from the demands of the flesh.

The window stood open as before. It was placed at an inconvenient height to shimmy through. He scraped his back on the sash and banged his head on Susie's dresser.

The smell of her death tainted the air. He tripped over something on the floor and crashed onto the bed, which wasn't where it used to be. With care, he crawled to the door, encountering more unexpected obstacles. He turned on the light.

Dresser drawers lay scattered across the fuzzy carpet, undergarments strewn amongst them. The mattress had been sliced open, the dresser toppled away from the wall. The contents of the closet decorated the top of the wreckage.

Kasker moved to the living room. The bedroom light illuminated couch cushions ripped open, the lamp overturned, the braided rug shoved into a rumpled mess at one side.

Susie lay on a mound of stuffing just two steps inside the door, a single red hole in her back. Kasker pictured her killer searching the house for Decker's diary. When he didn't find it, he waited for her to return and shot her through the bloody throw pillow now on the floor beside the body.

If the wraith of her soul still clung to her corpse when he arrived, she'd been shot four hours earlier, or around four that afternoon. Or perhaps she'd lain wounded on the floor for some period before death overtook her, in which case, she could have been attacked earlier.

A large pool of blood spread under Susie. He wasn't sure what that meant in relation to the time of the shooting. He checked to be sure there was nothing of interest under her or clenched in her hands. Turning her over had all the charm of wrestling a beached whale.

Beside her, a torn grocery sack contained chocolate syrup, raspberry syrup, melted peach ice cream, and a broken bottle of cheap white wine. She'd anticipated his return and remembered that he preferred raspberries to strawberries. Thoughts of where she would have applied the syrup flickered through his brain, and his flesh swelled. Goats! The timing of her demise was unfortunate.

He righted the lamp and turned it on. A few steps away, he found her voluminous purse dumped out amid the destruction. Cosmetics, hair brush, nail file, wallet containing twelve dollars, her ID, and another photo of the dog.

He pocketed the money.

A ring of keys, pen, checkbook, two paperback romance novels with half-naked couples clutched in suggestive embraces on their covers. The swollen bosoms increased the pressure of his woody.

No diary. He examined the check register. The last entry was for today at Wally's Food Mart. Tucked in the register was a receipt for a dollar and change from Postal Instant Press, a copy shop. It carried today's date.

So that's why Susie sent him on the wild goose chase to Decker Industries. She wanted a copy of the diary before she gave it to him. Why copy it? If it contained information Decker wanted to conceal from the cops, blackmail of Decker's associates came to mind.

But who knew she had the diary? Decker, but since Kasker had detected no untethered soul outside the bookstore door, it was unlikely Decker's soul survived. And if Decker thought he'd want it later, why hadn't he taken it with him? Why come back for it when the cops would be searching the place and Kasker would be hunting him? It didn't make sense.

Possibly Susie had already contacted someone from the diary, and they were responsible for her death. If that was true, whoever it was worked fast. They'd had little time to react. Holmes?

Kasker stuffed the receipt in his jeans with the money and left through the window. He had no leads to either Holmes or Decker. Seve wouldn't be pleased. Neither would his master. He had to think of something soon. Otherwise, he'd be forced to revisit the Oracle.

19

Kasker missed Susie. He'd found a brunette at a party to give him a blow job, but she'd been so drunk there'd been minimal pleasure in it. Susie had been the adventuresome sort who knew how to get a guy's rocks off.

There'd been no word of Susie's death either in the Sunday morning paper or on the radio news later in the day. Perhaps the neighbors hadn't smelled her yet. They would. It was just a matter of time.

The cops would find his fingerprints at Susie's. Then they'd come knocking. He'd cleaned out his stash of weed and wad of cash and made sure his apartment had nothing more suspicious in it than a six-pack of beer and a wedge of moldy cheese.

He wasn't worried. He had the mechanic to provide an alibi for how he'd spent Saturday afternoon. He hoped the guy wasn't still pissed about the walk to his truck.

But now it was time to focus on the hunt. In another twenty minutes, Lester Renquist would die from a ruptured aneurism. Kasker didn't understand how Seve could predict the exact time and cause of death, but he did. The foreknowledge robbed much of the satisfaction from the hunt.

When Renquist died, Kasker would devour his soul. He could smell the damnation burning sweet in his nostrils, taste the essence in his mouth, feel its silky texture sliding down his throat.

His foot pressed the accelerator, sending the Mustang charging through the night toward the luxury apartment building where the unsuspecting Renquist awaited. Cool salt air flowed through the window but did nothing to slow the heat building in his true skin.

Three blocks from Renquist's, he slowed. Renquist lived in the penthouse on the fifteenth floor. The height added to the logistical problem of getting his meatbag close enough that he could maintain his connection while he abandoned it to harvest the soul.

He crept along the street lined bumper-to-bumper with vehicles. Hot little sports jobs alternated with luxury cars as big as buses, all an ostentatious show of their owners' wealth.

A broad walkway led to iron gates that blocked entry to the building. Beside the gates, a silver panel of call buttons glinted under harsh security lights. At the building's underground parking garage, a guard dozed in a lighted kiosk, and a barricade barred the entrance. A sign proclaimed parking for residents only.

Goats! He should have come earlier and scoped the place out, found someone in the building to shag or a party to crash. No one noticed an unconscious guest at a party, at least not the kind he went to. He slid by, eyes darting left and right in search of a parking space. Renquist's brightness blinded his senses to the other surrounding souls.

At the corner, he turned left and narrowly missed the patrol car coming toward him. The guardian angel's presence in the passenger seat flickered like a lamp in a storm. The ward stomped on the brakes and stared.

Kasker continued ahead, sweat erupting on his brow and his stomach growing hard. He watched his rearview mirror. The patrol car U-turned. He turned left and floored it. Before he turned again, the cop cruiser's headlights appeared in his mirror.

Curses and cantrips! The wimpy guardian angel dared to stalk him. Him, the most dangerous hunter in Heaven or Hell. He dropped to the speed limit. A bead of sweat trickled down his ribs. So little time.

The dweeb might not recognize him now, but there'd be no mistaking what he was when he abandoned the flesh. If the angel found him here, found he'd been wearing a form not his own, there'd be Heaven to pay. Another bead of sweat joined the first.

Kasker hooked a right, keeping just under the speed limit until he was out of sight. He roared down a boulevard until the headlights reappeared. They'd lost two blocks, but the woman rushed forward.

Worse, they were getting farther and farther from Renquist's building. Soul lust set Kasker's brain on fire. He had to get back, had to satisfy the gnawing hunger.

Another left, another race down the asphalt. Another flash of headlights in his mirror. Time galloped by. His hands tightened on the wheel and his breath came in short, shallow gulps.

He spun right, raced to the end of the block, turned left, and darted into an alley. He killed his lights and navigated by the glow of the moon. A trashcan ricocheted off his fender, and he winced.

The pale flame of the angel rolled by on the street a scant seventy-five feet away, unaware of him sneaking back the way he'd come. It hesitated at the intersection but continued straight ahead.

The searing heat in his skin raced through his veins. Kasker threw back his head and howled. He'd outsmarted them. He drew a deep breath and exhaled, his focus returning to his victim.

Kasker left his lights off until he neared his destination, all the while scanning for the guardian angel. The angel might be a dweeb, but the ward... She had cast-iron determination, and it had been her at the wheel.

Seconds ticked down, and he hadn't found a place to stash his car or his corpse. His fingers drummed on the wheel, and he wiggled in the seat. The urge to devour crowded out rational thought.

No time to be picky. He sped to the back of the building and pulled into a loading dock plastered with signs forbidding parking.

20

I yanked the steering wheel, and we zoomed around another corner. The three boxes of files jammed in the trunk of the patrol
car thunked against the side wall.

"I'm telling you, it was Sleeth."

Dave grabbed a pile of file folders about to cascade onto the
floormats. "So what if it was? We're looking for a wino rifling cars,
not that hippie punk."

"He ditched us. Why do that if he isn't up to something nefari-
ous?"

"It's second nature. Everyone ditches a cop if they can. Especially if the cop is following them for no reason." Dave opened a
folder and played a flashlight over the contents.

"No reason? He nearly side-swiped us. That's driving in an
unsafe manner. It's my job to pull him over."

"Look at the hot water you've already gotten us into." He gestured at the file in his lap.

"How was I to know that Tad would ask his dad to put us on
the Slasher case!"

Tension stiffened my shoulders and neck, and sweat slicked
my hands where they gripped the wheel. I needed to redeem myself for the visit to Miss Brown's house, which I'd had to confess to
when Greene confronted me after his chat with the mayor. Bust-
ing Sleeth for drunk driving wasn't the spectacular collar I had
in mind, but maybe I could squeeze him for a few answers on the
way to the station.

Greene couldn't defy the mayor, so he put us on the case.
But in retaliation, he'd saddled Dave and me with a mountain of
paperwork to sift, looking for criminals who used knives in their

MOs. The new assignment didn't release us from our usual patrol duties. We'd become a rolling monument to dead trees.

"We're officially on the case, and Sleeth's the prime suspect. It's our duty to see what he's up to," I said. "Just one more minute?"

I peered into the blackness between the streetlights, hoping for a glimpse of a maroon Mustang. This time of night, cars came in just two colors: light or dark.

"You've already wasted five. By the time we catch the wino, he'll have vandalized another dozen vehicles, and the duty sergeant will chew our butts, not that he'll have much to work with after Greene's tirade."

I shot Dave an unhappy look. It bounced off. He jerked a thumb over his shoulder. I grumbled under my breath and headed back to Pleasant View Drive.

The investigation of Decker's murder had hit a wall. Maybe that would change once the detectives questioned Susan Brown about her association with Sleeth. The hippie was still the investigation's only suspect, but hard evidence remained in short supply. Try as I might, I couldn't get my questions out of my head. The answers might be the key to nailing the Slasher.

"What do you think Sleeth's doing in this neighborhood?"

Dave rolled his eyes. "I thought you were focused on Newell?"

"Sheesh! Can't a girl speculate?"

"Maybe for tonight we can speculate about where to find our wino?"

"For instance," I said, "why murder Decker in the bookstore? Was Calderon sending a message? Mess with me and this is what will happen to you? Or if a new player has come to town, why murder one of Calderon's associates there? Calderon doesn't own the store or even shop there. Old Man Clark isn't one of the city's shakers or movers."

Dave pointed out his window. "Let's check that Caddy. Looks like the door's ajar."

Dave had sharp eyes. Our vandal didn't risk slamming doors once he'd been through the contents of a vehicle; he eased them closed but not latched.

He'd turned over the Cadillac. The glove compartment hung open. Maps were strewn on the floor. Who knew what might be missing?

I made a note of the license plate, location, and time.

Dave grabbed the driver's seat, leaving me to juggle the files and the rapidly fading flashlight. As we rolled along, I ignored the files and kept an eye out for the perp.

"And how did Decker get to the bookstore?" I said. "Has Mack looked for his car? Checked for his last known whereabouts?"

"Have a little faith in the lieutenant," Dave said. "This isn't his first murder investigation."

I gritted my teeth. I'd vowed to focus on Tad and find a way back into the good graces of my superiors. Now here I was assigned to do useless busy work on the Slasher case and with the brass gunning for me. I began to wonder if my dream of economic freedom was worth the cost to my soul.

Reports from the past two nights indicated our car vandal liked to walk six or eight blocks checking for unlocked vehicles and taking anything of value. Then he'd move up a street and do it again.

Dave paused at the next intersection. "What'cha think? Left or right?"

We'd made it to the corner where we'd first seen Sleeth. I twisted my neck back to see all the way to the top of the high-rise on my right. Lots of rich folks living there. Was he muling drugs for Calderon?

"Take a right."

Dave complied, and I stared up at the building. It was a continental kind of place with a smooth stone face and little balconies fenced by iron railings. Rich people must not get up early like the working stiffs. A third of the windows had lights on despite it being twenty past eleven.

We turned right at the next cross street. An alley, dark and uninviting, ran behind the building. Something glinted halfway down. My breath stuck in my throat. My hand gripped the armrest.

"Back up, back up!" I said.

Dave slammed on the brakes, threw the shifter into reverse, and eased back.

"You see him?" He spoke in quiet excitement.

"It's Sleeth's car." My voice came out in a hiss.

Dave thwacked a hand on his forehead. "Give it a rest, Nicky."

I grabbed the flashlight and scrambled out before Dave had the car in gear again. My heart rat-a-tatted on my ribs. My shoes sounded loud on the pavement. I switched to tiptoes. The alley got longer and darker.

Sleeth sat behind the wheel. Was he waiting for someone? He didn't stir at my approach. It was an unnatural stillness.

I edged along to the driver's door and pointed my light in

Sleeth's face. He didn't jump like I expected.

His head lolled back. His tanned skin washed white in the light. His cheeks, his chest, his hands in his lap, all flaccid. His eyelids drooped low, but not closed. Eyes stared, vacant. I'd never seen anyone more obviously dead, not even Tad.

I choked and dropped my flashlight. In the corner of my eye, something shadowy glided past. Something black-on-black, the size of a pony. Something hot—searing hot.

"Shit!" It came out a squeak.

The skin on my scalp rippled, and the little hairs on my neck waved like centipede legs. My hand flew to my gun.

The flashlight rolled in a circle at my feet, flinging grotesque shapes against the building wall. I gulped, sucked in cool night air, and picked it up. A quick flash around assured me that I was alone.

My heart slowed. I glanced toward the cruiser, where Dave waited, looking over the roof at me. I hadn't expected to find Sleeth dead and wondered if it was the result of a drug overdose. I'd radio for an ambulance, but first protocol demanded I check for a pulse.

I turned my light on the car. Sleeth's cold blue eyes blinked and squinted. An arm rose to shield them from the glare.

A scream gurgled and died in my throat, and my hand squeezed the flashlight. I fell back a step.

Sleeth rolled down the window. A beatific smile lit his face. Rapturous eyes met mine.

"Officer Demasi." His soft tenor buzzed with ecstasy.

I took three deep breaths before attempting a reply. "Mr. Sleeth."

Whatever drug he was on, he was having a great trip. I leaned down to better see in his window, hoping he'd messed up and left his stash in plain sight.

"Are you all right? You appeared to be... in some distress when I arrived."

His smile pushed his cheeks up until crinkles formed around his eyes. It must have been a trick of the light. I thought for a moment a red glow reflected off his pupils.

"Everything is copasetic, Nicky."

"*Officer Demasi*, to you, Mr. Sleeth." The thought crossed my mind that if he was under the influence, he might be more inclined to reveal things he shouldn't—like those secrets he kept. Anything he divulged couldn't be used in court, but I wasn't fishing for a confession. I just wanted to know what was going on.

"What are you doing here?"

After a pause, he said, "Communing with the afterlife, *Officer Demasi.*"

"Have you been drinking, Mr. Sleeth?"

"Not yet. Good idea, though. You want to hang with me later, knock back a couple of brews? Maybe get it on?" His tongue wet his lips.

I want to slap your face. I reined in my anger. "You seem to make a habit of haunting dark alleys around midnight. Is there something you're looking for? Someone you're following? Perhaps you're making a delivery?"

Sleeth threw back his head and laughed. "I'm more a pick-up kind of guy, you know what I mean?" His eyes raked my uniform.

I unclenched my teeth and chuckled with him. "Is that what you were doing at the bookstore, making a pickup?"

He nodded, still grinning like a fool.

"What were you picking up, Mr. Sleeth?"

The smile faltered. The cold eyes blinked. I leaned closer. *Got-cha!*

Dave's whistle sliced the air, and Sleeth jerked, his neck and shoulders tightening. He glanced toward the patrol car. Brittle frost glazed his expression.

I resisted the urge to step back when his frozen stare focused on me. I was so close to getting something useful from him. All I'd needed was another few minutes.

Dave waved an arm. "Nicky, let's go. We have a call."

Sleeth's shoulders relaxed. "You'd better go, Nicky. Wouldn't want to get in trouble for harassing an innocent citizen, would you?"

His sleepy voice vibrated in my soul and buzzed painfully in my brain. I wanted to drag him out the window and work him over with my baton until he confessed to whatever he was up to. The sensation left me unnerved.

"Drive carefully, Mr. Sleeth." I stepped back and waved the hippie off.

Sleeth started the Mustang. He slid away into the darkness like a wolf disappeared into the shadows.

21

The Fifth Dimension's *Stone Soul Picnic* blared from the Mustang's radio, and Kasker joined in—except for the part about the Lord and the lightning. No point tempting Fate. He laughed at the irony of singing it while he was stoned on damned soul.

Seve should be pleased that Renquist's collection had gone without a hitch. Well, almost without a hitch. He wouldn't tell the demon about the guardian angel and his ward. The thought of how he'd almost spilled the beans to the ward made his skin crawl.

Of course the demon would ask about the diary and the quest to find Holmes. He wasn't Kasker's master, but Kasker decided it was best to hedge.

He turned between the stone monuments that marked a driveway and on through the open wrought-iron gates toward the doors to Seve's sprawling hacienda. Palm trees lining the route swayed in the cool on-shore breeze. The sliver of a crescent moon hung in a star-creased sky.

A burbling fountain occupied the center of the mansion's courtyard, and the reflection of discretely placed lights danced on the splashing water. The house walls were pale yellow stucco, and the roof was covered in red tile. Cool green vegetation lurked in the corners of the yard and crept up the lengthy front façade.

A second floor cloistered balcony overlooked the cobblestone circle that wound around the fountain. One section of the balcony glowed with light from the open French doors of the demon's study. All the other windows remained dark.

Seve knew how to live in style. It irked Kasker that he scraped by in only a one-bedroom apartment while the demon enjoyed such opulence. Imagine the orgies he could hold in such a palace.

Kasker left the Mustang beside the fountain and sauntered to the front door. Two bodyguards, one on each side of the door, watched his approach. Neither blocked his path when he reached for the ornate knob. Kasker chuffed a laugh. Word got about.

Inside, soft light shone from wrought-iron wall sconces in the expansive foyer and up the long staircase. Although the interior of Seve's home was immaculate, an ancient, musty odor hung in the air, an odor that followed the demon wherever he went. Kasker took the stairs two at a time, suddenly eager to be done with the meeting so he could bask undisturbed in the afterglow of his soul feast.

Old paintings in heavy gilded frames graced the walls of the upstairs hallway. The subjects were mostly humans suffering for their sins or depictions of damned souls cast down into Hell. They brought a homesick tear to his eye.

The study doors stood open. The spacious room was dominated by a wood desk polished to a dark satin sheen. A mace and broadsword decorated one wall above a mahogany credenza that served as a liquor cabinet. A black leather couch ran along the other wall, another of the old oil paintings above.

Two cowhide chairs were placed before the desk. Seve sat behind the desk swirling a glass of whiskey and ignoring his guest. Lamplight glinted off the glass. The whiskey's scent saturated the room.

Kasker flopped in a chair across from the demon. He could use a drink, but Seve didn't offer. Kasker considered helping himself.

"Renquist has been delivered to Hell," he announced, since the demon still hadn't uttered a word of greeting.

"About time you did your job right." Seve raised the glass to his lips and took a sip, rolling the liquor in his mouth before swallowing.

So the demon's insults were to be his thanks. Kasker deserved better. Hadn't he eluded the annoying angel with his cleverness?

Kasker jumped to his feet, crossed to the credenza, and grabbed the whiskey decanter. He pulled the stopper and took a long swig. The strong liquid burned like brimstone.

He coughed and plunked the decanter down to cover his discomfort. Seve had little appreciation for the hunt. Kasker would educate him.

"It wasn't a walk in the park, you know." He returned to his chair. "I had a guardian angel and his ward on my tail."

But wait, he hadn't meant to tell the demon of the angel. Too late. The demon's focus snapped to him.

"Angel?"

Kasker spread his hands. "Didn't I mention? The pigs who caught me at the bookstore."

Seve ground his teeth. "Heaven knows you're here in the flesh? The angel follows you?"

"No," Kasker said with a laugh. "The angel is a dork. He has so little power that he can't see me. I'm surprised that you weren't aware of him, you being the big bad boss in Solaris."

"Fool!" the demon said. "If he discovers you, there will be Heaven to pay, especially with these killings afoot. Do you think for a moment they will believe we're not involved? You could restart the war between Heaven and Hell. Our preparations are not complete. You could ruin everything."

Kasker dropped his eyes and crossed his legs. The high from his soul feast was clouding his thinking, slowing his reflexes. He should go before he said anything else he'd regret.

"What of Decker's diary? What of Holmes?"

"I'm working on it." Kasker leaned back in the chair, contentment fizzing like Alka Seltzer in his brain.

The demon's narrowed eyes gazed at him and his lips thinned. "Whose names appear in the diary?"

"I haven't had a chance to study it," Kasker lied.

"You know nothing of Decker's associates. Give the diary to me. I will tell you which of them might be involved in his sacrifice." Seve held out a peremptory hand.

Kasker shifted in the chair. "I don't have it with me."

The demon raised his eyebrows. "Bring it to the restaurant in the morning. Early."

Kasker squirmed, then stood. "I didn't get the diary from the secretary."

"Because you weren't strong enough to take it from her? I must meet this señorita who keeps the sabueso del infierno's tail between his legs."

In his stoned haze, the words slipped out. "You can't. She's dead."

Seve shot to his feet, a look of horror on his face. He bumped the desk hard enough to slop whiskey from his glass. "You killed her?"

"Of course not." Kasker shuffled his feet on the tile floor. This conversation couldn't go more wrong. "Someone shot her and took the diary."

The demon fell back into his chair. "Holmes?"

"Or another of Decker's acquaintances. I think she intended to blackmail those who appeared in it."

Seve wiped the back of his hand across his lips. His eyes locked on Kasker.

"You must return to the Oracle and learn where Holmes hides. He cannot be allowed to remain at large any longer. The danger is too great."

Kasker folded his arms over his chest. Just the mention of the Oracle's name caused a cold sweat to break on his forehead.

"The Oracle will not cooperate."

The demon seemed almost as uncomfortable with the topic of the Oracle as Kasker.

"Then how will you find Holmes?" Seve asked.

"There must be others who associated with Decker. They may have information about Decker's movements before he died, who he talked to," Kasker said.

Seve tapped a finger on his desk, lost in thought. Kasker wished he could go. He wanted to revel in what remained of his soul-eating high, not think about his problems.

The demon pulled a pad of note paper from the top drawer and took a heavy gold pen from a holder on the desktop. He scribbled a name and address and tore off the sheet.

"Decker cheated all his associates. I doubt he told them any-thing helpful—or truthful. But he liked to brag about his business conquests. Try this woman. She entertained him regularly." Seve pushed the paper across the desk.

Kasker snatched the paper and squinted at the demon's awful handwriting. He gave up trying to decipher it and stuffed it in his pocket. It would wait until tomorrow.

"Time runs short, sabueso. Find Holmes or face consequences."

22

Emmett Merkel. Mid-fifties, a little overweight, well dressed, filthy rich, and dead. He was our consolation prize. The rest of the Solaris PD was a mile from our location, responding on another Slasher killing.

Except for Merkel's car and our cruiser, the parking lot of the office building was empty. He'd parked next to the back door, in a spot with a reserved sign. Ornate lamps lit the lot. The one nearest the car was broken, casting this corner in gloom.

Visibility from the street was limited by a row of trees at the edge of the lot. The bus line ran two blocks south. The neighborhood had no apartment buildings. The odds of anyone passing on foot to see Merkel sprawled on the asphalt were slim.

Dave had his notebook out, pencil at the ready. "What did you see, Mrs. Sanchez?"

Mrs. Sanchez wrung the hem of her apron. Her dark eyes flitted to the body and away again. "I seen Mr. Merkel laying there by his car, so I checked, and he didn't look too good. That's when I called the cops."

I listened to the cleaning lady with half an ear. The Slasher had struck again. I knew it would happen. Anger churned in my gut.

"You didn't move him?" I asked too briskly.

"Are you kidding? I don't touch the dead." She crossed herself and mopped her forehead with her apron hem.

Dave nodded his approval. "Was there anyone else in the parking lot?"

"Not when I came out for a smoke."

"And what time was that?"

"I always take a break when I finish the fifth floor, around eleven."

Her statement jibed with the time we'd gotten the call. The left rear tire on Merkel's Lincoln Continental was flat. The trunk was open, the keys still in the lock. The jack and tire iron were on the ground by the flat, but the spare was still in its cover at the rear.

Merkel lay on his back near the car, one arm flung over his head, one sticking out at a ninety-degree angle. No bullet holes. No signs of strangulation or a bashed in skull. No scraped knuckles.

He wore black pants, a white shirt, and a black and red tie. The left cuff was missing the cufflink. The left wrist might have a bruise. I didn't see the cufflink on the ground. I'd make sure the ME checked his pockets for it.

His skin was cool to the touch.

"But you saw someone earlier," I said

"I saw a van from the window." Mrs. Sanchez pointed to the structure behind her.

The Merkel Building was a stately five stories on the western edge of city center. An elegant hotel built in the late 1800s, it had fallen into disrepair by mid-1950. Emmett Merkel, nouveau rich from his oil investments, bought the place and converted it to high-priced offices.

"What kind of van?" Dave asked.

She looked at Dave like he'd asked her to translate Chinese. "From up there, they all look alike. It was white with writing on the side, I think."

"When did you see the van?" I said.

Mrs. Sanchez checked her watch and frowned. "Must have been a little after ten-thirty."

"Had Mr. Merkel left by then?"

"Oh, yeah, he went out by ten." She shifted her weight from foot to foot and checked her watch again.

I pulled out my own notebook to make a quick sketch of the scene. "Was that typical?"

"He worked late a lot. I think maybe he wasn't in any hurry to get home, you know what I mean?"

Dave and I exchanged a look. Dave said, "You think he and Mrs. Merkel weren't getting on?"

"What do I know? I'm just the cleaning lady. But once I overheard him on the phone with her. It didn't sound friendly."

"Thank you, Mrs. Sanchez," Dave said. "If you think of anything else, please call us."

Mrs. Sanchez shuffled a couple of steps and stopped. "Sometimes those disciples of that phony church hang around on the corner. You know the ones I mean? They wear those green dresses. Mr. Merkel never liked having riffraff at his business, but that didn't stop them. If they were here, maybe they saw something."

The quasi-religious cults had followed the hippie invasion. Solaris street corners were painted in a riot of hues as each group chose a color and sent their acolytes to beg from those willing to work for a living. They'd become a rainbow plague on the city.

"Did you see them tonight?" I asked.

The cleaning lady shook her head.

Dave lowered his voice. "I don't see any signs of foul play. Looks like he just keeled over. Too much exertion for an old guy in his shape."

Something about the way Merkel lay bothered me. In my limited experience, people having heart attacks tended to grab their chest and fall forward. I shone my flashlight around the interior of the car.

An ambulance pulled up at the curb, red light strobing in the dark. Dave walked over to confer with the driver. Doors slammed and a stretcher rattled.

I stared at Merkel with little sympathy. We were stuck with him while the rest of the squad chased a killer. Of all the times to croak, he had to pick tonight.

I faced Mrs. Sanchez. "Did Mr. Merkel have a suit jacket when he left?"

She held a hanky over her mouth as though she thought it would prevent her from inhaling Merkel's death. "Of course. It's only proper for a man of his position."

Mrs. Sanchez tiptoed around the body and peered in the Lincoln's window. Her face wrinkled in a frown.

"I don't see his jacket. It was black. Italian silk, someone said. Real sharp."

Guys who wore expensive silk suits didn't fix flats. They called Triple A. "Was Mr. Merkel the do-it-yourself type?"

The cleaning lady took a step back and gave a vigorous shake of her head. "No way. He had a flat before, a couple months back. He took a cab home. Someone from the garage fixed it in the morning. He said it was the best part of being rich; he didn't have to get his hands dirty no more."

The ambulance attendants rolled the stretcher to the body.

"Hold it," I said, waving them back. "We need the crime scene boys."

"What?" Dave looked at me and then at the body. "That'll take hours, and this is open and shut."

I planted myself next to Merkel and crossed my arms. "We're on this case instead of chasing the Slasher because Emmett Merkel is a big financial supporter of the mayor's. What do you think Mayor Newell will say if the autopsy turns up foul play?"

"Where's the evidence of foul play?" Dave knelt beside the body and withdrew a wallet from Merkel's back pocket. He flipped it open. Credit cards were slotted behind a driver's license. Cash bulged from a side pocket.

"No sign of a robbery," Dave said.

"What about his coat?"

Dave chewed his lip for a few seconds. Then he threw his hands in the air. "Fine. I'll call it in, but Greene will skin us alive if Merkel died of natural causes."

23

Kasker twisted the top off his beer, sank into the couch, and placed his feet on the coffee table, knocking over two bottles standing empty on the surface. The Byrds' *Eight Miles High* reverberated from the stereo. He'd go to bed soon so the mortal vessel could rest, but for now, he reveled in satiety.

His thoughts drifted to Officer Demasi. They were more alike than he'd realized. She had a hunter's tenacity.

Too bad she was in the angel's care. She'd make an interesting conquest. What a trip, banging a cop.

The surprise on her face when he returned to the flesh was priceless. If only the annoying guardian hadn't interrupted them, he could have pushed her into attacking him. Imagine the blackmail value of an unprovoked assault.

The thumping beat of the bass no longer matched the music. A garbled voice joined the asynchronous hammering. Someone pounded on his door. The neighbors complaining again.

He sashayed to the stereo and cranked up the volume. The walls shook. He grinned and danced. Beer sloshed on the carpet.

Too late, the smell of cigarettes and sweat reached his nostrils. A hand wrenched his arm behind his back. Shoulder pain drove him to the floor. The music cut out. Three pairs of shiny black shoes filled his shrunken field of vision.

Handcuffs secured his wrists. The pain in his shoulder stopped. He was brought to his feet with a jerk. His bleary vision focused on the faces of the surrounding police officers.

"Kasker Sleeth, you're under arrest for the murder of Robert Haskell."

A voice droned on, reading him his rights. Through a haze of soul lust and beer, Kasker struggled to think. Who was Robert Haskell? The name brought no souls from his memory.

How incompetent could the cops be? They ought to be here about Susie's murder. Should he correct them? No, that was a bad idea.

"Do you understand your rights?" Lt. Mack asked.

Officers spread through the room, tearing cushions from the couch, opening empty kitchen cupboards. The sounds of similar mayhem drifted from the bedroom.

Kasker managed a cold smile. "It's your party, pig. Knock yourself out."

Mack stepped in so close Kasker could feel his breath. "We've got you this time, Sleeth. Give us Calderon, and we'll take the death penalty off the table."

Kasker giggled. "Skipped right over the part about innocent until proven guilty, didn't you? But hey, trials. Expensive, time-consuming. Who needs 'em?"

Mack's jaw worked back and forth. He flagged an officer. "Take him to the station. Get a blood alcohol and a drug test. If he's over the limit, we'll have to wait to question him until he sobers up."

Officers flanked Kasker and frog-marched him from his second-floor apartment down the metal stairs to the parking lot. Residents watched from windows, from balconies, and from little knots around the fuzzmobiles that jammed the parking lot, their red lights whirling.

Kasker gave them all a drunken smile. The pigs were fools to think he'd killed anyone. What evidence could they have when he hadn't done anything?

At his Mustang, an officer searched the back seat. He wouldn't find anything except old burger rappers and empty drink cups. Kasker should have tossed those on the roadside to avoid stinking up the car.

The officer pulled something out and dropped it in a paper bag. Kasker couldn't see what it was. The first niggle of apprehension crawled through his guts.

They took him for a blood test, and then to interrogation. They cuffed him to the table. He ran through possible scenarios about why he was there while his high faded. Fatigue and boredom set in.

He put his head down on his arms and napped.

The door slammed, and Kasker jerked awake. The wall clock told him he'd been asleep for ten minutes. His stiff neck and back said that he'd been slumped over the table far longer.

Mack claimed the chair across from Kasker, his face haggard but confident. Kasker lounged back and pulled one ankle up on the opposite knee. He'd aggravate Mack into throwing a punch. Then he'd scream for a lawyer and be on the street within the hour.

"It'll go easier for you if you confess," Mack said.

"Yeah, man, I confess," Kasker said with a laugh. At Mack's gleeful look he added, "I confess that I'm stumped about why I'm here. Maybe you want to clue me in?"

Mack's face darkened. "You murdered Robert Haskell. Considering the circumstances of his death, you're looking at the gas chamber."

A wave of uneasiness washed over Kasker. What kind of 'circumstances' would make the pigs arrest him when he'd had nothing to do with any murder?

"Yeah, right. You gotta prove I did it first."

An officer came in carrying a plastic-wrapped object. He dropped it on the table in front of Mack. It clunked when it struck.

Kasker stared at his tire iron, covered in blood and dusted with white powder. His jaw tightened. Goats! Holmes set him up for Haskell's murder—whoever the Heaven Haskell was. Another of Seve's damned souls?

"If you cooperate and give us Calderon, I can talk to the DA. He can ask for life."

"Go screw yourself," Kasker said, his voice filled with bravado he didn't feel. If his chase of Holmes was delayed while he procured a new corporeal container, his master would not be pleased.

Another officer entered. Another plastic-wrapped bundle plunked on the table, some kind of cloth saturated with blood.

"Blood type matches Haskell," the officer said.

Victory glowed in Mack's tired eyes. He pointed to the bundle. "A bloody shirt found in your car. A bloody tire iron with your fingerprints found at the scene. It's not looking good for you, Sleeth. Last chance. Give us Calderon and we take the death penalty off the table."

Kasker's foot dropped to the floor. A low growl rumbled in his throat. His true form hovered at the edge of containment.

"I want a lawyer."

24

"Damn it, Dave, there's something fishy about Merkel's death. Greene had no right to call off my investigation."

Dave sighed, but at least he didn't roll his eyes. "You heard the ME's assistant. Looks like a heart attack."

"There was a mark on his wrist! How does a heart attack explain that?"

Dave pulled open the station door and held it for me. "You think someone tied him up before they mugged him? And then they forgot to take his wallet?"

The station was the last place I wanted to be. The hallways buzzed about the Slasher murder.

"It's been a long night. Let's just file our paperwork and go home." Dave slipped past me into the squad room. Down the hall, Stutzman and Arndt regaled a uniform with details of their collar.

I stomped into the squad room and nabbed the desk with the typewriter that didn't jam. "What about the missing jacket?"

"Mrs. Sanchez might have made a mistake. After all, who wears a jacket in this heat?"

Dave took a seat at a desk and flopped his notebook beside the typewriter.

"Why didn't he call someone to change his tire? Or call a cab and worry about it in the morning?"

"I'll do Merkel. You write up our car vandal?" Dave fed a form into his typewriter and dropped the bale onto the roller.

Stutzman ambled into the room and parked his butt on the corner of my desk. His rumpled gray suit stank of cigarettes. I wished he'd go away.

"We bagged Sleeth," he said. "He's stitched up tight this time."

"Congratulations," Dave said. "How'd it go down?"

Stutzman removed his behind from my desk, driven away by my stony silence, and pulled up a chair beside Dave's. He put a foot on the seat and leaned his forearms on his knee. My fingers flew over the typewriter keys, making such a clatter that Stutzman had to raise his voice.

"We got him at his apartment. He never saw us coming. Found a bloody shirt in his car and his tire iron at the scene. Talk about your brainless criminal."

I looked up, puzzled. "Tire iron? I thought you brought him in for the second Slasher murder."

"We did. Same MO as last time: funny marks on the floor, victim gutted, knife stuck in the throat. The guy's face was smashed in, but the ME said that was done post mortem, probably to delay identification." Stutzman straightened and ambled toward the door. "We're all going to the Longbar to celebrate. You're welcome to join us."

I couldn't help myself; I had to know. "Did Sleeth say why he did it?"

"He ain't talking. He's lawyered up."

I checked my watch. Then I jumped up and ran after Stutzman.

"Hey, Jonas! What's the time of death on your vic?"

Stutzman's voice drifted down the corridor. "Between eleven and eleven-forty."

"You sure about that?"

Stutzman turned and gave me a scornful look. "Night watchman says the site was clear at eleven. He found the body on his eleven-forty rounds."

"The vic couldn't have been killed earlier and dumped there after he died?"

Stutzman's laugh boomed off the walls. "Not on your life. His blood covered everything. The ME corroborates the time of death."

Dave came to stand beside me.

"You know what this means," I said. "We have to tell Mack."

"They have hard evidence. A tire iron and bloody shirt."

I shook my head. "It'll fall apart in court. Sleeth will tell his lawyer we saw him."

"Leave it alone, Nicky. It isn't our case."

"The real killer is still out there." I crossed my arms and glared at him.

"Look, Sleeth's involved, and after tonight, we know he has an accomplice. Let the DA arrange a plea deal that gives us the other guy before you go charging in to rescue the hippie."

"I'm going to tell Chief Greene."

I walked out of the office. Dave hurried after me. By the time he caught up, I was already knocking on Greene's open door.

Inside, Lt. Mack rocked in the visitor chair and nursed a glass of whiskey. Greene lounged on the other side of the desk, his empty glass sitting on a stack of files, a grim smile on his face.

"Sorry to interrupt," I said, "but there's something you need to know."

Mack took one look at me, and a curtain of steel dropped over his demeanor. The legs of his chair thumped the floor, and he hoisted himself to his feet.

"You'll want to hear this, too, lieutenant." I ducked my head, adjusted my belt, and blurted it out. "Sleeth's not your killer."

"Bullshit," Greene said.

"At eleven-ten, we were chasing Sleeth around the Park View neighborhood."

Greene and Mack exchanged a look.

Mack huffed up like an angry bull. "It'd be close, but he'd still have time to get to the construction site and kill Haskell."

I wiped a hand across my mouth. "We lost him, but we caught up to him again by eleven-twenty. If the kill was between eleven and half past, he wouldn't have had time to drive back and forth and carve up Haskell."

Mottled red crept up Greene's neck and onto his cheeks. "What the hell were you doing chasing Sleeth in the first place?"

The room went so quiet that for a minute, I thought I'd gone deaf. I put my hands behind my back so Greene couldn't see my clenched fists. My chest felt like I was in the grip of an anaconda.

Then Mack slammed his palm on the desk and swore.

The redness in Greene's face shaded into purple. "There's just no end to your incompetence, is there, Demasi."

"It was a routine traffic stop," Dave said. "The vehicle was being driven erratically. We had reason to believe the driver was intoxicated."

"And did you write Mr. Sleeth a ticket for this erratic driving?" Mack asked.

"No, sir," I said. "I issued a verbal warning."

"We didn't want to give Mr. Sleeth grounds to file a police harassment suit," Dave put in. I could have kissed him.

Mack and Greene exchanged another look. The undercurrents were clear—they were thinking that only the four of us in the room knew Dave and I had seen Sleeth. And if Sleeth didn't kill Haskell, then what was his tire iron doing at the scene? How had he gotten the blood on his shirt? We had a conundrum.

Greene was first to test the waters.

"You were wrong about the time when you saw Sleeth. It was earlier. Or later."

If I told the truth, it would end my career. One way or another, Greene would get rid of me. I'd lose my house, my lifestyle, everything that meant anything. Would any of that matter if I was part of an illegal frame-up?

"No, sir, I'm sure about the time. I made note of it when we found a vandalized vehicle at eleven-fifteen. We saw Sleeth just before that but couldn't catch him. I spotted him again just afterward."

Greene dropped into his chair and put his head in his hands. "What a cluster fuck. I hope the mayor hasn't held a press conference yet."

"I'm not letting Sleeth go," Mack said. "We have evidence—"

"He has two of our officers as his alibi!" Greene's voice echoed off the walls.

"He's deliberately making us look like chumps," Mack said. "We can get him on accessory charges."

Greene waved a hand at the door. "Turn him loose before he gets it into his head to sue us. Then find a way to nail the bastard—one that will stand up in court."

"And you, Demasi." Greene punctuated my name with a finger pointed my direction. "I don't care that you and the mayor are best pals. One more screw-up like this and you're done."

25

Seve's high-priced mouthpiece hadn't arrived at the station yet, and already the police had turned Kasker loose without so much as a warning not to leave town. He wondered what happened.

The bloody shirt wasn't his, but it didn't matter. His fingerprints on the tire iron should have sealed his fate. Who could have found it at Decker Industries and known it was his?

Susie.

He stood on the steps of the police station and breathed in cool pre-dawn air. He was the hunter. But Holmes had turned the tables. Was Susie in league with Holmes? Had she been all along? The hair rose on the back of Kasker's neck, and his suspicious gaze swept the deserted street.

The bookstore had to be a trap to draw Kasker out so Holmes could identify his carcass, even though Kasker hadn't detected Holmes in the vicinity. To set the trap, Holmes must have known the exact date and time of Decker's death, and that was impossible. Only Seve had that knowledge. But how did Seve know?

What was the point of recognizing Kasker's flesh? If Holmes caused it some harm, Kasker would simply find a different cloak to wear while he hunted. It wouldn't stop his pursuit. It would only cause delay. So time was important to Holmes' plans.

Kasker strode away toward the commercial district. He'd find a cab, go to his apartment, and get his car. He'd pay Seve a visit. Then he'd find out about Haskell—whoever he was. Perhaps he'd order the demon to procure him new flesh. That should throw both the police and Holmes off his trail.

He'd gone three blocks when he encountered a man loading

the early edition of the newspaper into a paper box. The headline caught his eye. *Slasher Captured.* Below it, the subhead read *Robert Haskell Second Victim.* When the newspaper van pulled away, Kasker jimmied the lock.

According to the article, Haskell died at an eastside construction site between eleven and half past. He chuckled as a small puzzle piece clicked into place. So that's why he'd been released— the tenacious Officer Demasi and her powerless guardian angel had come forward to alibi him.

His delight at the irony faded. It was too much of a coincidence that Haskell would be killed at the same time Kasker was occupied harvesting Renquist's soul—a time for which, if not for the infuriating ward, he couldn't provide an alibi. And, according to the paper, Haskell's death had been another ritual killing like Decker's, not the bludgeoning murder Kasker expected.

His hands crumpled the paper. Goats! Did Seve own Haskell's soul? The demon would be furious if he'd lost another one. When he couldn't find a cab, he jogged to the construction site, all three miles. Sweat poured down his face and soaked his shirt. His feet blistered where his sandals rubbed.

Steel girders rose into the sunrise above a six-foot plywood fence that blocked access to the site. Two dozen construction workers crowded around a gate decked in yellow police tape. They argued with an officer who prevented their entrance.

Kasker watched from across the street. No souls—attached to a body or otherwise—remained inside the site. If Seve was right about the ritual, then somewhere nearby, another soul had been sacrificed to the universe so that Haskell's essence could occupy its discarded body.

Seven hours had passed between the ritual and Kasker's arrival. It would take a tenacious soul to remain untethered so long. But even a slim chance of finding a lead was better than returning to Seve empty-handed.

Kasker paced away, senses pushed to their limits. Without a body, he couldn't remain in this realm more than the few minutes needed to collect a damned soul. Clothed in it, he could stay as long as he wanted—half blind and muzzled. It made detecting a departed soul like swimming the ocean wearing concrete overshoes.

Already the buildings adjacent to the construction site sparkled with people starting their working day. Their blazing souls would obscure one fading remnant. He cursed Holmes for his skullduggery.

Kasker searched one block after another. More curses fell from his lips, and more blisters rose on his feet. Seve said the second sacrifice should be waiting right outside the door. He was wasting his time, but he plodded on anyway, desperate for a clue.

There! Faint essence clung to a patch of asphalt in the middle of the street where the occasional car whizzed past. Kasker couldn't feel power from any dark magic, and there weren't any runes drawn on the pavement. Why this place to obliterate a soul?

Regardless, the important thing was to identify the human. Then he would know what stolen mortal to hunt. He'd need a moment in his true form.

He squatted in the doorway of a dress shop pretending to adjust the buckle on his sandal. His true form would blend with the shadows of the recess. The few pedestrians who passed paid no attention to him. When none were close, he loosened his grip on the flesh.

His body lurched back and thumped against the door. Kasker had a dim awareness of a crack on the skull.

His vision sharpened. His nose detected the soul scent of the hundreds of humans occupying the buildings around him. His ears pricked, listening to the agonized screams of the damned trapped beyond this realm.

Before him, the soul thinned with each passing second. Kasker wanted to clamp his jaws on it and suck it down. But this one wasn't damned. To taste it was forbidden. Still, his mouth watered at the thought.

The soul was no more than a bright spot, a swirling fog. Kasker raised his heavy muzzle and sniffed. A tendril of essence wafted from the disappearing mass to tickle his nostrils.

Merkel. The dispossessed soul's name was Emmett Merkel.

The last vestige of the soul faded. Kasker bayed his excitement.

26

I'd gone home for a few hours' sleep. My churning brain made it anything but restful. When the sun rose, so did I.

No one on the force was speaking to Dave or me. Consensus was that while Sleeth set up his alibi by nearly ramming us, his accomplice was busy murdering Robert Haskell—the same accomplice who'd helped him kill Decker. An accomplice explained his bloodless clothes. He was playing us for fools.

Or was he? Were my fellow officers so sure of his guilt that they'd framed him with false evidence? And then I'd ruined their case when I'd alibied the hippie? Which one was Sleeth, killer or fall guy?

Nervous energy kept me pacing my kitchen. I had to do something. I needed to solve a case big enough to insulate me from any retaliation by Lenny Greene, but the Slasher case was off limits now. I drove to the station, ducked in, and spent the morning leafing through mug books.

I found one of Tad's pursuers quickly. The white guy with a cross tattoo on his neck was Jake Bronski. He'd done time for robbery and assault. His information included a list of known associates.

When I checked the associates, there was his buddy, Harold Warner, the acne-scarred Negro. Warner had been dishonorably discharged from the US Army, where he'd been a medic caught dipping into the drug supply. After the military, he'd been incarcerated for a year on drug possession charges.

When they weren't working scams, they were beating their girlfriends. But they didn't seem like big enough fish to engage in kidnapping or murder. Unless they were trying to mug Tad in front of hundreds of witnesses, the likelihood of them chasing him seemed remote.

I slumped in my chair. Perhaps in my eagerness to redeem myself, I was seeing crimes where none existed. I wondered whether Dave had encouraged me to look into the thugs as a way to distract me from the Slasher case. I hated to think that might be true.

A sense of dissatisfaction and impatience swirled in me. I still had hours before my shift started and nothing to focus on. I decided to throw my frustration at Emmett Merkel's untimely death.

My first stop was the medical examiner. According to a preliminary report, Merkel suffered from coronary heart disease and had for several years. His doctor said he managed it with a prescription for nitroglycerin and avoidance of hard physical strain. The ME hadn't found Merkel's nitro—or the missing cufflink.

Given the warm evening temperatures, Merkel's medical condition, and the stress of changing a tire, the medical examiner ruled the death a heart attack brought on by over-exertion. A drug screen was pending to see if Merkel had taken his nitro.

Over-exertion? Merkel hadn't even removed the hubcaps on the Lincoln, never mind straining on the lug nuts. Surely getting out the equipment to change the flat and unfastening one sleeve wasn't *that* much stress.

And the finding of death by heart attack didn't explain the missing jacket or the van that had pulled into the parking lot and out again without reporting a body on the pavement. But without the ME's backing, I'd have a hard time convincing Greene to investigate.

Perhaps Merkel's widow could explain the missing medication or tell me that Merkel left home yesterday without his jacket. I made her my next stop.

The Merkels lived in a neighborhood of older exclusive homes on the south side of Solaris. I rolled along their street and checked for addresses.

Three blocks ahead, a maroon Mustang slipped around the corner and disappeared. My foot came off the gas. Was it Sleeth? I plunged my foot to the floor.

By the time I reached the corner where the Mustang had turned, it was gone. Streets in this neighborhood meandered like a sidewinder through the desert. I drove a few of them, but the Mustang had vanished.

I returned to the Merkel house and chided myself for imagining it might have been the hippie. After all, he wasn't the only person in California who owned a maroon Mustang.

The Merkel house made me feel like I'd walked into *Gone with the Wind*. A butler answered the door of the white-pillared pile and made me ever so glad I'd worn my uniform instead of arriving in civvies even if I wasn't officially on duty. Merkel must be worth millions, which was a great motive for murder.

A huge wreath of yellow roses draped with a black ribbon stood in the foyer. The scent of the flowers overwhelmed the space. A crystal chandelier winked overhead. I asked to see Mrs. Merkel and informed the black-liveried servant that it was official business.

I waited ten minutes before Mrs. Merkel swept in. She was in her fifties. Her dyed-black hair was cut shoulder length, smooth on top and curly on the bottom. Her deep crimson lipstick slopped above her upper lip on the right side. Her face powder was applied unevenly.

Red rimmed her eyes, but I didn't think it was from crying for her dead husband. The face powder didn't quite hide the spidery nose and cheek veins of a heavy drinker. She wore a sleeveless peach satin jumpsuit that clashed with her lipstick. Over it, she had a sheer peach and green print robe that reached to her knees and swirled behind her like Batman's cape.

One hand held a crystal tumbler of amber liquid, the other a cigarette. She swayed a little as she stopped before me. I wondered if she always imbibed this early.

"You're Officer Demasi?" she asked. Her critical eyes looked me up and down. Then she seemed to realize she was staring. "Henry didn't mention you were a woman."

I assumed Henry was the butler. I murmured, "I'm very sorry for your loss, Mrs. Merkel."

"It was bound to happen eventually, wasn't it?" She took a sip from her tumbler. "I mean, we knew he had a bad heart. But his doctor didn't seem to think it was enough to stop him from working himself to death."

There was bitterness in her statement, like her husband had thought more of his work than her. I couldn't help looking at our opulent surroundings. Had she traded this comfort for a life in a loveless marriage? If I hadn't gotten my job with the Solaris PD, would I have done the same?

"What was it you came for?"

"Trying to clear up a minor detail," I said, pushing aside my questions about her happiness and my decisions. "Mr. Merkel's doctor said he took nitroglycerin tablets when his heart acted up.

Do you know if he had them with him yesterday?"

A little crease appeared between her eyebrows. "What a silly question! He never left the house without them. They should have been in his jacket pocket."

"Do you know what coat he wore yesterday?"

The crease was joined by frown lines across her forehead. "What does it matter what he wore? He's dead. Winning an award for best-dressed corpse won't bring him back. Now if you'll excuse me, I have arrangements to make."

She walked away with an uneven gait.

"Mrs. Merkel, wait," I said, following her.

She turned and glared at me.

"It's possible something happened in the parking lot last night. That someone was there with your husband."

She raised her cigarette to her lips, took a long drag, and blew the smoke toward the ceiling while she squinted at me through the cloud.

"My husband's death has been ruled natural causes. Are you implying it wasn't?"

"Not exactly." I squirmed under her scrutiny.

"What evidence do you have?" she asked.

"His jacket is missing," I replied.

"His jacket. That's it? A tramp could have wandered by and picked it up. Heaven knows Solaris has enough of them, lounging on every street corner with their bottles hidden in brown paper bags. Perhaps you should ask them who took it."

"His wallet was still in his pocket, Mrs. Merkel," I reminded her. "Why would a bum take his jacket and not his wallet?"

Mrs. Merkel watched me with rheumy eyes. Would she even remember our conversation later?

"Henry," she called, turning away. "See Miss Demasi out."

My face burned and my chin quivered. I clenched my fists at my sides. Seconds later, the butler appeared and showed me to the door.

I stopped just before stepping through, remembering the Mustang I'd seen as I'd approached.

"Have you noticed anyone different in the neighborhood? Any unfamiliar cars parked nearby?"

The butler looked down his nose at me. "No one but those hippie beggars from that phony church. When I shooed them away, they had the audacity to ask for a handout. I called the police, but by the time a squad car arrived, they'd gone."

I got in my baking Corvair and drummed my fingers on my

thigh. I'd find a pay phone and call Tad to arrange a meeting. I wanted to ask him if he know Warner and Bronski.

In the meantime, I was still officially part of the Slasher investigation. I squinted out the windshield at the heat waves rolling off the pavement. Why the bookstore? It was a question I couldn't silence.

27

Kasker parked down the block from the Luna Azul. A headache built behind his eyes. His earthly camouflage screamed for rest and food, but excitement kept him moving. Nothing sated like a good hunt.

Once he'd retrieved his car, he'd spent the long, hot morning ping-ponging between Merkel's home and office, hoping that the new inhabitant of Merkel's flesh would make an appearance. After all, what was the point of selecting a rich and powerful body to occupy if you didn't take advantage of its resources?

He pounded along the blistering pavement in the harsh noon light. Satisfaction curved his lips into a smile and puffed out his chest. He swept past the door guard without waiting for acknowledgment.

The restaurant was half-filled by customers who took advantage of the air conditioning to cool off while they lunched. The murmur of voices and the clatter of cutlery resonated in the air. The smell of food made saliva break in Kasker's mouth.

The two cooks and the kitchen helper jumped at his sudden appearance before moving away from him. Kasker grinned at them and raked his eyes over the skinny waitress, her hands filled with platters, who was just leaving the kitchen. Perhaps he'd have her serve him later, after he'd dealt with the demon.

Seve's Latino body guard waited at the office door. Kasker didn't see the Negro. The Latino took an initial step to stop Kasker, caught the look on Kasker's face, and backed away. Kasker swaggered in without bothering to knock.

The demon sat at his desk, pencil in hand, thick ledger open before him. His thin lips parted to reveal yellowed teeth, and the tension lines around his eyes deepened. Kasker lifted his chin and gave Seve a cold stare.

"Haskell was one of yours," Kasker said.

"Si. You devoured his soul?"

"Not yet." Kasker smirked. "He occupies the form of another, Emmett Merkel. I haven't found Merkel's corpse yet, but I will. Merkel's resources are too tempting to ignore."

Seve hissed through his teeth. He reached into the waste basket beside the desk and extracted the morning newspaper. The demon turned to a page near the back, folded the paper open, and slapped it on the desk. His finger stabbed an article, and his tone was surly.

"Try looking at the morgue."

The left column was filled with Merkel's obituary. Kasker's confidence spilled away like beer from a broken bottle. He dropped onto the chair opposite Seve and wiped a hand across his forehead.

"You've cost me another one, sabueso."

"Haskell isn't my fault," Kasker said, baring his own teeth.

"They're all your fault." The demon leaned over the desk. "Holmes' escape is your fault. You're incompetent and should be punished."

Kasker bit back a snarl and tightened his grip on his flesh lest his true form emerge to confront the demon. "If Merkel is dead, then the transfer was unsuccessful."

"You assume that Holmes' goal is to transfer the souls."

"You said that was the purpose of the ritual. Why else would he sacrifice those who've traded their souls to Hell?"

Seve stared at the ceiling and rubbed a finger over his mustache. "To spite Hell for his own incarceration? Or is he still practicing and not yet in full control of the magic? Perhaps he doesn't understand the distance limitations."

"Regardless," the demon said, returning his glare to Kasker, "you've failed again. Our master demands results—or you will pay the price."

Holmes motives were of little interest to Kasker, but the demon's warning stirred real concern in Kasker's belly. His hunter's mind turned itself to the problem. How did Holmes know whose souls were damned?

"Where do you keep the contracts?" Kasker asked.

The demon's eyes narrowed. "No one has access."

"You think Holmes has super powers? Or a crystal ball that tells him which ones to sacrifice?" Kasker spat on the floor. "Of course he doesn't. He's seen your precious parchments."

"Impossible." Seve slammed the ledger closed. "You think I leave them laying around for prying eyes to read?"

Kasker breathed in the office air testing for the scent of the damned. A succulent essence wafted up from the drops of blood spilled on the contracts. His heart thumped in his chest, and his skin prickled with soul lust.

"There." Kasker pointed to the floor. "Show me."

28

I'd found a phone and arranged a quick lunch meeting with Tad. I had time to kill, so I spiraled in on Clark's Books trying to answer one of my questions. Why use it instead of a safer, more secluded location?

If the neighborhood had significance to the killer, it eluded me. The bar across the street attracted late-night traffic, putting the killer at risk of being seen. If it had to be this area, why not use the flower shop, the bakery, or the dress shop, all on the opposite side of the alley from Clark's, away from the prying eyes of bar patrons?

A Closed sign hung on the front door of the bookstore. No one answered my knock. Bright light glowed in the room beyond the curtain, and the faint strains of chanting drifted through the glass.

I left my car out front and trudged around the block. A shiny blue and white Ford station wagon blocked the alley behind Clark's. The tailgate hung open, the interior crammed with bottles, jugs, buckets of rags, an ancient Hoover vacuum, brooms, and mops. Lettering on the front doors read *Blake & Sons Cleaning*.

Clark's backdoor stood ajar. The scent of vanilla and hot wax filled the alley. The scratchy recording of a cassette tape played from inside, repeating the slow chant *shree ram jay ram* while a stringed instrument and bells created harmony in the background. I squeezed past the car and into the bookstore.

Fresh wax on the scarred and battered wood floor gleamed under a powerful portable light. The walls and ceilings were three shades brighter and spotless. On the work table beside a cassette player, a white candle burned next to the photo of an ancient and shirtless East Indian guru.

"Can I help you, officer?"

A woman my age stepped out of the bathroom, cleaning rag in hand. She wore loose green coveralls, a blue bandana over her short, ebony hair, and bright yellow rubber gloves.

"I'm looking for Mr. Clark," I replied.

"He's across the street at the bar, waiting for us to finish." She picked up an empty pail and walked toward the door. "My sister's gone to get him."

"The place looks amazing." I'd imagined they'd have to gut the building to remove the bloodstains and smell.

"Thanks," she said with a nervous smile. "We almost didn't take the job, but money's tight right now."

I trailed her into the alley where she stowed her supplies in the back of the wagon. "I can understand why you wouldn't want to tackle a job like this one. Pretty gruesome."

"It wasn't the mess," she said.

She brushed past me into the store. I waited by the door. She unplugged the portable light, carried it to the wagon, and stashed it in the back.

"We've done jobs much messier than this one. Elderly people who died and weren't discovered for weeks. Suicide by shotgun. That was the worst. Bits of bone and brain everywhere."

My stomach flip-flopped at the thought. This woman was tough.

"Are you working this case?" she asked.

"My partner and I were first on the scene."

She went back inside, where she stopped the tape, blew out the candle, and collected the candle, player, and picture. She gave the place a final look, shivered, and walked out.

"I hope you did a cleanse afterward," she said.

"A cleanse?" I asked.

"To remove any taint of negative energy, especially since you were present right after it happened."

I stifled a laugh.

She must have read the expression on my face. She waved at the shop. "This is a place of power. That power was used to amplify an evil act. We did what we could to protect ourselves while we were here, but we're going straight to a sweat lodge, and then we'll meditate."

"It's a bookstore!" I protested. "Just a bookstore."

"It's a place of words, and words have power. And it's at a ley line intersection," she replied.

"A what?"

"Ley line intersection." Her voice took on the kind of patience that a teacher used with dull pupils. "John Michell, the English writer, lectures about them. They're psychic power lines that run between ancient spiritual sites. Some people can tap into that energy."

I didn't believe a word of this mystic crapola, but it didn't matter what I believed. What mattered was what the killer believed.

"How do you know it's an intersection?"

She opened the driver's door and fished a city map from the seat. When she unfolded it, it was crisscrossed with dozens of red lines.

"Here's the bookstore." She pointed to our location. "See how two lines cross?"

I stared at the map, my heart thumping in my chest. Another set of red lines crossed at the Robert Haskell kill site.

"Where'd you get this?" I took it from her hands.

"My sister and I made it."

"You and your sister are psychic?" Skepticism filled my voice.

She quirked an eyebrow at me. "Just because you don't believe doesn't mean these things don't exist. Besides, it doesn't take a psychic to draw lines between points on a map."

I reined in my opinions and used my neutral interview voice. "How'd you know what points to use?"

"They're from a list we picked up at our meditation center. It includes all the world's important temples and burial sites, like Machu Picchu, along with some lesser known local landmarks."

I nodded like I understood what she was talking about. A little thrill walked up my spine. I was close to nailing Sleeth.

"Who made the list?"

"No idea. It was meant as a guide for those who could afford to take spiritual pilgrimages. Then six months ago, my sister returned from backpacking around Europe with news of Michell's work. Suddenly everyone in Solaris was drawing ley lines on maps."

"And your name?"

"Amanda Blake."

I glanced at the name on the car door.

"There aren't any sons," Amanda said. "It's just my sister and me. People don't think women can cope with death. If they see 'Sons' in the name, they assume the company is run by men and hire us."

I understood how difficult it was to be a professional woman and thought none the worse of her and her sister for their ruse. A woman had to do whatever it took to get ahead. I wondered whether I could hire on with these two should I be fired.

"Can I keep this?" I asked, flapping the map at her.

"If it helps restore the balance between light and dark, you're welcome to it."

"It will," I replied. I walked back to my car feeling like I'd finally done something important. My feet seemed to skim the pavement.

If there were more murders, they'd be at the intersections of the lines on the map. I had the key to stopping them.

29

Seve glowered at Kasker. After some hesitation, he shifted a patterned throw rug from the hardwood floor beside his desk and opened a square hatch in the floor. A ladder led down into darkness.

Kasker climbed down into a room twice the size of the office above. The demon followed and flipped on a bare bulb that hung in the center of the musty space.

Deep wooden shelves rose floor to ceiling on three of the walls. Dusty boxes of liquor filled them. A heavy iron safe stood against the fourth wall, and next to it, a barred door.

The door to the safe yawned open. Ledgers and yellowed scrolls filled the dark interior. The scent of damnation strengthened. Kasker repressed the urge to howl.

"You leave the safe unlocked?" Kasker asked.

The demon drew himself up. "When I'm here using the ledgers. Otherwise, it's locked."

Kasker pointed to the barred door. "Where does that lead?"

"To a tenement building across the alley, and through it, to the next street over."

"Someone could sneak in while the safe is open and take everything."

"The lock on the other side is unbreakable, and no one can shift the bar on this side from there. Besides, you're not the only one who can detect a damned soul. I would know if Holmes visited."

Kasker snorted. "Like you, he may use minions to do his bidding."

Seve squinted at him. "The souls who work for me would never dare to steal my belongings. They fear my wrath."

"They wouldn't have to steal. Easy enough to copy the information."

Kasker walked to the safe. Alone on the top shelf sat a thick tome. The cover was charred and flaking. The title read *Book of the Dead*. Whole sections of pages were missing, the loss indicated by gaps at the spine.

Strange energy emanated from the volume, not unlike the energy from the dagger left in Decker's throat. Kasker stepped back and turned to the demon, eyes wide. He pointed an accusing finger.

"You keep a magical book. That's forbidden."

The black form of the demon surfaced on the human skin. "It's none of your concern."

Kasker's spine stiffened, and he bared his teeth. "So this is how you best your demon brethren and turn so many souls toward Hell. You know the future."

"The book does not reveal a soul's final alliance. It merely provides information to help decide which to approach."

"And when and where they will die," Kasker said.

"When, but not where," the demon replied. "And the pages are written only a short while before the soul's demise. Look for yourself if you don't believe."

Kasker had no intention of touching the book. If his master knew about it... Perhaps this was a way to ensure only favorable reports about his performance reached his master. Seve would not be anxious to be found with the contraband.

The next shelf held five fat ledgers. Below them, six brittle scrolls tied with black ribbons nestled. Their scent drew him like heroin drew an addict.

"Who knows about the safe?"

The demon frowned and ran a finger over his mustache. "Only my accountant. He fetches the ledgers and works on them in the office above."

"He has the combination?"

"No." Seve contemplated the safe. "But sometimes he has taken longer than necessary to retrieve a ledger."

"Fool," Kasker muttered. He climbed the ladder back to the office.

The demon followed and replaced the hatch and rug.

"Who is this accountant?" Kasker asked. "Do you have his blood?"

Seve's mouth pulled down into a grimace. "I had no need of

blood. He is weak, controlled by his vices and his fear. He is called Alan Mong."

Kasker growled his displeasure. "You have his address then?"

The demon sat at the desk, retrieved pen and paper, and wrote a list, which he handed to Kasker.

"These are the names and locations of the bookies he frequents. He lives with his girlfriend. Her address is the last." Seve looked him in the eye and spoke with sarcasm. "You are the great hunter. You'll have no trouble finding him—even without blood."

"Push me, demon, and the master shall hear of your book," he answered with a toothy smile.

Seve crossed his arms over his chest and scowled but said no more. Kasker kicked the chair from his path and stalked out.

30

I'd agreed to meet Tad at a hot dog stand he'd be passing as he rushed from one campaign event to another. When I reached it, I checked my hair in the rearview mirror and tried to curb my excitement.

I decided to skip eating despite the heavenly aroma coming off the grill at Dad's Dogs. I didn't want my uniform stained with mustard. I got a cold bottle of Coke and sipped it while I waited.

Tad arrived fifteen minutes late. He pulled into a loading zone across the street and limped over to me. A tingle electrified my skin. I couldn't wait to tell him what I'd found.

Tad gave me a lackluster greeting and bought a chili dog despite the baking heat building around us and the danger of spilling on his tie, which was loosened and askew. My excitement ebbed a notch.

We sat under a tatty umbrella at an outdoor table that hadn't been washed since Eisenhower was president. Flighty sparrows vied with fat, aggressive crows to grab stray crumbs dropped on the concrete.

"Did you interview Susie Brown?" Tad asked.

"Lt. Mack is sending someone else." I didn't tell him that I was stuck doing busy work. If he tattled to his dad about it, I'd be out on my ear. If she was involved, someone would eventually roll on her.

"They were drugged. At least Decker was, according to Chief Greene." He stared at his chili dog, picked it up, set it down unbitten. "This can't go on. The Slasher has to be stopped."

"We'll nail him." I spread the map on the table. "Sleeth won't make mugs of us again."

"How can you still think he's doing this when you're his alibi for the Haskell murder?" Tad clenched a fist, and his voice flowed with frustration. "Doesn't anyone get it? Some maniac is carving up innocent people, and all the cops think about how it can help them catch Seve Calderon."

I didn't want to argue about it. I knew Sleeth was involved up to his cold blue eyes, and he was Calderon's minion, so somehow, Calderon fit into the puzzle.

"I found out why he chose the bookstore. It's on a ley line intersection."

Tad gave me a blank look. I pointed to the lines on the map and repeated what Amanda had told me. "So either the killer really believes this mystic mumbo jumbo, or he's trying to throw the police off by making mob hits look like ritual killings."

Tad went still. "You think the mob had something to do with the deaths?"

"Yes, but I'm not sure what."

I could almost hear the wheels go round in Tad's head. He pinched the bridge of his nose like he had a migraine coming on.

"What about the men you saw outside the hotel?" he asked with an urgency he hadn't displayed before. "You said you believed they were chasing me? I didn't just step off the curb in a moment of carelessness?"

I pulled photos of the heavies from my pocket and laid them on the map. "Here they are, Harold Warner and Jake Bronski. Warner was in the service, but he was dishonorably discharged. Do they look familiar?"

The color drained from his face. After staring hard at the pictures for a full minute, he asked, "Do they work for Calderon, too?"

"If they do, it isn't in their files." I wondered why he'd think the penny-ante hoods were Calderon's men.

Seeing the concern I'd caused, I wanted to reassure him. "They're small potatoes, and you were in a very public location. It's probably just a coincidence that they were at the accident scene."

He didn't look reassured. "I'll keep an eye out for them. Maybe you could follow up? They may be more of a threat than I initially thought."

I studied the well-bitten nails at the ends of my fingers where they rested on the table. Now that I had the map, I wanted to focus on the Slasher case. I had so much ground to make up with my fellow officers and the brass.

"If I see them around, I'll ask."

"You've made great progress, Nicky, but you need to talk to Decker's secretary. If you're going to find the Slasher, you need her help."

Tad stood and dumped his untouched hot dog in a nearby bin. I rose, too. He took my left hand in both of his.

"I have to go," he said.

With that, he dropped my hand and limped away to his car.

I frowned after him. Why was he so fixated on the secretary?

I drove to the station in search of Lt. Mack. The duty sergeant informed me that Mack and Greene were at city hall personally updating the mayor. I paced the squad room.

When they returned, a hush fell over the station. I ducked out of sight until they passed. Mack's face looked carved in stone. Greene was a walking heart attack. Suddenly everyone had somewhere important to go. The place emptied in minutes.

Once Greene turned into his office, I screwed up my courage and followed Mack. He stood behind an orderly desk in a room cramped by half a dozen file cabinets and a lone visitor's chair. No photos or framed commendations marred the vacant walls, although word was he'd received numerous awards.

"What do you want, Demasi?"

I stood at ease, map in the hands I kept behind my back. "I know where the Slasher will strike next."

He squinted hard at me. "How's that?"

"Given the ritualistic nature of the murders, I asked around in the spiritual community—"

"You mean those occult nut jobs?" Mack cut in. His fingertips drummed on the desktop.

"Yes, sir. Given the unusual nature of the crimes, I thought those 'occult nut jobs' might explain the choice of locations." I brought the map out with a flourish and opened it on his desk. "It has to do with their belief in mystical power lines that connect places of old power. Intersections—the places the lines cross—"

"I know what 'intersections' means, officer. Get on with it."

My face heated. "As you can see, there's an intersection at the bookstore, and another where Haskell died. If we stake out the other intersections around Solaris, we can catch the Slasher in the act. Sir."

Mack placed both hands on the desk and leaned on them while he studied the map. I held my breath.

"What the hell is this?"

Chief Greene's voice boomed behind me.

I jerked around, face burning hotter. "I was just—"

"Officer Demasi has some ideas about where the Slasher may strike next," Mack said, his voice level and cold. He tapped the map. "She thinks we should stake out the intersections of the red lines, all thirty-three of them."

Greene crossed to the desk and looked at the map. His mottled skin darkened. "Don't you have anything better to do with your time, lieutenant?"

"And you, Officer Demasi." Greene snatched the map from the desk and slapped it against my chest. "The mayor had a call from Mr. Merkel's bereaved widow. Seems an officer came around questioning whether her husband died of natural causes, even though the medical examiner's office already ruled it as such."

I was too stunned to think. Mrs. Merkel hadn't seemed the least bit swayed by anything I'd said.

"I've had enough of your insubordination. You're off these ritual murders." Greene took a quick step toward the door, then stopped. "And once we've collared the killer so I have manpower available, you'll be back to a desk."

31

Kasker drove to the ratty apartment complex where Alan Mong lived with his girlfriend. After running up four flights of stairs to find the right unit, he didn't bother to knock. No souls were inside. He walked down the four flights, cussing and swearing.

He shifted his attention to the first of the bookmakers.

The address Seve had scrawled took him to Ernie's, a dumpy corner bar slumped in a neighborhood of decay. Lighted beer advertisements hung behind fly-blown windows. The door dragged on the concrete as Kasker wrenched it open. *Soulful Strut* played on the jukebox.

The interior reeked of cigarette smoke and grease. Kasker's stomach growled in protest. His mouth was so dry that his lips stuck to his teeth. He couldn't resist the kitchen's siren call.

Kasker grabbed a stool at the bar. A brawny middle-aged Negro sporting a huge Afro stood behind the bar and polished its surface. When he'd finished his cleaning, he walked Kasker's direction.

"Give me a beer," Kasker ordered the barman.

The barman ignored him and walked down the bar to remove the empty glass sitting before a grizzled old drunk who swayed on his stool. Kasker gritted his teeth, opened his wallet, and laid a twenty on the bar.

The barman hoisted a rubber tub of dirty glasses and marched by, headed for the kitchen.

"Give me a beer," Kasker said louder than before. "And a burger."

The barman disappeared around the corner without so much as glancing Kasker's direction.

Kasker shifted on his stool and looked around to see if anyone had noticed the barman's snub.

No more than a dozen patrons occupied the seedy joint, all of them Negroes. All of them had eyes on Kasker.

A group of three hard-looking men lounged by the pool table, their cue sticks rapping against the palms of their hands. They muttered among themselves and nodded Kasker's direction. One made a quiet comment. The other two enjoyed a nasty laugh.

The drunk down the bar returned Kasker's stare, slipped off his stool, and shambled out.

In a dark back corner, four souls watched. They were the real predators. Kasker could tell by their stillness.

The one in the middle had skin so dark he faded into the black upholstery of the booth. Only the glint off his sweating face gave him away. The other three glanced at this man every few seconds, waiting for his command.

The barman returned and swaggered along the bar carrying a tub of clean glasses. As he passed, Kasker leaned forward, snaked out a hand, and grabbed the man's forearm.

"Beer," Kasker said, looking the man hard in the eyes.

The barman turned a haughty look on Kasker. "That'll be ten dollars."

Kasker bristled, but he was desperate. He tapped the twenty.

The barman slid the tub under the bar, fished out a bottle of beer, and plunked it down unopened before Kasker. He snatched the twenty and walked away. He brought Kasker's change and slapped it down on the counter.

"And a burger," Kasker said.

"Kitchen's closed." He swaggered away.

Kasker twisted the top from the bottle and drank half in one go.

The front door opened, and a new patron entered, another Negro. He took a booth near the corner where the bookie held court.

Kasker swigged down the remainder of the beer and turned toward the corner. All eyes followed him as he ambled to the booth. The three thugs slid out and stood like an ebony wall between him and their boss. One had a hand in a baggy pocket, another a hand behind his back.

It would take no more than a moment to abandon the flesh and devour their souls. They would taste so sweet and probably deserved a place in Hell.

If he did, there would be consequences—dire consequences.

"You a little off yo' turf, whitie," the leader said with a sneer.

His dark eyes shot daggers.

Consequences, Kasker reminded himself, wanting more than ever to slip his corporeal transport and teach the soul respect. Despite his restraint, his mouth watered.

"Seve Calderon sent me," Kasker replied, hiding his distaste at being thought to be the demon's errand boy. "You see Alan Mong tonight?"

Invoking the demon's name caused a weakening in the ebony wall. Looks of uncertainty turned on the leader. For his part, their boss sat straighter and lost the sneer.

"Knowin' that suppose'ta make me jump to?"

"Never hurts to have a man like Calderon in your debt," Kasker said, pushing his will at the man, "for example, if you were having a problem with your competition."

The boss's face turned thoughtful. "What's he want with Mong?"

"A job," Kasker lied.

"Good. That cat owes me money. He ain't been in today though. You try his girlfriend?"

It was Kasker's turn to sneer. "Where else does he hang out?"

The bookmaker stiffened. "Don't know, man."

Displeasure rumbled in Kasker's chest. Or perhaps it was only gas from the beer. He stalked out.

Kasker strode to his car and fervently wished he had Mong's blood. All this talking with untrustworthy souls was an inefficient way to hunt. He longed for an exciting chase—one that ended in a tasty meal.

He was glad to see no one had stolen his hubcaps while he'd been inside. As he unlocked the driver's door, two men approached. He recognized one as the new customer who sat near the bookmaker. His companion—a Caucasian—stood out in this neighborhood like nipples on a cold female.

"Hey, bro, wait up," the Negro called.

Kasker tensed. He closed his fist around his keys, keeping one jutting between his fingers, and squared his shoulders. The hackles on his neck bristled.

"I heard you was lookin' for Mong," the Negro said. He was a big man, well-muscled in the upper body, but the beginnings of a beer gut overhung his belt. Dark eyes watched Kasker from an acne-scarred face.

"You know where he is?" Kasker asked.

"What's it worth to you?" the white guy replied. He stood next to his companion, chest puffed out, muscles taut, but the smell of fear rolled off him.

The Negro elbowed his mate hard and gave him an angry look.

"What?" the white guy protested. "We ought to get something for our trouble."

Kasker sauntered around the Mustang's nose and joined the men on the sidewalk. They took an unconscious step back. He drew out his wallet and removed a twenty.

"If you lie to me, I'll come for you," he said looking the white man in the eyes.

The white guy shrank away.

"Hey," the Negro said, "we ain't stupid. We wouldn't lie to Mr. Calderon."

Kasker raised the twenty, holding it near his chest so they were forced to move closer. The Negro reached for the bill but stopped when Kasker lifted his eyebrows.

"He's at a warehouse on Frasier, where it intersects Pomona. They hold dog fights there. On fight nights, Mong keeps the book." He checked his fancy gold wrist watch. "Fights will be over now, but Mong stays late counting the take."

32

My muscles were as taut as high-tension wires. I hadn't shown Dave the map, hadn't told him about my meeting with Mack. It was all I could do to be civil.

We drove through a neighborhood where neither whites nor cops were welcome. Dave insisted we look for the thugs I'd identified. I thought it was a waste of time. We'd tried Jake Bronski's last known address. He'd moved out months ago—without notifying his parole officer.

We were cruising toward Harold Warner's place when I saw the maroon Mustang. Sleeth stood on the sidewalk talking to Warner and Bronski. I slammed on the brakes, veered to the curb, and doused our lights.

"It's Sleeth," I said, choking on his name, "talking to the guys who chased Tad."

Dave recovered from my abrupt stop and looked where I pointed. His forehead wrinkled, and the corners of his mouth pulled down. He glanced at me and let out an exasperated sigh.

Warner took something that looked like cash from Sleeth's hand and stuffed it in his pocket. I leaned closer over the wheel and held my breath. My skin crackled with excitement.

Warner and Bronski were mixed up in something with Sleeth. And we'd witnessed a payoff. We'd just scored a big break.

Sleeth rounded his car and got in. The two thugs traded looks and stepped back against the building. Their body language shouted triumph. Why were they so happy?

"Did you see it?" I squeaked. "Those guys took money from Sleeth."

"He could have been repaying a loan," Dave said, his voice flat.

"Bull. Did you see how he was holding the money? He was waiting for something, and he got it."

Sleeth pulled away. Should we stay and question Warner and Bronski? Or should we follow Sleeth?

I shifted into gear, checked my rearview mirror, and pulled out. I cruised by Warner and Bronski. They gave us the eyeball before hurrying away.

"You can't go after him!" Dave said. "Greene will skin you alive. Pull over and we'll question those two."

"Sleeth's at the center of whatever's going on. He's the key. Wherever he goes, murder follows."

I crawled along waiting for Sleeth to get two blocks ahead, and then I locked onto his retreating lights.

Dave slapped a hand on his forehead. "We should question Warner and Bronski about why they were following Newell and tell Mack about their meeting with Sleeth. He can follow up, and we'll stay out of trouble."

"You think he'll follow up on a tip from us? Ha! By the time he sends anyone to check, who knows how many more victims will die." I squeezed the wheel. "I can't let that happen."

Dave shook his head. "If you follow him now, you'll not only lose your spot on patrol, Greene will see you're kicked off the force."

Dave was right. By following Sleeth, I risked everything I'd worked so hard for. I almost turned around. Then I thought of Decker on the floor of the bookstore. No one deserved to die like that. If I could just cage Sleeth long enough to question him, I could stop anyone else from suffering Decker's fate.

"Everyone has blinders on. They're so sure it's Sleeth that they aren't thinking about other possibilities. What if there's another explanation? No one will find it because no one's looking."

A new thought popped into my head, and it turned my stomach to ice.

"What if Warner and Bronski were trying to snatch Tad when he ran into the street? What if Tad was supposed to be another victim?"

Dave's face paled in the dim light of the streetlamps. "All the more reason to report this up the command chain. If you're right, Newell should be assigned protection."

"They'll never believe us. Greene will say I'm trying to use my influence with the mayor to horn in on the Slasher case."

Dave gave me a who's-fault-is-that look. My face warmed. As we neared the edge of our patrol zone, he called dispatch and told them we were on a break. I gritted my teeth and focused on follow-ing my prey.

Sleeth was headed west toward the industrial district. What was he doing out here? What went down in his exchange with the thugs?

Traffic was darn thin in this part of town once the sun went down. He'd spot us if I wasn't careful. At our next turn, I doused my headlights and dropped back another block while we drove past warehouses and factories. Parking lots stood empty. No one lingered on the streets.

We continued another mile, working ever deeper into the industrial neighborhood that bordered the train tracks. Hot wind kicked up trash in a vacant lot. A crescent moon rose above the skyline.

Dave drummed his fingers on the dash. "This is taking too long. We should call it in and get back to our area."

The Mustang's brake lights flashed, and it swerved to the side of the road. I drove a block closer, hid the cruiser on a side street, and ran to a spot where I could watch our suspect unobserved.

In a second, Dave was at my back. We both peeked down the street.

Sleeth got out and turned a slow circle, head up, as though he were looking for something. At this distance, I couldn't be sure, but I thought his eyes were closed. He walked cautiously to the door, hovered his hand over the handle before grabbing it, and disappeared inside.

"What do you think he's doing in there?" I whispered.

"I can't imagine." Dave checked his watch. "The place looks deserted. We need to leave. We're way out of our territory, and we're already overdue back from break. How will we explain to the duty sergeant?"

I trotted back to the patrol car, fished out the map, and shone my flashlight on it. Electricity buzzed up my neck. Two ley lines crossed through our location.

"What's this?" Dave asked, looking over my shoulder.

I tossed the map onto the seat. "This is the site of the next kill. We have to stop him."

I jogged down the street. I heard Dave's low voice calling me, but I didn't stop.

The building rose twenty feet into the air and occupied a full city block. The lower walls were unbroken sheet metal painted rust red. Or maybe the metal was rusty.

The upper walls had small windows spaced every ten feet,

enough glass to give the interior daylight but make access impossible. No light shone through the cracked panes.

Twenty feet from the entrance, I slowed. The sign on the wall read *Southwest Freight*. No light filtered around the solid steel door, but a faint glow came through a grimy window high above the sign. Somewhere inside, an innocent victim was about to be murdered.

The patrol car's headlights brightened the pavement in front of me. It purred to a crawl on my left. I set my jaw.

"Nicky, what are you doing? Get back in the car," Dave said, voice low, face drawn into a scowl.

"Either Sleeth's in there killing again, or he's been set up. Either way, someone's about to die." I kept my eyes on the door. "What if it's Tad Newell? They tried for him once. Maybe they got him this time."

33

The warehouse was cavernous—and stuffy, despite the ventilators in the roof that ticked and creaked as they spun in the wind. Their noise almost drowned the scratching of foraging rats.

To Kasker's right, against the distant wall, stairs led up to what must be an office overlooking the warehouse floor. Nothing moved behind the office window, from which dim light emanated.

On the concrete floor around him, stacks of boxes, crates, and shipping containers rose like a forest into the darkness overhead. The boxes smelled of musty cardboard, and the pallets they rested on of raw wood. Traces of diesel fumes from forklifts and spilled fuel clung in the torpid air.

A cleared path arrowed the block-long length of the building toward access to the suspended office. The rest of the floor seemed a jumbled maze.

Kasker veered away from the passage to the office and slipped along a narrow rabbit trail that led deep into the warehouse. He passed through a large open space where boxes enclosed a circle. Blood, the stale sweat of excited men, and pine cleaner tainted the air.

Canine blood, not human. Dark spatters marked the sides of the boxes. He'd found the makeshift dog-fight ring.

His sandals whispered over the floor, his senses of hearing and smell attuned to his surroundings. His eyes grew more accustomed to the dark, and he moved faster through the labyrinth.

He found his objective near the back of the building. A recently departed soul clung to its stinking corpse. His nose detected the scent of blood, this time, human.

In the dim light, he couldn't identify the body sprawled on the floor. No ritual killing for this man. Just a deep slice across the throat.

Remembering the painful lump on his skull from abandoning the meat puppet at the jewelry shop, Kasker sat with care, braced himself into a corner between two crates, and loosed his connection to his flesh. His true form sprang free, muzzle twitching, drool hanging from his lips.

Soul essence wafted into his nostrils, strong and sweet and tempting. He licked his chops. Alan Mong, dead perhaps two hours. The white fog of Mong's soul shimmered and twisted, confused by its sudden, violent end. So enticing to take just a nibble.

Kasker clamped his jaws and reached for his flesh. A new scent tingled his nose and stayed his return. He sniffed, the hair of his true form rising along his neck and back.

Magic.

The same dark odor that had surrounded Decker in the bookstore.

Walking on cautious paws, he followed the smell, stretching his bond to his flesh. He halted every few steps, testing for the absent smells of the ritual sacrifice—blood and offal. Testing for Holmes.

His zigzag path led toward the front corner, where the stairs climbed to the office. A curtain of power, undetectable while he wore his corporeal suit, cloaked the area. A growl formed in his throat, and he slunk closer, each advance tentative.

The front door opened, and the ward stepped in, moving as silently as a shadow. He flattened to his belly. Goats! If the ward was here, could the guardian angel be far behind? Without his disguise to hide in, his true form would flare in the angel's sight.

Kasker scrambled for his vessel, galloping through the twists and turns of the aisles. His body jerked as he resumed control of it. His heart thundered in his chest.

He focused on the front door and worked to slow his breathing. Seconds later, the guardian angel blazed.

Summonings and invocations! Would the police give him no peace? What were they doing here? And at his feet lay yet another death.

He silently cursed the protoplasm's paltry sense of smell and hearing, its limited ability to detect whatever danger lurked in the distant corner. He'd avoid that area at all costs.

The officers conferred in whispered voices, and then they moved toward the office. So typical of an angel—always drawn to the light.

Kasker tiptoed away from it, looking for a back exit. Little illumination penetrated this far. He banged a shin on a protruding box corner and bit back a curse.

He waited, frozen, to see if his clumsiness had been heard. The ward and the angel paused, and then they continued their slow approach to the stairs. What would happen when they reached the concentration of magic? His curiosity was almost enough to make him hang around.

Kasker found the back wall and fumbled along it. The only escape was through large roll-up doors. They'd make a holy racket if he raised one. He might as well scream to be arrested.

If he wanted to sneak out and leave the cops behind, it would be through the front door. The foolish pigs had left it unguarded. It would be easy enough to do once they went into the office—assuming they got that far.

But what if they'd called for backup? More fuzz could already be rolling toward the warehouse. He hurried forward.

Kasker reached the wide front access aisle and peered around a stack of freight. His escape waited twenty feet to his right, tantalizingly close. To his left, the angel and the ward neared the end of the building and the pool of magic. They bickered in whispers.

He should go, while their backs were turned. He stepped into the open.

34

"Newell better be in here. This goes against every protocol," Dave whispered. "We'll be kicked off the force."

"Sleeth has to be up there," I whispered back through clenched teeth while I eased across the warehouse floor toward the office. "It's the only light."

"What if he is? He could have a perfectly legitimate reason for coming here. We sure don't."

"Then he won't mind telling us his 'perfectly legitimate' reason—and why he was talking to Warner and Bronski."

"We should have stuck with them, not hared after Sleeth," Dave said. "They aren't poised to sue the department for harassment, and they're only half as smart. We'd have a greater chance of getting them to talk."

Dave's frown was just visible in the illumination from the office window. No one passed before it while we crept closer. We didn't hear anyone moving, although with the clatter made by the roof vents, it would have taken an army marching to and fro for us to notice.

Dave hung back, still not committed to the mission, but unwilling to let me go alone. I was glad to have him behind me. The place was too eerie.

I walked on, holster unsnapped, hand resting on the butt of my gun, and blood pulsing in my ears. The hairs on my arms stood on end. The warehouse seemed to inhale and exhale with a life of its own.

I was ten feet from the base of the open metal stairs leading up to the office door. They were bound to rattle. I'd have to tread carefully.

"Nicky! Don't go," Dave hissed behind me, his voice plaintive. His quick footsteps sounded against the concrete, closing the distance between us.

Lightning flashed. A boom shook the walls. I ducked and staggered a step. A miniature electrical storm crackled at the ceiling, throwing flickering light against the towering stacks of boxes.

A trail of marks on the floor throbbed with a blood red glow, and I jumped back. They reminded me of the marks on the floor around Decker. Like the lightning, they'd appeared out of nowhere. I felt as though we'd stepped out of reality; we'd stumbled into a carnival fun house.

The marks curved around both sides of me. I couldn't take my eyes off them. I turned to follow their weirdly hypnotic rhythm.

Dave swayed behind me and clutched his hands against his chest. His stricken face glowed from within, the way kids' faces did when they shone a flashlight in their mouths. It added to the surrealism.

His knees gave way, and he sank to the floor. He stared at the symbols. His chest convulsed.

"Dave!"

I rushed back and grabbed him as he crumpled to the floor. I eased him into my lap. His hands glowed white like his face. He couldn't draw breath.

"Hold on, Dave. Hold on."

I loosened his collar with shaking fingers. It didn't help. The beat of the symbols sped faster.

Movement caught my eye. Sleeth stood near the door, eyes wide, brow drawn down in horror.

Dave's gaze followed mine. Something flared in his eyes. He raised a shaky arm and pointed at Sleeth. His lips parted to speak.

The light in his hands and face winked out. His pointing fingers fell on his unmoving chest. I shook his limp shoulders.

"Dave? Dave!" I looked at Sleeth. "Help me!"

Sleeth's horror changed to abject terror. He took a step back, and then another.

"Help me, God damn it!" My voice cracked.

My plea froze Sleeth in his tracks. His head cocked, as though he was listening for something, and wild eyes scanned the ceiling.

I struggled to lift Dave, to drag him from the flashing circle that gradually faded. The lightning ceased as abruptly as it had begun. Tears fell like rain from my eyes.

At the back of the warehouse, metal clanged and rattled. A cool, fresh breeze stirred the air. Someone had raised an overhead door.

Sleeth's head jerked toward the sound. His eyes narrowed and his lips parted in a snarl. His neck and arms corded with tensed muscles.

"Holmes," he said in a guttural voice that was as much growl as word.

He sprinted away. His sandals slapped through the darkness.

Rage closed my throat against a scream. I let Dave go, drew my gun, and ran after Sleeth.

35

Kasker wove the narrow trail at speed, crashing hips and shoulders against box corners. He cut straight across the fight circle, vaulting the walls to close with his prey faster, all the while reaching with his senses for the souls who had raised the door.

And reaching to detect more magical traps. Blinded and muzzled by his camouflage, he had little hope of avoiding one. There'd been none elsewhere in the warehouse when he'd walked in his true skin, but new ones may have been conjured in the interim. The tantalizing nearness of the prey drove him through his fear.

The ward followed. She ran quietly, her presence given away by bumps with unseen obstacles. He thought she'd stay with the downed angel's empty shell. He'd underestimated her hunter instincts.

Behind the warehouse, two souls flickered in and out of awareness. Why did they flicker? Something masked them, as though a gauze curtain had been pulled over them. More magic?

He thought they might be the men from the street, but the distance was too great. And it was getting greater. He sucked in air and ran faster.

The stimulation of the chase brought his true form to the surface. He strained to contain it and cursed the inherent weakness of human containers.

An engine roared, tires screeched, the noise of the motor faded as it pulled away. Kasker leaped over Mong's body, threaded the final ten feet to the open door, and burst onto a loading dock.

A flash of white was all he saw before the vehicle disappeared around the corner. He cursed the universe and bolted back into the warehouse.

He still held a fragile tendril of contact with the souls. If he cut through the building to the street, he might make his car in time to give chase. The Mustang had plenty of horsepower, and he knew their direction of flight.

His focus all for his quarry, he didn't notice the ward until too late. He slammed into her going full tilt. She ricocheted off a tower of freight but stayed upright. He stepped on Mong's arm and twisted his ankle.

He went down windmilling, fighting to hold his concentration on the fast-fading escape vehicle. His knee smacked the floor first, sending a lance of pain up his leg. His hands saved him from doing a face plant.

He scrambled up.

"Police! Halt!" the ward said, her voice high-pitched and tinged with hysteria.

Kasker ignored her and turned to run. Goats! In the fall, he'd lost track of the fleeing souls. No matter. He had their direction. With the dearth of souls in this part of town, he'd find them again if he got close enough.

His first step was his last. A foot connected with the back of his already bruised knee. He went down hard. His breath flew away in a whoosh. His head cracked against the floor. The already dark warehouse grew momentarily darker.

A hundred-pound wildcat landed on his back. She twisted his arm into a painful position and secured a handcuff. Then she added the other. Her weight released him, and he thrashed.

Surging frustration weakened his tenuous grip on his mortal tissue. A few bites would rend her soul beyond recognition and free him to continue the chase. He fought the urge to erupt in his true form.

She rolled him to an uncomfortable position on his back, the lump of his hands forcing his spine from the floor. He drew a ragged breath and clamped his jaws.

She straddled his torso and pointed her gun in his face. "You killed my partner, you bastard."

"You bitch!" he roared. "The trap was meant for me, not the angel. You're letting the one who set it get away!"

36

I wanted to pull the trigger. I wanted to splatter Sleeth's brains over the warehouse floor. Dave's voice stayed my hand. *You're a better person than that.*

Sleeth's eyes glinted red. It must have been a trick of the light. His body was as hot under me as asphalt in the noonday sun. In the streetlight shining through the back door, his face displayed a ferocity that would have set me on my heels had I not also been enraged.

In that moment of fury, I knew he'd spoken the truth. He, not Dave, had been the intended victim. Like a kaleidoscope twisting, the pattern of the murders changed.

My hand went numb on the gun. My legs trembled against Sleeth's flanks. I slumped off Sleeth. My bones had turned to rubber. I didn't have the strength to rise.

Sleeth squirmed away from me and levered to his knees. His rage had abated, replaced with fear. He listened and scanned the air above us.

My eyes fell on the body beside us. I blinked at it but couldn't take it in. Was it Tad? No, not tall enough. Had Sleeth killed him? I no longer cared.

Dave was dead.

"Am I under arrest?" Sleeth asked. He clamored to his feet, an awkward move with his hands behind his back.

My heart ached. I'd killed my oldest friend. What would I tell Cindy? I could never be forgiven.

"I'll wait outside." Sleeth took a tentative step away from me toward the front of the building, his eyes flitting around the darkness like he expected the boogeyman to jump out.

"Try that and I'll put a bullet in your kneecap," I said. He might not be a murderer. He was certainly an asshole.

The next hour was a blur. I called for backup. Half the Solaris PD arrived within minutes. Another unit carted Sleeth away. More units kept the media circus at bay.

The ME arrived with the meat wagon to take Dave and the dead man. Mack stormed around shouting at everyone. Lenny Greene looked on, hands on hips, face gray.

I sat in the front of my patrol car and watched it like a movie at a drive-in theater. It didn't seem real. Any moment, Dave would come to me and grouch about all the paperwork this incident would cause.

Eventually, Greene and Mack conferred with one another and came to my car. I climbed out, preferring to face them standing up.

"What happened?" Mack asked.

"My partner and I—" my voice cracked. I cleared my throat. "My partner and I were searching for two known criminals who appeared to be pursuing Tad Newell, the mayor's son, at the time of his accident."

Mack crossed his arms over his chest. "We know who Newell is, Officer Demasi. Get to the part about Sleeth."

My mouth had gone dry. I licked my lips, but it didn't help.

"When we found the men, they were talking to Sleeth."

"Did you overhear their conversation?" Greene asked.

"No."

"Did you question them?" Greene said.

"No."

"You just rushed off after Sleeth. Am I right, Officer Demasi?" Greene said. "You followed him here and entered the warehouse without permission from the owner, a valid warrant, or probable cause."

I nodded, too ashamed to speak.

"Why'd you go in?" Mack asked.

"This is one of the intersections on the map. I thought this was the site of the next Slasher killing, and I thought Tad Newell might be the intended victim."

"That damned map again." Greene tossed an angry look at the lieutenant. Mack clamped his jaws shut.

"Then what happened?" Greene said.

"We were approaching the stairs leading up to the office. We could see a light on up there. Then—"

What had happened next? It seemed like something out of a

nightmare. Lightning storms didn't erupt inside buildings. The glowing symbols had to be a trick.

Sleeth said it was a trap. How did it work? Why had it killed Dave but I'd felt nothing?

"There were electrical arcs. Dave—" I swallowed. "Dave clutched his chest and fell."

Greene exchanged a look with Mack. "The ME didn't say anything about burns."

"Maybe the voltage was too low to cause burns but was enough to stop his heart," Mack said. "That would explain why he didn't find any marks. The autopsy should tell us. Where was Sleeth?"

"We didn't see him when we went in. He was standing by the door when Dave went down."

"I'll get an electrician," Mack said. "We'll figure out how Sleeth set the trap."

Mack turned to go.

"I don't think Sleeth's responsible," I said. "I think someone set the trap for him, and we stumbled into it. Someone wants him framed. Or maybe dead. Who was the man at the back of the building?"

Greene looked like he might explode, but Mack answered anyway. "Alan Mong. Vice says he keeps books for Calderon."

"You think Sleeth killed him? If he works for Calderon, why would Sleeth kill one of his own?"

"Sleeth is Calderon's lieutenant. Calderon gives him the target. Sleeth plans the operation, sees to the execution, but doesn't get his hands dirty. He probably has Warner and Bronski for that. Vice has Sleeth at Calderon's restaurant when Mong died, based on the ME's preliminary findings."

"But if the trap was meant for Sleeth—"

"We aren't buying that bullshit." Greene hiked his pants up. "Sleeth crossed a line when he killed one of ours. We'll get him."

Mack didn't say anything aloud, but a whisper of doubt ran across his face. He walked away and yelled at a uniform to call an electrician. Greene rubbed a hand over his balding pate.

"I ordered you to stay away from Sleeth, and you disobeyed that order." Greene's face screwed up like a prune. "Give me your gun and badge."

In a daze, I handed them over.

"The union rep will notify you of your disciplinary hearing date. Until then, you're suspended without pay. Officer Tisdahl will drive you back to the station. Now get out of my sight."

Maggie appeared at my elbow and guided me to the passenger side of the patrol car. She took the wheel and headed for the station.

"Honey, I'm so sorry about Dave. I know how close you two were."

My throat closed on a reply, and tears threatened to spill from my eyes.

"I couldn't help overhearing," she said. "What's this about the mayor's son?"

I wiped my nose with the back of my hand. "Two small-time crooks were at the scene of Tad Newell's accident. He asked me check them out."

Maggie's head turned my way. "You're seeing the mayor's son? Is that smart?"

I didn't want to talk about Tad. If not for him, Dave and I wouldn't have entered the warehouse and my partner wouldn't be dead.

I stared out my kitchen window at my neglected backyard, a mug of coffee going cold on the counter. The first blush of dawn painted the sky. Seeing the sunrise was one of the things I'd missed most about working the night shift.

Every few minutes, another round of tears carved stripes down my cheeks. I hated weepy women, but I couldn't seem to control the waterworks.

The last time I'd cried hard had been ten years ago, when I heard about my father, gunned down chasing suspects from a liquor store robbery. He and his partner had been the first to respond. The store owner said the suspects weren't armed. He got it wrong.

My phone rang. There wasn't anyone I wanted to talk to, but I couldn't listen to a ringing phone without picking it up.

"Nicky, how are you?" Tad's voice asked.

Something inside me whimpered, but I stopped it before it slipped out my mouth.

"I'm okay," I said.

"I heard about your partner. You have my deepest sympathies."

I covered the mouthpiece and sniffed. "Thanks. He was a good cop. A great cop. A better partner than I deserved."

"I'm glad you weren't harmed." He drew in a breath, his voice thick with anger. "Too many people have died because of Sleeth. It would be better for everyone if one of your fellow cops pulls the trigger on him."

This didn't sound like the man I'd had lunch with. "Weren't you the one who thought we had it wrong? That we ought to cast a wider net? If Sleeth's innocent, putting a bullet in his brain won't stop the Slasher."

Tad went silent. Then he said, "Danger follows him like a shadow. Promise me you'll stay away from him."

I gripped the handset so hard my fingers ached. "I can't talk about this."

"Sure, sure, I understand," Tad said, suddenly conciliatory. "I'm sorry I pressed you."

I hung up without saying goodbye and stared out my window again. The sun inched above the horizon, casting an orange glow across my yard.

Sleeth didn't kill Dave. I did. I'd rushed into the warehouse to prevent another death, but in the back of my mind, I knew I'd also rushed in with the hope of salvaging my career. Bagging the Slasher would have erased all the black marks on my record, solved all my problems.

Instead, I'd sacrificed my partner and been suspended. Since I was the darling of the feminist movement, possibly the review board would stop at a reprimand and demote me back to a desk. But I'd still have a job.

If I went near the Slasher case again, there'd be no hope of saving my career. No hope of opening the way for other deserving women.

None of that mattered. I had to do the right thing, the hard thing. No more impressing Lenny Greene, no more worrying about what anyone thought. No thinking about what I stood to lose. I'd follow the evidence and catch the murdering bastard who killed my partner.

37

Kasker stepped out the front door of the police station and tensed. Morning sun slanted on the concrete and cast long shadows in doorways and alleys. His senses told him no souls lurked unseen in the dark, but they'd also said no one was in the warehouse.

That the angels hadn't swooped down to destroy him yet seemed a miracle—or an enormous oversight. Between Heaven and Holmes, it felt like the entire universe hunted him.

The thought of what he'd witnessed at the warehouse made him shake. The trap had crushed the angel, not just pushing it from the earthly form, but squeezing it into nonexistence. It wasn't a fate Kasker wished to experience first-hand, although the power differential between the angel and himself was the equivalent of the difference between a gnat and a fighter jet.

Had Holmes been at the bookstore, too? Cloaked by more of the magic he'd learned from the cursed book? How could Kasker hunt something he couldn't detect? How would he avoid another trap?

For a moment, he wanted to release the flesh, experience the world around him through his true form, reassure himself that no unseen runes were drawn on the pavement ahead. But other humans came and went through the station door, and one held steady just inside, watching.

Kasker's eyes raked the streets—and the skies. He'd refused a ride from the pigs to retrieve his car. He balled his hands into fists and headed west for no particular reason.

He'd need a new car, and a new place to stay. He'd be a fool to frequent any of his old haunts, including the Luna Azul. Goats!

That must have been where the men who'd given him Mong's location started tailing him. He'd need their names. He turned at the next corner.

A car glided to the curb. The front passenger door flew open in his path. Kasker stopped with a jerk.

"Get in," the ward said.

Kasker swallowed and scanned the sky, listening for the beating of wings. Hanging out with her was to invite disaster.

"I've had my fill of pork today," he said and squeezed past the door.

A car door thunked behind him, footsteps tapped the pavement, and the ward grabbed his arm. He stiffened against her restraint.

"If you want to ditch the detective tailing you, you'll get in the damn car."

Alarmed, Kasker looked toward the corner. "How do I know you're not lying?"

"Fine." She dropped his arm. "I'll go after Holmes by myself."

Kasker glowered at her. What did she know of Holmes? *How* did she know of Holmes? For that matter, how had she found him at the warehouse?

She was a determined hunter, he'd give her that. Perhaps he could use her. Nothing else he'd tried seemed to work.

He reached the car in two long strides and slid into the passenger seat. The ward pulled away before he'd closed the door.

"Duck down," she ordered.

Kasker crammed himself low in the too-small seat of her Corvair, pressing against her right arm and shoulder. His hand rested on her thigh. The scent of her soap mingled with the scent of her soul. His nether regions responded. Goats!

She watched the rearview mirror. At the intersection, she took a fast left. Her foot pressed to the floor, and her rattle-trap car spluttered down the next block.

"You can sit up now," she said, voice dry.

He removed his hand from her thigh, straightened in the seat, and spread his senses to check for following souls. Satisfied no one was closing in, he turned his attention to the ward.

She wasn't in uniform. Her legs were clad in blue jeans, and she wore a light blue cotton blouse.

"Why are you helping me escape, Officer Demasi?"

"It's not 'Officer Demasi' now, Sleeth. It's just pissed-off-citizen Demasi—and pissed-off-citizen Demasi wants to catch the person who killed her friend and partner. Maybe if we trade information, we can both get what we want. Or we can see how you fare when you walk into the next trap."

"You know where Holmes is?" he asked, his interest sharpening.

"What were you doing at the warehouse?" she countered.

The lie came out as smooth as icing on cake. He'd repeated it a hundred times while the pigs questioned him. He'd gladly trade it for her information about Holmes.

"Collecting a debt. Mong owed me money."

"I'm the only person in Solaris who believes you aren't the Slasher," she said. "Cut the bullshit, or I'll drop you back at the station."

Sweat broke on his forehead. If she'd found him there, then Holmes could, too. He needed to disappear, to hunt from the shadows. His stomach rumbled. He needed breakfast.

"Mong was the bait in the trap," she said. "They thought you'd see the light in the office and assume he was there."

Holmes must not be aware of his abilities, Kasker decided. He'd detected that the office was empty moments after stepping in the door. And Mong should have been taken farther away before the kill. If Holmes underestimated him, it gave Kasker an edge.

"But you and your... partner walked into the trap instead," he said.

Her face jerked toward him. Her eyes were unusually red and her skin splotchy. With a smidge more concentration, her expression could have turned him to a pillar of salt.

"Why were you after Mong? He works for Calderon, same as you."

"No," Kasker said, irked by her assumption. "I don't work for Calderon."

She raised an eyebrow. "You and the mobster are just drinking buddies?"

How much should he tell her? Did she know what her partner was? He didn't think so.

Souls were to be kept in the dark about how things really worked. It was a clause demanded by Hell in the peace accords with Heaven. No manifesting demons, no overt miracles. Best to play by the rules.

"Seve's doing my boss a favor by loaning me a pad and some wheels while I'm in town."

For the next minute, they drove in silence.

"While you're in town?" she said. "You've lived here all your life."

Witches and water torture! The ward was quick. The thought of her status made the hair rise on his arms.

"Mong may have sold information about Seve's business relationships to Holmes. If Mong did, he might have known Holmes' whereabouts." Kasker watched her through narrowed eyes. "Do you know where Holmes is?"

"So Holmes snuffed Mong to keep him quiet." She pursed her lips then asked, "Who knew you were looking for Mong?"

She was inordinately good at avoiding his question. "Seve Calderon, a few people in the bar where I stopped to ask about Mong."

"Warner and Bronski?"

"Who?"

"The two guys you talked to on the sidewalk outside the bar." Kasker blinked. "You *know* them?"

Perhaps he *wasn't* the greatest hunter in Heaven, Hell, or the universe. Perhaps *she* was. Her extraordinary ability might explain the guardian angel.

"Only by their rap sheets."

She turned another corner and cruised through the retail district, glancing again in her rearview mirror. Traffic was sparse this early. If the pigs knew what to look for, they wouldn't be hard to spot.

"Where can I find them?" he asked.

"With Holmes?" She pulled into a vacant parking lot, taking a spot in the shade of a withered oak. "Tell me about him."

The ward killed the motor and turned to face him. Her eyes were keen and her body tense. She smelled anxious.

"You tell me about Holmes," he said, "since you're so interested in him."

"Well..." Her Adam's apple bobbed, and her face took on a rosy hue. Her eyes slid from his. "It's the name you spoke right before you ran to the back of the warehouse."

"You've been shining me on! You don't know anything." He grabbed the door handle.

"I knew the name of the guys who set you up." She reached across to stay his hand. "And I know where the next killings will be. I can help you find Holmes."

Her arm was warm across his chest and her fingers soft on his hand. His mortal transport already yammered for a woman. The slow smile formed on his lips, the one that melted female resistance.

No, he reminded himself. She was of the angels. Screwing her would be the mother of all mistakes.

She withdrew her hand, and a curtain of reserve fell over her posture. "Who's Holmes? Why does he want to kill you? Why's he buying information about Calderon's dealings?"

Kasker stared out the windshield. He'd need to watch his tongue. But if she knew where the next kill would be...

"Holmes broke a contract with my boss. I've been sent to collect, which is why he framed me and set the trap."

"Who's your boss?"

Kasker eyed her. "You wouldn't know him. He's not a local."

The corners of her mouth turned down. "What's Holmes look like?"

"No idea." At her disbelieving look, he added, "He's changed his appearance and taken a different name."

"Wonderful." She tucked a strand of loose hair behind her ear. "Was Haskell doing business with Calderon, too?"

Kasker started. She knew about the contracts?

"Is Holmes attempting to take over Calderon's turf? Is that why he killed Decker? Decker had business dealings with Calderon?" she asked.

His shoulders relaxed. She was thinking in the context of mob wars, not damned souls. He'd encourage her false assumptions.

"Possibly," Kasker said.

"But why the ritual killings? Is it a scare tactic?"

Kasker shrugged.

"You don't know any more than I do," she muttered. She tapped her fingers on the steering wheel. "Is there anyone besides Warner and Bronski who might know where Holmes is—and who isn't already dead?"

Kasker shifted in the seat and wiped a hand across his damp neck.

"There is someone."

38

Who was Sleeth working for? What kind of 'contract' had Holmes broken with Sleeth's boss? Why did Holmes slice and dice his victims? If he was killing people to send a message to Calderon, what was the message? Why was Robert Haskell a victim?

Sleeth adamantly refused to give me answers despite my continued badgering. Asking the questions kept my mind off Dave.

Sleeth wiggled in the seat like a little kid frantic for a visit to the restroom. His head swiveled constantly, and he seemed incredibly interested in the weather overhead even though it was the same clear blue sky every time he checked. The guy was wacko.

We stopped at a burger joint while we killed time until we could visit his mysterious source. I had no appetite. Sleeth downed two burgers and a mountain of fries. To my embarrassment, he leered at the carhop.

"What did you see when you ran out of the warehouse?" I asked.

Sleeth made sucking noises as he drained his cup. "The flash of a white vehicle turning the corner."

"Make? Model?"

"Couldn't tell."

Another white mystery vehicle. I didn't see how Merkel's death could be connected to the Slasher killings. Had to be coincidence. Lots of white cars in California.

"What about the trap? How was it done?"

The hippie shrugged.

"Why didn't you go to the office in search of Mong?"

He squirmed in his seat, and I was pretty sure a lie was coming.

"I thought I heard someone at the back of the warehouse."

Yep, another lie. I jingled the keys where they dangled in the ignition and thought about ways to torture Sleeth until he told the truth.

When it got to be nine, he directed me to a little shop just north of downtown, *Hawaiian Mike's Meditation Center*. In my time on the force, I'd never heard it. It didn't look like the establishment of a well-connected mob source.

"He's a powerful man. He hears things, knows things," Sleeth assured me, worry in his voice. "Be careful what you say."

Sleeth was slow getting out of the car. He trailed me to the door, casting suspicious glances both directions of the street. His caution put me on edge.

A heavy-set Hawaiian wearing a billowing t-shirt emblazoned with a screen-print of a surfer riding a curling wave stood behind the counter. His attention went to Sleeth first, and when it did, the hippie stopped dead.

"I see you found her." A jocular smile crinkled the Hawaiian's face.

I glanced at Sleeth, puzzled by the comment. He stared, first at the shopkeeper, and then at me, his eyes going round and his lips parting.

The shopkeeper chuckled and addressed me. "Solaris has a leash law. Maybe you wanna get him a collar and license."

He must have me mistaken for someone else. I didn't know him, and I didn't own a dog.

I examined the merchandise. It was typical occult junk: brass bells, incense burners, and crystals. I didn't see any obvious drug paraphernalia.

"I'm Officer Demasi." I advanced to the counter. "Solaris Police Department."

"Are you?" he asked. "Cause that's not what your aura says."

Definitely one of those spiritual nut jobs, the kind who communed with aliens on a different astral plane. Or maybe I had a blazing *Liar* sign shining over my head.

"Sleeth says you might have information about a man we're seeking."

The big Hawaiian's eyes flicked to Sleeth. "Didn't tell her what she's looking for, huh? Won't matter. It'll find you."

To me he said, "Better keep him on a short leash. Friday's coming fast."

"What's so important about Friday?" I struggled to keep frustration out of my voice.

"Didn't he tell you?" The shopkeeper waved a hand at Sleeth, and Sleeth flinched. "It's the solstice, a time of change. If you're planning big changes, best do it when the energy of the universe is behind you."

The shopkeeper pulled a bag of colorful hard candies from under the counter and poured them into a glass candy jar on the counter. I glared at him and considered walking out. He offered me a candy.

"You don't believe?" he asked with a glint in his eyes. "Wot, you aren't a good Catholic girl?"

"No," I said, heat in my words, and then I wondered why I'd answered. I didn't discuss my religious beliefs—or lack of them—with anyone.

"No Heaven or Hell? No angels or demons?" he asked, but this time, he looked at Sleeth.

Sleeth backpedaled another three steps towards the door. His face paled under his honeyed tan.

"Belief is power," the shopkeeper whispered, as though he'd shared a special secret with me.

I snorted.

"When you believe in something you give your power to that thing. Stop believing and you take your power back. You want to be strong, the best place to put your belief is in yourself. Then you can do anything."

"That's a bunch of cosmic hooey," I said.

The Hawaiian raised his eyebrows in surprise. Or maybe it was amusement. "Here, I'll show you."

He stared at Sleeth, his brows lowered, his face serious. His voice took on a deep timbre that seemed to fill the entire room without being loud. "I don't believe in you."

Sleeth staggered back. His eyelids fluttered. His countenance looked dead, like it had when I'd found him in his car behind the apartment complex.

"Stop it!" I said.

I rushed to Sleeth and gripped his arm to prevent him from falling. His normally hot skin felt cold and dry under my fingers. My touch steadied him.

"Run," Sleeth choked, fear painting his eyes and his breaths coming fast.

"Buck up," I said. "He's messing with you."

I turned Sleeth loose and marched back to the counter.

"Go ahead, you try," said the shopkeeper.

"No! Just because he's gullible and believes in superstitious claptrap doesn't mean you should torture him. You should be ashamed of yourself."

The shopkeeper hung his head, and his lips curled up in a bashful smile. "Okay, okay. I'll play nice with the puppy—and you remember the lesson."

My patience fizzled out. "Do you know anything about the Slasher?"

The Hawaiian rubbed his jaw with a thumb and forefinger and lifted his eyes to the ceiling. "One, two, three, four, five. Yeah, five points on a star. He's got two. He'll be in a hurry to get the other three. Friday's almost here."

I turned to Sleeth to see if any of this garbled rant meant anything to him. He clutched a display rack like his life depended on it. Sweat rolled down his face even though the store was comfortably cool.

Useless, the pair of them. It looked like I'd be on my own to find Dave's killer.

39

Kasker slumped in the Corvair seat and cast a slant-eyed look at the ward. Goats! She'd shown no fear of the Oracle. In fact, the Oracle implied she had the ability to wish Kasker out of existence, too. Despite the boiling heat in the car, he shivered.

The ward thrust her key in the ignition, wrenched it over, and started the car. She stared out the windshield.

"Back to square one," she muttered.

Kasker wanted to jump from the car and run as fast as he could. He was a simple hunter. He had no business in the company of creatures as powerful as the Oracle or Officer Demasi. No wonder she survived the trap while the angel perished.

Could *she* read minds, too? The thought paralyzed him.

The Friday solstice had importance. Why else would the Oracle harp on it? Seve said the book gave Holmes the power to destroy Heaven and Hell. Was that the big change the Oracle hinted at?

One thing was clear: the ward was meant to be his companion during whatever danger lay ahead. But would she be his savior or his destroyer?

"We should investigate Mong, see who hired him to steal Seve's information," Kasker suggested.

"Decker first," the ward replied. "That's where everything started."

Goosebumps raised on Kasker's arms. "I've done that already. It's a dead end. Mong's a better choice."

"We'll pay a visit to Susan Brown."

Kasker's breath stuck in his throat. Hot panic flooded his brain with a buzz that prevented thought. He had to do something to divert her. He dug the address for Decker's companion from his jeans.

"If Decker knew Holmes by his new identity, he may have told this woman something."

The ward snatched the paper from his hand. She frowned at it, turned it upside down, turned it back.

"Where'd you get this?"

"A reliable source," he said. Perhaps she *couldn't* read minds.

"We'll see this Laverne Fritcher right after we pay a visit to Susan Brown."

"Susie Brown won't help us," he said in a rush.

The ward gave him a cool look. "Maybe if you'd spent more time talking instead of... Well, I want to hear what she has to say."

His heart thumped in his chest. How did she know he'd met Susie? She'd find the body, call her pig buddies, and they'd lock him up—again. Flight was the only option. He reached for the door handle.

Too late. The ward pulled into traffic. Kasker licked his lips. His gut full of burgers and fries threatened to empty itself on the floorboards.

Seve couldn't procure new flesh for him on such short notice. He'd be rotting in jail while Holmes destroyed Heaven and Hell. The ward had to be stopped.

"It's a long, unnecessary drive to Susie's. Laverne Fritcher is closer," he said, pushing temptation at her with all his will power. "Don't you want to see Fritcher? The fuzz don't know about her. It'll be your coup."

Her face scrunched in thought, and her hands tightened on the wheel. "Fritcher first, then Brown."

A sigh whispered past Kasker's lips.

The address proved to be an older, two-story clapboard house in the Solaris red-light district. A large covered porch shielded the front from the sun. Seve's Negro bodyguard lounged in a lawn chair at the top of the steps. Kasker bit back a growl.

As they approached, the guard rose and barred their way. The huge muscles of his arms knotted, his fists balled at his sides, and his jaw worked back and forth.

"We're closed," the guard said. A sheen of sweat erupted on his forehead, but he stood his ground despite Kasker's hard stare.

The ward pushed Kasker aside.

"Officer Demasi, Solaris PD." She stood, feet planted and hands on hips, while the guard scowled down at her. "You can let us in, or I can come back with my buddies from Vice."

Kasker admired her balls. The guard's obstinance faded to be replaced by confusion and uncertainty.

"This is your chance to screw your master for posting you here," Kasker whispered, pushing temptation at the man. "Let the nice officer in."

The suggestion took its sweet time to worm through the Neanderthal's brain, but eventually a gleam shone in the guard's eye. He stepped back and swept a hand toward the door. "Be my guest."

The ward brushed past, and Kasker followed. He could feel the guard's vengeful gaze on his back.

The front door opened into a parlor decorated in black-flocked red wallpaper and crushed red velvet furniture. The large front window was covered by heavy red drapes trimmed in gold fringe, leaving the interior dim and cool.

The place stank of spilled liquor, sweat, and sex. The odor reminded Kasker that the meatbag would crave a woman soon. He considered the ward, since she was convenient, but then reminded himself of her status with Heaven. He listened again for the sound of wings.

A middle-aged woman wearing a floral housecoat, fuzzy slippers, and a scarf over hair curlers vacuumed the red shag rug. When they entered, she switched off the vacuum and frowned at them.

"Didn't he tell you?" She gestured toward the door and guard beyond. "We ain't open yet. The girls need their beauty sleep."

"We're looking for Laverne Fritcher," the ward replied. Her eyes scanned the room, but her face remained neutral.

"Never heard of her." The woman switched the vacuum on again and ran it vigorously over the rug.

Kasker reached down and yanked the vacuum's cord from the wall socket. The appliance died. The woman glared at him.

"Seve sent us." He took a step forward and loomed over her. "Where's Fritcher?"

The woman jerked, and her eyes widened just a little. She took a half step back, her hands rising in front of her.

"You should of said sooner. I'm Fritcher. Listen, if it's about the receipts—"

"It's not." The ward stepped around Kasker and guided the woman to a couch. She tossed Kasker a disapproving look and jerked her head toward the opposite side of the room. "Sit down, Sleeth. Over there."

Kasker resisted the urge to snarl and parked his butt on a wing-backed chair opposite the women. Then he got it: good cop, bad cop. He'd be the bad cop. The very bad cop. He smiled. The woman shrank back.

The ward placed a hand on Fritcher's arm to draw the woman's attention from Kasker.

"We'd like to ask you about William Decker," the ward said.

"The two-timing skunk's dead," Fritcher snapped. "What else do you need to know?"

"What was your relationship to him?" the ward asked.

Kasker wanted to laugh. They were in a bordello. What did Officer Demasi think their relationship was?

Fritcher chuckled. "You ever been in a place like this before, honey?"

"You were doing business?" the ward said without missing a beat. "From your low opinion of him, I thought maybe there was something more between you."

Kasker smirked. Despite her time as a pig, Officer Demasi knew little of the world's seamy underbelly. Unlike Kasker, Decker paid dearly for the company of women.

Fritcher looked down at her hands. "It started out as business. But then he said he loved me. He promised he'd set me up with my own place, my own girls. I wouldn't be under Calderon's thumb anymore."

Kasker wiped the smirk from his face. Goats! How had the ward known? Until he'd given her the demon's note, she'd never heard of Fritcher. In seconds, she'd pried the woman's secrets from her.

"You know what it's like for a working girl past her prime? You have to work cheap, and you get all the weirdos. If I had my own place, I wouldn't have to service the clients. And I'd take better care of my girls than Calderon does." She shot Kasker an unhappy glare.

"I'm sure you would," the ward said. "I don't think William Decker set out to be murdered. If he'd lived, I think he would have kept that promise."

Fritcher's eyes narrowed. "I'm not so sure. Something was up, something he wouldn't tell me about."

Kasker sat straighter. "Any idea what?"

The woman lifted her chin and clamped her jaw shut.

The ward patted Fritcher's arm and leaned closer. "Whoever killed Decker also killed Robert Haskell. Last night that same person killed my partner. Anything you know could help us nail him before anyone else dies."

Fritcher turned to the ward, and her face softened. "I don't know much. This past two weeks, Billy'd been distracted and distant. When I asked him about it, he said it was nothing. He had some business with Calderon, that's all. Dealing with Calderon is enough to make anyone crazy. The next day, he brought me flowers. I was shocked. Billy never thought of anyone but himself. The day after, he was dead."

"Calderon," the ward repeated. Her gaze went to Kasker. He shifted on the chair and looked away.

"Do you think—" the woman stopped and studied her hands. "Do you think Billy mentioned me in his will?"

The ward smiled and patted the whore's shoulder. "I don't know. Maybe his lawyers can answer your question."

Fritcher wiped her hands over her cheeks and stood. "That's all I can tell you. Now I need to get back to work."

The ward stood and shook the hooker's hand. "Thanks for your help. If you think of anything else..."

The woman frowned and tapped her fingers on her lips. "There is one thing. The week before he died, Billy rented a storage locker. He put it in my name and asked me to hang onto the key. He said someone would come for it."

A thrill surged through Kasker's blood. He stepped forward. "Give it to me."

40

"What kind of 'business' was Decker doing with Calderon?" I asked when we were in the car.

"How should I know?" Sleeth said. "I'm only interested in Holmes."

His tone was tense, and he rubbed the key between his fingers. As I drove, his eyes darted around the streets, flicking frequently to the rearview mirror on his side. Nothing like working with a suspected felon.

The storage facility was a shoddy affair near the railroad tracks. Low rows of metal buildings with silver roofs and white siding marched across two acres enclosed by a six-foot cyclone fence. A ten-by-ten office building stood beside the open gate.

I parked outside the fence, and we walked to the office. It was empty. Sleeth didn't wait for someone to return. He strode through the gates and checked unit numbers. I jogged to catch up.

He stopped in front of a roll-up door, inserted the key in the padlock that secured it, and removed the lock. The door opened with a screech.

The unit was ten by fifteen, concrete floored, and stifling. A jumble of cardboard boxes packed the space. I stepped to the wall to flick on an overhead light.

Sleeth marched to the pile, grabbed a box, and upended it on the floor. He flung the empty box aside.

I rushed over, planted a hand on his chest, and pushed. My shove had no effect on his six feet of muscles and sinews.

"Knock it off!" I said. "This is evidence."

"So?" he said.

He squatted and stirred the pile of papers that had fallen from the box. Before I could join him, he rose and reached for another box.

"Enough." I inserted myself between him and the pile. "We'll do this my way, or I'll do it alone while you're rotting in a cell."

His chest swelled, his eyes narrowed, and he stepped closer to loom over me like he'd done with Miss Fritcher. His strong-arm tactics with Fritcher had angered me, but I couldn't argue the point in front of her. Now was a different story.

I sucked in a breath, puffed out my own chest, and poked a finger against him with each word I spoke. "And you can knock off the intimidation stuff. It won't work on me."

For a moment, I thought I'd made a terrible mistake. Instead of backing down, he huffed up more and leaned closer, so close his body heat rolled over me in waves. A low growl rumbled in his throat.

I screwed up my courage, leaned in, and locked on his cold blue eyes.

"My way or the highway, Sleeth. What's it going to be?"

The hippie blinked first. He stepped back, lifted his chin, and crossed his arms over his chest. I knelt by the mess on the floor so he wouldn't see me exhale the breath I'd been holding. Threatening a psycho. How dumb could I get?

In a minute, he joined me. He didn't say anything or touch the bank statements and cancelled checks scattered in a three-foot circle. If he'd tried, he would have gotten a sharp jab.

I organized the statements by month and sorted the checks into the appropriate groups. Then I read through each statement.

Decker never bought groceries, at least not with a check during the past six months. He dined out daily at all of Solaris' best restaurants. Travo's seemed to be a favorite.

He made outrageous mortgage payments. He also made sizeable payments to Jamelko's, the only auto dealer in town that sold foreign sports cars. I hadn't seen anything in the case files about anyone finding his car near the scene of his death and wondered what had become of it.

In the final two weeks of his life, he'd made several very large deposits to his checking account. About the time Miss Fritcher said he'd seemed worried, he'd withdrawn ten thousand in cash. On the day of his death, he'd withdrawn all but a few hundred. Where was all that cash?

I retrieved the discarded box, replaced the statements, and moved on to the next box. Sleeth walked to the door, checked the alleyway, and returned. Fifteen seconds later, he'd paced to the door and back again. I ignored him and moved to another box.

"Find anything?" he asked ten minutes later.

"Give me a break! Financial records take time."

Sleeth continued to pace. I continued to dig. The sun climbed out of sight over the building, and the stuffy storage space got hotter.

"This is a stupid waste of time. Let's go." Sleeth headed to the door.

I looked up and shook a thick sheaf of papers at him. "About two weeks ago, Decker took out all the cash advances he could against his five credit cards, got a second mortgage on his house ostensibly for remodeling, and sold his business inventory—including goods he hadn't paid his suppliers for yet."

Sleeth's look of annoyance told me he didn't get it.

"He liquidated assets, whether they were legally his or not. He deposited the funds in his personal checking account and withdrew nearly all of it as cash the day he died."

I started on another box.

"He planned to run," Sleeth said. "Fool."

"Maybe." I pawed through the contents of the new box. "Or he might have used the cash for a payoff."

The next box was much like the last. The one after included legal documents for the incorporation of Decker Industries. Tucked between the pages was a pamphlet for the Temple of Enlightenment, a counterculture hippie church that probably only called itself that for tax purposes. On the corner, someone had written *10k* in smudged ink.

I wondered about the notation. The only place I heard metric used was the drug trade. The Temple of Enlightenment was familiar. Someone had mentioned it to me, but I couldn't remember who or why.

Was the temple a front for a drug supplier? Had Decker decided to buy into the operation? Had Calderon ordered Decker killed because he'd dared to go into business on Calderon's turf? Maybe the bizarre murder ritual was meant to implicate the temple.

A queer feeling crept over me, and I glanced at Sleeth. Was I working with a killer caught up in a drug war? If that's what it took to get to the man who murdered Dave, so be it.

The next box contained dozens of bundles of hundred dollar bills. I'd never seen that much cash and sucked in a breath. Sleeth noted my reaction and came to look over my shoulder.

"I was right," he said, expression smug. "He hid the money here so he could get it later."

"Or he was killed before the handoff." I was unwilling to cede my theory to his.

Sleeth put the lid on the box and picked it up. He walked toward the door.

I ran after him and grabbed the box.

"This isn't ours." I wrested the box from him.

"Finders keepers." The hippie snatched it back.

I grabbed the box but couldn't jerk it out of Sleeth's grasp.

"This money should go to the people Decker cheated."

We stood there tugging on the box like two kids arguing over a favorite toy until another storage unit renter walked into view.

"If I scream," I whispered, "you can be sure he'll call the cops."

Sleeth's lips drew into a thin, hard line. He let go of the box.

I placed the box with the others, escorted Sleeth from the unit, and locked the door.

"Key." I stretched out my hand.

Sleeth held out his own empty hands. "Must have left it inside."

"Bull." I wiggled my fingers in a gimme movement.

The hippie stalked away to the car. I clenched my teeth and followed. We got in my baking Corvair, the late afternoon sun slanting through the windshield.

We sat.

We sweated.

"Key," I said.

Sleeth glared at me. Then he dug the key from his pocket and tossed it on the dash. I scooped it up and put it in my pocket.

"We should see Mong's girlfriend," Sleeth said.

"Right after we interview Susan Brown."

Sleeth went still. I backed out of our parking spot and pulled onto the street.

"We won't learn anything from her," he said. "It's a waste of time. Mong's girlfriend might know who he stole the information for."

I glanced over at the hippie. He was positively rigid. The air blowing in the open windows had done nothing to staunch the trickle of sweat running down his temple.

"Susan Brown first. Then we can question Mong's girlfriend."

Sleeth rubbed his palms on his tatty jeans. "I had nothing to do with it."

What the hell was he talking about?

"Someone slashed my tires. You can ask the mechanic who sold me new ones. I was tied up all Saturday afternoon."

The little whisper of worry pulsing along my nerves erupted into a full-blown storm.

"Why should I care where you were Saturday afternoon?"

His neck flexed when he swallowed. He didn't look at me.

"Susie's dead. Someone killed her Saturday afternoon."

41

The ward stomped on the brakes and swerved to the curb. Kasker braced a hand on the dash to keep from colliding with the windshield. She stared at him, open-mouthed.

"You didn't report her death?"

Kasker snorted. "So they could arrest me?"

The ward's hands dropped to her lap. "Christ! Another murder?"

Kasker glanced up, waiting for the lightning strike. "Don't take the Lord's name in vain. He's a vengeful god."

Officer Demasi blinked at him. Then she laughed in a scary, crazy way that made him twitch.

"I've partnered with a psycho to chase a murdering lunatic. Imaginary deities are the least of my worries."

For the briefest moment, Kasker had that melting sensation, the same one he'd experienced in the Oracle's shop. The world faded. He struggled to hold onto his disguise, remain in this realm.

"Are you all right?" The ward placed a hand on his shoulder.

His true skin burned under her touch. Fire coursed through his veins. His lungs sucked in air. His heart resumed its regular beat.

"I'm cool," he said, voice shaking and vision clearing.

The ward withdrew her hand. "I assume you searched Miss Brown's house after you found her."

Kasker nodded.

"Why would anyone kill her?"

He cleared his throat. "She had Decker's appointment diary. I think she tried to blackmail someone in it. Whoever killed her took the diary."

The ward banged a hand on the steering wheel. "Tad was right. I should have questioned her sooner."

"What?" he asked.

"Nothing."

He slumped in the seat. He'd expected her to run him in, or at least to call her pig friends and send them to Susie's. But she didn't. How could he use that to his advantage?

She checked traffic, signaled, and pulled away. They drove in silence until they reached a neighborhood business district where a grocery store, pharmacy, and hairdresser's shop shared a block with a gas station.

The ward turned into the parking lot. Perhaps she had the munchies. She hadn't eaten at the burger joint and it was supper time. He could use a meal, before his corporeal veneer began its incessant nagging.

"Come on." She fished a purse from under her seat and got out.

Kasker popped his door and unfolded from her crappy little car. Goats! He missed the comfort and power of the Mustang. He missed the control of being in the driver's seat.

The ward stopped beside a pay phone. She dug in her purse and pulled out a dime.

"You're going to call the police and report a suspicious smell coming from Miss Brown's house," she said.

He crossed his arms. "Screw that."

"Show some respect for the dead. You know it's the right thing to do."

"It's a rotting corpse. Why should I care what happens to it?"

The ward's jaw tightened. She dropped the dime in the slot and held the receiver out to him while she twirled the dial. He reached past her to thump two fingers on the hook. The dime tinkled into the coin return.

"My fingerprints are all over her pad. The pigs will take me in."

The ward smacked his wrist bone with the hard plastic handset. He jerked his hand away and glared at her.

Officer Demasi returned his glare. "The longer her body decomposes, the harder it becomes to determine time of death. Your alibi won't be worth a plug nickel if they don't find her soon—assuming your flat-tire story isn't fiction."

He growled at her. She retrieved the dime and placed it in the slot again.

"Tell them you're a neighbor, but you don't want to get involved," she said.

He snatched the receiver from her hand, gave the operator who answered the story of the mysterious smell, and hung up. The ward nodded her approval and headed to the car.

"Where's Mong's place?" she asked.

Kasker directed her to Mong's apartment. He climbed the four flights of stairs behind the ward, admiring her tight ass and trim figure. Blue jeans enhanced it more than her ugly uniform. His desire for her almost overrode his fear.

He'd been foolish to challenge her directly. Lies and deceit were the safer strategy. He longed to be rid of her, to return to the hunt—in his true skin and alone.

The skinny waitress from the Luna Azul opened the door to their knock. A sticky brat of perhaps five clung to her hip. When the woman saw Kasker, recognition and fear flashed in her dark eyes.

Before the ward could speak up, Kasker crowded her over. "Seve sent us."

He extracted his wallet, drew out a wad of cash, and held it towards the woman. "He wants to make sure you're all right."

The woman's dark eyes flitted beyond them to the empty balcony, and her hand trembled where it held the door. She didn't take the money.

"We're very sorry for your loss," the ward said. "May we come in?"

After more hesitation, the woman snatched the bills and opened the door. The interior of the apartment looked much like Kasker's place after the police search. Mong's woman shooed the child away to a bedroom, cleared toys and magazines from a worn-out couch, and indicated they should sit.

The ward offered her hand. "I'm Officer Demasi. You're...?"

The woman sucked in a breath. Her gaze jumped to Kasker. Her thin frame shook.

"I don't know anything about what Mr. Calderon does," she said. "I just work in the restaurant."

"This isn't police business," the ward assured her. "And we don't care about Calderon."

He'd assumed she'd lied, but now Kasker realized Officer Demasi told the truth when she'd said she wasn't a cop anymore. That should give him some leverage.

The woman didn't take the offered hand. She clutched the money and glanced toward the bedroom where the child sang the alphabet song off-key.

She turned to the ward. "Eva. Eva Rodriguez. What do you

want?"

The ward bowed her head and spoke softly. "I know this is a difficult time for you, and we don't want to make it worse. We have some questions about Alan. If you can answer them, it may help us find his killer."

The suspicion in her eyes turned to confusion. She addressed Kasker. "Calderon didn't... ? The police said you..."

"No," Kasker said, "I didn't. Neither did Seve. But he'd be grateful to know who did. Very grateful."

Kasker's gaze fell to the cash in the woman's tight grip, and he pushed temptation at her. The ward's cheek twitched, and her hand went to her temple. Rodriguez glanced down at the money she held.

"What do you want to know?" she asked.

The ward helped Rodriguez down to the couch. "Did Alan meet anyone new recently? Someone who offered him a job?"

Rodriguez scrunched her brow. "A month ago, he started talking about moving away. San Francisco, he said. Or maybe Seattle, where no one knew him. I thought it was just talk. He owed Calderon more than he could ever pay off. But he said he'd have a lot of cash soon."

"Who offered him the money?" Kasker asked.

"He never told me." The woman wrung her hands. "Then that man, Decker, got killed in the bookstore, and Alan got jumpy. He said we had to go right away."

Another dead end. Kasker wanted to throw something. Bite something.

"Did you ever see him with these two men?" The ward drew pictures of Bronski and Warner from her back pocket.

Mong's woman stared at the pictures. Her eyes went wide. "They came for Alan, a couple days ago. He met them in the parking lot. I thought one of his bookies sent them to collect." She hung her head. "He gambled."

The hint of a smile tightened the muscles in the ward's face, and a new sharpness showed in her eyes. "Did you see their car?"

Kasker stopped breathing. He stared at the woman, willing her to speak.

"A white van, I think—with writing on the side. My eyes, I'm nearsighted," she said. "I couldn't read it."

The ward rose, reiterated her condolences, and thanked Rodriguez for her cooperation. They left the apartment and clomped down the four flights of stairs to the parking lot.

In the ward's car, Kasker drummed his fingers on the dash.

They'd learned nothing new. He'd hoped for more.

The ward clicked her nails against the steering wheel. "The white van again."

"What I saw last night," he said.

"The same one Mrs. Sanchez saw at the Merkel building?" she muttered. "What does Merkel have to do with this?"

Kasker couldn't follow her reasoning. When he'd read Merkel's obituary, he'd realized the man died in an ambulance on the way to the hospital. It explained why he'd found Merkel's soul in the middle of the roadway. Thousands of humans departed the realm of the living every day. They weren't *all* Holmes' victims. Being anywhere near the site of Haskell's death was pure coincidence.

He brushed aside the ward's comment. That he'd spent so much time and raised uncomfortable blisters on his feet without finding the sacrifice angered him. When he found Holmes, Kasker would enjoy every luscious bite. *If* he found Holmes before the damned soul destroyed Heaven and Hell. The terrifying thought of Hell's imminent destruction raised his hackles.

42

I got a newspaper from the box outside the Denny's and followed Sleeth in. The sun had dipped to the horizon, and we were no closer to finding Holmes' lair.

We'd looked into Decker and Mong. In the morning, we'd start on Haskell. I didn't have high hopes about turning up vital clues.

We took a booth, looked over the menus a waitress provided, and ordered. I didn't have much appetite and went with an egg and toast. Sleeth ordered a burger basket.

The front page of the paper was devoted to the Slasher killings. The writer rehashed their gruesome nature and emphasized the inability of the police to stop the killer. The story continued on page five.

I flipped pages. Sleeth drained his water and flagged the waitress for a refill. She rushed right over, ignored my own half-full glass, and filled his to overflowing.

Page five included additional stories detailing Decker and Haskell. I found nothing new or startling in Decker's bio. Haskell was another matter.

"Robert Haskell was a professional bowler?" I'd expected him to be another businessman. "Why would Holmes choose him to frame you? Did you know Haskell?"

"Does it matter?" Sleeth's gaze followed the swing of the waitress's hips as she returned to the kitchen. His eyes grew heavy, and a lecherous smile curled his lips.

"Of course it matters," I hissed at him. "You said Holmes wanted to take over Calderon's turf. What kind of business would Calderon be in with a pro bowler?"

The hippie turned his stone-cold eyes back to me. "I only said it was *possible*."

I sorely missed my police contacts. Five minutes gossiping in the canteen would have netted me the information about connections between Sleeth and Haskell or Haskell and Calderon. Or I should have asked Tad when he called to offer condolences.

I set the paper aside, tapped a finger on the table, and frowned across at my new, unhelpful partner. It didn't elicit a more helpful answer.

"Merkel as a victim makes sense. He was a man of power, of money, like Decker," I muttered.

"Too bad the dude croaked on the way to emergency, not in a rune circle." His voice dripped with sarcasm and anger.

"Where'd you hear that?" I asked, forcing myself to remain calm.

Sleeth must have sensed my tension. His attitude became guarded. "His obit, I think."

I'd read the obituary published by the paper. It hadn't mentioned a trip to emergency or even the cause of death.

"He never went near a hospital. His body was found in the parking lot behind his office."

"Bullshit," Sleeth replied with certainty. Then he clamped his jaw shut and turned his gaze out the window.

He knew something about Merkel's death, and he wasn't telling me. Getting answers from Sleeth was like navigating a maze blindfolded—too many dead ends.

"The death was suspicious," I said, just to see his reaction.

That got his attention. I swear I could hear the clack of wheels turning inside his head. "Why?"

"His jacket and heart meds were missing from the scene."

Sleeth snorted. "Probably stolen by some junkie."

"The building cleaning lady said she saw a white van in the parking lot shortly before she discovered the body."

The waitress arrived and set our plates in front of us. She asked Sleeth if he needed anything else. He didn't seem to see or hear her despite her flirty smile and flouncy moves.

"The Oracle said Holmes needed five by Friday," he mumbled more to himself than me. "If Merkel died before they were at the construction site..."

"You think they snatched Merkel, and when he keeled over, they grabbed Haskell instead?" I asked. "Merkel was another one of Calderon's business associates?"

Sleeth ignored me and dug into his burger. I'd dealt with drunks, spouse beaters, drug addicts, and raving lunatics. None of them irritated me more than the hippie. I wanted to reach across the table and shove the burger down his throat.

"It's too late tonight. Tomorrow we'll talk to Haskell's family and see what we can learn about him," I said.

"Someone will die tonight." Sleeth took an enormous bite of his burger, which he talked around. "You said you know where the next ritual will take place."

"Every incident happens at a ley line intersection. There's about thirty intersections in the Solaris area."

"Which one will he use?" He crammed a wad of fries in with the remains of a burger bite.

My stomach did a slow roll, and I addressed my answer to the tabletop so I didn't have to see his gaping maw.

"How should I know?"

Sleeth's voice dripped derision, along with a streamer of ketchup. "You said you knew, not that you had a long list of possibilities."

"He doesn't kill every night." I used my toast to mop up egg yolk. "Or at least he hasn't so far."

"The Oracle said he needed five by Friday—"

"And you believed that gibberish about points on a star and Heaven and Hell?"

The hippie dropped his burger and braced both hands flat on the table while he swayed. Color drained from his face. I wondered if he had some kind of seizure disorder or suffered from narcolepsy.

"Hey, are you okay?" I touched his right hand.

He leaned back and sucked in a deep breath.

"We need a shortcut," I said. "A way to get in front of the murders instead of traipsing around a day late."

Sleeth straightened and resumed stuffing his face. I stared into the darkness out the window and racked my brains.

"I want to talk to Calderon," I said after several minutes.

Sleeth froze in mid-bite. His chest didn't rise. His eyes didn't blink. The burger eventually made a slow descent to the basket.

"Why?"

"We're getting nowhere chasing dead men. If you're right and the victims know and trust Holmes, then someone may have been approached already and can give us a description or even tell us how to find him. Calderon is the connection behind Decker's murder and your frame-up. Maybe he's tied to Haskell, too. Since you don't know anything about Calderon's business dealings, I'll have to ask Calderon. He may know who Holmes will go after next."

After a long moment, he said, "Calderon won't talk to you. I'll ask."

"Look, Sleeth, you can introduce me or I'll go on my own, but I'm talking to Calderon first thing tomorrow."

A low rumble carried across the table. Maybe he was growling at me. Or maybe his stomach was fighting back against his steady diet of burgers and fries.

"His bodyguards won't let you in."

"They have to let a police officer in."

Sleeth raised his eyebrows. "Thought you weren't one anymore."

It was my turn to grit my teeth. I might have fooled the idiot at the brothel without showing my badge, but Calderon's guards weren't so gullible. I was stuck.

Sleeth knew it and smirked.

"I'll pick you up—early." I flagged the girl to bring our check.

"Where?" Sleeth asked. "I can't go to my pad. The pigs will be watching."

"Get a hotel."

The waitress brought the check and flashed her pearly whites at Sleeth. He undressed her with his eyes and gave her his most sultry smile. She jotted something on the check and put it beside his empty basket.

"I'll stay at your place," he said.

"Like hell you will," I said.

"I doubt your place is anything like Hell," he replied, a wistfulness in his tone. "The pigs would never look for me amongst their own."

He had a point. Still, I could only imagine what the neighbors would say if they saw me come home late with a man. Maybe I could sneak him in unseen after dark.

"Fine. You can use the guest room."

He turned the sultry smile to me. I resolved to lock my bedroom door. He tossed a couple bills on the ticket and shoved it across to me.

I noted that he'd shorted his half by a buck, and the waitress had added her phone number at the bottom of the bill. I didn't point it out to Sleeth. I added more bills and a stingy tip.

"You have any beer?" he asked. "Or weed?"

"House rules." I rose from the table. "No booze, no dope if you want to stay with me."

"Lighten up, Officer Demasi." He trailed me to the door. "Live a little. Tune in, turn on, drop out."

"Call me 'Officer Demasi' again and I'll drop you at police headquarters."

43

The ward pulled up before a squat, dark house in a working-class area just after ten. Kasker wondered why she'd taken the long way. They could have arrived half an hour ago.

No lights were on—anywhere. All the dull suburbanites were tucked up safe in their beds. He'd hoped the ward lived in a sprawling apartment complex, one with an active party life he could crash after she'd gone to sleep. The flesh craved a joint and a woman.

This neighborhood was as boring as a pre-school full of innocent children. Too many innocent souls who never broke the rules. Never pursued their true desires. Would never sate Kasker's growing lust for a damned soul.

Except in the ward's home, where a tainted soul moved from the front picture window to the middle of the house. It hasn't crossed the line into 'destined for Hell' territory—yet—and so wasn't quite fair game—yet.

Perhaps he could change that. A little temptation here, a little nudge there. His master would be pleased if he delivered such a gift. It might mitigate some anger over Kasker's slow restoration of Holmes' soul to Hell.

Why would the ward associate with a tainted soul?

"Your boyfriend gonna be okay with me dropping in?"

The ward turned a hostile look on him. "None of your business, but I don't have a boyfriend."

"Just asking. Don't have a cow." Kasker tilted his head. "Roommate?"

"Not even a dog."

Good. No whining, snapping cur to give away his true being.

A pig buddy from work then? Plenty of dirty cops in the world. They joined the force thinking they'd be impervious to the temptations of power, only to have their good intentions sucked out of them. Kasker chuckled at the thought.

He and the ward got out. She gave a nervous scan of the neighborhood and hustled around the car. Her tension made his caution rise.

No lights on in the ward's house. Strange that a visitor would hang around in the dark. Perhaps he'd fallen asleep while waiting for the ward's arrival.

Officer—no, Citizen Demasi—grabbed his arm and towed him beneath a scraggly tree to the front door. She must be in a hurry to greet her guest.

After a brief fumble, she stuck her key in the lock, twisted, and pushed the door open.

The soul inside had gone still. The smell of overpowering fear slapped Kasker in the face. In that moment, he knew they'd walked into a trap.

He grabbed the ward's arm and dragged her down and back. The sharp crack of a gun split the night. An angry bee buzzed over his head. A second bullet followed the first.

"Police! Drop your weapon and give yourself up," the ward shouted into the darkness.

Kasker admired her quick thinking and courage—even if she trembled against him like a sapling in an earthquake. The man inside sprinted for the back door.

Kasker dumped the ward on the porch and charged in. A lamp beside the door toppled as he brushed past. His shin caught the corner of a chair or sofa, the light in the room too poor to reveal the object.

The back door banged. He hopped three steps nursing his bruised leg and rushed into the kitchen where he caught his hip on a counter. Goats! The place was designed for midgets.

The ward grabbed him by the arm. "Let him go! He's got a gun."

"He's a lead to Holmes."

Kasker shook her hand away and slammed through the back door. Lights had come on in the house to his left. Souls stirred. A child wailed.

The shooter was already across the yard and leaping the fence. Kasker bared his teeth and ran after the assassin. The blisters on his feet screamed their protest.

Behind him, the screen door thumped closed. No footsteps

followed him. The ward might be a superior hunter, but it seemed she had no stomach for danger. Kasker laughed and vaulted the fence.

Kasker's prey rounded the corner of the neighbor's house and paused. *Setting another trap.* He wouldn't be fooled by such an ancient and simple trick.

Kasker cut sharp right around the opposite side of the building. On the way, he tripped over a wheelbarrow and sprawled on the grass, cursing. The barrow clanged onto paving stones.

The soul of the shooter stepped back from his strategic location at the house corner, alerted to Kasker's flanking movement.

Growling, Kasker regained his feet. He hugged the shrubbery, blending with the shadows. He burned to be free of his human cloak, free of binding mortality, so he could pursue his prey in his true form. He rounded the corner.

The shooter backed toward the street, gun raised. He fired high and wide. And fired again. A woman cried out in alarm.

Kasker dodged and grinned. The human was a coward and a bully, the type who shot others in the back. By his actions, he'd denied himself entrance to Heaven, but as yet, he hadn't assured his place in Hell. When he died, his soul would perish into the universe.

Kasker cursed the waste. He hungered for soul. Saliva broke in his mouth and washed over his lips. He was the hunter. He bayed his excitement and ran forward in a zigzag line.

The shooter went rigid. Then he turned and bolted.

More windows brightened. Porch lights switched on. Doors opened. Men stepped out.

The shooter dug in a pants pocket with one hand. With the other, he pointed the gun over his shoulder and fired until the gun clicked empty. He tossed the weapon away and ran harder.

Kasker didn't waste breath on a laugh. He closed ground. The puny shooter was no match for Kasker's superior physique. In another five seconds, his fate would be sealed.

The man reached a junker car parked on the street. He scrambled in and started the engine before closing the door. With a chirping of tires, he pulled away, the driver's door first swinging wide before slamming shut.

The grin fell from Kasker face. He raced down the middle of the street, pushing muscle and bone to its limits. His only focus was the swirling light and dark of the tainted soul as it fled.

44

Sleeth was either the bravest man alive or certifiably insane. My money was on mad as a hatter. I had to find the shooter before Sleeth got himself killed.

My family-oriented neighborhood wasn't the kind of enclave where hit men settled. The shooter must have a car stashed nearby. When he reached it, he'd get away. Chasing him on foot was plain stupid.

I started my Corvair, threw it into gear, and floored it. I circled to the opposite side of the block.

Neighbors stood in small knots on lawns discussing the night's events. I didn't see a body on the pavement and breathed a sigh of relief. But I also didn't see Sleeth. Someone pointed west. I hurried on in the indicated direction.

Three blocks farther, Sleeth ran down the middle of the street like the hounds of Hell pursued him. No one ran in front of him. Was he chasing the shooter or running away?

I closed up, but he was oblivious to me. He didn't look around until I tooted my horn. Then he stopped so abruptly that I collided with him.

Sleeth rolled across my hood, landed on his feet beside my door, and jerked it open.

"Move over." He didn't wait for me to comply but crowded in. The car rolled forward when my foot was forced off the brake. I pulled myself into the passenger seat, ready to read him the riot act.

"Quiet," he said before I could breathe a word.

Sweat rolled down his face and his chest heaved. His eyes were half closed in concentration. It must have been the reflection of the dash lights. His pupils glowed red.

He didn't bother to adjust the seat even though his legs were jammed against the steering wheel. He screeched away.

We tore through the quiet residential neighborhood like we were running for the finish of the Indy 500. I fumbled my seatbelt on and braced a hand on the side door. I didn't see a car ahead of us.

"What's he driving?"

Sleeth spun the wheel, and we careened around a corner. Still no taillights before us.

"Where—"

"Shh." His brows pulled down hard, and he leaned forward.

Five more blocks, during which we topped ninety. I didn't know the car could go that fast. Animal eyes sparkled, and a cat darted across in front of us.

"Watch out!"

Sleeth growled in reply. I had the arm rest in a death grip and vowed never to let him behind the wheel again, assuming I survived.

We blew through a stop sign and fish-tailed around another corner. I'd seen nothing of the killer's car. How could Sleeth still be following it?

A police cruiser, light flashing but running silent, ripped through an intersection a block ahead. I guessed they were the backup for the first unit responding to shots fired at my place. Their presence didn't slow the lunatic driving my car.

Sleeth weaved along an arterial, whipping into oncoming traffic to pass vehicles slowing him. I held my breath and gritted my teeth. A head-on at our speed would kill us both.

"There." Sleeth pointed, a triumphant grin on his face.

An older two-tone Datsun sedan sporting serious dents and gray primer patches rolled along a block ahead. Sleeth didn't let up on the accelerator.

"Back off. He'll see us," I said.

"I'll force him off the road," Sleeth replied.

"Not in my car you won't." I reached for the ignition key.

Sleeth caught my wrist. As we struggled, he swerved from one side of the road to the other. We missed sideswiping a parked car by less than an inch. My heart jumped up to block my throat.

The suspect noticed our erratic behavior. He romped on it. Sleeth did the same.

I withdrew my hand from Sleeth's grasp and braced it against the dash. Every muscle in my body locked up tight. This whole chase was insane, but I was powerless to stop it.

We'd reached the outskirts of Solaris and raced into an area of new home development. Stretches of bare lots were studded with houses at various phases of construction, only one in four of them complete and inhabited. Streetlights burned, but most of the sidewalks were missing or outlined in wooden forms.

Our suspect twisted and turned through rolling hills and meandering streets. He didn't seem familiar with the area. Too late, he realized he'd turned into a cul-de-sac.

Sleeth bared his teeth and pounded the wheel with a hand. "I got him."

When the shooter hit the end of the asphalt, he kept going. His Datsun bounced across the rough yard of an unfinished house and over a rise. A billowing cloud of dust hung in the air to mark his trail. Sleeth followed.

"Slow down," I said. "You don't know what's out here. If you bust an axle, he could get away."

The hippie tossed me an unhappy glance but complied. The car jumped and bucked. My teeth clacked together with each landing. I could barely breathe in the dust-laden air.

A thunderous crash carried over the engine and tire noise. Sleeth went for the brakes. We skidded off the dirt and onto pavement.

When the dust settled, the headlamps illuminated an eerie scene of contrasting light and shadows. Skid marks on the pavement indicated the driver's unsuccessful attempt to stop before he plowed across a street and into a telephone pole.

The sheared-off pole lay on top of the collapsed passenger compartment. Steam hissed from the radiator. Nothing moved inside the car.

"Come on," I said. I unlatched my seat belt and cracked open my door.

"You go. I'll wait here."

"Because you'd rather he shoot me?" I put as much sarcasm as I could into my tone.

"He tossed the gun before he got in the car."

I stared at Sleeth. This was the man unmoved by Decker's gruesome body, the man determined to run into a hail of bullets to follow a clue, and now he wouldn't get out of the car.

"Then what are you afraid of?"

The hippie huffed up. "I'm not afraid of anything. The guy's dead. Nothing to see."

At the next lot over, lights came on in a house. If I wanted a chance to search the car, I needed to move. I snatched my keys from the ignition.

"Get out of my seat," I said.

By the light of the Corvair's headlamps, I trotted over to the Datsun. Little eddies of dust created a haze that caught in my throat. The darkness outside my puddle of light seemed surreal and unfriendly.

I looked in the crunched driver-side window. A white male of approximately thirty slumped over the wheel. He hadn't taken the time to buckle up. The top of his head was a flattened bloody mess. I clenched my teeth on the urge to vomit and didn't bother checking for a pulse.

The house door opened. A man in a bathrobe stepped onto the porch. He peered my direction but didn't come any farther.

"Call an ambulance," I said, raising my voice so he could hear.

He gave me a wave and went inside. He'd be back.

I jammed my hand behind the shooter, searching for a wallet. I found one. A wave of heat washed over me from behind.

I spun around. Nothing was there. The hairs on the back of my neck stood up. It had to be a trick of the erratic breeze blowing heat from the motor over me.

In the light from the Corvair, I glanced through the contents of the wallet. My hands shook so bad I almost dropped it. No ID.

I stuffed the wallet back where I'd found it and circled the car. The passenger-side door wouldn't open, but the Datsun was tiny. I reached the glove box through the open window. I'd hoped to find the vehicle registration. No such luck.

In the corner of my eye, a shadow slithered past on the opposite side of the car. I gasped and jumped back, staring hard at the driver and out through the slit of window where I'd seen... something.

Nothing moved. I glanced back at the Corvair but was blinded by the headlamps.

I hurried back to the Corvair and got in. The interior burned like a furnace despite the open windows and cool night.

Sleeth slumped in the passenger seat. His arms wrapped his torso. He looked ready to upchuck on my floorboards.

"I didn't find any identification." I drove away fast. "What a bust."

"Herman Marks," Sleeth said in a tight voice. At my look, he continued, "The guy in the car, Herman Marks."

"You know him?" My voice rose with a mix of surprise and anger.

He stuttered and cleared his throat. "Seen him around."

It sounded like a big fat lie. "At Calderon's?"

"No, no," Sleeth said too quickly while holding up his hands and shaking his head. "Just... around."

We drove in silence while I replayed the events of the night. I started with Sleeth's questions about my living arrangements and moved on to how he'd dragged me out of the way a split second before the shooter fired. How he'd followed the shooter for blocks without seeing any trace of the sedan.

"You knew he was in the house," I said. "How?"

Sleeth floundered, hemming and hawing.

"Spit it out man," I said.

"I saw the curtains move."

"Bull. I don't have curtains, I have shutters. Tell me the truth."

Sleeth squirmed and rubbed a hand on his neck. "You won't believe me."

"Try me."

"I'm psychic. I 'saw' he was there."

I thought about that for a long minute. Then I laughed.

"You're right. I don't believe you."

Sleeth's eyelids fluttered, and he slumped against my shoulder. My arm gave under the sudden weight, pulling the steering wheel with it. The car jumped for the right curb.

With a shove and a shout, I pushed Sleeth away and corrected our course. He sucked in a breath and sat up, pale as a ghost, looking more sick than he had minutes earlier.

"What the hell's wrong with you?" I asked.

My attention shifted from Sleeth to the knot of police cars, their red lights flashing, parked in front of my house three blocks ahead. I took a quick left and pulled over to think.

I couldn't go home, not while I had Sleeth in the car. And I had a lot to process, some of which I wouldn't want to share with former fellow officers. I pulled out and drove into the night.

45

Kasker moaned as alternating waves of chills and fever swept through him. He'd succumbed to temptation and eaten the tainted soul even though it was forbidden. He'd never done that in thousands of years, and if he survived, he swore he'd never do it again.

In the lighted motel office across the parking lot, the ward arranged rooms for the night. She'd ordered him to wait in the car so he wouldn't be seen—after forcing him to hand over all his remaining cash. She had much to answer for.

Another wave of nausea battered his gut. He opened the car door and barfed on the pavement. His true form swirled, dizzy and barely controlled. The tainted soul that lodged in his craw refused to budge.

What if it was stuck there for eternity? The very thought brought another wave of spewing, even though nothing remained in his stomach. Perhaps if he abandoned his human masquerade... No, the ward already marched toward the car, keys in hand.

"Let's go," she said.

The ward retrieved a shopping bag of toiletries purchased at an all-night pharmacy, crossed the parking lot, and trotted up outdoor stairs to the second floor. Kasker dragged behind her.

A short walk along a railed balcony brought them to unit twenty-one. She unlocked the door and entered.

"Where's my room?" Kasker trailed her in. He needed to be rid of her—her and his restrictive human carcass. His head spun.

"You're looking at it," she said.

"Oh." His gaze swept the cramped room with its two sagging beds, chipped desk, and malodorous smell of cigarettes mixed with astringent cleaner. His nose wrinkled. "Where's your room?"

"You're looking at it," she said.

His eyes narrowed. "Where's my money?"

She swept an arm around the room. "You're looking at it."

"A hundred bucks for this?"

"You gave me fifty-six, and renting a room without ID costs extra." She took the shopping bag into the bathroom.

Kasker slumped on a bed. All he wanted was to go home to Hell. Go back to being a simple hunter. Let someone else more qualified save Heaven and Hell.

Now there's an idea.

He stared at the bathroom door. The ward was the Chosen of Heaven. Why else would she have a guardian angel? And she was a powerful entity of the universe. The Oracle said as much. Surely with Heaven behind her and no opposition from Hell, she could bring Holmes to task—alone—couldn't she?

What would his master say to such a suggestion? Would he be allowed to tell her who Holmes really was? Who *he* really was? She didn't believe his lie about being psychic.

The ward returned from the bathroom, checked outside the window, and closed the blinds. She fastened the chain on the door. For extra measure, she braced the desk chair under the knob.

He flopped back and closed his eyes. So much for sneaking back to the car long enough to dump his disguise. Perhaps her cop training made her paranoid about break-ins. He'd wait until she fell asleep and then do whatever it took to expel the tainted soul.

The ward's footsteps paced the carpet. He cracked an eye open to watch. Her back-and-forth motion made him seasick. He closed his eye.

"Damn it, Sleeth! How can you just lay there?"

He opened his eye again. "Food poisoning."

"Sorry, I didn't realize..."

She returned to pacing.

A moment later she said, "No one knew we were working together except for the three people we interviewed today."

"So?"

"No one knew you'd be at my house. It means the trap was supposed to kill me, not you."

Kasker opened both eyes. "Well huzza-huzza. Welcome to the club."

She glared at him. "And maybe the trap that killed Dave

wasn't meant for you, either."

He thought about that for a moment. It made his head hurt.

The ward wouldn't let it go. "Maybe someone Dave arrested in the past went after him. Maybe I saw something in the warehouse I wasn't supposed to."

"Maybe you're nuts," Kasker said.

The ward stopped at the foot of his bed and glared at him.

"You weren't the one framed for Decker and Haskell," he said. "You weren't the one lured to the warehouse by those two goons. If anyone wants to kill you, it's because you're forever sticking your nose in where it doesn't belong."

Her glare turned to ice. She paced.

"You're sure the shooter was Herman Marks? Did you get a good look at him?"

Kasker moaned. "Absolutely sure."

"We should follow up on him in the morning. What do you know about him?"

"Nothing." Kasker rolled to his side and put a pillow over his head.

The ward slapped his foot. "Pay attention. Would Calderon know him?"

Kasker thought again about telling her everything. But what if she didn't believe him? She could wish him out of existence. That would be an even worse fate than swallowing a tainted soul.

Let Seve tell her. If she didn't believe, she could wish the demon away instead of Kasker. He congratulated himself for the idea.

"You can ask Calderon yourself in the morning," he said. "I'll take you to him. Now can we get some sleep?"

The ward returned to the bathroom, where a lot of splashing and gargling occurred. She came into the bedroom, took the other bed, and turned out the lights.

It didn't help. Despite the closed blinds, the lights from the parking lot made the room as bright as if a full moon shined from the ceiling. Kasker waited for the sounds of rhythmic breathing that signified sleep. All he heard was the ward tossing and turning.

Out of patience, Kasker slunk from the bed to the bathroom, locked the door, and collapsed on the floor, what there was of it. The place was designed for dwarfs.

He released the flesh and squeezed his true form into the bathtub, a fixture that wasn't nearly large enough. Tail jammed against one end, head between front paws, he heaved with all his might. The tainted soul didn't budge. He heaved again. And again.

Hours later, Kasker returned to his body, the soul finally expelled. The mortal remains were chilled and racked with tremors despite the broiling temperatures caused by his true form confined in the tiny space. He tottered to his feet and staggered to bed.

Seemingly only moments later, the ward switched on the lights and announced it was time to go. Kasker groaned and buried his face in the pillow. The ward slapped him on the legs. Twice.

Kasker's empty stomach tied itself in a hard knot. He insisted they stop for food before seeing Seve. The ward reluctantly agreed and drove to an IHOP nearby while the sun slowly crested the horizon.

Kasker strode to the restaurant door, the smell of food tantalizingly close. The ward stopped at the newspaper box.

"There's been another one." She lifted a paper from the box.

Kasker hurried back and snatched the paper from her hands. He scanned the story.

"Goats! Eight blocks from here."

The ward grabbed the paper back. "We should have patrolled the ley line intersections last night. We might have Holmes by now."

"Let's go." He turned for the car.

"Why? The police will have the scene cordoned off, and if they see you there, they'll detain you."

"Psychic, remember?"

The ward rolled her eyes. "Yeah, right. How could I forget?"

Dizziness touched Kasker. He braced his feet. "Just get me as close as you can."

She glanced at the restaurant with longing, sighed, and dug her keys from her pocket.

They drove the eight blocks to Lovejoy's Roller Rink. As the ward had suggested, yellow tape ringed the building, a police cruiser occupied the front lot, and uniformed pigs guarded the doors. Spectators and reporters gathered in clots outside the tape.

"Circle around back again." He extended his senses as best he could.

The faintest tickle of soul essence wafted to him. He sucked it in, but it wasn't enough to identify. He either needed to get much closer, which wasn't possible, or he needed to shed his corporeal cloak momentarily. How could he get rid of the ward?

"Park there." Kasker pointed to the parking lot of Wong's Chinese restaurant.

He pushed temptation at her. "Don't you want to go mingle

with the reporters? Ask them what they've heard?"

The ward rubbed her temple and squinted into the morning sunlight. "Not especially. It's the police who will have the details."

Kasker resisted the urge to snap at her. "Perhaps one of the reporters has an anonymous source inside the department."

"Like they'd tell me if they did. Why don't you go talk to them?"

He looked over the group. "The pigs might recognize me. Besides, most of the reporters are men. Being female, you'll have a better chance. Use your charms."

The ward's face turned bright red. She gave him a cold stare but got out of the car. He smirked. She slammed the door.

When she was twenty feet from the car, he leaned the seat back and loosed the flesh just a little.

The world of souls jumped into sharp relief. Bright torches of light mingled at the tape. A few more stood near the outer walls of the skating rink.

In the loading area behind the back door, one faint and fading soul hovered. Kasker strained to reach it while maintaining contact with his camouflage. Inch by inch, his true self emerged.

At last, a wisp of soul trailed to his nose. *Erick Richards.*

Kasker retreated to his human costume and grinned. A quiver of anticipation raced over his skin. Come nightfall, he would find the body of Erick Richards and devour the damned soul that now occupied it.

46

"Bastard," she said. The woman beside me glared at a middle-aged man farther along the fluttering yellow tape while he directed a disinterested photographer where to point a camera. "Thieving bastard."

"What happened?" I asked.

"Reynolds stole my story, that's what."

She looked about my age. Her fine blonde hair was cut short in the style that Twiggy made famous. Her eyes were ringed with black eyeliner, and thick mascara clumped on her lashes. Royal blue eyeshadow clashed with her green eyes. She wore a striking red sleeveless shift dress that ended at mid-thigh. The square neckline set off her scrawny neck and protruding collarbone.

She turned her attention from the man to me, and her thin eyebrows pulled down. "Don't I know you?"

"Who's Reynolds?" I countered, although I'd seen his byline on a hundred crime stories published in the Solaris newspaper.

"He's the jerk my editor assigned as soon as he realized this was another Slasher case, even though I was the one who spent the night cozied up to the police scanner. Can't have a junior reporter on the city's hottest story, especially when the victim is one of our own."

"You knew the victim personally?" I couldn't believe my luck. But if she recognized me, the game would be up.

"Matthew Shertleff, former Arts and Entertainment writer for the Solaris Daily News. Of course, he quit after he became an infamous novelist last year." She squinted at me and tilted her head. "You sure look familiar."

"You must be devastated after losing a close colleague," I said.

"Did you still keep in touch?"

"Ha! After his smutty novel sold a million copies practically overnight, he turned into a hermit. Wouldn't answer his phone or his door. Had his groceries delivered." She shook her head. "He'd spent years trying to hock his literary masterpiece, but he couldn't sell it to save his soul. So he writes trash, and he's an instant sensation."

Recognition lit her eyes. "Hey, aren't you that officer that saved Mayor Newell's son? The one whose partner died?"

I glanced down at my watch. "Wow, look at the time. Gotta go."

I strode away from the tape. The reporter's flats slapped the asphalt behind me.

"Wait a minute! I want to interview you!"

I bolted. The sound of her footsteps dwindled by the time I hopped in the car. Breathless, I started the Corvair and peeled away from the curb.

Sleeth barely noticed my haste. He hummed under his breath and drummed his fingers against his thighs in time to a tune I didn't recognize. Any moment, I expected him to cut loose with an air guitar performance.

Back at the restaurant, Sleeth made an energetic recovery from his food poisoning and gorged on sausage and eggs. I felt tired and grumpy and stuck with tea and toast. He showed no interest in the details I'd learned about Shertleff.

I'd spent most of the night unable to sleep, listening to him moaning and cacking in the bathroom. My eyes were gritty, my head ached. Paying for Sleeth's breakfast didn't help my mood.

Worst of all, I'd soon have to reveal to the hippie that Calderon's place was under surveillance.

After breakfast, I drove to the Mission. Despite its name, there was nothing Spanish about its architecture. It occupied a converted warehouse. One end housed a chapel, the large center section provided space for dining tables where the homeless ate an evening meal, and the other end contained a kitchen and storage rooms.

"Wait here," I said.

I slipped from the car before Sleeth could ask any questions and approached the rear kitchen doors.

The place hummed already. Under Mrs. Hemstreet's supervision, a small army of volunteers prepared food for the evening meal. I ducked unseen into the storage room. It was jammed with canned goods, donated clothing, blankets, and props for the morality and seasonal holiday plays the Mission provided as entertainment.

I scrounged for the items we'd need to sneak into the Luna Azul unrecognized. I piled my loot in an old wheelchair, scurried through the kitchen with my head down, and rolled the chair down the sidewalk to my car.

Sleeth turned a puzzled look on me. He didn't get out to help while I wrestled the chair into the trunk. We headed back to the hotel.

"What's all that junk for?" he asked.

"So we won't be recognized when we go to Calderon's."

A look came over him. It must have been the first time he considered how I knew he worked with Calderon.

"How long have the pigs been watching?"

Heat inched up my face. "I'm just—was—a lowly beat cop. I don't know anything."

The hippie snorted. He wiggled in the seat and went back to humming.

Back at the hotel, I handed him a makeup case and a stack of clothes. His nose wrinkled at their musty smell.

"What am I supposed to do with these?"

"Pretend it's Halloween and you're going dressed as a Mexican peasant. There's coloring for your hair in the case.

He set the garments on the bed and pulled off his tank top. When he reached for the button on his jeans, I fled to the bathroom with my costume.

I stripped to my underwear and started with the padding usually worn under the Santa suit. Over that, I added a flowing orange and red skirt that reached my ankles, and an oversized white blouse. I covered my head with a red scarf and finished the look with black-framed men's glasses.

I cracked the door open and hoped Sleeth was decent. He sat at the desk using the mirror on the wall. He'd changed into the brown work pants and red checkered shirt I'd brought. He'd streaked the dye through his loose hair so skillfully that I could have sworn it was naturally black threaded with gray strands. He pasted a stringy, drooping mustache on his upper lip and turned to face me.

"Whoa, Chiquita, looks like you need to ease back on the tortillas." His fake Mexican accent sounded like something from a cartoon.

We parked three blocks from the Luna Azul. By the time we reached the restaurant, sweat trickled down my ribs under the padding. I hoped I wouldn't drop from heat stroke before we left.

I dragged the wheelchair from the trunk while Sleeth watched but didn't offer to help.

"Get in," I said.

His brows rose. "Why me?"

"It's part of your ensemble." When his face turned belligerent, I sighed. "They know you, your build, your height, your swagger. In the chair, they won't see any of that."

Sleeth grudgingly sat in the chair. He settled a sweat-stained straw cowboy hat low over his eyes, caved in his manly chest, and slumped his shoulders. He curled one hand in his lap as if it were useless.

Too bad he'd gone to the dark side. If he'd kept his nose clean, he might have had a stellar acting career.

We bumped and rattled our way to the restaurant. I was chugging like a freight train and sweating like an ox by the time we arrived.

One of Calderon's men stood outside. He barely glanced at us and held the door open while I pushed the chair in. Sleeth chuckled, and the man gave us a second look.

"To the kitchen, Chiquita." The hippie gestured to the door at the back.

"Call me Chiquita again and I might accidentally push your chair in front of a bus," I muttered over his head.

Threading around the nearly empty tables was murder. We'd gotten within fifteen feet of our destination when the mobster appeared in the doorway, one hulking goon flanking him, and another approaching us from a nearby booth. I drew in a sharp breath.

Calderon's flat eyes took in the hippie first. The disguise didn't fool him for a moment. Then he regarded me.

A chill came over me despite my stifling outfit. The dining area seemed suddenly darker, as though Calderon sucked away the light and good cheer. Behind us, the chatter of patrons and the clank of cutlery died.

"My Chiquita has questions," Sleeth said, amusement in his voice.

The damn hippie thought this was funny? I expected us both to be wearing concrete overshoes and swimming with the fishes before noon. I should have let him come alone.

Calderon stared at Sleeth a good thirty seconds. He gave a flick of his hand, and the goons parted like the Red Sea. The mobster spun and walked into the kitchen. Sleeth rolled the chair forward. I scrambled to keep up.

When we reached Calderon's office, Sleeth abandoned the

chair and walked inside, leaving me to move the chair to clear the doorway. The mobster stood behind his desk, his face hard. We stood opposite.

"The pigs have eyes on you," Sleeth said.

Calderon's gaze flicked to me before returning to the hippie. "Si, of course. Who is this señorita?"

"*Citizen* Demasi," Sleeth said. "Formerly *Officer* Demasi, the... fuzz who found me at the bookstore."

For a split second, Calderon's eyes widened. New caution slowed his speech. "Where is her partner?"

"Perished." Sleeth let the word hang in the air.

The mobster's lips parted. He dropped into his chair. Like the hippie, he glanced up and cocked his head, listening.

"He stumbled into a trap meant for me." Sleeth splayed his hand on his chest as though pleading for sympathy.

Calderon's shock quickly turned to anger. "You brought her here?"

"Alan Mong is dead," I said. "And so is Matthew Shertleff. I'm tired of following Holmes' bread-crumb trail of bodies. I want to get in front of him. You did business with Decker, and I'm willing to bet you had a relationship with Haskell and Shertleff. Tell me about your other associates."

Calderon's anger surged to barely controlled rage. He turned it on Sleeth. "What have you said to her?"

Fearless, the hippie stared down the mobster. "Nothing. But little time remains to stop Holmes. If the stakes are as high as you believe, maybe you should explain..."

"Risk the master's wrath if you will," Calderon said, "but *I* want no part of it. What you suggest is forbidden."

"She has power," Sleeth countered. "The Oracle says so. And she's Chosen. How can there be objections?"

Their conversation had shifted into the Twilight Zone. When had Solaris become an asylum for all California's lunatics?

"The victims never fought back," I said. "Decker at least made preparations to either pay off Holmes or to run away. That means he had contact with Holmes before his death. If we can find some-one who's heard from Holmes—and is still alive—we can use the information to track Holmes to his hideout. I need to understand why and how Holmes targets his victims and know who he might go after next. I need a list of all your business associates."

"*All?*" Astonishment widened the mobster's eyes.

Sleeth sighed. "Some must be more... *interesting* than others. Those are the names we need."

Calderon tossed the hippie a black look and bared his teeth.

"The master would not be happy if he learned that you imped-ed the hunt for Holmes," Sleeth said in a pious tone.

The mobster's jaw tightened. Sleeth looked smug. The mobster rubbed his fingers on the edge of the desk, his eyes focused on a closed ledger.

"The killings aren't about business," Calderon said at last. "I belong to a secret organization. Its members sign contracts swear-ing to silence. Holmes lost faith and left. Now he commits this butchery because he believes it is the only way to loose the others from their vows."

From the corner of my eye, I caught a flicker of surprise from Sleeth. This wasn't what he expected. The question was, did he know the real truth and this was a lie? Or was what Sleeth thought the lie, and Calderon's revelation the truth? It all made my head hurt.

"I need a list of the other members," I said.

The mobster pulled a pad from the desk drawer and scrawled the list. He handed it to Sleeth, who frowned at it, shook his head, and tucked it in his pocket.

"Sabueso, you will accompany her during questioning." Calde-ron glared at the hippie. "You will protect our interests—or the master will hear."

Sleeth bristled. "Don't flip your lid, man."

"What do you know about Herman Marks?" I asked.

Calderon leaned back in his chair, his face shuttered. "Why do you ask?"

"He tried to kill the— He tried to kill Citizen Demasi last night," Sleeth said. "But he screwed up and killed himself in-stead."

The mobster's eyebrows twitched, and he glanced at the ceil-ing. Sleeth did the same. "He's untrustworthy, an addict. And he's a stooge for the police."

Calderon's revelations didn't seem helpful, but I wasn't going to press. I counted myself lucky to still be alive.

"I need more pesos, compadre." Sleeth held out a hand.

The mobster clamped his jaw.

"Living on the run's expensive, man." Sleeth shot me a look.

Calderon's lip curled. He reached in a desk drawer, pulled out a bundle of cash, and tossed it on the desk.

"Go."

Sleeth grabbed the cash, walked to the office door, and dropped into the wheelchair. "Let's go, Chiquita."

I grumbled a curse under my breath and pushed the hippie through the kitchen. Calderon's shoes clicked on the floor behind me. All the hairs stood up on the back of my neck.

"Be careful, sabueso," the mobster said when he stopped at the kitchen door. "You play a dangerous game."

Sleeth sniggered and waved a dismissive hand.

47

Back in the hotel room, Kasker nibbled a fingernail and fought to keep his true skin contained. Anticipation coursed through him. Tonight, he would devour Matthew Shertleff's damned soul. Hiding in Erick Richards' body wouldn't save Shertleff from his fate.

Had Shertleff remained in his own body, who knew how long a life he might have enjoyed before his final demise? Now that he'd separated his soul from his mortal remains, Shertleff would make an express trip to Hell. Kasker ran his tongue over his lips, sucking back the drool forming in his mouth before it dribbled down his chin.

"Isn't 'sabueso' Spanish for hound?" the ward asked when she emerged from the bathroom. "Why does Calderon call you that?"

"Because I'm a dog with the chicks." He cackled and tossed her a sly look.

The ward scowled. "Give me the list."

Kasker opened the paper Calderon had given them and squinted at the spidery writing. Eight names straggled down the page, each with an address and a note describing their occupation.

"First on the list is Debbie Peck. She's hot. Miss Southern California, 1966." At the ward's deepening displeasure, he added, "Just sayin'."

The ward snatched the list from his hands. She scanned it, and her frown deepened.

"William Decker, businessman; Robert Haskell, pro bowler; and Matthew Shertleff, writer, all dead. That still leaves five people to interview."

"Four," Kasker corrected.

"Because eight minus three equals four?"

Goats! How would he explain that Lester Renquist—although not a Slasher victim—was already deceased? The sweet taste of the crooked lawyer's soul sliding down his gullet brought a momentary smile to his lips.

"Whatever. Math's not my thing." He walked to the door while he searched frantically for a lie to explain his knowledge of Renquist's untimely death. "Let's bug out."

The ward trailed behind, the paper rustling in her hands. "Merkel isn't on here. If Holmes is sticking to members of Calderon's cult, his name should be listed."

Merkel was on a list, it just wasn't the mobster's. Holmes didn't choose his sacrificial receptacles randomly, Kasker realized. Holmes expected the damned souls he'd shifted to new bodies to be beholden to him, and he'd want them in positions of power where they could serve his interests, cover his crimes.

Merkel, a rich man with influence in business and politics was exactly the kind of victim Holmes would target. Like Merkel, Erick Richards—the recipient of Matthew Shertleff's soul and a respected judge—fit Holmes' victim profile perfectly. Who else might Holmes target? The city offered too many choices.

The ward drove to a working-class neighborhood of apartments and scanned property numbers for their destination.

"What's she do now?"

"Who?" he asked, pulled from his thoughts of his coming rendezvous with Shertleff.

The ward tossed him a glare. "Deborah Peck, the beauty contestant at the top of the list."

Kasker shrugged. Debbie Peck's day would come, and he would devour her soul, but Matthew Shertleff was ready now. He wanted to ditch the ward, race to Shertleff's location, and suck down the sweet taste of sin.

Unfortunately, Erick Richards/Matthew Shertleff's new incarnation would be at the court house this time of day, surrounded by pigs. Kasker wouldn't get his flesh within a mile of the damned soul without being arrested.

The ward turned into a parking lot and squeezed the car into a visitor space. They walked past an office and into a courtyard dominated by a large swimming pool. The chlorine stung Kasker's nose.

A hot babe sunning in a skimpy pink bikini caught his eye. A full salute rose in his jeans. The meat puppet had been without a woman for two days. *Two days.* It seemed an eternity.

The ward led the way up a flight of stairs and along a balcony that overlooked the pool. No souls blazed in most of the units, not surprising for a Wednesday noon. If they didn't find Peck in her apartment, he would convince the ward to go for lunch while he got it on with the chick in the bikini.

They stopped in front of a door, and the ward knocked. Kasker shifted from foot to foot, eager to answer the call of Shertleff's damnation. He could use the Mexican peasant disguise to get into the courthouse undetected. All thought of the woman by the pool fled.

The door opened. A shapely blonde dressed in a sleeveless t-shirt and shorts stared out at them. The alluring scent of damnation drifted through the warm air to Kasker drawing his attention from Shertleff. Her eyes flicked from the ward to him. He gave her a wanton smile.

"Officer Demasi, Solaris PD. Are you Deborah Peck?" the ward asked.

A little crease formed between Peck's eyes, ruining the near-perfection of her face. "I'm not interested in contributing to the Police Department Benevolent fund."

Kasker caught a slight rise of the ward's eyebrows and a shift in her stance. He dragged his attention from Peck's breasts pushing on the soft fabric of her shirt to consider the ward's reaction.

"This is official business. Can we come in?" the ward asked.

Peck hesitated. Kasker barged past.

The main room looked more like an illegal sewing factory than a living space. It contained no comfortable furniture for entertaining. Bolts of cloth were stacked against the walls. Hand-drawn pictures of blouses, skirts, dresses, and swimsuits hung above them.

A large table covered by a layer of silky fabric, paper patterns, and straight pins took up the center of the room. A portfolio containing a pile of drawings sat open at the far end of the table. An old-fashioned Singer sewing machine stood in front of the window. A dress-maker's mannequin squeezed in next to it.

"Calderon sent us," Kasker said. "Where's Holmes?"

Peck's shoulders lifted, her face stiffened, and one finger pointed to the door. "Get out!"

Kasker thrust out his chest and took a threatening step toward Peck. The woman clenched her jaw. Her pointing finger didn't waver.

The ward shot him a fierce look, stepped between them, and faced Peck.

"My apologies," the ward said. "Ignore him."

Peck's hand dropped, but her anger didn't. "Anyone who works for Calderon is lower than a rat. Lower than a worm."

"We don't work for Calderon," the ward said, voice low and calm. "And I couldn't agree more. Calderon is the scum of the earth. He ought to be in jail."

Kasker chuffed a breath and crossed his arms over his chest. The ward had been more than willing to consort with the demon when he had something she wanted, and from her scent, she'd been plenty afraid, too.

The ward took Peck's elbow, turned her ninety degrees, and gestured to the walls. "These are amazing. Are they your designs?"

Peck's gaze flickered to the pictures and back to the ward. "Yeah, they're mine."

"What did Calderon promise you? That he'd get you a job at a fashion house? Is that why you joined his cult?"

Surprise blossomed on Peck's face. It morphed to anger. "He promised I'd win the Miss Southern California title. I thought that the fame and prize money would be enough so I could start my own fashion house."

Peck's hands balled into fists. "But I didn't have enough cash to do it alone, and banks won't loan money to young single women who want to start a business."

"Tell me about it. So you're selling privately?" the ward asked.

"At consignment shops. If I can get a rich patron to back me…" A flash of hope crossed her face but drained away. "Calderon cheated me."

"You got what you bargained for," Kasker said. Stupid, gullible humans. Always wanting short-cuts to a happy-ever-after. The demon hadn't given her anything she couldn't have gotten by herself.

The ward shot him another withering look.

"We think you might be in danger," the ward said.

Peck's brow wrinkled, and alarm shone in her eyes. "From Calderon?"

"From the Slasher. He appears to be targeting people who signed contracts with Calderon."

The woman relaxed. "Thanks for the warning. I'll be careful."

Peck walked a few steps toward the door. "Now I have work to do."

"Has the Slasher contacted you?" The ward drifted in Peck's wake. "He may have used the name Holmes, or he may have used an alias."

"How stupid would a killer be to contact his victims?" the

woman said.

"We think he develops a trust relationship first so he can lure them to their deaths. Have you been approached by someone who's taken a sudden interest in your designs?"

Peck opened the apartment door. "Sorry, Officer. I'll be sure to let you know if anyone does."

Kasker followed the ward out. The door thunked closed behind him.

Goats! What a waste of time. All they needed to do was arrive at each murder scene early enough for him to identify the victims to which the damned souls transferred. If Kasker devoured them after the transfer, then Holmes would never get the five the Oracle claimed Holmes needed for whatever ritual he planned.

The ward marched away along the balcony. He strode after her and ground his teeth.

The scent of Peck's damned soul had tormented Kasker. His peasant disguise was at the motel. He could claim a return of his food poisoning, go back to their room, don the costume, and head to the courthouse while the ward continued her useless interviews without him.

Once inside the building, he could hide in the men's room and wait for the judge to be alone in his chambers. Shertleff's demise would take only moments. Saliva broke in Kasker's mouth.

"She's lying," the ward said as they neared the car. "She's getting ready to run."

Surprise stopped Kasker in his tracks. *Could* the ward read minds?

"She'd moved most of her drawings to her portfolio. She's going soon."

Kasker sneered at her assumption. "How do you know they weren't already in the portfolio?"

"Because there were thumbtack holes in the walls where they'd previously been hung."

"Maybe she ran out of space."

"Plenty of space with no holes," the ward said. She opened the car door and looked across the roof at him. "She also had a suitcase open on the bed."

48

Sleeth no longer hummed under his breath. Instead, his leg jiggled non-stop, and his brow creased in a frown. The tapping of his foot drove me crazy.

He'd tried to convince me he wasn't feeling well and needed a nap at the hotel. I'd told him I'd be happy to drop him there, but I wasn't coming back for him—ever. He'd made a remarkable recovery. I hadn't figured out why he wanted to ditch me.

I also couldn't figure out why Merkel wasn't on Calderon's list. Sleeth knew too much about the millionaire businessman for him not to be involved in this mess somehow. I put Merkel aside to focus on Calderon's cult list.

All the murders occurred after dark. I decided to keep on with the interviews and loop back to stake out Deborah Peck in the evening. To that end, we pulled in down the block from the Solaris Youth Shelter. Late afternoon sun blinded us as we trooped to our destination. Heat rolled off the pavement in waves.

The shelter occupied an old store-front in a flea-bitten neighborhood just east of downtown proper. Runaway and abused teens could shelter there, get a hot meal, and talk with adult volunteers who could help them sort out their messy lives.

I pulled the door open and stepped into the dim coolness. Three scruffy youths played pool at a threadbare table to the left of the door. In a lounge space to the right, an attractive dark-skinned girl and a Latino boy watched an old movie on a big, square black-and-white console TV.

"Can I help you?"

A woman in her mid-fifties crossed the room to greet us. Curling salt-and-pepper hair created a soft halo around her broad face that was at odds with her stick-thin figure. She was clad in a dark brown skirt that reached below her knees and a plain white blouse. She wore sensible black shoes.

"Sister Magda?" My words came out strangled. I'd last seen Sister Magda when I'd graduated St. Charles Catholic School. She'd taught math there.

Her face clouded in concentration before recognition dawned. "Nicola. Nicola Demasi."

She was the last person I expected to belong to a secret cult run by a mobster. She'd been one of the most honest and devout people I'd ever known. I'd never seen her in civvies and stared at her attire.

"It's just Magda Krohn now," she said with a wistful smile. She placed a hand on my arm and lowered her voice. "I'm sorry for your loss. You and Dave were inseparable all through school. How's Cindy holding up?"

Tears pricked my eyes. I blinked and sucked in a breath. "Is there somewhere we can talk?"

She led us through a door at the end of the room, down a claustrophobic hallway past stairs leading up, and into a tiny, cluttered office at the back of the building. She took the ancient wooden swivel chair behind the desk. I squeezed into a visitor chair. Sleeth stood in the doorway looking unhappy, although there was a second chair.

Sister Magda looked expectantly at Sleeth. He crossed his arms. She turned to me.

"Oh, sorry," I said, my face heating. "This is Kasker Sleeth. He's assisting with the Slasher investigation."

Sister Magda arched an eyebrow at me. "He's a police officer?"

Sleeth snorted and rolled his eyes. Sister Magda's lips drew into a hard line. I'd seen that look before and expected her to pull out a ruler to rap Sleeth's knuckles.

"I don't know how I can help you," Sister Magda said to me. "I don't know anything about the horrible murders that have afflicted the city."

"We believe the Slasher targets individuals who..." I clasped my hands in my lap and screwed up my courage, "have signed secret agreements with the mobster, Seve Calderon. Your name is on the list."

Sister Magda's shoulders drooped, and her gaze shifted to the desk. "Yes, I sold my soul to Calderon."

"Why?" I asked. "No one had more faith than you."

She straightened her spine and looked me in the eye. "Giving up my habit doesn't mean I lost my faith. I tried to convince the diocese that we needed a youth shelter. They said having a safe place to go would only encourage more children to run away. I couldn't change their minds.

"So a year ago, I did a deal with the devil. Calderon got what he wanted. I got a free twenty-year lease on this building."

Sleeth sneered at the surroundings. "You got ripped off."

Sister Magda gave him a cold stare. "What's done is done."

"But you'd back out of the contract if you could," Sleeth said.

"As God is my witness, a bargain is a bargain."

Sleeth shifted uneasily and glanced toward the ceiling. Sister Magda had scored.

"We believe the Slasher targets people who have regrets and want to be released from their promises," I said. "Has anyone contacted you?"

Sister Magda's hand went to her throat. "There was a letter a month or so ago. Don't ask who sent it. I don't know. There wasn't any signature or return address. The sender claimed I could get out of my contract with no negative consequences. If I was interested, I was to tape a blank white sheet of paper in the lower left corner of the front window. They'd get back to me."

"But they didn't," said Sleeth. "Bet that broke your heart."

Color suffused Sister Magda's cheeks. Her lips moved like she counted soundlessly.

"Sit down," I said, turning on the hippie, "and keep your mouth shut."

Sleeth's eyes narrowed, but he obeyed my command. Sister Magda gave me a stern look.

"Sorry, Sister," I said automatically and ducked my head. "Did they try contacting you a second time?"

"No, I never heard from them again."

"You have no idea who it might have been?"

She shook her head. "I wish I could be more help."

49

The ward tossed Kasker a disapproving glance... *another* disapproving glance. The sun had dropped below the horizon, pole lights pushed back the shadows in the parking lot, and the sounds of splashing and laughing carried from the pool in Peck's apartment complex.

On the pretext of a trip to the john, he'd snuck out of the IHOP during dinner and called for a taxi to pick him up here at ten. He had Erick Richards' address. He could be there and back in under an hour. If Peck bolted while he was gone, the ward would follow. He'd catch up later.

Kasker shifted in his seat and drummed his fingers on the arm rest. The scent of Shertleff's damnation called to him like the smell of baking bread drew a starving soul. But the taxi he'd ordered hadn't arrived yet.

The ward had parked close to the main entrance of the complex. Kasker had to twist his head to see the street where the taxi would arrive. When he looked for the fifth time in five minutes, the ward turned to look as well.

"What's the problem, Sleeth?" she asked.

A surge of panic washed through Kasker. Then he had the answer to his problems ditching the ward.

"We're sitting ducks. One of us should watch for Peck while the other watches our backs."

On the street, a yellow cab pulled to the curb and tooted its horn. A thrill coursed through Kasker's blood. He squashed the urge to erupt in his true skin.

"Bad idea," the ward said. "We might need to move in a hurry. We stay together."

The cab honked again. If he didn't respond quickly, it would pull away without him.

Kasker threw open his door. "I gotta piss. Back in a sec."

"Where do you think—" The slamming door cut off the ward's question.

Kasker paced to the landscaping at the edge of the complex and pushed through a hedge to the next property, which consisted of another ugly block of apartments. Out of the ward's sight, he ran for the street.

The cab was already leaving. Kasker charged into the street, his arm waving. The driver stopped before hitting him, but it was a near thing.

He gave the cabbie Richards' address and vaulted into the back seat. A glance out the back window showed a vacant street. He smirked and promised a ten-dollar tip if the cabbie hurried.

Kasker's tongue caught a string of drool at the corner of his mouth. His true skin, hot and black, swirled beneath his covering of humanity. He tapped a foot on the floorboards.

The Who's *I Can See For Miles* whispered from the driver's radio.

Kasker scooted forward. "Turn it up."

The driver, who looked to be a college student picking up party money, cranked the volume.

Kasker thumped his fists against the seat in time to the music. He barely contained the urge to howl. The driver's reflection in the rearview mirror showed a big grin, his head bobbing along. Kasker considered paying the promised ten, then dismissed the idea.

They reached the judge's neighborhood in record time. It was one social class closer to downtown than Merkel's place. He'd be back to Peck's apartment sooner than he thought. Kasker ordered the driver onto a side street and told him to wait.

The kid wasn't born yesterday. He demanded payment of the fare first.

Kasker shelled out the fare, but not the extra ten. He'd stiff the kid after they returned to Peck's apartment.

He didn't need to read the house numbers to find Richards' place; Shertleff's damned soul blazed like a spotlight on the second floor of a faux-Tudor house in the middle of the block. He jogged closer.

The house to the right still had lights on, and like Richards' house, little in the way of cover. The house to the left stood empty, a for-sale sign staked in the shriveled front lawn.

The branches of an old, withered willow cast deep shadows over the yard. Kasker glanced around to be sure no one watched before he hurried under it. He dropped to the ground, mindless of the cat pee stench that permeated the area.

Once safely hidden behind the tree, Kasker stepped free of his flesh and licked his heavy chops. He bounded over a low hedge into the back yard of the deserted house and over the wooden fence to Richards' yard.

A cat screeched and ran. Kasker ignored it. Down the block, first one, and then a chorus of canine voices rose in alarm. He threw back his head and bayed.

The neighboring dogs fell silent. A light switched on upstairs. Kasker bayed again and charged for the house.

50

Sleeth was up to something. I just couldn't figure out what. As I'd followed the taxi, I thought he might be headed to Emmett Merkel's place. But the taxi pulled over while we were still half a mile away from the millionaire's mansion.

I wondered if Calderon had passed him a note in the bundle of cash. Or maybe Sleeth had called the mobster when he slipped away from the table at dinner. Did he expect to find Holmes here?

I parked behind the cab. The driver glanced back at me. I walked to his door.

"Hey," I said, nodding to the driver. "Your fare changed his mind. He won't need you any longer."

The driver, a white male a year or two younger than me, drew his face into a disappointed pout.

"He promised me a sawbuck if I waited."

I sighed and dug in my pocket. My ready cash was dropping faster than rain in a tropical storm. I'd collect from Sleeth when I found him.

The cabby snatched the bill from my hand and gunned into the night.

I walked back to the corner. Nothing stirred on the street ahead. Where had Sleeth gone? I tread on silent feet toward the next corner.

A cat yowled, dogs barked, and then a frightening howl sent shivers coursing through me. Whatever made that noise, it had to be big—and possibly feral. The neighborhood pack went dead quiet.

The savage lament had come from the darkness on my right. I peered into the gloom as I edged forward, every muscle taut. Nothing moved.

Something lumpy lay under a willow in the front yard of a house advertised for sale. I stepped onto the grass and parted the drooping, desiccated tree branches. A body stretched on the ground behind the trunk.

In the dark, I fumbled my hands over the head and felt Sleeth's ponytail. He didn't stir at my touch. I thought I found a thready pulse in his neck, but I couldn't be sure. I needed more light.

I grabbed Sleeth's wrists and dragged him toward the front of the yard where the streetlight did a poor job of illuminating his inert form. His skin was pale, flaccid, and cool. His chest rose in a shallow breath once every ten seconds. I didn't see any wounds.

Despite the terrible racket I'd heard, the surrounding houses remained dark. In this neighborhood, I doubted anyone would answer the door this late. I wished I hadn't dismissed the cab. The driver could have radioed a request for an ambulance.

The hair on the back of my neck came to attention. In the deepest shadows under the tree, a pair of glowing red eyes watched me. A darker black patch that might have been an enormous dog if they got that big shifted left. For something that size, I'd be little more than a morsel.

I rocketed to my feet and reached for my gun, remembering too late that I was no longer a pistol-packing patrol officer. My breath hitched. I swear I heard a chuffing breath, like someone stifling a laugh.

Twenty feet to my left, something small blurred past. I whipped around and identified a cat high-tailing it across the street. A dog barked in the direction it was headed, and it jigged right thirty degrees but didn't slow. More dogs joined the chorus.

With my heart pounding in my ears, I spun back to the willows. The eyes were gone. At my feet, Sleeth stirred and sat up.

"What's the matter, Officer Demasi? Seeing things?" Sleeth asked, an edge of amusement in his tone.

He got to his feet and brushed grass from his jeans. His attitude and lazy smile made me want to pound him back to the ground.

"What the hell are you doing here? And don't call me that."

"Catching some air, looking for some action," he said.

He stepped closer. Heat rolled off him, and the lazy smile turned into an eye-crinkling grin. He looked me up and down in a way that made me uncomfortable.

"You want to get it on?"

"We're on a stakeout and you run off to get high? If Peck dies tonight, it will be on your head." I stepped around him and marched toward my car.

"No great loss." Sleeth trailed a step behind me. "She's damned whether she goes now or later."

I whirled on him, and his chest bumped me before he stopped. "You are the most disgusting excuse for a human being I've ever met."

Sleeth's brows raised in surprise. "Thanks."

I threw up my hands. "We're done."

I spun around and stormed back to my car. Once inside, I locked the doors. Sleeth sauntered up and waved goodbye, a sly grin curving his lips.

I drove away fast and headed to Peck's apartment, glad to be rid of Sleeth. When I'd cooled down a few minutes later, I thought about what a mistake I'd made. Sleeth might have been in that neighborhood to meet his drug supplier, but I doubted it. Now that I'd cut him loose, I'd never know.

By the time I got back to Peck's complex, the lights were off in her apartment. I risked doing a walk-by. Her door stood ajar. I pushed it gently open and stepped in.

The apartment was dark and still. Faint sounds from her neighbor's TV whispered through the wall. I reached out a hand to find the work table in the center of the living room. Once I'd anchored my position, I felt my way around until I faced the single bedroom.

I cast off from the table and fumbled forward. My hand found the door frame. The door was open. I stopped to listen, every muscle taut. No snoring, no quiet breathing. I flipped on the overhead light.

Except for the absence of the suitcase, the room looked much as it had earlier. The bedroom light illuminated the living room enough to show the portfolio of Deborah Peck's designs missing from the work table. She'd flown while I'd chased Sleeth.

I cursed Sleeth with every four-letter word I knew while I walked back to my car. Inside, I drummed my fingers on the wheel. Our best lead to Dave's killer was blowing in the wind. All the swearing in the world wouldn't fix that.

I flipped open the glove box and pulled out the ley line map. Lt. Mack said there were thirty-three intersections. I didn't think Holmes would reuse a location. That left thirty scattered over the city. I plotted a course to the closest, started the car, and drove out of the lot.

Four hours later, at my twenty-second stop, I found Deborah Peck. Like the others, she was alone, spread-eagled in a rune spiral, and very, very dead.

51

Kasker sprawled in the back of the cab and rubbed his aching feet. After the ward abandoned him, he'd been forced to walk thirty blocks to find a pay phone. Fortunately, the phone was located beside a late-night convenience store that sold beer.

Unfortunately, the driver who responded to his summons wouldn't allow open containers in the back of the vehicle. He also wouldn't accept Kasker's generous bribe to break the rule. Kasker made the driver wait while he downed two bottles. He left the remainder of the six-pack on the sidewalk.

Now the beer sloshed in his belly and fog swirled in his brain. He giggled aloud. The Latino driver eyed him in the rearview mirror.

Kasker congratulated himself on ditching the ward—and for his new, brilliant plan. He wondered why he hadn't thought of it earlier.

All he needed to do was trail behind Holmes devouring the damned souls after they'd moved to their new bodies. As long as he got to the murder scenes before the displaced souls were swallowed by the universe, he'd have no problem identifying the new container worn by the damned.

His mouth watered at the thought of the feast that awaited him. Of course, eventually he'd have to devour Holmes or incur the wrath of his master. Still, he'd enjoy the extra damned souls on a timetable earlier than the one Fate intended.

The cab stopped three blocks from the freight warehouse where the angel perished two nights earlier. Kasker instructed the driver to wait, but the man refused and demanded payment.

Once the cab was gone, Kasker moved into the shadows, sat

against a building, and loosed his grip on his anchor to this realm. He detected no magic nearby, and no souls, either. On silent paws, he trotted away to the end of the block and peered around the corner.

The Mustang remained parked in front of the freight warehouse. No pigs waited in the vicinity. They must have given up their surveillance. Kasker returned to his carcass, strutted to his car, slid into the driver's seat, and tooled away.

All he needed now was a place to lay low for a few hours while he waited for the morning edition of the paper to arrive. He should find a party, smoke some dope, and sate his transportation's yammering appetite for a woman.

His high mellowed into a pleasant afterglow, and he began to rethink his strategy. Perhaps Holmes took the other damned with him to each ritual. If Kasker arrived before they departed, he could identify whose bodies they'd stolen. Then he could pay his respects to each and devour them one by one.

Kasker licked his lips and decided to follow Peck to her rendezvous instead of waiting for the morning papers. He wound through side streets, avoiding the main arterials, until he reached Peck's apartment complex.

He drove past, checking for the ward's car or the flicker of her soul. He detected neither. He made a U-turn and pulled into the crowded lot.

No lights were on in Peck's apartment. No souls waited inside. She must have left for her rendezvous with Holmes. A niggle of worry crawled up his spine. He pushed it aside. Back to Plan A. He'd wait for the morning paper to give him the murder location.

That left plenty of time to party. He hadn't driven far before a fuzzmobile passed him going the other way. His unease rose. The more he drove around, the more likely he was to be spotted by the pigs.

Kasker rolled into the parking lot at the IHOP and swung behind the building where the Mustang would be out of view from the street. He tilted the seat back and snoozed in the car for an indeterminate amount of time.

When he awoke, the sky had lightened. He crawled from behind the wheel, stretched, and sauntered around to the front door. The morning paper showed its headlines behind the glass of the display box. They appeared to be a rehash of the Slasher case.

Kasker jimmied the box and withdrew a paper. He perused it while he headed into the restaurant. He barely noticed the perky waitress who greeted him.

At his table, he pored over the front page. Finding no mention of Peck, he turned to the inside sections while worry gnawed at his guts. The discovery of Peck's body was conspicuously absent.

Goats! Had the incompetent pigs not found the body yet? Or did they discover it too late to make this morning's paper?

Kasker abandoned the restaurant and hurried to the Mustang. He turned on the radio, twisting the dial in search of a news broadcast. Another murder ought to be the talk of the town, but no one reported it.

Now how would he find Peck? Perhaps he'd been too hasty in abandoning the ward. Thinking of her reminded him of her map. If he had the map, he could check each location until he found Peck's body. Would she still be at the hotel room they'd shared?

Each passing minute meant less chance that the displaced soul could be identified. He roared from the parking lot and sped the short distance to the hotel he'd shared with the ward. The sun slipped above the horizon.

As he'd hoped, her car remained in the parking lot. He waited while a man in a suit and tie loaded luggage in the trunk of a Cadillac. When the Caddie pulled away, he crossed the lot to the ward's gutless Corvair.

The doors were unlocked. Kasker popped the passenger door and pawed through the glove box, leaving a messy pile of items on the floorboards. He grabbed the map, slammed the door, and returned to his Mustang.

52

I took a last glance in the mirror. My white cotton blouse still showed the creases from hanging on the rack at Woolworth's. The black skirt I'd found there was a size too big and drooped unevenly just below my knees. I wore my white sneakers without socks. It wasn't suitable attire for a funeral, but it was the best I could do without going home.

I walked into the morning sunshine. It seemed inappropriate weather for so solemn an occasion. My guilt over Dave's death hung like a dark mantle from my shoulders.

I reached my car and slid in before I noticed the contents of my glove box strewn on the floor. The ley line map was missing.

Sleeth.

Burning anger ignited in my chest and spread to my arms until I clutched the steering wheel in a death grip. I wished it was his neck. I blamed him for Deborah Peck's death. And I blamed myself, just as I did about Dave.

I'd elected to skip the mass at St. Charles and attend only the short graveside service at Holy Trinity Cemetery. When I arrived, I parked at the end of a long line of vehicles a quarter mile from the burial site.

A river of dark blue uniforms flowed toward a white canopy erected beside an open grave on a gentle hillside halfway up the rolling lawn. I kept my head down, too ashamed to make eye contact with my fellow officers.

"Nicky!" Tad took my right elbow. "Thank God you're okay. When I heard there was shooting at your house…"

I looked into Tad's worried face, and then around at those nearby, concerned about what they'd think seeing us together. I wasn't the mayor's little darling anymore.

Tad seemed thin and haggard. His bruises had shaded to a nasty yellow-green, and the scrapes were still fleshy pink. Dark semi-circles smudged the skin under his eyes.

"Shooting at my place? I don't know anything about it. I've been away for a few days," I said.

Tad spoke barely above a whisper. "Susie Brown is dead. I'm convinced Sleeth did it."

I lifted a brow. "How can you be sure? Have you asked him?"

Tad glanced around like he expected a bogeyman to jump out any minute. "He's dangerous. Stay away from him. Stay away from the Slasher case."

"Look," I said. "The Slasher killed my partner. I'm going to get him, no matter what it takes. If I can't do it as a cop, then I'll do it on my own."

Tad started to speak, glanced behind us, and stopped. If he'd looked worried before, he looked positively spooked now.

"I just wanted to offer my condolences on the loss of your partner," he said, his voice louder than it needed to be.

With that, he strode ahead, his limp nearly invisible.

A hand touched my arm. "Hey, how you doing Nicky?"

I turned to Maggie Tisdahl and did my best to smile. "I'm okay."

Maggie tugged at the hem of her uniform jacket. The temperature was already climbing, and a sheen of sweat showed through her thick makeup.

"I stopped by your place to check on you, but the neighbors said they hadn't seen you in a couple of days, not since that shoot-out in your neighborhood. I was worried."

"I've been staying with a friend," I said, glad to note that my face didn't heat while I lied.

"You and I should go for coffee when the service ends," Maggie said.

I glanced around at the swelling ranks of officers. "Are you sure you want to be seen with me?"

Maggie gave me a disbelieving look. "I don't care what the others say. I know you. You didn't do anything wrong."

So my workmates thought I'd screwed up and gotten my partner killed. I blinked back tears and focused on the ground for the next hundred feet.

"You hear the news?" a male voice said behind me.

"That the Slasher struck again?" A second voice asked. I thought it might be Benny Rositto, but I didn't turn around to check. I sucked in a breath and held it, sure that the operator must have recognized my voice when I'd made my anonymous call to the station telling them where to find Peck's body.

"Naw, everyone knows that—everyone except the press," the first voice said. "Me and Steve got called out to Judge Richards' house this morning. He keeled over sometime last night."

The first voice had to be Larry Monroe. A quick glance over my shoulder confirmed my suspicions. He and his partner patrolled the lower South Hill—the same area where I'd found Sleeth.

"For real?" Benny said. "I'm supposed to testify before him next week."

"I never saw anything like that before. The judge was laying in bed. His hands were up at his shoulders like he'd been trying to push something away. And his face... He musta had a bad dream or something. It sure wasn't peaceful."

"Foul play?" Benny asked.

"ME says it was a heart attack. How would anyone get into the judge's place? He's got one of those fancy alarm systems, and the housekeeper said it was on when she got there and found him."

Unless someone was psychic and didn't have to enter the building to kill the judge? I didn't like coincidences, and I didn't trust the hippie. No normal person was that cold.

"Listen, honey," Maggie said, "I think I forgot to lock my car. You go ahead, and I'll catch up to you after. Then we'll get that cup of coffee."

I nodded my agreement even though I didn't intend to go anywhere with Maggie. I'd hang out on the fringe of the crowd and slip away before she could find me. I had Calderon's list, and I intended to make sure the three remaining names on it didn't meet the same fate as all the others.

At graveside, Dave's family and Solaris PD VIPs filled a row of chairs under the awning. Everyone else stood in a semi-circle behind them. There must have been a hundred people. I couldn't see the priest for the wall of bodies.

The priest cleared his throat and the crowd of mourners stilled. He began his prayers. The Catholics in the group responded where appropriate. Someone stepped up at my left shoulder.

I glanced sideways. It was Lt. Mack. He noticed my glance and nodded. I clamped my jaw and stared at the ground until the priest finished.

I turned to go, and Lt. Mack fell in beside me.

"We responded to a report of shots fired in your neighborhood night before last."

I trudged across the dry grass toward the paved drive. "Good to know Solaris looks after its citizens."

Stutzman came out of nowhere to flank my right shoulder. Lt. Mack stepped in front of me. I frowned up at him.

He wasn't getting me to admit to anything. I wasn't the one blowing holes in the neighbors' houses, and I had places to go, things to do. I kept my face passive and stared back.

"Sorry, I can't help you. I haven't been home the last couple days."

"Look, Demasi, I have a killer to catch. I don't have time for games. Jonas will drive you to the station."

53

Kasker followed the winding drive up the hill to the county park set amongst the scrub. The park overlooked Solaris to the west. To the east, the foothills rose into national forest lands. It was his thirteenth stop.

Ahead, the narrow paved access road widened to provide gravel parking on each side. The road separated a baseball diamond on his left from a picnic area shaded by spindly pines on his right. Swings at a children's playground just beyond the diamond creaked in the gentle breeze. Beyond the swings, basketball backboards stood at each end of a concrete patch.

Past the play area, the road curved behind thick brush and out of sight. A sign indicated more parking on an upper level. The lower level was empty. No one enjoyed the play area or lounged at a picnic table.

The scent of blood wafted through the open window. Kasker slammed on the brakes and scanned the area more closely. He couldn't detect a displaced soul, but it was mid-morning already. Any hope of finding the victim of Peck's body swap had dwindled away hours ago.

A lump on the basketball court caught his eye. He stiffened, and then he pulled into a parking space.

The lump was too far away to identify, but the wind came from the right direction for it to be the source of the blood scent. A crow fluttered down from a nearby tree, landed a few feet away from the lump, and waddled over to take a tentative peck.

Abandoning the overcoat of mortality this far away would tell him little he didn't already know. He wouldn't venture across the sun-splashed playground in his true form. But if he walked to the thicket where the road curved, he could take his true form and traverse back through the brush to inspect what he was now sure was a body.

Kasker stepped out of the car and swept his eyes over the park. Song birds chirped in the trees. A squirrel rooted around the base of a picnic table. The swing continued its annoying squeak. The wind brought the scent of coyote scat and barbeque ash.

Kasker edged up the pavement, his senses extended to their limits. More crows gathered in the treetops beyond the basketball court. Two flew down to join their flock-mate. Rowdy squabbling ensued between the newcomers and the first bird.

The lump on the basketball court resolved into a body spread-eagled on the gray pebbled concrete. Behind the court, farther up the hill, a flash of reflection cut through the dense brush. Kasker walked faster to the thicket.

As soon as he reached cover, he dropped to the ground and shed the flesh. The world of souls leaped into sharp relief—as did the magical emanations surrounding the body. He growled, low and quiet. The hackles rose along his spine.

Staying in the shadows of the thicket, he moved closer to examine the Slasher's latest victim, caution checking every step. When he was still fifty feet away, he stopped and sniffed.

Something about the tableau was off. The runes seemed sloppy and didn't spiral out to a portal. In fact, there was no portal at all in this setting. There was the usual gutting, but he couldn't detect the soap and clove oil of the ritual washing. The body reeked of booze and piss and disease.

He crept three steps closer and flattened to his belly, his lips curled back. The magic he detected wasn't from the charcoal-drawn runes around the body. It emanated from a second ring disguised in the grass around the concrete slab.

Cloaks and cauldrons! Holmes had set another trap. If Kasker had approached in his disguise, he would have stepped into it without warning. This sacrifice wasn't one of the damned souls but simply a decoy used to lure him here. A chill cooled his skin. He stepped back, growling.

He turned his attention to the upper parking lot, above the play field, where he'd seen the reflection. Two souls waited. He'd been smart to look for cover instead of trotting openly to the corpse displayed on the concrete.

Kasker retraced his steps and then wormed uphill through the thicket until he stood hidden at the edge of the parking lot. The only vehicle was a white van. The name on the side read 'Temple of Enlightenment.' The two men, Warner and Bronski, who'd sent him to the freight warehouse, stood in front of it, watching over the playing fields.

The white man peered through binoculars, sweeping them left and right. "I still don't see him. Why hasn't he gone for the body?"

"Give him a minute," the Negro said. "Maybe he's taking a leak in the bushes."

The white tossed a nervous glance at his partner. "What if the trap doesn't work?"

"Then we'll do it the hard way" The Negro patted a pistol thrust into his belt.

Kasker's lips twitched. Saliva dripped from his mouth. Unlike Holmes' minion who tried to kill the ward, these two had sealed their fates. In time, their souls would be his. His body shook with his desire to burst from cover and devour them.

He slipped back through the thicket, reclaimed his camouflage, and considered his next move. Holmes' latest trap worried him. What if, when he found Holmes, the man stood inside another trap? How would Kasker get close enough to retrieve him?

He needed the ward. She could walk through Holmes' traps unscathed. The thought made him grind his teeth. If she apprehended Holmes, she'd drag him clear of any trap he might set. Then Kasker would pounce. He grinned at the thought.

All he had to do was find the ward and trade her renewed partnership for the name he'd gleaned from the side of the van.

But first, he had to get back to his car.

54

Everyone at the station looked grim and haggard. A few of my fellow officers nodded to me as we walked through the halls. Most seemed too preoccupied to notice.

I thought Stutzman would take me to an interrogation room. To my surprise, he showed me into Lt. Mack's office. I took the lone visitor chair and stared at the bare walls.

Five minutes later, Lt. Mack trudged in, sank into the chair behind the desk, and lit a cigarette. He took a drag, blew toward the ceiling, and squinted at me through the haze.

"What happened at your place?"

"I don't know. I've been staying with a friend."

Mack's tired eyes bored into me. "I'd ask for your friend's name, but it's a cock-n-bull story. Witnesses saw your car."

Mack waited in silence. I'd read a bit about how to conduct interrogations, and I knew he wanted me to fill that silence. The urge squirmed inside me, but I kept my mouth shut.

The lieutenant ran a hand over his hair. "You've been hounding Sleeth. As a consequence, he and Herman Marks took a shot at you. Marks bought it when you chased him into a telephone pole. Don't deny it. A witness identified you at the accident scene. Where's Sleeth?"

At last, something I could answer truthfully. "I don't know, but he's not your guy, and you're wasting time if you're focused on him."

"Susan Brown is dead," Mack said, expression cold.

Neither Sleeth nor Tad had mentioned the circumstances of Brown's death. Considering Judge Richards' unusual demise, I wanted more information about Brown.

"Sorry to hear that. How'd she die?" I asked.

"Single GSW in the back. Her place had been tossed. We found Sleeth's fingerprints."

Cold fingers of doubt tiptoed up my spine. Sleeth might not be the Slasher, but if he wanted information from Brown, how far would he go? He claimed he had an alibi for the time of Brown's death, but he always told lies. And then there was the business with Emmett Merkel's death, of which Sleeth seemed to know too much and wouldn't share.

"Look Demasi, Internal Affairs is on the fence about what to do with you. You cooperate with me, and I'll put in a good word. Sure, they'll still give you a slap on the wrist and assign you to a desk for a few months. But then they'll put you back on patrol. In a couple of years, it'll be like nothing happened.

"Or, I can tell them that you're unwilling to cooperate in the Slasher investigation. That you learned nothing losing your partner, and you're still disobeying orders to stay away from the case." Mack leaned back in his chair and took another drag on his cigarette. "What's it going to be?"

Knuckles rapped on the door. Det. Arndt stuck his head in.

"We have another one, up at Highgate Park."

Another one? My stomach lurched. The Slasher was accelerating his timetable.

Lt. Mack looked like he wanted to throw something. He settled for grinding his cigarette into the ashtray. "I'll be right there."

Arndt closed the door. Mack stood, his face gray.

"We'll finish this conversation when I get back."

Mack hurried out. I sat in the uncomfortable chair, tapping my foot at the passing minutes. Highgate Park was on the outskirts of town. By the time Mack drove there, supervised the scene, and drove back, it would be mid-afternoon.

What should I do? Should I tell the lieutenant everything? He didn't know the half of the 'interfering' I'd done while I was on suspension. Did I want my career back? Regardless of what it did to my career, I decided I'd tell him all I'd learned. The Slasher had to be stopped.

I sat there fidgeting for an hour before the duty sergeant stuck his head in the door.

"Hey, Demasi, you know where Tad Newell is?"

I arched an eyebrow at him.

He had the good grace to blush. "Mayor Newell's on the horn. He says his kid missed some public appearance and a lunch date. He wants me to roll out the National Guard. I can't find Chief

Greene, and Lt. Mack's still out at the latest Slasher scene. I heard you and Tad were an item. I thought you might have some ideas about where we could look."

My breathing stopped. I couldn't move a muscle. Had Bronski and Warner finally succeeded in kidnapping Tad? Why did they want him? He wasn't on Calderon's list.

"No," I said at last. "No idea where to find him."

The desk sergeant frowned and left.

Mack needed the information I had about the Slasher. But if Holmes had Tad, he could be butchering Tad while I waited. I had to stop Holmes, and following up on Calderon's list was the best bet.

I leaped from my chair and bolted for the door. Then I stopped and rushed back to Mack's desk. I found a tablet in a drawer, scribbled a note giving him the names of the remaining members of Calderon's cult, and telling him they would be the Slasher's next victims, probably within the next twenty-four hours. I added the list of ley line intersections and Holmes' intended kill sites.

I snuck out the back of the station and took a cab to the cemetery to pick up my car. I'd visited most of the ley line intersections looking for Peck. I'd start again and hope I found the right location before Holmes killed Tad.

55

Kasker waited in the shade of a tree and watched the cemetery caretakers fill the grave of the angel's rotting, abandoned flesh. The ward's car stood in the blazing sun a hundred yards down the lane.

Where had she gone? Why was her car still here? He'd swung by their hotel room first, figuring that the funeral would be long over. When he hadn't found her there, he'd tried this longshot.

The hot afternoon dragged on. The meatbag wanted a cold beer and a joint, or at least a burger. His stomach rumbled its complaint.

He'd thought about stopping for food, but it had taken an hour to lure Holmes' stupid goons far enough into the woods that he could make a getaway without being shot. If he'd missed the ward here, goats only knew how he'd find her again.

At the cemetery entrance, a cab pulled in. Kasker straightened. The ward climbed from the back seat, paid the driver, and jogged up the drive despite the insufferable temperatures.

Kasker sauntered to her car. When she saw him, she stopped. Her face tightened, her fists bunched at her sides. She marched forward.

"Out of my way, Sleeth." She stretched a hand toward the driver's door.

Kasker leaned his butt against the door. "Where've you been?"

She planted fists on her hips. "I don't have time for your crap. And give me back the map you stole."

Kasker narrowed his eyes. She was more hostile than he'd anticipated. Being of the angels, she should respond contritely to a reminder of her promises. He lifted his chin and kept the smirk off his face.

"We made a deal. We'd work together to get Holmes. You broke it."

"You cut out, and Peck died. Deal's over. Now get out of my way."

He scowled. Her behavior wasn't very Heavenly. "You didn't have to follow me."

Her face stiffened. "Last chance. Move."

Kasker crossed his arms and opened his mouth to argue. Her knuckles planted in his solar plexus. Air rushed from his lungs. He tipped forward, surprised by a wave of pain.

Her hip jammed into his groin, her hands laced behind his neck, and he was airborne over her shoulder. He smacked down, his spine connecting with the asphalt. More pain shot through his bones. He yipped.

The ward's key rasped in the lock. The car door opened and slammed.

Kasker gasped in a breath and rolled to his stomach. Anger flared in his true skin. He fought the urge to shed his corporeal costume.

The ward wrenched on the ignition. The Corvair coughed and started.

In a moment, she'd be gone. He needed her. He lifted a hand.

"I know where the white van is," he shouted. It came out as a rasp, barely louder than the engine.

She didn't hear him. She stepped on the gas. The car lurched forward—twenty, thirty, fifty feet—off-kilter. She stopped with a jerk, got out, and circled to the passenger side to inspect the front tire.

Kasker smirked openly before wiping the expression from his face. He picked himself up, brushed off his jeans, and strutted to her car, determined to mask his aching back.

He'd let the air out of her tire so they would take his Mustang. That way, he'd be in control. He congratulated himself on his fortuitous planning.

"Bummer," he said. "Hope you've got a spare."

She glared at him. "Tell me about the van."

So she *had* heard him. But she'd left anyway. Why?

"It was at the park, where Holmes made another kill."

Her face registered shock. "He was there? And you let him get away?"

Indignation flared. "Of course I didn't let him get away. He wasn't there, but his minions were. It was a trap."

He snapped his jaws shut. He hadn't meant to tell her that part.

She stared hard through narrowed eyes. "You caught them at the scene of the murder, but you didn't call the police. You didn't follow them. You ran away."

"They were armed." He puffed out his chest. He could have followed them, but that would risk running into another trap.

She didn't look impressed.

"By the time I got near a phone, they were long gone. And what would your pig friends think when I called in another murder?"

"You've got nothing." The ward stormed to the rear of the Corvair and opened the engine compartment.

Kasker scrambled after her. "I've got the name from the side of the van."

She stopped loosening the bolt holding the spare and turned to face him. Tension draped like an aura around her. She seemed suddenly eager to listen to him. He took a step back.

"Where have you been?" he asked in a suspicious voice. "The funeral ended hours ago."

"The mayor's son, Tad Newell, is missing," she said. "I think Warner and Bronski kidnapped him for Holmes, although I don't know why Holmes wants him. He has nothing to do with Calderon."

Kasker's heart sped up, and a smile curved his lips. He knew exactly what Holmes intended to do with Tad Newell.

"I'll tell you about the van, but only if you promise not to call the pigs. Calderon wants this kept in the family."

The ward bit her lip while she considered, and then she nodded.

"We'll take my car," he said and strode away.

Kasker pulled the Mustang over a block from the Temple of Enlightenment. After detecting the trap at the park, he wasn't taking any chances. He'd need to get the ward out of the Mustang long enough to check the area in his true form before he'd go closer.

The ward shaded her eyes and squinted into the sun setting behind the building. There wasn't much to see. In a previous life, the storefront had been an expansive record shop. But the neighborhood around the shop had become increasingly industrialized and decrepit, driving customers to more friendly locations.

The windows were painted over with scenes meant to depict

Nirvana. Acolytes in green robes worshipped deities or strolled through fields of wild flowers. Kasker couldn't tell if lights were on inside. The large parking lot in front of the building yawned empty and litter-strewn.

"Let's go." The ward slipped from the car.

With reluctance, Kasker opened his door and stepped out. He perused the street. No inset shop doors. No parked cars to shield him from the ward's sight. He trailed after her as she paced quickly toward their target.

At the corner, Kasker stopped. The hair bristled at the back of his neck. Rivulets of sweat trickled over his temples and ran from his armpits. His hands knotted into fists. Under his breath, he cursed the insensitive flesh.

The ward, now four steps ahead, turned back. "You coming?"

Half a block to his left, an alley yawned. The breath he'd been holding whooshed from his lungs.

"In a minute." He marched toward the alley.

The ward's footsteps pattered on the pavement behind him. Ten feet short of the alley, she appeared at his shoulder. He grimaced.

"I'm not letting you out of my sight," she said.

He squinted at her. *Curse the ward!* He walked to a dumpster parked near the mouth of the alley and unfastened his fly, one slow button at a time.

He gave the ward a lecherous grin. "Let me know if you see anything you like."

Scarlet bloomed on the ward's face. Her nose wrinkled in disgust. She scuttled back past the corner of the building.

Kasker darted behind the stinking dumpster and dropped to the ground. He loosed his true form, focusing his senses on the temple across the street.

The bright prick of the ward's soul shone just beyond the alley mouth. It was Friday night. Few other points of life flickered in the surrounding buildings. None glowed in the Temple of Enlightenment, nor did he detect any magical essence.

Kasker withdrew to his corporeal cloak and stood. He glared at the empty building that the ward was determined to visit. His empty stomach rumbled.

Searching the temple was a waste of time, as was chasing after the mayor's son. If they went to Seve, Kasker could get the contracts for the remaining damned souls. Once he tasted their blood, he could track them to their rendezvous with Holmes. He chided himself for not thinking of the contracts sooner.

Holmes killed after nightfall, when dark magic was strongest. The sun hadn't set yet. He and the ward could stop for burgers and still have plenty of time to locate the damned. All he had to do was convince her to give up this foolish pursuit of Newell.

Kasker buttoned his fly and stalked back to the ward.

56

Sleeth and I weren't speaking. He'd insisted no one was at the Temple of Enlightenment. I'd demanded we get inside to look for Tad or clues to his whereabouts. Sleeth broke out a window, climbed through, and unlocked the door.

We'd found nothing. I'd wanted to call the police. Sleeth reminded me of my promise not to and stopped for burgers. His callous attitude towards Tad's safety left me cold.

Sleeth claimed that Calderon would supply people to help stake out the remaining members of the mobster's cult. Since finding Holmes seemed like the only way to find Tad, I agreed.

We'd donned our costumes, and I wheeled Sleeth over the sidewalk to the front door of the Luna Azul. The doorman let us in. For a Friday night, the place wasn't that busy. I maneuvered the wheelchair between tables and guests until we reached the kitchen door.

Calderon met us there, flanked by two of his hulking bodyguards. His flat black eyes regarded Sleeth, and then he walked through the kitchen to his office. Sleeth abandoned the chair and followed.

"Now what?" the mobster demanded when I'd shut the office door.

"We need your help," I replied before the hippie could open his mouth. "Holmes has three potential victims. We think he'll go for one of them tonight. We can't cover them all."

Calderon stared, first at me, and then at Sleeth. "So, sabueso, you admit you're incompetent? You ask me to do your job for you?"

Sleeth squared his shoulders and sneered at the mobster. "I

don't need your help. Give me the contracts."

The mobster's face set hard. "It's not their time. If they're harvested now, there will be Heaven to pay."

A sly smile spread Sleeth's lips. "That's not a solution I considered, but it *would* prevent Holmes from breaking more of your precious pacts."

Calderon set his fists on the desk and leaned forward. "No. Now get out."

I wanted to slug Sleeth, but I held my temper in check.

"Okay, Sleeth, you had your chance to do it your way." I gestured at the mobster. "If your buddy doesn't want to get involved, we'll do it my way. I'm calling the police."

I'd taken a single step toward the door when a distant voice shouted "Police! Hands up!" A gun barked. A cacophony of voices shrieked. China shattered. Heavy objects thumped. More shots rang out.

"It's a raid," Calderon said through gritted teeth. "You idiot. The police weren't fooled by your disguise. They've come for you."

Sleeth loomed over the desk. "The solstice is tomorrow noon. If I don't stop Holmes by then, he'll destroy Heaven and Hell. Get me out."

Calderon bared his teeth. He yanked the desk drawer open. I expected him to draw a pistol and plug Sleeth where he stood. Instead, he tossed the hippie a ring of keys and bent to move a carpet beside the desk.

"Go through the barred door," the mobster said. He pulled open a hatch in the floor. "It exits in the vacant shop across the alley."

Sleeth jumped through the open hatch, landing with a thud. I used the ladder. I wouldn't run far on a broken ankle. By the time I reached the bottom, Sleeth had a light on. The mobster dropped the hatch. I'd expected him to follow us.

Sleeth rushed to an iron door in the wall and unlocked it. Then he ran back to a huge old safe and snatched an armload of moldering scrolls from the bottom shelf. He brushed past me into the dark passage.

This was nuts. I'd done nothing wrong and had no reason to run. On the other hand, I'd be forever tainted if I were found here, not to mention the hours I'd lose giving a statement. Heavy footsteps clomped overhead, and a door slammed. I gritted my teeth and ran after Sleeth.

As promised, the passage ended at another ladder that led up to a vacant shop across the alley from the Luna Azul. Through the walls, the sound of the gun battle continued. I thought about the innocent customers caught in the middle of it and felt sick.

Sleeth darted out the front and ran like the wind to the Mustang. I thanked my lucky stars I'd worn plain, sturdy shoes and caught him before he pulled out. I had the feeling Sleeth wouldn't wait for me.

We tore away headed west. Sirens split the night as backup units and ambulances responded.

"Slow down," I said. "You look like you're fleeing the scene."

Sleeth glanced my way with a grimace but eased back on the gas. When we'd driven a dozen blocks, he pulled into an A & W parking lot. I couldn't believe he was making another burger stop.

He reached between the seats, retrieved the crumbling scrolls, and unrolled one. He didn't bother reading. He checked the signature at the bottom and tossed it into the back.

I wondered what the scrolls were and fished out the one he'd tossed. By the time I'd pulled it into my lap, he'd tossed another one and opened a third.

The paper was rough, dry, and gave off an ancient, musty smell. I recognized Calderon's awful scrawl from the list he'd given us. I turned it toward the window and began to read.

By the time I reached the signature, my hair stood on end. Sister Magda had said she'd sold her soul to Calderon. I thought she'd meant it as a metaphor. But the paper I held in my hands was a contract for Matthew Shertleff, the Tuesday night Slasher victim, to hand over his soul in exchange for a guarantee that he'd become a best-selling author.

Sleeth held a contract in front of him. His long pink tongue flicked out and touched the rust-red signature. My stomach rolled. His eyes drooped closed, and a look of bliss transformed his face, as though he'd inhaled the vapors of a fine wine. When he opened his eyes, they glinted red.

A dark, primal fear raced up my back, the kind that made my ancestors throw another log on the fire and huddle closer. Every inch of my skin crawled. I would have gotten out right there, but paralysis set in.

"What the hell's going on?" I whispered.

Sleeth looked at me and smiled. It was the kind of smile a panther gives its prey just before it leaps. I stopped breathing.

"I'm the hellhound," he said, his voice laced with pride, superiority, and drunkenness. The red in his eyes flashed like hot coals, and a dark shadow passed over his face. He rattled the parchment at me. "I collect the souls of the damned when they die."

I didn't believe him. He and Calderon were kooks. They were deranged, playing at crazy games where people signed away their souls.

"Calderon thinks he's Satan?" I asked. My voice trembled. I was trapped in a car with a lunatic.

"No, just a garden variety demon sent to entice humans to sign on the dotted line." His eyes narrowed and the smile vanished. "He's very good at it because he cheats."

"And Holmes?"

Sleeth shifted, uncomfortable with the topic. "America's first serial killer. Or at least he's the first serial killer the pigs caught. He murdered dozens of women, children, and even male business associates who thought they could trust him."

"*H. H. Holmes?* The man who ran a murder hotel during the Chicago World's Fair?" I edged against the door. "He's been dead for nearly seventy years."

"His soul escaped Hell three months ago. I'm here to retrieve it—again."

I'd humor him until I could get away. "Escaped Hell. Does that happen often?"

Sleeth jerked back like I'd slapped him. "Never. He must have had help. Someone from your world of souls opened the way, perhaps with the magic book that explains the ritual to transfer the souls of the damned. Whoever it was, he wears their flesh."

I nodded like I agreed with every word while I kept an eye out for a passing citizen who might help me escape. A magic book. What other delusions lurked in his insane mind?

"So Holmes is moving souls around between bodies. That's what the murders are about?"

"He kidnaps a recipient. At the same moment that he finishes the ritual on the damned soul, the recipient is sacrificed. The damned soul transfers to the still-warm body and animates it."

The red in Sleeth's eyes dimmed. I wondered how he pulled it off. He must have contacts, and it was a trick of the light.

"Emmett Merkel was meant to be a recipient. He died too soon, and the transfer failed. Haskell's soul was lost to the universe." Sleeth shifted the Mustang into gear and drove toward the exit. "If Holmes grabbed Newell, then he intends to use Newell in the ceremony tonight."

"Won't these 'damned souls' of yours still go to Hell eventually anyway?"

Sleeth shook his head. "Their blood binds them to the contract. Once they leave their original body and take a new one, the blood no longer binds them. Seve thinks Holmes needs the damned to destroy Heaven and Hell."

Destroying Heaven and Hell sounded like a darn good idea to me. I was no fan of religion.

"You killed Judge Richards," I said.

My hand clutched the door handle, and I prepared to roll out before the car picked up speed on the street. Sleeth was too fast for me. He screeched out of the driveway.

"Killing humans is strictly forbidden," Sleeth said, expression solemn. "Richards perished at the roller rink. I found his lingering soul in the alley. Once Matthew Shertleff 'died' to leave his body, his soul became mine. I removed it from its ill-gotten new abode in Richards."

Sleeth headed north.

"Where are we going?" I asked, unclear on the distinction between removing a soul from its abode and murder.

"Now that I've tasted their blood, I can track the remaining damned. We'll follow them to wherever Holmes intends to hold his ritual." He tossed me a cheery grin. "Then you can rush in and arrest him."

Maybe I could talk him into stopping for help. "Calderon's list still has three names. We can't follow them all at the same time. We need help."

"Two," the hippie replied, eyes focused on the road.

I recited names from memory since Sleeth had the list in his back pocket. "Colleen Hobert the nurse, Frank Zachary the sanitation worker, and Lester Renquist the lawyer."

Sleeth licked his lips in a way that turned my stomach. "Only two left. Renquist died Sunday night."

Renquist. Died Sunday night while Dave and I chased Sleeth through the Park View neighborhood—Renquist's neighborhood.

I'd believed Sleeth when he said he didn't kill Susan Brown. He had alibis for Brown and Haskell. But as the body count connected to Sleeth climbed, I wondered if the hippie was a stone-cold killer.

"Why didn't you tell me all this sooner?"

"It's forbidden."

I gulped. "Does that mean that once we catch Holmes, you'll have to kill me?"

His eyes got a thousand-yard stare. It was the same look he'd had when we chased the shooter away from my house. He leaned over the wheel and accelerated.

"One of the damned is on the move."

57

We raced through the night heading northeast to the Solaris city limits. Sleeth ran every light. My white, shaking hands gripped the door handle. I was terrified of the madman in the driver's seat, and more terrified we'd smash into a telephone pole or another car and die.

I'd heard stories about spaced-out druggies displaying super-human strength. Some people said dropping acid activated latent psychic powers, something Sleeth claimed to have. I'd never heard of anyone's eyes glowing red.

The hippie eased back on the gas. "Look at the map. Is there a ley line junction ahead?"

Maybe if I humored him, I'd live to see the dawn. We were leaving a residential neighborhood behind and moving into an area of undeveloped scrub punctuated by widely spaced farms. The desolate countryside wouldn't give me a lot of options to find help, and I wasn't sure I could outrun Sleeth.

I dug the map out from under a burger wrapper and an empty drink cup at my feet. There must be a way I could use it to get us back to civilization. It was my only hope for escape.

I flipped on the dome light. The paper was spotted with grease. We were already at the edge of the map, but if I traced some of the lines beyond Solaris, I could visualize other possible junctions. If I told him there were none nearby, would he turn around?

Something nagged in the back of my mind. I'd been too worried about escaping Sleeth to let it surface. I stared hard at the map and rubbed the paper between my thumb and finger. Something we'd seen earlier... The connection snapped into focus.

"That brochure that Decker had," I said, my voice barely a

whisper. "It was from the Temple of Enlightenment."

"We already know about that." Sleeth pressed the gas pedal down again, and the Mustang leaped forward.

"The brochure said they had a commune in the country. It's out this way."

Had the Slasher taken Tad to the compound? Was he preparing Tad for sacrifice as we approached? A shiver wriggled through my gut.

All the other murders had taken place around midnight. We were already on the far side of ten. How much longer before the Slasher started his slice and dice?

I had to get to the commune. I had to free Tad, even if it meant going along with the lunatic at the wheel. No time to call for back-up, assuming Sleeth would allow such a thing. Besides, without probable cause, the police were unlikely to charge onto the property.

I dropped the map and stared out the windshield. In the darkness ahead, our lights reflected off the back of a white van. It sped up as we closed with it.

Sleeth growled and pumped a fist in the air. "Colleen Hobert is mine."

"You think she's in the van?"

"She's in the van," he said with certainty. "So are Holmes' minions."

"You know that because...?" I grabbed the edge of my seat while we careened around a corner.

His eyes blazed hot and red, and a smile danced on his lips. "We're close enough for me to feel their souls."

I should stop asking him questions and expecting sensible answers. Somehow, I couldn't help myself. I clamped my mouth shut.

The pavement ended, and the road turned to gravel. The van threw up a choking cloud of dust that obscured its tail lights. The landscape stretched into darkness on both sides of us.

Bits of rock pinged against our windshield. I jumped with every hit. The road took a gentle bend to the right, and the Mustang shimmied around it. We must have been doing seventy, which was double the speed limit.

What would we do when we caught the van? A stealth approach was off the table. Sleeth said Warner and Bronski were armed, and I wasn't carrying a weapon. I suspected the hippie would be worthless in a fight.

A road sign warned of an approaching stop at a T-crossing.

The van decelerated sharply, and Sleeth ran up its tail. Our front window was so coated in dust that I could barely see the van's white bulk before we kissed its bumper.

The van swayed around a sharp right turn. In the blink of an eye, a curtain of pulsing red surrounded us. An electrical storm crashed overhead. Sleeth howled and slumped over the wheel.

The Mustang shot through the stop sign and across the road, bumped over a shallow ditch, and plowed through a barb wire fence. I grabbed for the dash. My head bumped the ceiling while we covered a hundred feet of deer grass clumps and rocks. We stopped just short of a copse of live oaks.

Out the back window, a red glow still emanated from a circle of throbbing symbols laid out to encompass the entire intersection. Miniature lightning bolts flashed over the circle.

Sleeth hadn't moved since we'd run off the road. His throat felt clammy under my fingertips. I couldn't find a pulse. The dash lights illuminated dark blotches roiling and shifting under his skin like trapped clouds of smoke.

They'd killed him, just like they'd killed Dave. A cold lump formed in my stomach. I was alone now, just me against the Slasher and his cohorts. I swore I'd nail the bastard's hide.

The van had stopped fifty yards up the road. Warner and Bronski were walking back to where the Mustang had torn through the fence. Warner carried a pistol.

I killed the Mustang's headlights, grabbed the keys from the ignition, and swung my door open. Bronski pointed. Warner raised the gun.

I slammed the door, dowsing the dome light. Darkness swallowed me. I couldn't see the ground and fumbled to the front bumper.

A smothering blanket of dust hung in the still air. Ahead, the treetops were defined by the stars they masked. In the distance, an owl hooted.

The gun barked, dust kicked up a foot to my right, and I dashed for the trees. I stumbled over the rough terrain, zig-zagging until I reached the oaks.

In the cover of the woods, fallen twigs snapped under my feet. My ankle twisted, and I went down. My breath came in ragged, terrified gulps.

Running footsteps crunched on gravel. I caught glimpses of the two thugs silhouetted by the light from the van. They left the road and trotted to the car where they argued in voices too low for me to understand.

I couldn't raise enough spit to swallow. Dust clawed at my throat and scratched my eyes. If I coughed, I'd give away my position. Bronski gestured toward my hiding place. I got up on hands and knees, prepared to flee deeper into cover.

Warner shoved Bronski aside and opened Sleeth's door. He dragged the hippie from the seat, and together, they carried him to the back of the van.

Bronski opened the door. A woman dressed in a stark white nursing uniform huddled inside. She had to be Colleen Hobert. They tossed the hippie onto the floor and slammed the doors.

What did they want with Sleeth? Was he still alive? How had he known Hobert was in the van with the two men?

The van peeled out in a spray of gravel.

58

I counted to fifty to be sure the thugs weren't sneaking back to ambush me. Then I stumbled through the dark to the Mustang.

The little muscle car looked no worse for wear despite its off-road adventure. I started it, turned on the lights, and drove back to the road.

What the hell were the flashing red symbols? Why did they have such a profound effect on Dave and Sleeth but not on me? If I was about to walk into the lion's den, I wanted to understand what I was up against, but I didn't stop to examine them. Tad might die before I reached him.

Who was Holmes really? Probably someone with mental health issues who'd been sucked into Calderon's crazy cult. I could imagine the flat-eyed mobster applying drug-induced brainwashing.

I turned the headlights off and navigated by the running lights. Despite the tension in my shoulders urging me to hurry, I advanced down the road at a careful pace.

I almost missed the sign for the turn into the commune. A dirt driveway disappeared through a hedge of sycamores. I stayed on the road until I passed over a rise, and then I parked the Mustang.

When I checked the map, it looked like two of the ley lines crossed somewhere inside the commune. I hadn't passed any other farms. The thought of walking into the commune alone gave me the willies.

I needed a weapon. Nothing in Sleeth's car presented itself. No switchblade in the glove box. No Saturday night special stashed under the seat. He didn't even have a tire iron in the trunk.

I quit stalling and followed the driveway onto the property. It cut between two large fields planted in neat rows. The scent of tomatoes and damp earth hung in the air. The place looked like every other California truck farm.

The driveway seemed to stretch endlessly into the dark, but it couldn't have been more than a quarter mile. It opened into a space ringed by buildings. Lacking any cover, I crouched in the dirt to take stock.

A series of huts that were originally intended for migrant workers stretched off to the left. To the right, a stately two story farm house nestled among giant live oaks, a weak porch light shining beside the door. The white van was parked in front of the house, along with two sedans and a jeep. No light shone through any of the house windows.

Straight ahead, a monster packing shed loomed dark and quiet. The whole place had a deserted air. Where were the acolytes? Where were Holmes and his goons?

No guards. They either didn't expect me to follow, or they weren't worried if I did. Goose bumps rose on my arms.

A car engine growled on the road. Headlights winked through the sycamore hedge, and the vehicle slowed.

I leaped into the field on my right, pushed through a row of tomato plants, and flattened to the ground. Twin beams lit the road. A station wagon rolled past and parked on the far side of the van.

I rose to hands and knees. A car door slammed, and a man walked to the porch. Was this the final name from the list, Zachary Frank, the sanitation worker?

Bronski opened the door before the new arrival knocked. The man slipped inside. Bronski stepped out, glanced around, and then went back in, closing the door. Moments later, a light came on in a small second floor window.

I tiptoed closer to the vehicles. Tad's blue Impala was flanked by a black Olds Cutlass Supreme and a red Scout. I passed the cars and circled wide around the house, keeping to the deep shadows under the trees until I reached the back.

A round patio table and four chairs stood on a patch of lawn outside the back door. Jasmine climbed a trellis against the wall, its flowers scenting the air. Light filtered through the curtains of a second-floor window and also a first-floor window at the far corner.

I darted across the lawn and flattened myself against the back of the house. My breathing was shallow and fast and much too loud in the silent night. I wished I had my gun.

All the house windows were opened to let in the cool evening air. I could peer through the screens to see who was inside, although in the dark, I wouldn't see much. But that wouldn't help with the second story.

The jasmine trellis didn't look strong enough to support my weight. If I wanted to search both floors, I'd have to get inside. The very thought sent hot fear lancing through my chest. *One step at a time, Demasi.*

I started with the first floor windows. The one closest to the back door was a yawning black hole, small and set higher than most of the others. The smell of fried onions and grease drifted through the sweet odor of jasmine. Kitchen window, no sound of anyone moving inside.

The next window was also small, high-set, and frosted. Water drip-dripped inside. The downstairs bathroom?

Two large windows remained: one was dark, the other was the lighted window at the corner of the house. I couldn't see or hear anything in the darkened room. I slid past to the lighted corner window.

A window shade was drawn three-quarters down, leaving a couple-inch gap at the bottom. A desk lamp did little to light the room, which seemed to be some kind of office or study. No one spoke, but fabric rustled.

Someone wearing dress slacks and a formal cotton shirt passed by the window so close that I jumped back. I froze while I waited to see if I'd been discovered. The midriff crossed again going the opposite direction.

"Sit down, Newell. Pacing won't help," a voice said.

I knew that voice. It was Chief of Detectives Lenny Greene. Greene must have addressed Tad. The pacing figure was too tall and thin to be the mayor. I edged close to the screen and tried to see whether anyone else was in the room.

"I should have told Nicky everything."

"If you'd told her, you'd be locked in an asylum now," Greene said.

"She's smart, an excellent detective. She would have figured out the Slasher's identity if she'd just had my diary."

"And she'd be dead like your secretary," Greene added. "Don't you see? We can't stop what's coming."

"This is wrong," Tad said. "We're helping a murderer."

"Don't you forget it. If we don't help, we'll be the next victims."

Their conversation left me confused. Was Tad working undercover for Greene? Why hadn't the two men kicked out the flimsy window screen and escaped?

Tad strode to the desk and yanked open the top drawer. He

pawed through the contents.

"What are you doing?" Greene asked.

Tad pulled out a letter opener and tested the flexibility of the blade. "Someone has to stop this madness."

He tucked the blade in the waistband of his slacks, under his shirt. He checked the remaining drawers before returning to his pacing.

"Psst, Tad," I whispered, afraid I might be overheard by Bronski or the man who'd entered the house.

Tad's surprised face appeared at the gap under the shade.

"Nicky? What are you doing here?"

"Everyone's looking for you." I ran my hands around the edges of the screen. "We have to get away and find help."

Greene moved beside Tad. He looked different, although I couldn't say why. He still wore the black suit he had on at Dave's funeral. His mouth was opened in surprise, and one hand splayed on his chest.

Tad raised the blind and unlatched the hooks that held the screen in place. I lowered the screen to the ground. Tad grabbed the edge of the window and raised a foot to the sill.

Greene grabbed Tad's arm. "You can't go. You know what will happen."

Tad's lips set in a hard, thin line. "For once in my life, I'm going to do the right thing. Stay if you want, but I won't be part of this anymore."

Anymore? How was Tad involved with the Slasher? And what was Greene afraid of? None of it made any sense. The place still seemed as lifeless as a tomb, but that might not last. We needed to move.

Tad clambered through the window and straightened beside me.

"Where is everyone?" I asked.

"I heard the commune members are on a pilgrimage to some ruins in Mexico. I don't know who else is here," Tad said. "How did you know where to look for me?"

"Sleeth and I followed Colleen Hobert—until he ran into a trap just like the one that killed Dave."

"Sleeth's here?" Tad's face paled in the dim light from the window.

"That's right," said a voice from behind me. "I finally have the hellhound."

I turned around to face Maggie Tisdahl. Her pistol pointed at my chest.

59

"You work for Holmes," I said when I'd recovered my voice. "You're helping the Slasher?"

Maggie's eyes blinked, and a change came over her. Her head tipped forward, a smile curved her lips, and her posture relaxed.

"I *am* Holmes." Her voice had deepened and taken on an East Coast accent. "Maggie and I have shared this body since she released me. Lucky for me she found that old book and used its contents as part of her meditation chant."

A frightening intensity came over the personality who looked at me through Maggie's eyes. "Tomorrow, after I have sacrificed Sleeth to destroy Hell, you and I will get better acquainted. It's been a long time since I've enjoyed the entertainment of a woman."

She'd had some kind of personality split, or a psychotic break. I had no sympathy for her. I wanted to plant my fist in Maggie's face, scratch out her eyes, make her suffer the way I'd seen Dave suffer.

"You're the one who killed Dave," I said, my voice flat. My hands clenched at my side.

"It's your fault he's dead. If you'd done as you were told and stayed away from Sleeth, Dave would still be alive," the voice of the Holmes personality said. "I never wanted to hurt your partner, but I had to have Sleeth. He's the hell mouth. Rupture him to rupture Hell."

Criminals always blamed others for their actions, but some part of me still cringed with guilt at the accusation that I'd killed Dave. I diverted the guilt into rage and focused it on Maggie.

I jerked a thumb at Tad. "And will it be Tad's fault when you kill him? What about Chief Greene? What sin did he commit that entitles you to murder him in cold blood?"

Maggie laughed, a sound that chilled me with its madness despite the warm night. She flicked the gun barrel at Tad. "Go ahead, tell her who you are."

Tad's brows pulled down, and his hands rubbed his pant legs. "I'm sorry, Nicky. I should have told you sooner, but I didn't think you'd believe me. I didn't think *anyone* would believe me. They'd say it was because I banged my head in the accident.

"I'm Bill Decker. Tad Newell died when he was hit by the car, and I stole his body."

Tad was right; I *did* think he'd hit his head too hard in the accident.

"All I wanted was to get out of my contract with Calderon." Tad's eyes filled with sorrow. "When she contacted me, I thought I was buying a new identity, a new life somewhere that Calderon couldn't find me. I didn't know she intended to murder me or anyone else. None of us did."

My eyes tracked from Tad to Maggie to Greene, who leaned out the window. I waited for Greene to say something, to refute the madness.

"When you tried to warn me about the Slasher, you said he was a man. But I'd spoken to a woman," Greene said.

"She won't help you," Maggie said, her voice back in its normal range.

She *who?* Maggie and I were the only females present. She couldn't mean—

"I hadn't intended to take Greene," Maggie said. "He's small potatoes, not the kind of rich and powerful associate I prefer. But Calderon helped the hellhound. That had to stop, and Greene had the authority to do it."

I stared at Greene. "You ordered the raid at the Luna Azul."

"She has my heart," Greene said. "If I don't do what she says, she'll kill me."

"What about the innocent victims caught in the crossfire?" I asked. "You swore to protect them when you took the job."

"She swore nothing," Maggie said. "Nicky Demasi, meet Deborah Peck."

My eyes widened, my lips parted, and my breath stuck in my chest. Greene ducked his head. His ruddy face flushed. Was I the only sane person left on the planet?

"If you'd just shot Sleeth at the freight warehouse, this would all be over," Tad murmured at my shoulder, his voice laden with regret. "She can't hold the ceremony without him."

The porch light blazed. Warner banged through the screen door and joined Maggie on the grass. The light revealed dried blood on Maggie's hands. My stomach churned. Was it Sleeth's?

"Hobert's resting upstairs," Warner said. "Frank Zachary finished his shower, and Bronski gave him his sedative. He'll be out soon."

"Good. Time's running short. We need to get them back to their ritual locations," Maggie said. She nodded at me. "Put her in the basement."

The strange shift came over Maggie again, and the deeper Eastern voice spoke. "I want her secure but comfortable. When you're done, you and Bronski go after Judge Innes. Take Peck with you. The judge will open the door if he sees his ol' buddy Chief Greene."

Maggie looked at me with a sad smile. "Another failure to add to your list, Nicky. If you hadn't let Sleeth take Matthew Shertleff's soul from Judge Richards' body, I wouldn't need a replacement."

Warner pulled his pistol from his belt and stepped over to me. He grabbed my arm in a grip as tight as a vise and jerked me toward the back door. Inside, we crossed the kitchen to a locked door.

Warner shoved his gun in his belt and dug a key ring from his pocket. The door yawned open to dark stairs leading down. He drew his gun and flipped a switch. A bare bulb hanging overhead came on. We moved forward.

We stopped before a second locked door at the bottom. My captor used a different key to unlock this one. It swung open on well-oiled hinges. Warner turned on another light.

The room encompassed half the footprint of the house. Ceiling-mounted fixtures cast light on a scene that made me stop in my tracks.

A steel table, the surface of which sloped to a drain at one end, stood in the space closest to the door. Straps hung from the edges. Beside the table, a tray displayed gleaming surgical instruments laid out in neat rows. Beyond the table, chain manacles hung from a ring set in the concrete wall.

At the far end of the room, a huge brick furnace took up much of the remaining space. It had a small metal door near the floor and a larger door at waist height. A chimney rose in an L to vent the furnace out the side wall.

No one needed a furnace that size to heat a house in Southern California. It looked more like— My throat closed.

Warner dragged me to the wall and fastened manacles around

my wrist. They bit into my skin. He glanced at the furnace, which had captured all my attention, and then looked at me.

"Don't worry," he said in a gravelly voice. "By the time you go in there, you won't feel a thing."

60

I sat on the cool, hard concrete floor, my arms stretched over my head, my wrists already raw from the rough edges on the cold iron bracelets. I should have jumped Warner before he brought me down here. I'd rather be shot than face my dark future on the dissection table.

How had I missed Maggie's severe mental illness? How had she sucked so many other people into her delusions? How could I stop her from committing more murders?

She'd been after Sleeth all along, and I hadn't seen the significance of it. We could have set a trap using Sleeth as the bait. Maggie would have come to us. If we had, we wouldn't both be her prisoners now.

The door opened, causing me to jump. I discarded my regrets, scrambled to my feet, and faced Warner.

The hoodlum crossed to me at a brisk pace. He pulled handcuffs from his trouser pocket and fastened them on my wrists before removing the manacles. The gun was tucked in his waistband. I thought about making a grab for it, but he never gave me the opportunity.

We climbed the stairs, exited the kitchen, and emerged in the yard. Despite my feeling that endless hours passed while I was chained to the wall helpless, stars still twinkled overhead. The thinnest line of light lit the eastern horizon.

We walked to the packing shed, a two-story metal-sided building with two large delivery doors and a smaller door for foot traffic. Inside, a single bulb beside the door did little to light the cavernous, echoing space.

Slatted wooden crates were stacked in a jumble along the wall to my right. Two refrigerators, a stove, and worktop demarked a kitchen area to my left. I made note of it. Kitchens were usually stocked with knives.

At the back of the space, pinpricks of light flickered. Warner pushed me across the open expanse of concrete floor.

When we were closer, the pinpricks resolved into candles, five of them in a circle. A naked body lay spread-eagled in the center of a rune-inscribed spiral. It was Frank Zachary, the man I'd seen enter the house earlier, and the last living member of Calderon's cult.

A second man struggled against the ropes that held him to an old army cot placed at the outer edge of the spiral. Even with the tape over his mouth and the poor light, I recognized Judge Innes. His eyes rolled my direction, filled with terror and pleading wordlessly for help.

They'd ripped open Innes' shirt to bare his chest. A glass bottle of clear fluid hung upside down from a stand, and a tube trailed from it to his arm.

Bronski waited next to Innes. An overturned crate beside them held a rubber tourniquet, an Ambu bag, and a filled syringe. A defibrillator stood beside the crate.

Maggie stepped from a dark corner to meet me. Her face glowed with excitement, and her eyes shone too bright. She wore a long black robe that smelled of blood, and she carried a white-handled knife, the quintessential lunatic executioner.

"Welcome to the Temple of Enlightenment," she said. "Lt. Mack seems to have listened to you after all when you told him about your map. He's staked out the site I intended to use for Mr. Zachary's transfer. I'll have to make do with this one. That's unfortunate. Using the same site twice drains the power. But our five damned souls should be sufficient to overcome any difficulties."

Maggie swept an arm over the tableau before us. "You'll be my witness. You'll see the mighty Judge Innes cut down to size."

I blinked. As a man, Innes wasn't well-liked. He came across as crusty and opinionated, and he didn't look favorably on career women. But he'd always been fair on the bench. If you made a solid case, your perp went down.

"Why him?"

Maggie's demeanor changed, and the deeper voice replied. "It's good to have friends in the criminal courts."

So Holmes was lining up people who could protect him from the consequences of what he intended to do in his basement torture chamber. I'd be his first customer, but no one would ever find my remains. It turned my stomach.

Warner handed me to Bronski and picked up the syringe on the crate. He inserted the tip into the catheter on Innes' arm. Maggie walked to the rune spiral and knelt at Zachary's head. Her eyes closed, and she began to chant strange, unintelligible sounds. Bronski shifted his feet.

The rune closest to Zachary glowed red. In a few seconds, a second rune colored. One by one, the runes lit up. When half of them glowed softly, they began to pulse in a heartbeat-like rhythm, each beat sparking another in the chain.

Fear blocked my throat and steeled my muscles. I took an involuntary step forward. Bronski jerked me back with a grip sure to leave a bruise.

When the last rune closed the circle, Warner pressed the plunger on the syringe. Innes recoiled in pain and stopped breathing. Maggie swept the dagger down and ripped Zachary from sternum to groin.

Blood fountained from Zachary's chest. Maggie plunged her hands in, and after a moment, came away with his heart. She held it aloft with a grim smile. Then she stabbed the dagger into Zachary's throat and rose.

Sweat ran from Warner's brow, and worry lines formed at the corners of his eyes. The IV line no longer drip-dripped but ran wide open. He'd removed the tape from Innes' mouth and replaced it with the Ambu bag, which he squeezed twice. Then he dropped the resuscitator and picked up the paddles of the defibrillator.

The device whined and beeped. Warner punched the buttons to release their charge into the judge's chest. Innes jerked and fell back, still. Warner swore, set the defibrillator to recharge, and tried again.

After the second shock, Innes' chest heaved up, stuttered, and settled into an erratic breathing pattern. Warner checked for a pulse in Innes' neck. Satisfied with what he discovered, he rocked back on his heels and worked to untie the knots in the ropes.

Maggie walked over to stand beside Warner. She held the dripping heart in her hand.

"How is he?" she asked.

Warner glanced up at her face, then at the heart. His gaze returned to Judge Innes.

"He's good to go."

A triumphant look settled on her features. "Bronski, take Ms. Demasi back to the basement. When she's secured, help Warner get the judge to a bedroom. Then clean up this mess."

Bronski jerked me away towards the door. He seemed in a hurry to get out of the shed. Drops of sweat beaded on his upper lip. He stared at the ground, paying little attention to me.

This was probably my only chance of escape. I waited to see if anyone followed us to the house. When no one emerged from the shed behind us, I clenched my fists and swung at Bronski's face.

Bronski flinched, and my fist connected with his cheek instead of his nose as I'd intended. He shoved me forward and down. His fist came like a freight train. Pain shot through my head, and the lights went out.

61

I burned in Hell. That's how it felt. Sweat drenched my face. The air was too hot to breathe. My jaw ached, and my head throbbed.

When I opened my eyes, I was in the basement chained to the wall. Murmuring voices and a metallic rattle drew my attention to the far end of the room.

Warner and Bronski wrestled a blanket-wrapped form through the upper furnace door. The glow of hot flames flickered beneath it. I sucked in a breath and stared.

When they'd finished, Warner mopped his face with his forearm. Bronski shifted from foot to foot and watched the furnace, nervous energy overcoming the heat-induced lethargy he should have felt.

Warner walked down the room to me, pulled a ring of keys from his pocket, and removed the single manacle bracelet fastened around the center of the handcuffs. He hauled me up.

A new wave of pain swept over me, accompanied by nausea. I swayed, and the light in the room dimmed. Then the blackness receded, and Warner pulled me to the door.

"Where are we going?" I asked.

"You're to watch, so you understand who's boss," Warner said. He didn't look happy about it.

Bronski led the way out of the basement and into the cooler air of the kitchen. We traipsed through a dim hallway and onto the front porch.

Blistering light blinded me. I squinted at the sky. The sun stood directly overhead. We'd reached the solstice.

Bronski hesitated, eyes shifting between Warner and the packing shed.

"I don't like it," Bronski said. "There's something about that Sleeth guy. We should have done him in, not brought him here."

Sleeth was alive. One more person I should rescue. If only I could rescue myself.

"You want to get paid," Warner said, "you'll do what she says."

Warner didn't wait for Bronski to respond. He dragged me across the lawn and dusty yard at a brisk pace. Too soon, we reached the packing shed.

"Don't do this," I pleaded. "Help me stop her. I'll put in a good word with the DA."

Warner grunted and opened the shed door.

Inside, light shone through skylights in the roof, giving the space a large, airy feel. Warner marched on while Bronski's footsteps slowed behind us. If I could talk to him alone, maybe I could convince him to turn on Maggie and help me escape.

As we approached the rear of the space, the body on the floor caught my eye. Sleeth lay spread-eagled over smears of blood and charcoal dust, on top of a freshly-drawn pentagram. His eyes were closed. Under his tanned skin, shadows roiled and writhed.

Black candles flickered at each point of the star, and just beyond them, runes formed a closed circle. Outside the circle, one at each candle, Maggie's kidnap victims waited.

When Tad saw me, he took an involuntary step my direction. His hand lifted toward me, and his eyes were haunted with worry. Then both his hand and face fell. He turned away.

Maggie crawled on hands and knees, scrawling a second circle of runes six feet beyond the first circle. No spiral here, just the rapidly closing scribbling of a madwoman.

"Hurry up," she said and gestured us inside the outer circle.

When we moved through the gap, she drew the final shapes. She pulled a dagger from under her black robe, pricked her finger, dropped blood on the last rune she'd drawn, and muttered something under her breath. The second rune circle pulsed to ruby life.

Maggie faced us all and pointed to the outer circle. "Step over that and you die."

Stunned silence greeted her proclamation. Bronski licked his lips and raised a hand to rub his chest. Warner looked grim and tightened his grip on my arm.

Maggie distributed scraps of paper to each of the people gathered around the circle: Tad, Chief Greene, and Judge Innes. George White, a rich businessman and supporter of Mayor Newell's, stood at the fourth point of the star. He must be the man kidnapped and possessed so Colleen Hobert could be free of her contract with Calderon.

"When we begin, you will repeat what's on the paper until I tell you to stop," Maggie said in that eerie voice I associated with her Holmes personality. "The hellhound must remain trapped in the body until the body is destroyed.

"If you don't cooperate and I succeed, you leave me no choice but to destroy your heart for your disloyalty and lack of gratitude. I saved you from a fate so horrible you can't imagine it. I will save all Mankind from ever facing the fires of Hades again.

"If you don't cooperate and I fail, the hellhound will be set loose. It will take all our souls to Hell. You would condemn those standing with you to eternal torture. To prevent its escape, you must chant until the ceremony is complete."

These were normal, intelligent people listening to the threats and ranting of a madwoman. I had to stop the insanity before they killed Sleeth.

"Don't do it," I said. "You've done nothing wrong yet, but if you help her, you'll be accomplices to Sleeth's murder."

Maggie's fevered eyes focused on me. "Sleeth is long since dead. It's the unholy creation of Satan that animates his remains. I've trapped the hellhound there, and when I destroy the sinew and blood, I'll destroy Hell's conduit for the damned. All the incarcerated souls will be released from their punishments. Satan's realm will be destroyed forever."

I turned my attention to the others in the circle. They were my only hope. But would they believe me?

"She kidnapped each of you, pumped you with drugs, and brainwashed you into accepting this hogwash about saving you from Hell. She's a vicious murderer, not Mankind's savior. You have to stop her."

Doubt crossed the faces of the judge, the businessman, and the chief. Tad frowned, and his gaze shifted from Maggie to Warner and back, a calculating look in his eyes.

"You see my power in the runes, don't you?" Maggie gestured to the pulsing outer circle.

"I've seen an elephant disappear and a guy teleport out of a locked chest at the bottom of a river. None of it was real. Your fancy lights aren't, either."

I lowered my voice and looked into Maggie's crazed eyes. "Maggie, you're a cop and a good one, not a cold-blooded murderer. Put the knife down and let us go. I'll get you the help you need."

Tad edged closer to me but spoke to the other three kidnap victims. "Nicky's right. If Maggie gets help, she won't be able to hurt *anyone.*"

Warner's grip tightened on my arm, and his other hand drifter closer to his pistol. "You're not pinning everything on us while she skates with an insanity plea."

Judge Innes flexed his hands and looked at Warner. Beads of sweat stood out on his forehead. "Shoot her. We're influential people. We'll testify that you didn't know what she intended to do and saved us all once you did. You'll get off all charges. No one would believe us if we told the truth anyway."

I went stiff and waited for Warner's reaction. If he drew the gun, I'd make a grab for it. Once he started shooting, he might see that it was more expedient to kill *all* the witnesses to his crimes.

"You say that now, but when the case came to trial, you'd send Warner to the gas chamber," Maggie said.

Greene shook his head. "No we wouldn't."

Rage rippled over Maggie's face. Her hand plunged into a cloak pocket and withdrew a human heart that looked remarkably fresh. She held it aloft.

"Disloyal ingrates! I'll show you power." Her fist squeezed the organ.

Innes gasped, clutched his chest and dropped to his knees.

Maggie turned a vicious stare on me. "If she speaks again, shoot her."

Warner drew the pistol from his belt and pointed it at me. His expression said he'd have no problem following his instructions.

I gritted my teeth. I'd come so close to persuading the others until Innes' psychosomatic display. As long as Maggie could threaten them, nothing I could say would make a difference. We were all doomed to play our part in this mad tableau.

"Places." Maggie waved the heart around the circle before returning it to her cloak.

Innes struggled to his feet. The other three reluctantly took positions behind the candles at Sleeth's hands and feet.

Maggie stood inside the inner circle near Sleeth's shoulder. She pricked her finger and dripped blood on the rune at her feet before moving to his side. She nodded to the others to begin.

Her eyes closed, and she chanted unintelligible consonant and vowel combinations that sounded a little like a Catholic mass. The others stumbled over the foreign words as they joined in. The runes shimmered to life in pairs, one to the left and one to the right of Maggie's position. When the circle closed, the runes flared and settled into a pulse that matched the outer circle.

The dark shadows swirling under Sleeth's skin coalesced into a black mass centered down his midline. Maggie raised the dagger in front of her chest and chanted on.

The hair on my neck and arms stood on end, as though I'd touched something electrified. Overhead, the first crackle of miniature lightning arced across the circle. A second bolt followed.

The four chanters stuttered at the display. Maggie's eyes opened, and she shot them a mean look. They resumed their chants, slightly out of sync.

Bronski shifted back, his eyes wide, his face white. His arms were stiff and his fingers splayed. Sweat glistened on his brow.

Warner's lips pulled into a hard line. His fingers dug into my arm. The barrel of the gun never wavered.

Beside me, Bronski screamed. In a blind panic, he spun and lunged toward the door. When he hit the outer line of runes, a curtain of red light blazed, just as it had when Dave died. He raised his hands in a defensive gesture, but his speed was too great. His momentum carried him over the line.

The curtain flashed brilliant, blinding red. More lightning split the air. Bronski plunged to the floor just beyond the runes and rolled to his back. His eyes were wide and unseeing, his face pulled into a terrible death rictus.

62

The four men between the circles stopped chanting and stared at Bronski's still form. Their faces were pale, their lips parted in shock and surprise. Greene made the sign of the cross.

"Stop this lunacy!" I said. "It can't harm you if you don't believe in it."

In the silence, distant sirens wailed. Everyone turned toward the sound.

Maggie pointed a finger at Bronski's twisted form. "There's your proof that it's real. No more interruptions. Warner, shoot her."

Warner lifted the pistol. At the same time, Tad spun around and leaped, the letter opener glinting in his fist. His impact with Warner shoved me free. I stumbled and fell.

The two men twisted as they wrestled. Their struggle took them closer to the outer circle. I had to get up, had to help Tad.

Before I could rise, Warner grunted, and his face screwed up in pain. The gun went off. Locked together, the two of them dropped to the floor.

Tad rolled off Warner. I crawled to help him. His eyes were half closed and already clouding with death. A flood of blood ran from a black-rimmed wound high in his ribs.

Warner pressed calloused hands against his belly. They did nothing to stem the tide flowing from a gaping slice across his midsection. He reached a bloody hand my direction, a silent plea for help.

His gun lay on the concrete two feet from his shoulder. I snatched it up and faced the circle.

"Chant, damn you," Maggie shrieked at the other three.

"Chant or it will escape and seal your fate: eternity in Hell."

I pointed the gun at her and hoped I wouldn't have to use it. There'd been too much death. "It's over Maggie."

The other three fell silent, their attention shifting between Maggie, the bodies on the floor, and me. The blackness under Sleeth's skin dissipated to swirl in a frenzy over the whole of his body.

Maggie's hand dipped into her cloak pocket and retrieved another heart. She pricked it with her knife. "Chant or die."

Lenny Greene grabbed at his chest. The blood drained from his face. His lips parted, and the strange chant stumbled out. The other two, eyes wide, joined him.

"You can't stop me. I will destroy the hellhound." Maggie raised the knife and muttered more incomprehensible gibberish.

The crazy Hawaiian's words rang in my head. *Keep your power. Believe in yourself.* I might not be able to best Maggie in a battle for the belief of her victims, but I know how to control Sleeth.

"I don't believe," I said.

The rune circles flickered and dimmed. The blackness under Sleeth's skin faded to gray. The chanters stopped, struck dumb by my audacity.

Maggie stared at me in surprise. Her voice was a whisper. "What have you done?"

"Your magic tricks can't hurt me. Watch this."

I took a step forward and kicked over the nearest candle, smudging her carefully drawn runes.

"I don't believe. Heaven and Hell are myths. And you can't do magic."

The runes winked out. The remaining gray in Sleeth's skin vanished, leaving his body a sickly white.

I gestured at Sleeth. "See, nothing but an unconscious hippie. No denizen of the Underworld."

"No!" Maggie screamed in the voice that was Holmes. "I won't go back. I have to destroy it."

The knife plunged down into Sleeth's stomach.

An instant too late, my finger squeezed the trigger. My ears rang from the boom. The gun bucked in my hand. Maggie toppled to her side. A spreading patch of red blossomed on her temple.

My gorge rose, and my hand shook. I set the gun on the floor, afraid I might discharge it accidentally. No one moved. The sirens wailed louder.

Blood ran in a burbling steam from Sleeth's wound and spread into a puddle at his side. My brain kicked into gear. I moved to help him.

The other three charged Maggie's fallen form. While I used the hem of my peasant costume to staunch Sleeth's bleeding, the men dug into Maggie's cloak, each retrieving a heart.

I pitied them. Despite everything, they still believed. I shook my head and felt for Sleeth's pulse. I couldn't find it.

"Come on, you sick son-of-a-bitch. You can't die on me now," I muttered under my breath. "You hear me Sleeth? Stay with me."

Sudden heat blistered my skin. Blackness enveloped me and doused the sunlight pouring down from the roof. A savage bay split my ear drums.

A male voice screamed. The blackness and heat moved away in a bound. I froze.

An enormous black hound faced the three men who cowered beside Maggie's body. His coat was a wall of black flame. In the flames, hundreds of tortured faces screamed while their hands clawed at some invisible barrier.

Burning slobber dropped in fiery strings from the dog's maw. It snapped and snarled at the men, its eyes blazing like hot coals. The hound lifted its muzzle and howled, making the same preternatural sound I'd heard in Judge Richards' neighborhood.

In that moment, I knew I'd glimpsed the hound before. Felt its heat before. Seen those glowing red eyes before.

Terror gripped my chest so hard I couldn't draw in air. Primal urges told me to run as far and as fast as I could.

The hound leaped. It landed on Chief Greene. Greene went down hard, screaming and lifting his arms to ward off the dog. The hound buried its muzzle in Greene's chest and ripped.

The chief's chest appeared undamaged, but a silky gray cloud came away in the dog's jaws. Streamers of the mass trailed down into Greene's body. The dog chomped twice, and the cloud slid down its throat.

Greene's arms dropped. His eyes rolled back, and his face went slack. Innes shrank back, and White rose to make a break for the door.

The hound snarled and jumped on White. It buried its muzzle in White's chest. Like Greene, White collapsed in a heap, his face frozen in an expression of horror, his body intact.

Innes screamed and scrambled for the gun. He shot the beast at point-blank range. The slug had no effect. The hound ripped a gauzy mass from the judge's body, and the judge went still and silent.

The hound padded to Maggie. It lifted its massive head and

bayed, the pure joy of the hunt ringing in its piercing voice. It snarled down at Maggie's lifeless body, revealing a row of sharp, white teeth.

The jaws gaped open, and it tore into Maggie. Like a terrier with a rat, it ripped gauzy substance loose and shook it hard before swallowing it down. It dove in for a second attack, ripping more of the stuff away.

When it had finished with Maggie, it turned toward Tad's fallen form. The tail wagged. The jaws opened. The pink tongue lolled over the teeth. The dog stepped forward and chuffed what sounded like a happy laugh.

63

"You can't have him," I said. My voice shook. My body quivered.

The hound peeled back its lips and took another step forward. The eerie red eyes swung to look into mine.

"He gave his life to save me. His sacrifice qualifies him for redemption."

The hound's body swelled. Its head lowered, and the ears pricked forward. Hackles rose along its spine. It snapped powerful jaws at me.

Fear sizzled up my spine and danced across my scalp.

"If you're still hungry, go dig up a bone."

Suddenly the hound dropped to its belly. Its ears pinned back, and a whimper escaped it. Its eyes looked beyond me, and it quaked.

I turned.

Two shimmering angels stood beside Tad's body. They weren't your Sunday-school cherubs. Both stood at least seven feet tall. Their wings topped out another two feet above that and swept down to brush the floor. Blinding white light radiated from them and hurt my eyes.

Their expressions were anything but Heavenly. The hound's snarling countenance couldn't hold a candle to the anger, the ferocity on their perfect, chiseled faces.

One stooped to Tad's fallen body and gently scooped a cottony mass from it. The angel cradled it like a new-born.

The other angel pointed a long, accusing finger at the hound. Then they were gone.

When I turned, the dog still cowered on the concrete.

Sirens split the air. The rumble of motors filtered through the shed walls. The cavalry had arrived five minutes too late.

The hound rose on enormous paws and glared at me, the hint of a snarl wrinkling its muzzle.

"Beat it, dog. You're done here," I said.

I blinked and the hound was gone. Warm liquid oozed over my fingers. Blood still drained from Sleeth's wound. I pressed harder. I couldn't staunch the flow.

"God damn it," I muttered, my voice a shaky croak. "The least the damn angels could do is perform a miracle while they were here."

The shed door opened. Uniformed officers wielding shotguns darted in. They took up crouching positions to each side of the door, their guns pointed my way.

Someone shouted 'Clear,' and more men streamed in. One by one, they checked the bodies on the floor.

Lt. Mack strode through the space. He assessed the situation, and his face was grim.

When he reached my side, he crouched by Sleeth. His fingers went to the hippie's throat for a pulse check.

"Stutzman!" Mack said over his shoulder. "Get a chopper. We need an emergency evac. And bring the first-aid kit. Make it snappy."

"I can't stop the bleeding." The horror of the scene I inhabited flooded over me. Tears misted my eyes.

"Let's see." When I didn't move, Mack lowered his voice while he nudged me aside with his shoulder. "I was a medic in Korea."

I moved out of his way.

He pulled my skirt off the wound. His eyes looked worried. His fingers probed deep into the wound. The bleeding slowed.

"What happened here?" he asked.

I swallowed hard. As Tad had said, no one would believe the real story. And I wasn't sure what constituted the real story.

"Maggie." The words tumbled out in a jumble. "She's the Slasher. She hired Warner and Bronski to kidnap her victims. I shot her, but I was too late. She'd already put the knife in Sleeth."

"Arndt, get these cuffs off Demasi and get her out of here," Mack said. "Call the ME. And get a barricade on the driveway. I don't want the press crawling over my crime scene."

Arndt helped me to my feet. He removed my blood-covered handcuffs, dropping them in a plastic evidence bag. Then he guided me out to the yard.

Heat drifted down from the sun high in the cloudless sky. A fly zipped past my ear. Birds sang in the distant sycamores. It was a glorious first day of summer.

As the adrenalin drained away, I couldn't feel anything except a hollow void where my love of Dave, my concern for Tad, even worry about Sleeth used to live. I'd wake up in the morning to discover this was all a bad dream. I'd take my three mile run, pull on my uniform, and get back to the normal world.

At the house, heat waves shimmered above the chimney. The fire in the basement burned hot and smoke-free. No one had noticed.

"There's a furnace in the house," I said to Arndt. "They're cremating a body. I think it's Frank Zachary. If you hurry, you might recover enough to identify it."

Shock showed on Arndt's face. He steered me to a patrol car parked beside the Scout and left me on the front seat, the door open. He rounded up a uniform. They disappeared into the house.

Time passed. My eyes sagged, and I slumped in a stupor. I should remove the Santa padding before I dropped from heat stroke. I couldn't find the energy.

The thrum of rotors drew my gaze to the sky. A helicopter dropped out of the blue and landed at the edge of the tomato field. Two EMTs carried a stretcher and a medical kit to the packing shed. I hoped they'd come in time to save Sleeth. Someone had to be saved.

A little later, a dust cloud rose along the sycamore hedge. The radio in the patrol car crackled to life, the roadblock officer requesting backup. The press had arrived. Uniformed officers moved to the perimeter of the property to prevent anyone from sneaking in.

One of the big loading doors in the packing shed rattled opened. I stood up to get a better look.

Four officers toted the stretcher, a body slung on the rack. An EMT held an IV bottle in the air. They made remarkable time crossing the yard. They wouldn't hurry if Sleeth was dead.

The stretcher went in the helicopter. The bird lifted off. I looked away to shield my face from the dust it kicked up.

The Scout beside me seemed familiar. Maggie's vehicle, I remembered. A worn leather-bound book rested on the front passenger seat, a tiny circle of silver runes gracing its cover.

It had to be the magic book that convinced Maggie of her mystic powers. Rage kindled and burned in the pit of my stomach. If only she'd left the damn book alone.

So much death all because of one book. Evidence or no, the book had to be destroyed. I glanced around the yard. No one looked my way. I opened the Scout's door and snatched the book.

I got back in the patrol car. A minute of squirming and wriggling lodged the volume in my underpants, beneath the Santa padding. Satisfied, I leaned back and awaited the endless questioning to come.

64

I sat in the empty canteen nursing a cold cup of coffee, waiting for the interrogation to begin. Seven hours after the cavalry's arrival at the commune, the station was still in an uproar.

The ME was overwhelmed. Three innocent bystanders died in the assault on the Luna Azul, along with an officer and a couple of Calderon's bodyguards. The mayor wanted to know whether the customers had been hit by friendly fire or cut down by Calderon's thugs. Their autopsies were a priority.

The ME'd barely started the postmortems when he'd been swamped by the bodies from the commune, too many of whom were VIPs in the community. I wouldn't want to be in his shoes.

Lt. Mack appeared at the door of the canteen. He nodded to me but made a beeline to the coffee urn. When he'd filled a mug, he trudged to my table and sank into the chair opposite me. His face was lined with fatigue and had a gray pallor.

"I need to ask you some questions," he said.

"Do I need legal representation?"

Mack ran a hand over his tired face. "No. There are a few things about the Slasher case I hope you can clear up, but you're not a suspect."

"Ask," I said, wanting very much to go home and mourn the loss of so many friends.

"Why were you at the compound?"

"Sleeth and I got a tip from Calderon about who the Slasher's next victims might be. We followed Warner and Bronski when they picked up Colleen Hobert."

"You worked with Sleeth and the mobster? That list you left me was from Calderon?" Mack looked both surprised and unhappy at the company I'd kept.

"I would have worked with Satan himself if it meant I could collar the person who killed Dave." *And maybe I had.* "How did you know about the compound? Did you follow Frank Zachary?"

"No. By the time we wrapped up at the Luna Azul, Zachary was gone, and so was Colleen Hobert."

I tilted my head and gave him a puzzled look. "Then how did you know to come?"

"We had Calderon in interrogation. We'd been at it all night, but he wasn't saying a word. Then just before noon, he had a fainting spell or something. When he came to a minute later, he told us about the arrival of a drug shipment at the commune. Said we'd have to hurry or the supplier would slip through our fingers. He didn't ask for anything in exchange."

Mack took a sip of his coffee and grimaced. "I thought it was fishy, some kind of trap. But after the botched takedown at the Luna Azul, we had nothing on him. If it meant I could nail him on a drug charge, I couldn't afford to ignore him. So we rolled."

I nodded. Maybe Sleeth was psychic after all, and he'd broadcast a message to the mobster. Or maybe Sleeth had a hotline to Hell and his 'master' interceded. It seemed unlikely that Calderon would risk a long prison stretch unless, as Sleeth claimed, the mobster was a demon. Or perhaps he knew he'd go free when no drug shipment was found at the compound.

"How did Calderon know who the Slasher would go after next?" Mack asked.

"Calderon formed a cult. He made members sign over their souls as part of their membership. In return, he helped them achieve their goals." I pitched my voice for derision. "Maggie thought her sacrificial ritual would free them from their pacts. She had a personal vendetta against Sleeth, which is why she lured him to the bookstore, framed him for Haskell's murder, and set the trap at the freight warehouse."

Mack blew out his cheeks. "That's nuts."

My shoulders relaxed. He'd arrived at the conclusion I'd intended, and I hadn't told a lie.

Open questions still niggled at the back of my mind. "I wondered how the Slasher bypassed the alarm system at the bookstore. Maggie moonlighted at the alarm company, didn't she?"

Once again, Mack looked unhappy. "We saw her name on the list of people with access to the alarm codes and never checked her out. She was one of our own—and a woman. Why would we?"

We both stared at our coffee cups and thought about what ifs and unintended consequences.

What if Maggie's unfaithful husband hadn't cheated on her? Would she have turned to the occult? Would she have slaughtered so many people?

What if Mack had checked on Maggie? Would he have discovered the money Decker and the others paid to escape their fates?

What if I'd waited for backup at the freight company? Or taken the time to call for help before sneaking into the commune? How many of the dead would still be alive?

"Sleeth didn't kill Susan Brown," I said. "He has an alibi for the time of her murder. He thinks she stole Decker's appointment diary and tried to blackmail Maggie."

"Ballistics matched the bullet that killed Brown to Warner's gun," Mack said. "We found Decker's partially burned ledger in Maggie Tisdahl's fireplace. We're no longer interested in Sleeth."

Mack sighed and sipped his coffee. "You were right to raise a stink about Merkel's death. We found his jacket in the van at the commune, his nitro prescription in the pocket. Since everyone involved is deceased, we won't reopen the case."

Mack shifted in his chair. "The mayor wants to know how his son died."

His son got mowed down by a Camaro a week ago while trying to escape a kidnapping. But the mayor wouldn't believe that. I wasn't sure I did either.

"I tried to stop Maggie. She ordered Warner to shoot me. Tad jumped him. If he hadn't—" I swallowed a lump in my throat. "He's a hero. That's how the mayor should remember him."

I wished I could tell Decker's girlfriend, Laverne Fritcher, what a brave and honorable man he'd turned out to be. She'd never believe me. Or maybe she would. We try to see the best in those we love.

"We wanted to believe she'd kidnapped him along with the others. But in the aftermath at the crime scene and considering who we found there... things were a little confused. We had trouble telling the victims from the perps." The lieutenant looked me in the eye, searching for the truth and finding it. "That news will give him some comfort."

"I'm not coming back," I blurted.

Mack nodded. "Good. When you went out on your own, you damaged your credibility with the department. They see you as a liability, a loose cannon. That weighs more heavily than solving the Slasher case, especially considering the outcome. If the brass don't demote you to clerical permanently, it'll take years for you gain back trust and work your way up to detective. That would be a shameful waste of your talent."

I stared into my cup and thought I'd heard him wrong.

"Here." Mack slid a business card across the table to me. "If you're interested, call this number."

I read the card. *AAA Investigations*, followed by an LA address and phone number.

"The owner's an ex-partner of mine. He can help you get through the licensing requirements so you can go into business for yourself."

He heaved to his feet. "I want a full report on my desk first thing Monday morning. Now go home and get some rest."

65

The morning sun warmed the pavement outside Hawaiian Mike's Meditation Center. I had so many questions. I wondered why I thought this merchant might have the answers.

I sighed and reached for the door. Bells tinkled as I pushed in. The place was empty except for the big Hawaiian waiting behind the counter.

His brows lifted in surprise, and he looked over my shoulder. "No dog?"

My steps faltered. How did he know about the dog?

I walked to the counter and laid the book on the glass top. "Maggie Tisdahl came here, didn't she?"

He gave a sage nod. "Once or twice. She didn't get what she came for, though."

"What was that?"

"What everyone wants—a sense of self-worth. Of purpose. Like we're here for a reason. The belief you have to find inside yourself."

I fought against rolling my eyes. "And Sleeth?"

"He's a dog," he said. "A party animal. Chasing women, breaking rules. He needs a trainer with a firm hand. Sure wouldn't want him running loose."

"I saw—" I couldn't make myself say it. "—things that weren't there. Things I don't believe in. Why?"

Hawaiian Mike shrugged. "Our lives are the stories we tell ourselves. What we believe shapes our stories. Each story is a chapter in the bigger story of the universe. Since we all got human brains, there's a lotta overlap in what we create. If enough people believe the same thing, that thing can manifest in the story of the universe."

"That's nonsense!" It sounded like a load of New Age hooey.

"You can see the manifestation even though you know it isn't real. Kinda like watching a magician. You see the trick, but you don't believe it's real."

I held up a hand and shook my head. "But I influenced the dog. If it isn't real, how can I do that?"

His expression became serious. "Every now and then, the stars align, the astral planes intersect at just the right angle, and someone is born who has a lotta influence. What that person believes influences the universe more than what dozens of others together believe. People like that can change things in a big way. The power leaks out in everything they say or do. Even the most inconsequential remark can have unintended consequences to create or destroy."

I frowned at him. "You think Maggie—the Slasher—was one of those special people."

"Not Maggie. Holmes had that kind of influence. He was an extraordinary con man." His voice had the patience of an ancient teacher. "But he wasn't the only one with influence. You have it, too. You can send the dog away with a wish, destroy Hell forever, make everyone stop believing in religion if you work at it long enough."

I laughed, but the pain came through. "I couldn't stop Maggie. I couldn't keep her victims from helping her."

"Changing other people's beliefs is hard and takes practice. But the dog, he's another story—an insubstantial story easily influenced by belief. You wished him out of her grasp. Temporarily out of existence."

"So many people died." Tears welled in my eyes. I blinked them away.

His voice softened. "Maybe you forgot winning has a cost."

Anger and grief bubbled in my chest. "If I could, I'd wish away Heaven and Hell. I'd get rid of cults that take advantage of the weak. I'd make everyone stop believing in superstitions that make them hate people they don't understand."

"You sure about that?" he asked. "You'd take away people's faith in Heaven when maybe that's all that comforts them through the loss of a loved one, an illness, a disaster?"

"Okay, they can have their damned Heaven and their angels," I grumbled. "We can do without Hell."

Mike's eyes twinkled. "The universe seeks balance. Yin and yang, Heaven and Hell, angels and demons—and hellhounds. When someone does great good, it has to be balanced with great evil. Better to stick with small acts that help individuals than big ones that save the world, 'cause payback's a bitch."

I scowled at the shopkeeper. I didn't want to be special. I didn't want to believe any of what I'd heard.

"That... thing that came out of Sleeth, I could get rid of it by wishing?"

"The hellhound came for Holmes. Once he knew where to find Holmes' soul, he shoulda given up his illegal occupation of a human, taken Holmes, and gone home. But you called him back."

My mouth dropped open. "No I didn't. I'd be thrilled to never see that thing again."

Mike grinned. "You mean you saved Sleeth by accident? 'Cause when you told him to live, you bound him to you. He's your dog now."

"My dog!? I don't want anything to do with him."

Mike leaned on the counter and chuckled.

I rubbed the back of my hand over my mouth. "He's evil, and he hurts people."

"That depends on who you ask. Lotta cultures have a hellhound myth. In some, he's the embodiment of evil. In others, he protects the recently departed on their trip to the afterlife. Seems like who he has as a master—or a mistress—makes all the difference." He quirked an eyebrow at me. "You know anything about dog training?"

I raised my hands, horrified at the thought of taking responsibility for Sleeth. "Why can't he just go back to Hell?"

"You upset the balance, the natural order of things. Maybe you should ask him where he wants to go."

I felt more confused now than when I'd walked in the door. I tapped a finger on Maggie's book.

"What's this?" he said.

"It's the magic book Maggie used to justify the murders." I flipped the book open. "It's blank. There's nothing on any of the pages."

The Hawaiian gave a sage nod. "Course not. There's no such thing as a magic book."

66

The hellhound rested his head on his paws and stared into the enveloping white mist. The trill of an anxious whine slipped from his throat. He knew this place. He'd crossed it thousands of times retrieving the souls of the damned.

But those crossings were like pushing through a thin curtain. This space was vast and empty. He'd wandered lost for hours, unable to find the way to Hell, and that worried him.

The ward had sent him here. Her actions confused him. First she'd freed him from Holmes' magic by pushing him out of the human realm. Then she'd called him back. He'd devoured Holmes and all the damned souls. The memory of his drunken feast still resonated.

But then she'd stopped him from taking Decker's soul. Moments later, the angels appeared. Had she called them? When they'd gone, she'd ordered him away. Was this what it was to perish?

The muffled clop of hooves approached, and he lifted his head, hope kindling in his chest. Out of the swirling fog, the demon that had worn the flesh of the mobster, Calderon, materialized. The hellhound rose on his paws, his tail wagging with excitement.

"Demon," the hellhound said, "you've left the realm of souls?"

"Observant as always." The demon's skeleton jaw sagged open in what might be construed as a smirk. "I bring word from our master."

The hellhound's muscles tensed until he quivered. So his master knew he was stuck here and had done nothing about it. It must be punishment for his slow recapture of Holmes.

"Get on with it," the hellhound said with false bravado, "unless you wish me to tell the master of your magic book."

The demon clacked his teeth. "Heaven wants retribution for their lost angel."

The hellhound drew in a sharp breath. Would he be destroyed to appease Heaven?

"The angel wasn't my fault."

"No, but a damned soul in your charge was. To Heaven, it is all the same. They wish you to perish."

The news hit the hellhound hard. He sank to his haunches. The demon seemed to delight in his discomfort.

"For reasons I will never understand," the demon said, "the master values you. He made a deal with the angels."

The hellhound rose again, relief surging through him. "What kind of deal?"

"The master convinced the angels to accept restitution in place of vengeance."

The demon was definitely enjoying himself, perhaps too much. The hellhound lowered his head and growled, suspicious.

"And the terms of this restitution?"

"Angels prefer to occupy mortality from the beginning of its existence. They have no one of appropriate age available to serve as the ward's guardian and don't want her unescorted until a new vessel matures."

The demon gestured at him with a bony arm. "You, on the other hand, have a suitable vessel that is already acquainted with the ward."

The hellhound's jaw dropped open. "I'm to be the ward's guardian? *Heaven agreed to this?*"

The demon laughed openly. "Ironic, isn't it? The master argued that since you'd saved her life once already, you were clearly qualified. As for motivation to why you should agree, if the ward were to 'meet with an accident' before her Fate-appointed time, the deal is off, and Heaven will demand your existence as payment.

"Our master sees this as a unique opportunity. While you play guardian, you are tasked with turning the ward toward Hell. She would be a powerful ally and could hasten the shifting of balance to our favor. The master will not be pleased if you fail."

"But..." He stared at the demon. "What of the retrieval of damned souls?"

The demon wagged a finger at him. "No hunting allowed while you're on guardian duty."

"No," the hellhound whispered. "It can't be. How will the army of Hell grow if I don't acquire more damned souls?"

"We'll manage," the demon replied.

Another cold thought traced a path through his brain. The ward didn't like him. "What if the ward won't have me?"

"Then you'll also perish." The demon strolled off at a leisurely pace.

"Wait! Where are you going?"

"Home to Hell," the demon said over his shoulder. "Seve Calderon died in his cell. I saw to it that the body was battered and bruised before I abandoned it. The pigs will be hard pressed to explain how it happened when the mobster's sister claims the remains."

"What of me?" the hellhound called at the fading demon. "How do I get out of here?"

"Not my problem," the demon said as he vanished.

67

I stared up at Angels of Mercy hospital. I'd thought about what to do on the half hour drive from Hawaiian Mike's, and I'd finally settled on a course of action.

The best thing for everyone was to wish the hellhound back to Hell. That's where he belonged, not here in the land of the living. I had a lot of stressful changes coming in my life. The last thing I wanted was responsibility for a psychopath.

I parked at a meter, dropped a dime, and headed into the hospital. The interior was cool and hushed. The sound of a floor polisher echoed from a side corridor. Two clerks chatted in the florist shop off the main lobby. The scent of flowers mingled with the biting odor of bleach.

I took the elevator to the fourth floor and walked to the nurses' station. A nurse in a crisp white dress and nursing cap looked up at my approach.

"I'm looking for Kasker Sleeth's room," I said.

"Room 410, down the hall to your right," the pretty, dark-haired nurse said, her face serious. "Are you a relative?"

"Distant," I replied.

"He's not conscious," she said. "The doctors can't explain his coma. They've tried everything to wake him up. They're still hopeful he'll recover."

I thanked the nurse and tread quietly down the hall to Sleeth's room. I took a deep breath and stepped through the open door.

Sun filtered through partially closed blinds and glared off the white walls of the four-bed suite. Three of the beds were empty. Sleeth occupied the one nearest the windows. An IV bottle hung beside the bed, and a tube led down to his arm.

I walked to his bedside and looked at his still form. Lank blond hair spread like a halo around his head. His skin above the covering sheet was pallid, his respirations were slow and shallow, and his eyes were half-open in that dead state I'd seen whenever he collapsed.

The lights were on, but the dog wasn't home.

"All right, time to wake up."

I waited to see what would happen. The body before me continued unchanged. Maybe I wasn't as powerful as the big Hawaiian thought.

I put a hand on Sleeth's shoulder. "Damn it, dog. Quit screwing with me. Wake up."

Sleeth's chest stuttered. It expanded with a deep, indrawn breath. His cold blue eyes blinked open and squinted up at me.

Pain wrinkled his face. His hand slid to his belly, and he winced. A moan slipped from his throat.

I felt a moment of guilt for using such a sharp tone. Waking up with a knife wound in his gut couldn't be fun. It was my fault he'd been stabbed.

"Officer Demasi," he said, ending with a dry cough. Wariness glazed his cold blue eyes.

I filled a glass with water from a carafe on the bedside table. I placed a straw in it and held it before his lips. He looked at it like he thought it might be poison.

"I've told you before, I'm not a police officer. Drink."

Sleeth's lips gripped the straw, and he sucked down half an inch of water.

"How did Sleeth die?" I asked

His eyes widened for a split second. "I didn't, thanks to you."

I glared down at him. "Did Calderon kill Sleeth so you could occupy the body?"

He gasped in shock. "Killing is strictly forbidden."

I crossed my arms. He hadn't gotten any better at answering questions.

Sleeth plucked at the sheet and mumbled, "Drug overdose. It's possible Seve pointed him to a dealer with tainted product."

His gaze met mine. "He had free will. No one forced him to get high."

I threw up my hands. "And that absolves you and the mobster of responsibility?"

"I had nothing to do with it. I wasn't even in this realm when it happened."

I heaved a sigh. He was a creature of Hell, and we were debating morality. I was nuts to think he'd feel guilt for what he'd done. I walked to the foot of the bed.

"If you're not a p— not a cop now, what will you do?" he asked.

I rocked on my heels and glanced at my shoes. "I'm going to open my own investigation business."

His cold eyes sparkled, and his lips twisted in his heart-melting, come-hither smile. "You'll need a partner. I'm the greatest hunter in the universe and the logical choice. We made a great team."

My anger rose, and my brows went with it. "We were never a team. You lied to me. You withheld important facts. You abandoned the stakeout at Peck's apartment. If you hadn't, we could have caught Holmes before so many people died."

His chin lifted. "But you wouldn't have found Holmes without me."

"You should go back to Hell where you belong."

Sleeth's lips parted. Panic flashed in his cold eyes. His voice dropped to his smooth tenor. "The body will die without me. Its family will be bereaved. You'd be responsible. You don't want that, do you?"

An irritating buzz gnawed at my brain and stabbed at the back of my eyes. I'd been fine a moment earlier. Sleeth watched with a strange intensity.

My eyes narrowed. "Whatever you're doing, stop it."

He looked away, his face awash in desperation and fear. No regret, though.

"Why don't you want to go back to Hell?"

He couldn't have looked more surprised. He swallowed and cast his eyes around the room while he floundered for a plausible lie.

"Out with it," I said.

"I'm forbidden from hunting by using a human disguise, but it was the only way to find Holmes. Now that Heaven knows what I did, I will be destroyed if I leave this realm."

I was tempted to wish him away that very moment, but Hawaiian Mike's warning about upsetting the natural order gnawed at me.

"You can stay with Calderon," I said.

"Seve's dead," he replied, voice flat.

"No, he's in jail, but he'll be out soon. They don't have anything on him."

Sleeth shook his head. "He died in his cell, beaten to death by the pigs."

"Bullshit. Mack wouldn't let that happen."

He shrugged. "You'll see."

His fingertips rubbed the sheet near his wound. He wasn't telling the whole truth. Eventually I might worm the rest of the story from him, but not today.

What was I going to do with him? Hawaiian Mike implied he'd become my responsibility. The last thing I wanted was a hippie hellhound in my life.

But Mike had also implied that the hellhound wasn't all bad, that he could be a force for good with the right mistress. Maybe the dog's rehabilitation was my penance for getting Dave killed.

"You'll be an employee, not a partner," I said. "When you're on your feet, call me."

Relief blossomed on his handsome face, and stiffness went out of his shoulders. "I'll need a place to stay while I recuperate."

I crossed my arms on my chest. "What's wrong with your apartment?"

His expression turned sly. "Can't afford it with Seve gone, and can't work until I'm patched up. You wouldn't put your walking-wounded partner on the street, would you?"

"Not a partner," I said through gritted teeth. "You can use the spare room until you find a new apartment. No dope in the house. And no bringing home women."

Sleeth grinned. "No problem, Nicky. We'll be buddies. I'll show you how to have a good time."

I rolled my eyes and walked out of his room worried that I'd regret my offer. What would my neighbors say? Maybe I could pass him off as a long-lost cousin recuperating from an illness.

I climbed into my car, focused on the tasks ahead—training to attend, business license applications to complete, groceries to stock up on. I wondered whether Sleeth liked Milk-Bones.

Light bulbs talk to River Madden; God doesn't. When the homeless schizophrenic unintentionally fractures a dimensional barrier and accidentally steals a gym bag containing a million dollars, everyone from the multiverse police to the local crime boss—and an eight-foot tall demon—is after him. Can he dodge them long enough to correct his mistakes and prevent the destruction of three separate dimensions? If he succeeds, will the light bulbs stop singing off-key?

For more information, visit http://www.ksferguson.net/touching-madness.html.